Kathryn Haig w
an officer in the
civil servant and a computer program
now lives with her husband, daughter and an
assortment of animals in the New Forest. Her
previous novel, *Apple Blossom Time*, is also
published by Corgi.

Also by Kathryn Haig

APPLE BLOSSOM TIME

and published by Corgi Books

A TIME TO DANCE

Kathryn Haig

CORGI BOOKS

A TIME TO DANCE
A CORGI BOOK : 0 552 14538 6

First publication in Great Britain

PRINTING HISTORY
Corgi edition published 2000

1 3 5 7 9 10 8 6 4 2

Copyright © Kathryn Haig 2000

Set in 10½/12½pt Sabon by Kestrel Data, Exeter, Devon.

Corgi Books are published by Transworld Publishers,
61–63 Uxbridge Road, London W5 5SA,
a division of The Random House Group Ltd,
in Australia by Random House Australia (Pty) Ltd,
20 Alfred Street, Milsons Point, Sydney, NSW 2061, Australia,
in New Zealand by Random House New Zealand Ltd,
18 Poland Road, Glenfield, Auckland 10, New Zealand
and in South Africa by Random House (Pty) Ltd,
Endulini, 5a Jubilee Road, Parktown 2193, South Africa.

Reproduced, printed and bound in Great Britain by
Cox & Wyman Ltd, Reading, Berks.

For Hugh and Rachel

Early one morning, just as the sun was rising
I heard a maid singing in the valley below:
'Oh don't deceive me, oh never leave me,
How could you use a poor maiden so?'

*Regimental quick march of the
Women's Royal Army Corps*

PROLOGUE

To everything there is a season
and a time to every purpose under the heaven . . .

So many things gave her pleasure. She would have enjoyed it all so much.

The homely garden flowers, unpretentious, late floppy roses, perfumed like myrrh; absolutely no chrysanthemums; the drowning scent of lilies – there was a spatter of pollen across Lydia's cuff, a difficult stain to remove, but she'd have known what to do, she knew things like that. The sunlight fragmented on the pale stone flags, throwing down a pall of scarlet and blue, translucent, so you could still read the words beneath, though they had been scuffed by centuries of careless feet.

Aetatis suae 73 . . . mourned by his grieving relict . . .

She'd always stepped so tenderly around the words, going crabwise along the edge of the pews. 'It mattered so much to them – to be remembered. I'll not rub them out, if I can help it.'

Lydia didn't think she cared very much whether or not she would be remembered. Things like that weren't important.

And the music. The vicar had asked if relatives wanted to make a choice, but Lydia had left it to the choirmaster. He'd know. He'd known her long enough. And he hadn't let her down.

Be not afraid, thy heaven is nigh . . .

Such certainty.

The sound bounced back from the low barrel roof and, for a moment, Lydia could hear her.

That voice was difficult to silence, a fruity contralto, limited in range but enormous in power. She'd always sung too loudly in school services and an octave lower than the squeaky schoolgirl voices. Other people's mothers were tidy little women, in neat, tweedy suits and sensible flatties, with pearls and smooth hair and fluting voices. Not large and somehow billowing, too colourful, too . . . too noticeable, too *different*. At fourteen, Lydia longed for her own to look like a mother should. Little prig! She'd cringe and jab her mother with her elbow and beg her not to make so much noise.

'Everybody stares. They know it's you.'

'Nonsense,' she'd say briskly. 'It's not me that's loud. The others just whisper. Why not sing up and enjoy it?'

Hopeless.

The little church was nearly full. All the women her mother had employed were there, some dragging along their husbands, to pay their last respects. Lydia hadn't realized there were so many. It had been a thriving little business. What would happen to it now? What would happen to them all?

And *they* were there, of course, sitting in a row together, halfway down the church. Not vying for the front pews with those who thought their standing demanded it. Not creeping in at the back with those who'd just popped in off the street for a nice funeral and a bit of a sit down.

Not wearing black. Well, she wouldn't have wanted black. She liked bright colours, unsuitable colours, some might have said, for a woman of her age. Emerald and acid drop yellow and episcopal purple. They hadn't let her down.

They didn't look unseemly in their colours. Funny. It was everyone else, respectful in black or navy or a good grey, who appeared out of place. But they all looked as though they'd been crying. And one definitely looked as though she'd needed a stiffener or two before she'd been able to face the service. They sat shoulder to shoulder, not caring if they touched, four straight backs, four sets of coat-hanger level shoulders.

United. But now divided.

Be not afraid . . .

Had she been afraid, when the moment had come? Had there been a split second when she had known, had seen her death, coming towards her through the low evening sunlight, along the towpath?

She'd been attacked from the front, the pathologist had said. She hadn't had time, hadn't thought to run. Perhaps she'd even called out a cheerful 'Good evening' in passing.

Had the first blow been the merciful one? Or had she felt the others, the ones that had turned

13

her head into the pulp that no-one could identify?

Frenzied, the newspapers had called the attack. Ugly, ugly word.

How much pain had she endured before the compassionate darkness fell? A faceless woman out for a walk, without a handbag, without car or house keys, a crumpled Waitrose receipt in one pocket, the last two of a packet of Polo mints, two paper clips and an elastic band in the other, a dog lead in stiffened fingers. It had been forty-eight hours before anyone had spotted Polly shivering and whining and scratching at an unlocked door.

The last time . . . the last time she'd seen her alive . . . How could anyone recognize that the last time had come? The husband who goes to work and drops dead in the office. The child who sets off to school and bicycles under a bus. A day like any other and then horribly, for ever transmuted. And you'd always think . . . the last time. You'd always think . . . I could have done more, I could have shielded, have saved. There must have been something . . .

The last time Lydia had seen her, she'd been rummaging in a drawer for Polly's vaccination certificate.

'I know I put it in here. It's always in here. Oh, are you off, darling? Have a lovely time. The weather's set fair for you, anyway. I'm sure Polly's jabs are overdue. Give my love to Daniel . . .'

The last time . . .

And the nausea began again, the clamminess at the back of Lydia's neck, the tormenting, dancing

14

black spots in front of her eyes. She could feel herself on the verge of fainting, sliding into quiet darkness. It wasn't the fainting that was so distressing, it was the coming back.

But not now. Not now. Lydia gripped the edge of the pew in front and took command of her breathing, slowly, slowly, that's better.

If she'd gone for that walk an hour earlier or an hour later. If I hadn't taken up that chance offer of a berth on a yacht sailing to Cherbourg and on to Honfleur. If . . .

Don't think of that day. Don't think at all. Smell the flowers. Watch the sunlight. Keep your eyes away from the plain, no-nonsense box in front of the altar. Listen.

Be not afraid . . .

Lydia could only hope.

A lovely service, they all said so. She would have enjoyed it so much. Oh God, I miss her so badly . . .

So little, really, to show for a life. A good life.

A rented cottage. A few sticks of furniture, not much, because the cottage was tiny, but all of it good and all of it battered. Nothing ugly. But nothing much, most of it from Woolley and Wallis's auction room at the back of Castle Street, discards from their better sales.

A few clothes that might have been worn by the raggle-taggle gypsy-oh. A couple of bin bags of washed underwear and battered shoes – even the Salvation Army might draw the line at those. A patchwork cot cover in most un-childlike colours

15

– coppery velvet and peacock taffeta and violet silk –
half completed, that had been meant for Lydia's
cradle and now, so her mother had joked, might just
be finished in time for Lydia's as-yet-unconceived
children.

More flower pots than anyone might reasonably
be expected to accumulate. On the kitchen windowsill a row of Canterbury Bells and Brompton stock,
potted up and ready for overwintering, now flagging
with thirst. Some saucepans with warped bottoms
that wouldn't sit steady on the Rayburn, punished
by twenty-four years' wear. Tesco's cutlery
scrambled in the drawer with Georgian silver
serving spoons, pointed and thin with use, hallmarks
polished to a blur. The wedding present dinner
service, with more chips than she remembered, interleaved with market stall earthenware.

What was she going to do with it all?

There were a few nice watercolours. She remembered her father trying to sell them when things had
got a bit tight and there were school fees due. But
they weren't in fashion – nothing Victorian was,
then – and he'd come home with the pictures still
under his arm and his shoulders bowed.

'Just as well,' Lydia's mother had said. 'That one
was covering a hole in the plaster.'

And the one-day-I'll-sort-it-all-out box. Or, knowing her mother, Lydia thought, the one-day-I'll-
chuck-it-all-in-the-bin box.

And in the morning, there'd still be the office to
face. A most unlikely person, her mother, to run a
domestic cleaning agency and a good one, at that.

16

The Houseproud Cavalry. Lydia was pleased with the name. She'd chosen it herself.

It was a venture started in need after her father's death at Bluff Cove, when they'd discovered how inadequate was the pension offered by a grateful government to the widows of those who had died for their country – or for their political masters – one and the same.

'If there's one thing I learned while I was in the army,' her mother had said, 'it was how to clean.'

So she'd advertised in all the garrisons on Salisbury Plain. She'd offered 'marching out' cleaning at a reasonable price, knowing from past experience how traumatic were those last few days in a married quarter when, husband already hundreds of miles away, boxes packed and children squalling, a wife would struggle to return her house to the condition demanded (and so rarely achieved). Floors, paintwork, windows, carpets, curtains, loose covers, mattresses, saucepans, cookers – especially cookers – everything was supposed to be cleaned to a terrifyingly high standard. And frequently wasn't.

The one-woman Houseproud Cavalry would arrive, spreading good cheer and Ajax. She knew all the tricks. She'd strip the cooker down, soak all the pieces in ammonia and tie them up in a bin bag for the night. The next day, they'd come out clean enough to pass inspection. Even the sticky black bits.

The odd thing was, she'd said often, that it was much easier to work for someone who had been junior to her husband, than for someone who'd been senior. Funny, that. You'd have expected it to be the other way round. The soldiers' wives who'd known Major and Mrs Strickland as the Company Commander and his wife were always ready to muck in, always ready with sympathy, a reviving cup of coffee and a good laugh. The senior officers' wives really couldn't cope with the idea of having their bathrooms scoured by a woman they'd last met at the General's cocktail party.

'Jilly Harrington pretended she didn't know me,' she'd said one evening, as she washed out dirty dusters ready for the next day. 'Silly cow! She just couldn't stand the idea that we'd shared the same plant stall at the SSAFA fair and now I'm scrubbing her floor. Letting the side down! Her husband remembered me, though – he suddenly remembered he'd tried to grope me on the terrace at the summer ball!'

Soon the Houseproud Cavalry had more work than one woman could cope with, so she hired another ex-soldier's wife and then another. And not all her workers were women. When redundancies began to bite, she took on their men, too, men who weren't too proud to do a decent day's work for a decent day's pay to keep their families. The Houseproud Cavalry rode to the rescue in shiny red vans all over Wiltshire.

What would happen to them now?

The evening was settling in and the chill struck up from the red brick floor and into Lydia's knees. She crouched by the fire and struck a match. The log basket was full, the fire neatly laid, waiting for her mother's return. But her mother had not returned.

18

Finding the carefully arranged pyramid of paper and kindling had been one of the worst moments of the day. Silly, really.

At the scratching of the match, Polly crept in from her basket and settled by the fire with a sigh. She laid her whiskery face on her paws and watched Lydia through toffee-coloured, lonely eyes.

Polly licked a stray fragment of Chum off the tip of her nose. The blood on her whiskers had stiffened and set by the time she'd been found. It had taken Lydia a long time to wash it off. Gently, gently. Her mother's blood. Not like cleaning the terrier when she'd gone after an unlucky rabbit. Unthinkable, unnatural action.

Lydia leaned forward to scratch the stiff little ears, but Lydia was the wrong person and Polly turned away.

Lydia dragged a cushion onto the floor and sat cross-legged on it. She upended the box to be sorted and stirred the contents dispiritedly.

The room was full of the little creaks and shudders of an old building settling down for the night. The lop-sided plastic clock, a pony with a swinging tail that Lydia had made in technology class, made its irritating, not quite even sound – tick, *tick*, tick, *tick* – it had done that for fourteen years. The hands went round in jerks.

'Leave it alone,' her mother had once said. 'I love it – and it works.'

The water pipes gave off the juddering drone that meant one of the Lovells next door was having a bath. The spider that always seemed to appear

19

about this time strolled across the floor. Polly's ears pricked at the sight of it, but it was an old acquaintance and she left it alone. Besides, it was massive.

Everything was going on as usual and it was all wrong.

The phone rang and Lydia let it ring. It went on and on – twelve rings, twenty – and she knew it was Daniel. He was a very persistent man. That was his strong point and his failing. But even he had to give up in the end.

For more than a moment, Lydia wished she'd allowed Daniel to stay with her, as he had wanted. He would have been quiet, sympathetic, have plied her with tea, have walked the dog. He'd have said all the right things at that terrible graveside parting. He'd have helped her to shake all those hands. He'd have cheered her by day and warmed her by night.

But Daniel was still in Battersea, staring miserably at the phone and Lydia knew that was the best place for him.

For how do you explain to anyone that, after twenty-five years, your mother was not your mother?

The post-mortem report had been admirably brisk. It itemized the head injuries in language that, somehow, sanitized the brutality. It succinctly described the rest of the body: the scar on the right hand (a dog bite, Lydia remembered); the big toe distorted from being broken (a too frisky pony); the appendectomy scar; all the wear and tear of forty-six years of living.

And, almost in passing, it mentioned that the deceased had never borne a child.

Never.

Lydia stroked Polly's rough head. The fire had warmed it on one side, the other side was still cold. That's the trouble with inglenooks, her mother had always said, all the heat goes up the chimney, keeping the sparrows warm. You cook on one side and freeze on the other.

She looked at the detritus spread over the rug. Programmes from school concerts that Lydia had played in. Menus from past military dinner nights. Orders of service and parade programmes.

And photographs. A picture of the Queen presenting a standard on some unrecognizable parade ground. The Queen Mother presenting the Military Gold Cup at Sandown to Lydia's father – young then, younger than his daughter now, spattered with mud and grinning. Any number of school photos, with Lydia getting bigger and bigger, but always squinting into the sun. Regimental photos, with her father slowly becoming more senior and moving closer to the front.

Lydia's birth certificate.

He wasn't her father, of course. Lydia had always known that. The column on the certificate where a father's name should have been was blank, but she hadn't minded. The word bastard never seemed to apply to her. The man she'd called Daddy had been the only father she'd known and the only one she'd wanted.

A father isn't necessarily a father, but a mother is

21

always a mother. She was the woman named on the birth certificate. But she had never had a child.

So?

So thousands of people are adopted and don't always know about it. Perhaps the truth comes out by accident. Maybe it comes as a shock at first, but you come to terms with it. It's normal. It happens. Maybe your parents aren't your parents, but that hasn't stopped them from loving you for as long as you can remember.

But in Lydia's hand, the printing on the document was quite plain. She couldn't argue with it. Her birth had been registered as the birth of a female child to the woman she called Mother. As far as the state was concerned, she was who she had always thought she was. And that was that.

Only she wasn't.

One more photograph. And there they were. The five girls in uniform and one of them the woman that Lydia had always thought was her mother. Five faces scarcely framed by hair, so scraped back was it. Five starched white collars. Five pairs of hands neatly folded on laps, right over left. Five sets of legs, ankles crossing right over left and ending in enormous black shoes.

And underneath, stapled to the picture, a slip of paper typed with names: Vernon; Blakeney; Cleeve; Tedder; Cameron.

As good a place to start as any.

1994

A time to laugh . . .

These days Nell didn't bother to get up. Well, there didn't seem much point.

He'd always been an early riser, up and out for a run, punishing his body, disciplining it, determined, as each year passed, to stay as fit as the youngest man in his command – fitter, probably. Nell would be in the kitchen when he got back, dripping, and his kiss would be salty and the place between his shoulder blades where her hands met would be sweaty, so he'd have a quick shower and change and there'd be tea and scrambled eggs or grilled tomatoes and a rasher of bacon – just one – and toast and the *Daily Telegraph*. And Jago would be trying to cut a token off the back of the cereal packet before it was finished and Jessica would be banging her spoon on the high chair tray and there'd be Farex on the dog and Frosties stuck to the DS pink – the official Directing Staff solution to the problem that his Staff College student syndicate had been labouring over all night – and Nell was happy.

These days, she was just in the way, really. Now, Mrs Parr would be in by the time Oliver got back from his run and Nell would hear him in his dressing room, the shower running, the gurgly, toothpasty noises, the drawers and doors slamming and she'd know that downstairs would be a perfectly laid table for one and that the house sergeant would be overseeing Bombardier Kane, who would be bringing perfectly bright shoes up to a more perfect shine. Mrs Parr and Sergeant Lofthouse had been at Kabul House longer than anyone could remember. The house ran beautifully, precisely, as it had for the Hawtreys' predecessors and would for their successors.

It didn't need Nell. Why get in the way? But if, for one moment, she'd thought he'd wanted her . . .

'I thought you were going out this morning?'

'I am, but it's lunch – Winchester. Plenty of time.'

'Don't leave it to the last minute. You know what you're like. I don't like Kane bashing along the M3, doesn't look good, speeding in a staff car.'

He bent forward and peered in the looking-glass, checking that the sleeves of his shirt were rolled up to the same point on each arm, just to the bend of the elbow. It was the first of May, the first day of shirt-sleeves order, come rain, hail or shine. And of course he knew that Mrs Parr would have rolled and ironed in each fold to hair's-breadth accuracy. And of course he checked. It was important. One of the many subtle ways of identifying an officer from a distance, even in combat kit, was the height of the rolled shirt sleeve. Soldiers rolled theirs much higher, so that the biceps and tattoos could be better displayed.

On the right sleeve, halfway between epaulette and elbow, on every uniform shirt or jacket he possessed, the dark and light blue feathered wings of the SAS were neatly stitched.

As he bent, his back swept in a smooth, lean line into neat buttocks and long, long legs. 'Really fanciable,' Nell had heard one of the subalterns' girlfriends whisper at that drinks party the other night, 'gorgeous bum.' And then she realized she'd been heard by the General's wife and had taken a hurried gulp of her curry puff and burnt her tongue. Silly girl. Why should Nell mind? It *was* a gorgeous bum.

'Oliver, I thought . . .' Nell began, ridiculously nervous. 'I don't need the staff car . . . I thought I might drive myself.'

'Is that such a good idea?'

'Why not?'

'Hen party – old girls' reunion – I can't see you sticking to water and you know how hopeless you are after a small sherry. Kane can drive and then you don't have to worry.'

'I don't want Kane. Anyway, I've asked him to pick up Jessica from school. It may have skipped your attention, but she's coming home this afternoon – study leave before the exams.'

'Study leave! No docking the time at home off the fees, I suppose,' he growled. 'Kane can do both. Drop you, then go on to Ascot, pick up Jessica and her piles of rubbish and be back in Winchester in

27

time to bring you home. That's not a problem.'

'But I want to drive myself in my own car.'

'Aren't you being a bit silly?'

'I don't want . . . well, if you must know, I don't want to arrive in state and play the General's wife. They're my friends, Oliver.'

'Sentimental twaddle. I don't know why you're so keen to go, anyway. Reunions are never all they're cracked up to be, I always find. You see Ruth often enough, don't you? She's Jago's godmother, for heaven's sake, you saw her at his confirmation.'

'Three years ago.'

'That long? Really? And if you haven't seen the others for twenty-five years, then what sort of a friendship do you call that? Oh, have it your own way. I haven't time to argue. Watch your drinking and don't forget we've people coming at six.'

He pecked her briskly. She listened as he ran downstairs. She could hear Harry Dowland greet his superior. He must have been standing in the hall all the time they'd been arguing – had it been arguing? she wondered, is that what you'd call it, or had she just been whining on, as Oliver so often said? Had Harry heard? Probably not. Oliver never bothered to raise his voice to her. Not any longer.

There was a pause while Oliver picked up his hat from the hall table and put it on. Then Nell heard the front door slam, the passenger doors, the driver's door and heard the Rover 800 crunch slowly down the gravel drive.

She thought about getting up.

*   *   *

28

Ruth was going to make up her mind at the last minute. She'd left things open at work, fixed it so that she could have the day off or come in, depending. If it was a good day, she might just take the risk and go to Winchester. If it was a bad day, there wasn't a chance.

Good days were all pretty much the same. Rare as hens' teeth and a whole lot more desirable. Bad days came in all sorts of disguises. Sometimes they signalled themselves well in advance, giving plenty of warning, time to cover your head and duck. Sometimes they just crept up when you weren't looking and grabbed you by the scruff of the neck. For no reason at all, a day could start out good and finish bad.

That wasn't strictly true. There was a reason. But it was a reason no-one else seemed to admit. And if everyone else was right, all the people who ought to know – the doctors, the politicians, the Ministry of Defence, the Pentagon – and there was no physical reason for Tim's distress, then he was mad.

It hadn't always been this way. But the last two years had seemed longer and tougher than all the other twenty-odd that she'd been married to Tim.

Syndrome. She'd looked up the word in the dictionary, anxious that they should be using it correctly. *A concurrence of symptoms*. Thus – Gulf War syndrome. The newspapers bandied the term around (but only in very short articles and never on the front page) as though they understood it. Well, if they did, they were the only ones. Tim certainly didn't.

A concurrence of symptoms. So what did you do when the symptoms were different every day? Good days and bad days.

Good days were when he could get out of bed without weeping. Good days were when he had the energy to get down to the Job Club, have a cup of coffee, compare notes with the others, catch up on what was new in the job market. Good days were when he could manage to cut the grass without wheezing or get in to Tesco's to save Ruth having to shop after work. When he didn't resent Ruth going to work every morning, in the red Renault van with HOUSEPROUD CAVALRY emblazoned on its side and the logo of Don Quixote carrying a mop and bucket in place of his lance and shield.

Bad days were when the post brought the replies to the latest batch of job applications. Seventy-one applications. Eleven short lists. Three interviews. No job. Bad days were when he didn't care what the postman brought, anyway. When even the weight of the bedclothes hurt his joints. When his bones felt as though they were made of glass. When the raw skin in the folds of his elbows, his knees, his neck, his groin erupted again.

Good and bad. Two sides of the same coin. Bad that Joanna had had to change schools in her GCSE year. Good that Henry would never have to be sent away to school, as his sisters had been.

The worst days were when Ruth had to leave Tim writing letters. He'd write careful, densely argued reports to the army pensions people, to their MP, to the Director Army Medical Services, to a self-help group called WAGS – War Against Gulf Syndrome – in America, to the newspapers, to anyone he thought might listen. And all the letters said the same thing – that he, and hundreds like him, had been poisoned by the cocktail of drugs they'd been ordered to take during the Gulf War. Anti-nerve-gas drugs, insecticidal organophosphates, anti-diarrhoea drugs, anti-every-bloody-thing, all warring inside his body. No wonder his immune system was shot to pieces. And what the hell was anyone doing about it?

When Ruth would come home, she'd find screwed-up paper littering the floor beneath the desk. Tim would be cursing his own feeble body and the army that had left it that way and Ruth for being the breadwinner and the children for being too noisy or for creeping around and not saying a word.

And when the outburst was over, he'd put his face in his hands.

'God, I'm a bastard. Did you see the way Henry looked at me? As though I'm some sort of monster. You'd be better off without me.'

Ruth would take him in her arms (if that didn't hurt too much) and kiss the top of his head where the hair was thinning and rock him, waiting for the spasm of self-loathing to pass.

He'd turn his face in to her breasts, burying himself like a child in a nightmare, but knowing that he wasn't going to wake up.

'I'm no good for you, Ruthie. I can't take care of you all the way I should.'

'We're all right. We've got your pension and my job. We've nothing to complain about.'

31

'I'm useless . . . we don't even . . .'

Don't even make love any more, Ruth could have finished for him, don't even sleep in the same bed any more. No tenderness, in the shortening space between the children falling asleep and their own exhausted sleep. No waking to turn to each other in that warm moment as night makes way for day. How long since she had caught and answered that unspoken question when the children went off to spend a Sunday afternoon with friends. *Gardening? Ironing? Let them wait.* Not any more.

But if Tim couldn't make himself say the words, Ruth wasn't going to fill in the gaps.

'Useless . . .'

The fear would grip her heart and squeeze it so hard she was sure that Tim could hear it struggling to cope. One day . . . one day she might come home and he wouldn't be there.

'It's all right,' she'd whisper. 'It's all right.'

It was, Ruth saw with relief, going to be a good day. Or at worst, a fair to middling one. Tim came downstairs as she was filling the teapot. Slowly, it's true, but under his own steam. He pushed back the hair from the nape of her neck and kissed the mole he revealed.

'Good night?' Ruth asked. A wife ought to know if her husband has a good night or not. But Tim had long ago moved to a separate room – 'For your sake, love,' he'd said. 'I don't want to keep you awake' – because sometimes he couldn't bear the touch of the sheets, let alone the weight of Ruth's limbs next to his.

'Not bad,' he answered. 'Thought I might take Henry in to school today and then see what's going at the Job Centre. Postman been?'

'Yes,' Ruth answered, carefully casual. 'There's a postcard from Joanna. It's by your plate. Sounds as though she's having a wonderful time. Going to all those parties must be doing wonders for her German. I hope. Nothing much else.'

No bills, she meant.

Tim pulled out the heavily cushioned chair that was reserved for him and sat at the table. Ruth poured out some tea for them both, managing not to look too carefully at Tim as she did so. The early summer sun was especially cruel. It seemed to strip away his flesh. She could look right through him to the ghost of the Tim she remembered.

He had gone to the Gulf hard and fit, a hockey-playing, squash-playing, cross-country runner. He had come back little changed on the surface, thinner maybe, but complaining of a painful cough. Then had come the night sweats, and that was just the beginning. Ruth had put away the photo that had always stood on the bookcase, of them both in Winterberg, the army skiing centre, in the days before the children. She couldn't bear to look at it now.

But the smile was still there, shy and oddly inno-cent, the smile she had fallen in love with even before she knew the man. It was a parody of the original, but Ruth still treasured it.

Henry was pouring a double helping of Coco Pops. The milk turned a swampy brown.

'Like shit,' he announced, 'shitty, shitty milk.'

He waited for the adult response and looked disappointed when it didn't come. He slurped some of the milk down his school tie and wiped it off with the cuff of his white shirt.

'Henry . . .' Ruth protested weakly.

'Wot?'

'Never mind. Give Lucy another call, will you, poppet. Tell her breakfast is on the table and if she isn't down in five minutes, she won't get any.'

'She doesn't want any. She says pig meat is gross and if we knew what was in the bread we wouldn't touch it with a bargepole – what's a bargepole?'

Jasmine jumped on the table with a friendly chirrup and stuck her waterproof Elastoplast nose into the Coco Pops. Without lifting his eyes from *The Times* appointments section, Tim stretched out his hand and put the cat back on the floor.

'Daaaaad . . .' Henry complained. 'Milk's good for her kittens.'

'And chocolate's bad for them. Ask Lucy. She'll tell you everything you want to know about food.'

The May morning sun, scarcely brighter than the yellow check curtains, turned Henry's gingernut head to fire, camouflaged the grey in Tim's and gilded the tip of each separate tabby hair right up to the curl at the end of Jasmine's tail.

Ruth smiled. With any luck, it was going to be a good day.

*   *   *

Alice was still in bed when Juliet left. She was in a sulk and had been since the day before, when they'd had a major confrontation about a Jamiroquai concert in Bournemouth.

'But everyone's going – absolutely everyone. I'll be the *only* one who's forced to stay at home . . .' she'd wailed.

Simon barely looked up from the *Independent* as he laid down the law. 'You should have thought of that before you ploughed your mocks. What good will seven Ds and two Es do you? Mmm? Even shelf stackers these days have higher qualifications than that. If this is called study leave, then you study. Every day. OK? And no late nights and *no* sleep-overs with Louise.'

'That's so unfair.'

'Plenty of time for concerts after your GCSEs.'

'But that'll be too late. There won't be another concert for years – ever, probably.'

'That's what you said last time.'

'You don't understand. You're just trying to make me look a nerd. I'll be completely out of it if I don't go. *Everyone's* going . . .'

Alice flopped forward onto the table, face on her crossed arms. Her dark brown hair, a shade lighter than Juliet's own, fanned across the cloth in un-brushed profusion. Her grubby fingertips, finishing in chipped black polish, looking like fat, black-headed maggots, splayed from frayed cuffs.

'For heaven's sake,' Simon growled. 'Spare us the tragedy queen. No means no.'

Galvanized by fury, Alice stood up, rocking her

chair backwards with a crash. 'You're an absolute dinosaur. You treat me as though I'm six years old. I wish you were dead.' She slammed out of the room and up to her bedroom.

Twenty-four hours later she was still in self-imposed exile. Juliet knew what she was doing, as certainly as though she'd been allowed into the malodorous den Alice called her bedroom – which she wasn't – *ever*. Alice would be lying on her bed, brooding over the portrait of Kurt Cobain, which had been black-shrouded ever since the singer's suicide, and deafening herself with headphone-silenced Nirvana.

It was enough to make a mother worry. But Juliet had heard her in the night, rummaging in the kitchen. She'd heard the fridge door, the microwave door, the rattle of plates and forks. So Alice wasn't starving. Most unlikely. She could feed off herself like a camel for at least a week.

Juliet despised herself for allowing the thought headroom. You couldn't go around thinking things just because they were true. Where would that lead? Mothers who criticized their daughters' weight ended up weeping over anorexics. At least Alice was healthy.

It was just a question of who had the most determination – her daughter or her husband. Knowing Simon, Juliet would have been prepared to risk a sizeable bet on him.

'The trouble is,' she reminded Simon that morning, 'that you've got a very short memory.'

'What?'

He always said it like that, Juliet thought. As though his untenanted body was sitting at the table eating toast while the important bit, the thinking bit, was already on its way to his consulting rooms in the Nuffield hospital twenty miles away.

'Simon, for God's sake, put down that paper and listen to me.'

'What is it? I'm late and the M27 traffic is murder. They've been digging up that bloody road all spring.'

'You've forgotten what it's like to be young. You've forgotten what we used to get up to . . .'

That startled him. 'Good God . . . not at sixteen . . . I hope.'

'Well, no. But . . .'

'Stop making excuses for her. She'll do as she's told.' He came round the table and kissed Juliet briskly. His skin was beautifully shaved, sleek as a seal's pelt. He smelt of Trumper's Lime. He slipped on the coat of his three-piece suit. Juliet was sure that he hadn't put on a pound since he'd been a harassed medical student. 'I've a late appointment tonight. Some captain of industry who's killing himself with booze and stress. Don't know when I'll be back. Go ahead and have dinner without me. Tempt Alice down with something she likes.'

Juliet laughed. 'A Chinese take-away it is, then.'

When he'd gone, Juliet sat for a while, enjoying her third cup of coffee and the silence that would last until Mrs Welton began thumping the vacuum cleaner around the house.

Elbows on the table, she cradled the cup comfortably in both hands, in a way that would have called for a reproof if she'd seen Alice do it. What had been acceptable for Simon and Juliet in 1968 was certainly not acceptable for their daughter a quarter of a century later. 'That's the trouble with men,' Juliet said to herself. 'They all have such very short memories.'

The best thing about that building where they had all been mewed up was that it was easy to get into. The flat roof of their sitting room – only of course the army called it something else, the ante-room – could be easily reached from a man's willing shoulders. Then it was just a quick bunk up into Nell's room.

Nell never seemed to mind. Her bed was under the window and they'd flop through it and onto her feet. And as long as they – well, Juliet, actually, most of the time – didn't make too much noise, Nell never complained about being woken up. Good little Nell. Always safely tucked up. *Her* room was never empty when a truant climbed in.

2359 hours was such a ridiculous time to expect adult women to be inside. Not midnight, because officially that didn't exist. (What would you call it? 2400 hours or 0000? A typical military nicety.) And at 0001 hours the front door was locked.

Old enough to vote, but not old enough to stay out after midnight. You could always apply for a late pass, but the Company Sergeant Major scrutinized every application and you had to have a jolly good reason for more than a couple of late nights a month.

So it was cars left at the bottom of the rhododendron-lined drive, creeping past the Sergeants' Mess – oh, God, Sergeant Millett hasn't drawn her curtains – a last cuddle in the leafy darkness behind the building and in through Nell's window.

Juliet wondered how much Nell could hear. She'd asked her once.

'Nothing at all,' Nell answered quickly. Then why did she blush?

Juliet did have her rules, of course (which is more than could be said for some, but that's an old story, best forgotten). Nothing below the waist, she said and stuck to it. Nothing below *her* waist, that is. She wasn't sure whether or not the rule extended to *his* waist. It certainly didn't seem to.

If you were really out of luck, you tangled with the orderly officer on late rounds, flashing her torch round the dustbins. Then it was a quick button-up and into the bushes, holding your breath. If it was one of the younger officers, she wouldn't want to catch you, wouldn't dream of trying. But heaven help you if you were unlucky enough to be cornered by one of the crusty old spinster majors . . .

Juliet had enough trouble now getting Alice home before midnight and she was only sixteen. If Juliet couldn't fetch her herself, she was very strict about taxis and always made sure Alice had enough money for the fare. But sometimes she wondered how long it sat outside – and, more to the point, *where* – meter ticking, before Alice bothered to come out to it. It was worth it. Juliet could remember the boys who used to drive her home . . . but not at Alice's age. Surely?

Simon and Alice had endless rows about curfews. Juliet kept out of it. At sixteen, she'd never seen the point, either. But then, at sixteen she'd still been in ankle socks and sandals. *Her* curfew rows had been about whether she'd be allowed to go along to the coffee bar after Guides, walking home with Brenda Matthews from next door by ten o'clock.

'But Mum, *everyone* my age is allowed out until ten. I'm the *only* one who has to come straight home.'

'If Mrs Matthews chooses to let her daughter run riot round the town all night, that's none of my business,' her mother had replied tartly. 'But no daughter of mine is going to roam the streets after dark.'

And then Juliet had met Simon . . .

Juliet allowed herself a reminiscent grin. The harder you rein them in, she thought, the quicker they break out. And she went into the kitchen to make up a tray of cereal and toast for Alice.

By the time Nell had driven three times round Winchester's one-way system, she wished she'd been more sensible. Kane would have dropped her off at the front door of the Forte Crest hotel and picked her up again at any time she'd stipulated. What he did, where he went in between times, she would never know. At a guess, he'd probably have used the hours to spare before going on to St Mary's in reading the *Sun*, parked on the nearest double yellows, and fending off traffic wardens with his army identity card, his MoD Form 90, and a whole lot of Brummie cheek.

Yet the thought of arriving in the big black car, of the uniformed driver leaping out and opening her door, of the saluting and stamping, made Nell cringe. It just wasn't going to be that sort of day. At least, she hoped it wasn't.

With relief, she finally squeezed her Clio into the staff carpark at the back of the concrete horror of the hotel, between the dustbins and a wall. She squinted into the driver's mirror, fluffed up her hair, checked the butterflies on the backs of her pearl studs, slicked on some more lipstick, regretted it and tried to blot it away.

Her expression was apologetic. It seemed to have become stuck that way about five years ago, about the time she and Oliver started to have a house full of staff looking for instructions. She tried a brighter look, but it didn't work. Silly, really. It was only a hen party, after all, as Oliver had dismissively said. Five middle-aged women. What did it matter how she looked?

But it did. She was thinner, now, than they would remember, even slim, she could say truthfully and her hair wasn't *all* that grey – just sprinkled – it would scarcely be noticed in a man of her age. But that wasn't good enough. She wanted to look . . . she tried all sorts of words – smart, sophisticated, well dressed – but the only word that fitted was the one thing she couldn't be. Young.

Twenty-five years.

There'd been the weddings, of course, one after the other, tumbling like skittles. Who would have believed it? Not even the brides. All those hopes, all those ambitions, smothered in white lace.

Nell first – a fantasy wedding in the Royal Memorial Chapel at Sandhurst, with Oliver in 'blues'. A white Grecian portico against a duck-egg sky. Low autumn sunlight glinting off the arch of swords and striking sparks from the tiara that held Nell's billowing veil.

Then Juliet – in a small, smart ceremony held in a pretty country church where neither family worshipped – but just too perfect, said Juliet's mother. A lavish reception in a country house hotel, finished by fireworks as Juliet and Simon left for Heathrow and the flight to Simon's new appointment in Hong Kong.

Next came Ruth – marrying Tim quietly because his father had recently died, on a freezing December day so misty that the smiling figures in the photographs looked insubstantial, vaguely disembodied. Tim's mother looked on the verge of tears in every one. Five days later, Tim was patrolling the streets of Belfast.

Three down and three uniform allowances to be repaid.

And last came Hope – a surprise, that, for all of them, not least, they suspected, for Hope. Between Christmas and New Year, in the dead days when everyone is exhausted by too much jollity, she rang her friends and told them to turn up at the Register Office in Salisbury to wish her and Chris luck.

'Chris?' they each asked. 'Who's Chris?'

'The man I'm going to marry.'

And so she did, looking so calmly happy, in that unattractive setting, that Nell felt a pang of envy that she mistook for the stirrings of her two-month pregnancy.

All gone. All married within the year. Who'd have thought it?

All except Isa. But that didn't surprise anyone.

Twenty-five years. They'd been friends, but were they still? And would she even recognize them? If Ruth hadn't already arrived, how would Nell know where to go, where to look? She could feel her breathing quicken at the thought of walking into a hotel lounge and having to keep on walking all the way round, staring at any likely groups of women, wondering, hoping.

When she finally decided that she was sufficiently late for everyone else to have met up, she found that she'd parked so neatly that she couldn't open the door. She flicked the rear hatch lever, climbed over the seats and struggled out of the back.

And there they were. Ruth and Juliet, Isa and Hope. Smiling and waving and beckoning Nell over. They'd changed, of course – why not? Nell had, too – but each was unmistakably, unforgettably *herself*.

Juliet was still smart and slim and her scarlet Jaeger suit fitted as exactly as once her uniform had done. And if her fragile skin had collapsed into a mesh of wrinkles, cruelly exposed as she faced the

43

window, she could still display legs and ankles to die for.

Hope had put on weight, though. Not too much, but her outline was matronly. Yet the mass of russet hair – grey-streaked but still undisciplined, a sergeant-major's nightmare – and the dangling tribal earrings made her still the least likely person ever to have been a soldier.

Whereas Isa could scarcely have been anything else. Not that there was anything muscle-bound or butch about her, Nell didn't mean that. Although she looked fit and tanned and toned in a way that none of the others did, she was very much a woman. Too thin, if anything, Nell thought. The cords in her neck stood out as she turned her head and the hollows below her cheekbones weren't the result of an artful application of blusher. Yet round her cheeks and eyes, Nell noticed, she was unusually puffy, doughy, as though, if you pressed her with a finger, the mark would remain. Odd, Nell thought, and dismissed the idea. Isa didn't stand out, like Juliet in scarlet, or make a statement, like Hope in her ethnic prints. She wore honey-coloured cashmere. You could sense its softness yards away. Yet there was something about the way she sat, relaxed but very much in command of the situation and of herself, that reminded Nell of Oliver. They were two of a kind. Isa was the perfect woman general.

And Ruth . . . oh dear, Ruth. Very much still the soldier's wife, pie-frill collar and gathered skirt, pearl stud earrings and flat patent shoes. Perfect. A clone, almost a travesty of the traditional image. But everything washed too often, ironed shiny, neatly darned. Nell felt a surge of guilt. She should have seen her more often. She ought to have kept in touch, invited Ruth to lunch, had the children over, perhaps – although she could guess what Jessica might have said about that.

'What – *all* of them? You've got to be joking. Joanna's such a sad case and Lucy's a blob and Henry's a vandal. Don't expect me to be around. I'd rather *die*.'

Nell had replied, of course, full of sympathy when Ruth had written to say that Tim had been made redundant, but she hadn't actually *done* anything. If there was anything to do . . . Perhaps Oliver might have . . . if she'd asked him, if she'd thought. But redundant officers were a glut on the market, post-Gulf War.

Twenty-five years.

Nell wondered what they thought of her as she walked across the lounge. She was glad she'd never know.

They looked as though they'd been there half the morning. There were empty coffee cups on the low table. Champagne stood in an ice bucket and glasses were ready on a tray.

'Come on, Nell. Late as usual,' Hope called and her laugh sounded exactly as Nell remembered.

'A good soldier is always five minutes early for everything,' Juliet reprimanded her, 'and we can't get on with the champagne without you!'

Suddenly everything was all right. It was as though the years had never been.

1968

A time to dance . . .

It was easy to guess which girls had just left school and which had left another job to join the army. The ones from school came in Humber Super Snipes or Rileys, sweeping smoothly through the metal gates decorated with incongruous ladybird crests, with fathers to carry trunks that had school and house names painted over and mothers to inspect ablutions and each other. The girls carried battered teddy bears and patchwork gonks and tennis rackets in wooden presses.

The working girls came in the minibus from Bagshot station and humped their own suitcases up the treacherously polished open-tread stairs. And their skirts were shorter.

'It's not quite as bad as I feared, darling,' Nell's mother said, somehow managing to inspect the room in one quick, prowling sortie. She glanced out the window at a flat roof below, flung aside the sliding doors that disclosed a basin and cupboards and peered under the bed. 'It's quite – quite modern really and very clean.'

She looked around again at the freshly white-washed brick walls, the G-plan furniture, the seaweed-coloured lino topped by a seaweed-coloured rug. It was clean all right, ferociously clean, untouchably clean. Their entering feet had left squidgy marks on the layer of floor polish.

'Thank heaven you don't have to share,' she went on, casting her eyes through the open door at another mother carrying an eiderdown. 'Did you *see* that girl in the skirt up to goodness knows where? What does she think she looks like? The *view* going upstairs. Hardly officer class. Not at all the type I expected.'

Nell's father touched his wife's arm. 'We'd better be off. Better for Nell to settle down without her old parents hanging around, eh?'

'I still don't know what you can be thinking of, Eleanor. Why do you have to do this? Why couldn't you settle for university like all your friends? You're being so . . . so perverse.'

'Now then,' her father warned. 'Don't start. We've been through all this. Nell must do as she pleases.'

He gave his daughter a rasping, awkward kiss and she wanted to snuggle into his embrace and beg to be taken home. When her mother kissed her, lipsticked lips somehow slid off Nell's cheek and settled somewhere near her ear. Then their cheeks briefly touched. Her mother's earrings were pointed and scratchy.

Her mother checked a tiny, marcasite wristwatch, the face too small for any practical purposes – a cocktail watch, she'd have called it, when it was new.

'Oh, yes, we must be off. The thing is, darling – Daddy and I thought we'd go the pretty way home, perhaps stop in Marlow for dinner . . .' *And drinkies*, Nell thought bitterly, *don't forget the little drink or two, before, during and after.* 'You don't mind, do you? Of course not. And remember, darling,' she reminded her for the third time that day, 'if you hate it, you can always come home. You don't have to stay. It's no disgrace.'

But Nell knew it would be.

When they'd gone, Nell was overtaken by an awful lethargy. She felt rootless, homeless, placeless in that fierce, white, blank room. Her trunk stood un-opened in the middle of the floor. To open it would be a declaration and she wasn't at all certain that she was ready to make that gesture yet. Or at all.

'Ready?' A girl stuck her head around the door. Her wiry mass of hair, like a gigantic, rusty Brillo pad, startled Nell. With her jangling, silver filigree earrings and naked face, the girl looked more like a hippie than a potential army officer. But her smile was wide open and frank, taking in the untouched suitcases and Nell's ready-to-run stance. 'Oh, haven't you unpacked yet? Aren't you stopping? You'll feel better when you've got a few of your own things scattered around. I'll help you later, shall I? Come on, we're due at a pep talk downstairs.'

She picked up a badge from the top of the book-case and pinned it to Nell's jersey. It seemed to refer to an efficient, unflappable stranger called Officer Cadet Vernon, shortened, in a set-in-stone military abbreviation, to *O/Cdt VERNON*. Her own badge read *O/Cdt BLAKENEY*. 'There you are,' she said, looking at Nell's. 'Now we know who we are officially. But I'd rather you called me Hope. And you're . . . ?'

'Eleanor,' Nell called after her as she clattered downstairs. 'That's Nell, if you like.'

Downstairs, they found the senior cadets gathered, looking intimidatingly neat in lovat green uniforms, brightly buttoned, with hair scraped back, strangling collars, and shoes that glittered in the late afternoon sunlight.

Will I ever look like that? Nell wondered. *I must have thought so once, or I wouldn't be here.* But now, faced with the real thing, she wasn't so sure. It seemed unlikely, absurd even. How could she ever imagine that she might gain that poise, that – oh dear, the only word that filtered into her head was arrogance. *I'm certain they're not*, she told herself. *It's just the uniforms, it's just that they sit straighter, hold their heads higher than I'm used to. I'm sure they're perfectly nice, really.*

Conscious of their shortcomings, the new bugs perched on the edges of orange-upholstered chairs, eyeing each other – she looks nice, she looks pushy, what amazing hair – trying to look enthusiastic and cool at the same time and managing only to look anxious.

Juliet leaned forward and admired her new pink suede boots, laced to the knee. She turned her foot in a slow circle, enjoying the way the suede moulded around her fragile little ankle. Simon said she had legs like a gazelle – of course, he *might* have been exaggerating. Or not. The boots had been a super buy. Some of the other girls looked frightfully dowdy. She did hope they weren't going to be as dull as their clothes. Apart from that one in the floppy, patchwork velvet, of course. What *did* she think she looked like?

Hope lounged – as far as lounging was possible in the straight-backed chair – with her legs stretched out in front, keeping up an insouciant front that she was pretty certain would annoy the shit out of the bandbox neat girls in front of her. But what the hell – the whole place looked as though it could do with a good shaking up. *And just look at that cool blonde over there*, she said to herself. *She could suck an ice cube and it wouldn't melt. I can't see how she's going to mix in with the rest of us.*

Isa cast an assessing eye over the four girls with whom she expected to share the trials of the next eight months. *Oh, my God*, she thought, *just babies. They're going to be eaten alive. A hippie, a dolly bird and one who's escaping from home – you can always tell the escapees, they have nervous eyes that roll around at every sound behind them, as though they expect to be dragged off home again. The only one who looks as though she's got any substance at all is the tall one on the end – tougher than she appears, probably, she'll be able to bend with the wind and stand up again when the storm's over. And that's a trick they'd all better learn – double quick!*

They're rather overdoing it, Ruth thought, staring

calmly back at the uniformed girls, with a composure that, although she didn't know it, annoyed the senior girls, who rather expected the new entries to be appropriately humble. *Those supercilious glares – or perhaps it's just that their hair is pulled back so fiercely it makes their eyes look slitty. Just trying to make us feel small, I suppose. A sort of power politics. Worse than school prefects. OK, maybe we're new and ignorant. But we won't always be. So I'll just let it slide over me. That girl across there looks really rattled already.* She aimed an encouraging smile towards Nell and was rewarded by a nervous return, not quite a smile – the girl looked scared as a rabbit – but her response was instant and friendly. *A good start*, Ruth thought; *at least someone else out there is human.* And she turned her attention to the speaker.

'Right. I'm Alison Barkwith and I'm an officer cadet sergeant and the senior cadet. You're the lowest of the low here,' the pep talk began. 'So you'd better start getting used to it.'

The Commandant said much the same thing next morning – less aggressively, but her meaning, though wrapped in milder words, was unmistakable.

Commandant's Address the timetable read. And 0900 hours – better get used to a whole new way of telling the time – found the new girls, not girls any longer, but junior officer cadets, sitting nervously in a classroom.

Juliet was trying not to tap her fingers. She was dying for a ciggy and it looked as though she wasn't going to get one until coffee break at 1100. *God, it's just like being back at school*, she thought. *I don't know why I bothered. I wouldn't have, if I'd thought it was going to be like this. Same wooden desks. Same chairs that squeak across the lino. Same chalk and talk. Even the bloody headmistress . . .*

They all rose to greet the entrance of Colonel Marjorie Appleby, OBE, Commandant WRAC College. Red band around a gold-braided cap. Red tabs on her collar. She was the most senior officer they would see for a very long time. She was God.

Like Reverend Mother at school, Ruth mused, studying the portly little woman with detached curiosity. *Only trotted out on high days and holy days.*

How odd, thought Hope. *She looks quite motherly – a bit like the Queen Mother, in fact, same well-corseted figure and perfect perm – but there's not a spark of humanity there. Not that I can spot, anyway. I wouldn't like to turn to her, if I was in trouble. She'd just get me to fill in a form in triplicate.*

Colonel Appleby began with a little military pleasantry. 'We were going to call you the mini-course, because we've never had such low numbers before – a sign of the times, I suppose, the young have so little true patriotism today – but now I see that we shall have to call you the bun-course.' She waited for the little ripple of laughter. It was rather slow in coming. 'All of you with long hair and all of it tied up in buns. It makes it rather difficult to tell you apart. Still, I'm sure we shall manage.'

The Commandant spoke of them as raw material, young and impressionable, clay to be shaped – *Not the most original simile*, thought Nell, with a touch of the intellectual arrogance that four As at A level had given her – with undoubted potential, but a potential that had to be moulded, coerced if necessary, into the final product.

'And even then . . . even then you will be untried and inexperienced. Even then you will be learning. In fact,' she finished, with a wintry smile, 'I'm still learning, even after thirty years.' *Crumbs, she must be dim*, scribbled Hope on a scrap of paper and shoved it over to Juliet, who sniggered and blew her nose. 'You young people never fail to surprise me with your energy and enthusiasm. I'm sure we can put it to good use, if you will allow yourselves to be directed.'

Suaviter in modo, fortiter in re.

The motto of the Corps, beneath the crowned lioness badge, was flashed up on a slide. Gentle in manner, resolute in deed.

Colonel Appleby left them all in no doubt that they'd have to be resolute indeed, if they were going to survive the next eight months.

'Water in the sink? Water in the sink! What's a sink for, for heaven's sake?'

They all clustered in the orderly room, trying to snatch a glimpse of the comments written by the orderly officer after their first room inspection.

'Of course there's f . . . flipping water in the flipping sink,' Juliet cursed, irritated out of her ladylike pose. 'I'd only just cleaned the bloody thing.'

'You're supposed to polish it dry afterwards,' Isa informed her in a soft, Scottish accent that Juliet found primly know-it-all. 'No, don't look at me like that. I'm not being a clever-clogs. It's just the way the military mind works. Work it out and stay a step ahead, see. Less hassle. My tap drips, so I stopped it with a wodge of Kleenex shoved up the spout. It lasted until after inspection. Then who cares?'

'Smartarse,' Juliet growled.

'I've got smeary window louvres,' Ruth announced, peering at the book over Juliet's shoulder. 'I cut my fingers to ribbons trying to polish them up.' And she held out her hands. The knuckles were scraped raw. 'They looked fantastic until the sun came out and then I could have wept! Inspections should only be held on rainy mornings – someone should make that a new Queen's Regulation.'

Hope gave a rollocking laugh. 'O/Cdt Blakeney,' she read, '*your room is a disgrace. Re-inspection tomorrow at 0830.* What makes her think it'll be any better then? Do you think I'll be inspected every day until I get kicked out of this place?'

'Don't worry, we'll give you a hand tonight. It won't take half an hour if we all muck in. You'll have a room to be proud of tomorrow,' Isa promised.

The lowest of the low. Oh, and didn't they feel it? It was as though, during those first, terrible weeks, they were being tried by the system – ordeal by little pricks. As though every indignity, short of actual abuse, was being heaped on them, just to see if they could take it. As though the Women's Royal Army Corps had a corporate, malevolent sense of humour and they were its butt.

Uniform? What a laugh. It was issued in dribs and drabs. Far from being instantly transformed into sleek efficiency, they looked like refugees.

Beret? Yes, flat as a cow's pancake and much the same colour, flying off at a ridiculous angle until Isa taught them to soak the felt for a couple of hours and mould the dark green berets, wet, to their heads before careful drying.

Shirt and tie? Yes, and even those who'd been lucky enough to have worn a tie at school broke fingernails on the stiff collars and reluctant studs. Those who'd never worn a tie before took urgent lessons.

Jacket? Oh, no. There's a shortage in the right sizes. The sleeves need taking up or letting down. The bust needs letting out (or, in Juliet's case, taking in). Wear a khaki jersey instead, skin tight, finishing well above the waistband.

Skirt? Don't be silly. They need taking in/letting out/taking up/letting down. You'll have to make do with your PT skirts for a while. Dark green worsted and flared, barely respectable for the shortest amongst them and for the leggy Ruth, ridiculous.

Because they wore stockings, regulation shade, 60 denier, seamed stockings sized for some mythical Private Average, whose legs were shorter than anyone they knew. Even hoicked up as far as the elastic of the suspender belts could pull, their stocking tops showed every time they bent over or turned to straighten crooked seams or every time the wind blew. And Ruth showed them all the time.

'I'll get done for indecency,' she moaned, catching sight of herself in a window one breezy morning. 'You can practically see what I had for breakfast!'

'Don't worry,' Hope reassured her. 'You'll catch pneumonia first.'

Shoes? Not in the average sizes. Juliet got a pair, size 3, and Ruth's size 8 could be met from the quartermaster's store, but Hope and Nell, both size 6, finished off their outfits with black plimsolls.

Oh – and a handbag. Don't forget the matching green handbag! Somehow, it was the final indignity.

Kitted out like this, suspenders flashing, they scurried daily between the Officer Cadets' Mess and the classrooms.

'You needn't march, ladies, but you walk with a purpose. In step,' the Company Sergeant Major informed them. 'This isn't the King's Road. You're not dolly birds. No slopping around bent over like a lot of half-shut Swiss Army knives.' She chuckled at her ancient joke, repeated every four months to every new course for the years and years she had been at the WRAC College. 'You go quickly and smartly about your duties, in step at all times.'

Hope took a photo of them all. 'Evidence. You'll never believe it, one day. Go on – smile, Nell. It's a lark. Send it home to your mum. Let her see how smart her little girl looks in uniform.'

But she didn't. She didn't dare. Her mother would

have been down to Camberley like a tipsy whirlwind and dragged Nell home.

And when payday came – £4 10/- with the ten shillings going for compulsory mess subscriptions before they even saw it – they rushed down to Camberley on Saturday afternoon and bought things they'd never bought before – hairpins and bun nets. Hope wondered if the Camberley branch of Boots was the only one in the country to stock so many bun nets in so many shades, as she wrapped a ginger one around the floppy doughnut-shaped wodge of hair, which slid down towards her collar before first lesson, no matter how high it had been skewered before breakfast.

'Hair must be off the collar at all times when in uniform and that means you, Miss Blakeney. Even in the gym. Even when you're hanging upside down from the wall bars. If you can't keep it tidy, then it has to go. The college hairdresser will be happy to oblige.'

Only Isa looked like a soldier and that was because she was one.

'I'm a ranker,' she answered when asked why she already had a uniform. 'Didn't you know? I was still a corporal last month – an analyst special intelligence. If you look closely, you can still see the needle holes where the stripes were stitched. It's like the mark of the beast!'

Nell looked sharply at her, to check that she was joking. Isa's fair, pale face was utterly composed, utterly impassive. No-one ever knew what she was thinking. Not really.

'I bet you wish those stripes were still there,' remarked Juliet sourly, as she finished scrubbing black shoe polish from under her nails. She lavished fragrant cream on her hands, right up over the wrists, and massaged it well into the cuticles. 'Fancy coming here and finding yourself back at the bottom of the heap again. You must be barmy.'

'I don't suppose I'll last long. Didn't you notice Captain Hillcroft, when she was giving us that lecture on table manners?'

It had been one of the most embarrassing activities so far. *Mess Etiquette* the lecture had been labelled.

'Etiquette?' queried Juliet, with a quick lift of one mobile black brow. 'I really don't think I need that.' She looked around in quick apology. 'Oh, none of us, I'm sure . . .'

'A doddle,' explained Hope. 'Just a quick word on which way the port goes round the table and what to do during the loyal toast. And then a nice, long coffee break. My feet are killing me . . .'

Instead they found a full table setting – ranks of cutlery, a row of five varied glasses and a stiff napkin, folded like a water lily, all on a starched cloth.

And a very awkward Captain Hillcroft.

'Well, now,' she began, 'this is not my favourite lecture, so the sooner we get on, the sooner we'll get it over with. I'm sure I don't have to tell you, not all of you anyway, some might not be familiar, but I'm sure you are . . . anyway . . . I'm sure you all know how to use your cutlery . . . and if you're not . . . well, anyway, let's get on, shall we . . .'

They'd fixed her with steely, unblinking gazes, pitiless as basilisks, as she'd outlined the use of each knife, fork and spoon and the respective shapes of glasses. She demonstrated the correct way to hold a knife – 'never, never like a pen, but I'm sure you all . . .'

She caught Juliet's eye and Juliet gave a tiny, bored yawn, covering her mouth with fingertips that ended in manicured, shell-pink nails.

How does she manage to keep them like that? Nell wondered, squinting down at her own black-rimmed stubby ones.

Captain Hillcroft took a deep breath, fixed her gaze steadfastly on Isa and bashed on at a frantic pace. They were told on which side to expect the mess waiting staff to present food and from which side the used plates would be removed. They were told about the intricacies of seating plans, when a gentleman is expected to take the lady on his right in to dinner, but what do you do when the gentleman is the guest and the lady the host? Very delicate, so important not to dent masculine sensitivities.

Behind her, the mess stewardesses tiptoed in and out, like Victorian tweenies, carrying coffee pots and cups and biscuits, setting them on the buffet table by the door. Hope became distracted by the treacly scent of stewed coffee.

Their instructor got round to the loyal toast in the end.

'The President of the Mess Committee will stand

62

and say *Mr Vice* – only in your case it will be *Madam Vice* and that always causes a great deal of hilarity, so I don't want to see a ghost of a snigger – *Her Majesty the Queen*, or whatever title may be used by the regiment, for example the Queen is called the Captain-General in gunner messes. Then the Vice-President, usually a junior officer, will stand and say *Ladies* (if appropriate) *and gentlemen, the Queen* and the first few bars of the National Anthem will be played. Now this is the moment when subalterns think it killingly funny to tie Madam Vice to her chair with napkins, or hold onto her skirt, so she can't stand up, or whisk her chair away so that she can't sit down again. All I can say to you, ladies, is that boys will be boys – unfortunately. Keep your dignity and never, never join in such silly tricks yourself.'

'Didn't you notice?' asked Isa. 'She was watching me all the time, as though she expected me to pour coffee into my saucer and fan it with my beret!'

'Surely not,' Ruth argued, but mildly. 'She didn't know where to look, where to put herself. She said before she started that she always found it embarrassing to give that talk.'

'Well, she would, wouldn't she. You're all nice girls from nice schools. You don't need to be taught which fork to use to pick your teeth! But I'm a corporal and my father's a recruiting sergeant. I could just see her thought-bubble – suppose I disgrace myself by using the pudding spoon for the soup at our first dinner night?'

Hope raised her eyebrows. 'Does your shoulder ache?' she queried, with heavy sympathy.

'No, why?'

'Because you're carrying one hell of a big chip on it!'

The college was a cross between a finishing school and a reformatory, Juliet thought. After that awkward little interlude about table settings – and really, some things had to be said, Isa wasn't *quite* out of the top drawer, after all – had come flower arranging, not little posies but socking great arrangements, big enough to be seen across a very crowded room.

'The junior female in the mess is almost always Flower Member,' they were told. 'So you must be able to order flowers in correct quantities, without waste, arrange them and care for them. On grand occasions, you can always call on officers' wives for assistance.'

Some hope. Juliet could manage the dinky little table settings, but her big vases always toppled over.

'I thought I'd joined the army,' she grumbled, 'not the Constance Spry academy.'

Hope loved the original touch. She did a massive arrangement for the chapel that consisted only of grasses. Wild, waving and very, very green against the pine-clad walls, it looked marvellous on Saturday. By Sunday the grass was flat, shedding seeds all over the altar cloth. Another carpeting for Hope.

And makeup. The bare-faced look was not approved for would-be officers.

'Femininity in uniform, ladies, is *so* important,'

stated a representative from a well-known cosmetic house. 'Don't you agree? It's your duty to present a bright, agreeable and feminine aspect to the watching world. It was important during the last war – I should know, I always made sure my ATS girls wore lipstick, even on a gun site – and it's *just* as important to young serving women today. Now – who's going to be my *lucky* guinea pig today? How about you, dear? Yes, you, the tall girl by the door. You're rather pale. Are you getting enough iron?'

Ruth had no idea what was going on. She lay back with her eyes closed and listened to the murmur of the woman's voice and enjoyed the gentle slap-slap of strong fingers on her face.

'You have a very striking face, very elegant, but you don't make the best of it, dear. Always show a *bright* face to the world. It's a matter of pride. You owe it to yourself. Smile and the world smiles with you, I always say.'

It was oddly soothing. The opportunity to do nothing for half an hour was worth the crick in Ruth's neck. She lay in a warm, sleepy haze, while images of herself magically transformed into Celia Hammond floated by. She'd just got to the bit where she was being photographed by David Bailey when she had to wake up.

'There, dear. The new you. I just know you're going to *love* it. And all the cosmetics I've used come at a very affordable price.'

A mirror was held up to Ruth's face for her delighted inspection.

Hair still scraped back in a bandeau. Pencilled

brows. Shimmery lids, heavy with the weight of pearly shadow, shining blue above brown eyes. Neat little rouged cheeks, coquettishly pink on matt tan powdered skin. Joan Crawford lips.

'Oh, my God,' Ruth screeched. 'You've turned me into my grandmother!'

She turned in time to catch the frown of disapproval on Captain Hillcroft's flawlessly made-up face.

Nell quite enjoyed the academic work. She'd always been a bit of a swot. Bad luck on the officers chosen to teach some subjects. There wasn't a lecturer born who could make Pay interesting (there simply wasn't enough of it!), or enthral with the arcane mysteries of the subject called Quartering (sock counting and mattress inspecting). How could students be expected to spend an hour filling out a sample inventory book, when it was all a matter of common sense? She closed her book and looked round to see how the others were getting on. Surely it must be nearly time for tea. Nell's was the only head raised.

But military history fascinated her and current affairs gave everyone a chance to remember that there was a real world out there beyond the ladybird-decorated metal gates. These subjects were taught by academics from Sandhurst and were handled like university tutorials. During the oddly named Army Org., Nell could have recited a brigade or divisional ORBAT (Order of Battle) standing on her head, if asked. Then there was Service Writing – how to write anything from a full-scale brief to the

Chiefs of the Defence Staff to marking an operational map, from a formal submission to a senior officer (I have the honour to be, sir, your obedient servant) to a thank-you letter for a dinner party (the kipper pâté was delicious – do let me have the recipe).

Easy-peasy.

But always, mid-morning or mid-afternoon, came the anxious moment when the duty cadet would have to invite the current teacher to join them for coffee or tea. The girls could all relax if it was one of the civilian lecturers, have a giggle and enjoy the harmless, if sometimes outrageous flirting of silly old men. If it was a military lecturer, they were on their guard, even as they took coats, opened doors, poured tea, handed round cake. These were common civilities; they would have done the same for any guest in their own homes.

But here it was different. They were being assessed. Constantly. Watching, there was always some-one watching. And junior cadets were always on display.

So when their uniforms, supposedly tailored to fit, arrived at last, they were absurdly grateful and eager to stitch on the white gorget patches that signified their status as officer cadets and the narrow strips of felt – beech brown or green, designating company, Edinburgh or Windsor, and term, senior or junior – onto their sleeves. Hope was made to unpick hers twice, because she couldn't get the spacing between the strips right. With a circle of white felt behind the beret badge and a white strip of petersham behind the forage cap badge, they were complete.

The system worked. It had broken them down, made them ridiculous, and now they really believed that it would build them up again.

Nell looked in the glass on the first morning in uniform and saw a different girl. This one had a new assurance. Straighter, taller, surely, or was it just the way she stood? The collar was so tight that she had to keep her head high. Not thinner, though, she was sorry to see. Breakfast was a parade – they had to attend – and it was always cooked. Biscuits with morning coffee. Lunch often included seconds of steamed pudding. Tea and cake. Dinner. Being chivvied from pillar to post all day meant that she always seemed to be starving. Or perhaps she just ate because it was there. Oh, well . . .

Still, she thought she looked terrific. Perhaps they all had the same feeling. There was a new briskness in their walk. Their strides were longer. Their arms swung more freely. They were on their way to their first inspection by an officer.

'Fluff on your beret, Vernon, and hairs on your shoulders. The knot of your tie is off centre. Fluff on your beret, Cleeve, you need a smaller collar size – your collar is gaping and your skirt zip is sliding towards the front. Blakeney, if you can't do better than that with your hair, you must have it cut. It's escaping everywhere. Fluff on your beret. Unpick your company flashes and resew, please, by tomorrow. And there's a dirty thumbprint on your left gorget patch. Very nice, Cameron. Tedder, fluff on your beret. Don't press folds into your sleeves. Sleeves should be pressed, but not into knife edges.'

The administrative officer finished with the front and moved on to inspect their backs.

'Crooked stocking seams, Tedder. Good, Cameron. Blakeney, crooked seams and the back of your skirt looks as though you've slept in it. Crooked seams, Cleeve. Crooked seams, Vernon.'

And now she was at the front again, having completed her circuit.

'All of you – with the exception of Cameron – your shoes need a considerable amount of work before they're fit to be seen on parade. And a word about shoelaces. Shoes are to be laced like a ladder, not criss-cross, and the bow is to lie flat, horizontally across the foot, not vertically down the laces – Vernon. Thank you, Sergeant Major.'

'Thank you, ma'am. Officer on parade. Parade – dismiss.'

They didn't suppose Captain Hillcroft actually enjoyed demoralizing the little squad. She could have been a lot tougher.

'More in sorrow than in anger,' as Hope remarked. 'I know I'm scruffy. I'm one of nature's slobs. I mean, look at this, for God's sake.' She plucked hopelessly at the slipping knot of hair. 'It's like rusty barbed wire. You're just too perfect for words, Isa. I really ought to hate you.'

'Oh, don't . . .' Nell gasped. 'You mustn't say that . . .'

When everyone laughed, she joined in, knowing she'd said something silly, but not sorry for it.

Whatever happened, they mustn't fall out. Whatever happened.

'Don't be daft,' Hope consoled her, putting one arm around Isa's shoulders and one around Nell's. 'We've got to stick together – just like cowboys with the Indians circling. If we don't, they'll pick us off, one by one.'

Ruth joined the huddle and pulled Juliet in with her.

'We'll learn,' she consoled Hope. 'Soon we'll be the brightest, smartest, neatest cadets around – but it won't make us any nicer than we are already.'

'Anyway, don't worry about inspections. It's just the way things are,' Isa advised. 'Look on the bright side. At least we don't have to polish buttons these days. God bless stay-bright buttons.'

'We told you that you weren't fit to be seen,' said the senior cadets.

So they'd been wrong. The system still had some breaking down to do.

'A little word, Blakeney.' Captain McCall, Edinburgh company commander, popped her head round her door as she heard the junior cadets clatter off to coffee. 'In my office.'

'Now, ma'am?'

'Now, Blakeney. No need to wear your beret. It's just a chat. Sit down.'

Hope knew about little chats. The seniors had warned them. There was a recognized scale. A system of fine checks and balances. First the chat, if you were straying from the prescribed path. Then the Company Commander's interview, more formal, beret on and saluting. Then – and it was time to start worrying – Officer Commanding Cadets' interview. She would hand out Kleenex with her sentence: on review (watch it); back-terming (for the worthy but dim); official warning (one false move and you're out); finally, sorry, you're not one of us, no hard feelings and here's a railway warrant home. Then it was off to the Commandant for confirmation of the punishment.

You've wandered off the straight and narrow, Hope, she told herself. *I wonder what it's for this time.*

'Blakeney, at the cadet party last week . . .' Captain McCall began, taking off her spectacles and looking (piercingly, she believed) at Hope. Then she dithered, screwing the cap back on her fountain pen, adjusting the right-angled symmetry of her blotter.

'Yes, ma'am . . .' Hope encouraged her. As far as she was aware, she'd been sober, diligent and polite. So what next?

'You should be aware that there were certain questions raised . . .'

A little pause. The sunlight struck sparks off the officer's diamond and sapphire engagement ring. She was engaged to a carabinier without – rumour had it – a penny to bless himself with. The ring was a good one. Perhaps it had belonged to the impoverished fiancé's grandmother.

Another good woman bites the dust, Hope thought.

'Yes, ma'am,' she said again, with bewilderment.

'It occurred to several people ... we wondered ... were you wearing a bra, Blakeney?'

Hope gave a snorting laugh that only got worse when she saw her company commander's disapproving expression. A bra? Whose business was it what went on under her clothes? The whole idea was ridiculous.

'I'm not aware of having made a joke, Blakeney.'

'No, ma'am.' But Hope was still giggling. For heaven's sake, whose smutty idea of duty was it to stare at her breasts, anyway?

'This childish sniggering is an example of all the things about you that disturb me, Blakeney. I fear that this little chat will be the first of many, unless you come to your senses. Now – were you wearing a bra last Thursday night?'

Hope stared over Captain McCall's shoulder, her eyes glazing over with the effort of remaining serious. The Education Officer's corgi was relieving herself right in the middle of the parade square. The RSM would go mad.

'No, ma'am.'

'I thought not. And with a crochet dress. Blakeney, it was most unbecoming. There are standards of dress and decorum which are required of WRAC officers. We all – all of us – have to strive to uphold those standards. We are expected to be ladies as well as officers, and ladies wear underwear. Always. You are not to be seen again improperly dressed. And that – Blakeney – is an order.'

'Yes, ma'am. But it was a party, ma'am. I'm

always well strapped up in uniform. All that foot-stamping . . .'

Not a glimmer of response. 'There is no gulf between private and public life in the army, Blakeney. On-duty and off-duty are one and the same thing. Indivisible. Do you understand?'

She didn't, but what was the point of prolonging this little chat when there was coffee waiting? 'Yes, ma'am.'

'And while we're on the subject . . . it's not a personal criticism – you mustn't take this personally – to say that overall you are quite a . . .'

'Scruffy soldier?'

'No. Quite a . . .'

'Failure?'

'No. Will you let me finish? Quite a well-rounded . . .'

'Voluptuous?' Hope suggested with a grin. Just as well she hadn't used that word to Molly Greene, the other company commander, if the rumours were anything like accurate!

'That's not the word I was looking for,' came the humourless reply. 'You are quite a curvaceous young woman. Bluntly, you have a wiggle. This has been commented on . . .'

Suddenly, Hope wasn't laughing any more. The joke was over. She stopped looking over the Company Commander's shoulder and fixed her frank, grey eyes on the young officer's face. The poor woman looked down and tightened the already tight cap on her pen. There was a tiny sound as the plastic cracked.

'I'm only human, ma'am,' said Hope.

'Yes, of course, and I'm not suggesting . . . Blakeney, why don't you wear a roll-on? In uniform, at least?'

'I don't have one, ma'am.'

'Then buy one. It doesn't have to be restrictive. Something lacy. And there are quite pretty colours today, you know . . . I'm sure you know . . .' she finished, lamely.

'I can't afford one, ma'am.'

'Blakeney, you are quite determined to do this the hard way, aren't you?'

Hope stared silently.

'Very well. Let's be quite clear. You are not to be seen without a bra at any time and in uniform you are not to wiggle.'

'I'm not certain that's a legal order, ma'am.'

'What?'

'We were doing it in Military Law. Major Archer said that certain types of order are not enforceable and illegal orders can be disobeyed. For example, if you ordered me to shoot the prisoners-of-war . . . if there were any prisoners-of-war in the WRAC College and if I had a gun . . .'

'Blakeney . . .' Captain McCall could feel her little chat spiralling out of control.

'Or even if you ordered me to walk the Commandant's dog . . . if she had a dog . . . you could *ask* me, but if you ordered me . . .'

'Blakeney, that's enough . . .'

'Then I could say no and it wouldn't be disobedience.'

'I will not have you disputing points of law with me.'

'For instance, we were paid underwear allowance when we arrived to make sure we were fully equipped. And if I'm in possession of the full scale of underwear as laid down in WRAC Regulations, can you order me to buy something extra? And if so, am I entitled to an extra allowance to cover the cost?'

Captain McCall gave a sigh that seemed to come from a very long way down. 'I'll speak to the paymaster about it. Now, I can hear your squad on drill. Give Sergeant Millett my compliments and apologize for your lateness.'

'Yes, ma'am. Thank you, ma'am.'

'And Blakeney – you haven't made a very good impression so far. Just a reminder . . .'

Hope smashed her feet down on the tarmac of the drill square with more than usual fervour. *Whose business is it if bits of me wobble? Who cares if I fucking wiggle? It's my backside.* The metal-tipped leather soles made a satisfying crash. By the left . . . quick march. Squaaad – about turn. (Left, in, left, right, left, forward.) Change step. (Left, check, left.) Squaaad – squad, halt. *I don't bloody care.* Stand at ease. *The next person to stare at my bum will get a bloody earful.* Stand easy.

'Some of you, ladies, some of you – ' said Sergeant Millett, glaring at Juliet ' – are under the impression that we are ballet dancing out here. But we are not. We are soldiers. So we do not flap our arms like dying flipping swans – do we, Miss Cleeve? And we do not mince along like sugar plum fairies. There are no fairies here, are there? I hope not. Because we're going to do it again. Properly. Squad – stand at ease. Squaaad – squad, shun.'

Hope crunched her feet again and this time she ground her heel into the tarmac.

Nell wasn't sure which was worse.

There were the informal parties, when they were supposed to have fun. It was expected, required, even. Young people ought to be allowed to let off steam. It was healthy – like porridge for breakfast and cold showers. You weren't allowed *not* to enjoy yourself. Within limits. It would never do for the music to be heard in the Officers' Mess.

Then there were the formal ones, when the cadets spent whole evenings under the critical eyes of the permanent staff. Benevolent despots, they watched and listened while the girls circulated, made conversation, offered drinks, entertained official guests. They sparkled. God, *how* they sparkled. Alert, they were always alert, ready to grab every opportunity to demonstrate that elusive virtue, OQ – Officer Quality. And if you didn't have it – well, goodbye, it was time to pack the suitcases.

Nightmares, all of them.

Nell's personal nightmare started on a Saturday night early in the term.

She was shattered. They'd been orienteering around Minley Lake. At least, that had been the idea. Nell had got lost – the map didn't seem to bear any resemblance to what she saw on the ground –

stuck in a bog, caught in a rhododendron thicket, and was the last to struggle back to the minibus. The instructor, an elderly, passed-over Royal Signals major – the male members of staff were specially selected for their paternal attitudes and happily married status – had been bellowing as she came in sight.

'Come along, Vernon, show a leg.'

Only then did she realize that she didn't have a compass.

'Well, now,' he said, with a wicked uncle grin. 'You have a choice, Vernon. Officers should be able to make decisions – good training. You can get in the bus and face a charge of losing military equipment. Or you can go back and look for it and make everyone late for tea. Which will you choose?'

There wasn't a choice, really. On a cadet's pay, she couldn't afford stoppages to replace the stupid compass. So she turned and trotted off. A mile and a half away, she found the dratted thing on top of a gatepost. They were all glaring, even Hope, by the time she got back to the bus again.

'There was another option, you know, Vernon,' Major Archer informed her, looking more like Aladdin's Uncle Abanazar than ever. 'You could have told the others to go back without you and not forced them to pay a penalty for your carelessness. Did you think of that? Mmm? No? Well.'

Nell squashed into the minibus, silent and conscious of the smell of sweat rising from her.

'But you said last week – sir – that it was never a good idea to split up a raiding party into penny packets,' Ruth intervened, with her usual calm logic. 'You said it reduced the effectiveness of any action.'

'So I did, Tedder, so I did. Nice to know that someone was awake. Sometimes I think that all you girls are interested in is the best shade of lipstick to go with your uniforms.'

The tea was stewed and the seniors had eaten all the cake. Nell had to apologize all over again.

So all Nell wanted, that Saturday night, was to have a bath and get into her pyjamas. She could sit in bed and swot up on the *Manual of Military Law* for the test on Monday. She rather liked military law. It had a sort of anachronistic certainty. 'If this, then that . . .' No arguing. No maybes.

She'd got rather diverted by the sample charges.

The prisoner, No.—, Private—, —Battalion, —Regiment, a soldier of the Regular Forces, is charged with Malingering, in that he, at—, on—, with the intention of evading his duties as a soldier, counterfeited dumbness.

The prisoner, No.—, Private—, —Battalion, —Regiment, a soldier of the Regular Forces, is charged with Losing by Neglect his equipment, clothing and regimental necessaries, in that he . . .

Oh, Lord. This was the one they'd have got her on, if Major Archer had had anything to do with it. She could almost hear the charge being read out.

. . . in that she, at Minley, on 28 September 1968, was deficient of one compass . . .

Who the hell cared!

Someone put on a record in the anteroom below.

Mary Hopkin's thin, childlike voice rose and filled her room.

To everything – turn, turn, turn – there is a season . . .

Piercingly sweet, achingly sad, pure and wise and innocent.

. . . and a time to every purpose under heaven.

Nell was suddenly, wrenchingly lonely. Inside she was void, an aching nothingness. There was nothing for her here. She'd made an awful mistake. She was totally lacking in OQ – not a scrap did she have, not a saving vestige, nothing but a reasonably sharp brain.

She'd be turfed out and sent home, home to 'I told you so . . .' Only it wouldn't be put as bluntly as that, of course. Her humiliation would be treated with cutting kindness. It would be, at intervals, in varying combinations – 'Darling, such a relief. Now you can settle down at last. I can't imagine what made you think you could . . .'

She was going down in a welter of self-pity. All she wanted to do was pull the bedclothes over her head and howl. And that, in itself, was a pointer to her lack of OQ. She couldn't win!

'Nell, for heaven's sake, what're you doing in bed? Are you ill?'

Nell kept her face turned from Hope, to hide the tearstains, but she couldn't help the sniff before answering. 'No. Just muddy and sweaty and fed up.'

'Is that all? Pretty normal then! Did you have any dinner?'

'I wasn't hungry.'

'*That* serious, huh?'

'There didn't seem much point in getting dressed again after my bath.'

'Well, there is now. We're on parade.'

'What?'

'Don't panic. Only sort of. Some of the cadets from Sandhurst have come over to check out the new talent. Sorting out the sheep from the goats. Or, rather, the dogs from the dolly birds!'

'Cheek. I'm not available to be checked out by anyone.'

'You never know. They might be OK. Some of them even look old enough to shave! D'you realize, we haven't seen a man under fifty since we got here.' Hope darted towards the bed and whisked off the bedclothes before Nell could grab them. 'C'mon. It's Saturday night. Stop wallowing and get dressed.'

'Get off. I don't want to.'

'You don't have a choice.' Hope looked at Nell's sprawling figure with pity. 'Haven't you learned *anything* yet? You're not allowed to be different here.'

Nell had to sluice her face in cold water and slap on enough makeup to hide reddened eyes – make a virtue of it, why not, so she slicked on some Biba eyeshadow in a sludgy pinky-grape – and decide what to wear. None of her skirts were short enough. *With knees like mine*, she thought, *perhaps that's no bad thing*. So she settled on a skinny rib sweater and her only pair of flares, purple velvet. Her mother had winced and called them a terrible mistake – 'I really don't think, darling . . . Are you being sensible. With those thighs . . . ? I don't mean to be hurtful, but if your mother can't tell you the truth, who can?' But Nell loved the colour, though she'd never found the right time and place to wear them yet.

By the time she went downstairs, the visit had grown into a party. Already, the room had a squalid atmosphere, hazy with smoke, pungent with hair lacquer and *Je Reviens* and beer and damp tweed. All the lights but one by the bar had been turned out and replaced by candles in wax-encrusted Chianti bottles. The chairs had been pushed back and the carpet rolled up, leaving a little square of polished floor that half a dozen couples could cram to immobility. The record changed to a smoochy one.

'*Trains and boats and planes . . .*' Nell sang to herself.

Juliet was dancing, scarcely moving, rocking from one foot to the other, snuggled against a boy whose raw neck told Nell that he'd been in the army no longer than she had. Isa was sitting with a man on either arm of her chair, like heraldic supporters. Knowing Isa, they were probably reorganizing the Ministry of Defence to her liking. Ruth was stuck on the dance floor with a sandy-haired boy whose chin came up to her shoulder and whose sense of rhythm had gone absent without leave. Hope was cross-legged on a cushion on the floor, sharing a cigarette, sucking at it dreamily then passing it to a man who looked older, less skinned alive, than most of the others. It seemed odd.

That's not very hygienic, Nell thought. *I mean, I*

*know we're hard up, but surely Hope could afford a
cigarette of her own. Still . . .* Nell smiled and waved.
Hope raised a hand in a slow greeting. *At least they
look happy.*

Everyone seemed to have paired up already. Men
outnumbered women by about four to one, but the
unattached boys huddled in a daunting phalanx by
the bar. In uniform or out of it, you'd be pressed to
tell them apart. The patched tweed jackets, the cords
– yellow, most of them, in every possible shade,
lemon, canary, mustard, ochre, stiff enough to stand
up on their own – the desert boots, crêpe-soled
brothel creepers. Little boys in their father's castoffs.
They couldn't be anything but soldiers in mufti, with
the individuality already ground out of them.

Nell stood by the record player, ready to make
herself useful. It was a ploy she always used at
parties. Look busy – stack plates, empty ashtrays,
change records – and no-one notices you're not
talking.

She riffled through the stack of records, looking as
though she might be choosing the next one. She
went through them four times.

'Nice bristols,' she heard someone remark. Oh
God, were they talking about her?

'Shame about the legs,' came the inevitable reply.

'I always go for the air hostesses myself. They may
not have the brains, but they certainly have the
bodies.'

'And they're willing.'

Nell looked up and glared at the speakers.
Both older, by a couple of years, maybe, not from

82

Sandhurst. The cadets were having their rough edges scrubbed away, but these two had already been repolished, shaped to fit the mould. Subalterns, she guessed, probably from Aldershot garrison.

One had the manners to look away. She hadn't seen him properly, but she had the impression of a nose that didn't quite fit the rest of his face, a battered, kindly face, too gentle to speak those ugly words. The other held her angry glance and lobbed it back to her, defused with a laugh. He was gorgeous, blond and willowy, not the type she yearned after at all, but so perfect, Rupert Brooke reincarnated. And bloody rude.

Bloody rude. What did he expect her to do? Burst into tears and run off to hide? Nell yanked the playing arm and the needle slid off the record with a screech that caused a yell of protest from the dance floor. She picked something fast and bouncy. Juliet and her partner continued their static swaying, foot to foot, as though the music hadn't changed at all.

'Dance with me,' she demanded, holding out her hand to the beautiful blond. 'I know you think I'm dull and dumpy . . .'

'Hey, I never said . . .'

'But didn't you know, we plump girls are always good dancers. Light on our feet.'

'Listen, I didn't mean . . .'

Nell wondered if he had the grace to blush, but it was too dark to tell. Once she knew him better, she realized that he wouldn't.

'It's a modern myth, you know. Like the one

about coloured people and their natural rhythm. Strange but true.'

They danced to the end of that record and into the next and the one that followed was dreamy and he felt so good to her and her head nestled so comfortably into the hollow just beneath his chin.

Frank Sinatra's voice was soothing as honey and lemon.

Do people fall in love, Nell wondered, *just like that?*

He slid his hands down her back and around her waist, then down to her buttocks. The actions seemed to come naturally to him. That's what he always did. That's what girls always liked. He held her closely against him, closer than she meant to be, closer than she knew was sensible. He was hard and flat and bony. Without a jacket, she could feel the play of the long muscles down his back beneath her fingers.

'Hey,' he murmured. His lips moved against her hair. 'You're so tense. Relax. Come on.' And he stroked her, as though she were a frightened kitten. 'What're you scared of?'

Even Nell knew better than to answer, 'You.'

Their movements slowed to a sway, as though they waded through honey, as though they stood in an invisible pentacle and dared not leave its confines. Nothing could touch her, Nell felt, nothing make her afraid, for as long as the music lasted.

Then Alison Barkwith took her by the shoulder and turned her away from her partner. 'Sorry to butt in.' Like hell she was. 'I'm going to have to ask you to get changed, Nell.'

'Whatever for?'

'Because you're wearing trousers.'

Nell just gaped at her.

'You know the rules – no trousers unless they're part of a tailored trouser suit.'

Her partner just laughed. 'That's a bit petty, isn't it?'

Alison shrugged. 'I didn't make the rules. But Nell has to obey them.' She gave a little flick with her head towards the door.

Nell thought she was pretty good at not showing how humiliated she felt. She seemed to be getting plenty of practice these days. Stiff upper lip. Backbone of the empire. A different sort of protective camouflage. She didn't slam the door on her way out, but she bashed the door of her own room back against the wall. There was no-one to hear. She was too angry to cry. She thumped into the chair, grabbed a cushion and hugged it into her stomach.

Bloody Alison. And bloody, bloody, bloody rules . . .

She didn't bother to change and go back to the party. There didn't seem to be much point. She knew the type. He'd be with someone else by the time Nell reappeared.

And that was the first time she met Oliver Hawtrey.

'Nothing much going there,' Oliver complained as he nosed the E-type out of the gates and down the A325 towards Aldershot. 'Hardly worth the effort . . .'

'Oh, I don't know,' answered Harry. 'Nice girls, plenty of booze. What more do you want?'

'*Not*-nice girls!'

He gave a laugh that transmitted itself to the steering. The car swooped right and then back again, flinging Harry against the door. Oliver felt the tail slide momentarily from his control.

'Hey, steady on!' protested Harry.

'If you don't like it, get out and walk.'

'And you mustn't tease the babies. They're too young for you. That little plump one would have rolled over and let you rub her tummy.'

'Cute, though. Sometimes a nice girl is a bit more of a challenge than a not-nice girl!' His teeth flashed briefly as they passed the carpark lights of the One Oak. 'Bloody weather.' Oliver rubbed the Jaguar's tiny split screen, but his fingers were greasy with sausage roll pastry and smeared the glass. 'The old man's inspecting the Gurkhas tomorrow. He'll be expecting me to be standing smartly to attention behind him with the rain dripping off the end of my nose.'

'Cushy job,' Harry taunted. 'Think of me at dawn, won't you, trundling off down to Salisbury Plain to jump out of a Hercules.'

'More fool you. Wouldn't catch me jumping out of a perfectly good plane. God, it's an absolute monsoon. Open the window your side, will you? Let some air in.'

As they neared Aldershot, leaving the series of

roundabouts behind them, Oliver allowed the sleek machine to pick up speed. So easy. It scarcely waited for his foot on the throttle. He wasn't even certain that he'd made the decision. The engine was impatient, as though it knew what it was doing. Harry twisted sideways and squinted at the dials.

'Steady on,' he warned again. 'Even parachuting's not as dicey as driving with you.'

Past the Queen's Hotel and the final roundabout. The road stretched dark and slick ahead of them, shadowed by trees. On the left, the grassy expanse of Queen's Parade, mowed to a millimetre. On the right, married quarters where some of Oliver's friends slept blamelessly beside their wives.

Boring. Always a mistake to marry too young in the army. A man under thirty shouldn't even dream of it. Does your promotion prospects no good at all. Like living in military sin. Promotion and wives don't go together. Just so much baggage.

The headlights bounced back at him off the road. A cyclist pushing his bike, head down, unable to make progress against the slashing rain. A Land Rover going the other way, its engine note a high drone, water coursing away from its tyres, silver and gold and red.

And out of the black zone where light met dark, out of the black edge of consciousness, just beyond his vision, emerged a figure. Sturdy and white and heedless. Hunched and buffeted by the storm, a careless figure in flapping white. And, at the last moment, a face turned. In a terrified face, great

87

black holes, eyes and an open mouth, a screaming mouth.

Oliver kicked the brake pedal, then he was fighting the steering as the car spun round and round, tyres squealing, water hissing, spray and steam and smoke clouding his vision.

The lights pointing back down the road, slicing through the darkness, back the way they had come, but blazing down the wrong side of the carriageway. Silence. Then Harry Dowland's voice.

'Jesus Christ. Jesus Christ. Jesus Christ.'

Oliver still clutched the steering wheel and his forehead lay on his hands. A trickle of blood from a bitten lip found its way down his chin.

'What the hell were you playing at?' Harry demanded as his breath returned. 'You bloody nearly killed us.'

'I killed him,' Oliver replied flatly.

'What? Who? I didn't see anyone.'

'I killed him.'

'Oh, Christ.' Harry hauled himself out of the low-slung door. 'Get this thing back onto the right side of the road, will you, before some other idiot comes along.'

Bits of him hurt like blazes – knees and elbows and shins and forehead, all the bony bits had been battered against the car's unforgiving interior. A whiplash of agony coursed up his spine. Someone out in the darkness might be hurting a lot more.

But there was no-one there.

It was hard to work out where the car had been when Oliver hit the brakes. They must have travelled quite a distance, some of it sideways, some of it backwards, and Harry had lost all sense of direction as he was twirled about as though in an out of control fairground ride. There were no tyre tracks to guide him. The rain had slicked over them, covering the tarmac with a fine oily sheen.

He walked very slowly for two or three hundred yards in either direction. No-one. Nothing. Not so much as a dead cat. No dark stains on the road. No fragments of clothing. Nothing. But it was bloody dark.

Back at the car, he inspected the bonnet and wings. Only the scrape of khaki paint along the passenger door that showed where Oliver had over-taken a staff car too neatly a couple of days before. Not another mark. Then he pulled open the driver's door.

'Move over,' he ordered.

He drove very slowly along the route he had already walked. The car's lights, close to the ground, illuminated a wide arc. Nothing.

'Nothing,' he said. 'You nearly killed us for nothing, you crazy bastard.'

'There was . . . I saw . . . Jesus Christ, I saw . . .'

'What?'

'I saw . . . Perhaps he's crawled away.'

'No chance. Anything you hit at that speed, Noll, would stay hit. It wasn't going to crawl away.'

'I saw . . . again . . .'

'There was *nothing*.' Harry's voice rose, as though by sheer volume he might make some impact on Oliver's inward-looking horror. 'And *no-one*. There never is. You've got to get over this thing before it's too late.'

Nell reminded Oliver of their meeting once, and only once, after they were married and living in a boxy, semi-detached married quarter in Aldershot, with paper-thin walls and bits of the old parade square coming up in the garden every time she tried to plant something.

He just laughed and said, 'A man doesn't expect the same things in a wife as he does in a girlfriend.'

'And vice versa?'

'And vice versa,' he agreed and patted her bulging stomach.

She never spoke of it again.

'Can any of you – any one of you – tell me why you're here?' Major Ottaway glared round the room through glasses with upswept scarlet frames, matching the flash of the scarlet jacket lining that could be seen every time she moved her arm. The wings of the spectacles were decorated with little diamanté triangles that caught the overhead light and magnified the reflection from the glass. 'Why did you join the WRAC? Cleeve? Why did you?'

Bugger it, why pick on me first? If she'd been honest, Juliet would have said 'Because I look good in a uniform. I've got the figure for it. It was a toss-up between the WRNS and the WRAC, but green suits me better than blue.' Besides, it had seemed like a good way to escape Simon, who was much too keen on marriage. And marrying a junior doctor who worked one hundred and seven hours a week was not part of Juliet's life plan.

But even Juliet had been at the college long enough to learn that you give the answer that's wanted, not necessarily the truth.

'Because I was looking for responsibility, ma'am,' she answered glibly, her usually snapping black eyes for once wide and guileless.

'And Tedder? What about you?'

Ruth considered. Nothing ever hurried her, not even Major Ottaway. 'I like working with people,' Ruth answered, simply and honestly.

'Vernon? Why are you here?'

Nell was tempted, really tempted to tell the truth. *Because it was the only way I could think of to get away from home. The army was the only place my mother couldn't follow me.*

Instead, she dredged up one of the stock replies, highly recommended, rocking no boats. 'I want to serve my country, ma'am.'

'Mmm. I wonder.' Major Ottaway turned without much enthusiasm to Hope. She looked as though she was unlikely to believe any answer Hope might give, however praiseworthy. 'And why ever did *you* think you might find a career in the WRAC, Blakeney?'

'I want to specialize, ma'am. I'm good at languages. I'd like to train as an interpreter.'

Another mistake, Hope. Honesty was the last quality required here.

'I see. You think you're too intelligent for regimental work. That you're a cut above the rest of us poor mortals? Is that it?'

Hope squirmed. 'Not exactly . . .'

Major Ottaway gave her a look of utter contempt. 'I respect your frankness, if nothing else. Regimental officers are the backbone of the Corps. I hope none of you will forget that. We *Serve to Lead*, as the Sandhurst motto has it. Specialization is the icing on the cake – attractive, but unwholesome in quantity. Now, Cameron. I've left you until last because I'm hoping to get a sensible answer from you. How do you see your career in the WRAC?'

Isa was very calm. There was an unshakeable quality about her that endowed her words with the sound of prophecy. 'I'm going to be the first woman general,' and into the following silence intruded the sound of Major Ottaway's breath being drawn in sharply.

'I see . . .' she said slowly, blown off track.

Nell wondered if the Pope had felt any more shocked when he heard about Martin Luther burning the papal bull. This was heresy. This was insurrection.

In a few, quiet words, Isa had suggested that there was life beyond the confines of regimental duty. She had said that she didn't believe that the purpose of the WRAC was to administer itself, in a self-fulfilling spiral. She had cast doubt on the belief that the highest attainable position, the ultimate aim of every woman officer, was to be the DWRAC, the one and only woman brigadier who held the post of Director Women's Royal Army Corps.

In the silence, it was almost possible to hear the faggots being piled around the stake.

Then Major Ottaway looked down at the desk and shuffled her notes. 'I see . . .' she said again. 'Well, no-one can fault your ambition, Cameron, even if there must be serious doubts about your common sense.' Then she was up and running again. 'Very praiseworthy sentiments from all of you. Responsibility? Working with people? Serving your country? I wonder. But I have to tell you that not one of you will be serving your country in this uniform, unless you stop and think seriously about effort and commitment. Your junior term is three-quarters over. Soon you'll be going home for Christmas. When you come back – those of you who come back . . .' she looked threateningly around the room '. . . will be senior cadets, with responsibility for a new intake of juniors. And I certainly don't think you're ready for it. This intake is distinguished only by laziness, complacency and lack of initiative. Worst of all, there is a total lack of team spirit. I warn you, that unless you start working together as an entity, things are going to go from bad to worse . . .'

Phew!

The cadets stood as Major Ottaway left the room and let out a collective gust of breath.

'Don't worry about it,' advised Jo Fiske, the oldest of the senior cadets and the only one who'd had a civilian job before joining up. 'It's routine at this stage in the course. Week ten – the pull-yourselves-together talk. She's just putting a squib up your collective backside to see if it makes you fart . . .'

* * *

Ruth called a mass shoe-bulling session that evening. She called into the bedrooms and hauled out a tired and grumpy girl from each.

'This is important,' she urged. 'Yes, even more important than polishing your taps! Downstairs in five minutes. OK?'

And because it was Ruth and because she almost never became worked up about anything, they obeyed.

The seniors had been invited to Sandhurst to hear a guest lecturer talk about NATO and the Threat from the Warsaw Pact. For once, the juniors had the run of the mess and all met in the television room.

They brought their best pairs of shoes – their parade shoes – clean dusters and black Kiwi polish. Only Kiwi would do. Nothing else got up that sought-after, diamond-hard gloss. In the lid of each open polish tin was a little clean, cold water.

'The trouble is,' Ruth began, twisting a duster around the first and second fingers of her polishing hand, 'that the OC was right.'

'Rubbish. She was just trying to put the wind up us,' interrupted Juliet. 'Jo said so.'

Ruth contemplated her shoes with the serious expression of a surgeon about to make the first incision. 'I'm not so sure . . .'

Nell dabbed her duster-wrapped fingers into the water in the tin lid, smeared them through the polish, and began to work in tiny circles on the toe-cap of her right shoe.

The Sandhurst cadets had come up with all sorts of tricks for getting that Coldstream Guards best boots glitter. Some of the methods sounded a bit too much like voodoo – rubbing with a clean bone, for instance. Then there was smoothing the grain of the leather with the bowl of a red-hot spoon. Potential cavalry officers swore by champagne instead of water. The girls ignored it all and stuck to hot breath and cold water.

There was something oddly comfortable about the scene. The curtains were drawn against the late autumn darkness. Rain was battering the windows, carried on a wind that gusted across acres of sandy, heathery emptiness. The five girls sat in a circle, their polish tins open on a table in the centre. Juliet's ashtray was filling. Their first bottle of Blue Nun was nine-tenths knocked off. It was the military equivalent of a quilting bee, a sociable, friendly, gossipy fellowship of workers.

Or a vacuum. A closed, secret world in which an American electorate choosing Richard Nixon to be the next President, the most powerful man in the world, passed by without causing a flicker of interest, but in which the precise angle of a shoelace bow assumed gigantic importance.

'*These boots are made for walking*,' sang Hope, in an off-key imitation of Nancy Sinatra, '*and that's just what they'll do . . .*'

'*One of these days these boots are gonna walk all over you*,' Ruth finished.

Isa was breathing vigorously on her toecaps. Spit was no good, whatever old soldiers told you. If you'd just cleaned your teeth, you got toothpaste mixed up with the polish. And if you hadn't just cleaned your teeth, you got a bit of whatever you'd last eaten. Breath was much more efficient.

'When I was at the Centre . . .' she began and the others all stopped to listen. Isa didn't often talk about her days in the ranks, but when she did, it was always worth listening to her sound, Scottish common sense. '. . . in recruit training, we were divided into platoons, of course. And it was obvious that the platoons that worked together as teams, that stuck together and helped each other out, got through their training much better than the ones that were always bickering or out for number one. Of course, that was only six weeks. We didn't have time to get on each other's nerves,' she went on, with a wry smile in Juliet's direction, 'like we can in eight months. But we ought to think about it.'

'We get on all right,' said Juliet, a touch defensively, hunching a shoulder over her work.

'But, don't you see – all right isn't good enough . . .'

'That's what I've been trying to say,' put in Ruth. 'We've got to make a much bigger effort to stick together next term. If we can't rely on each other in this place, we're sunk.'

'All for one and one for all, eh?' laughed Hope, who seemed to be taking off more polish than she was putting on. She held up her arm in a clenched fist salute, spoiled by a dangling yellow duster. 'The people, united . . .' she chanted.

'. . . will never be defeated . . . Exactly,' Ruth agreed. 'And if not, we won't all make it until April.'

Nell was impressed by the idea. 'You've got my

vote, Ruth. If we don't help each other out, they'll pick us off, one by one. We've all got our weaknesses and we've all got our strengths. Put together, we make one pretty damn fine soldier!'

'But it means all of us,' Ruth continued. 'No exceptions. Watching each other's backs. No-one out on a limb.'

They all nodded solemnly, as though they'd been asked to take an oath. They'd grown out of childish spit-and-swear, but the atmosphere was much the same.

The television in the corner flickered and changed to the black-and-white face of a concerned newsreader. No-one paid much attention. Same old stories.

Civil rights marches in Londonderry. Defiantly banged dustbin lids and hurtling bricks and jeering women.

An anti-Vietnam demo in Somewheresville, USA. The American flag burning, flaring at first, then damply refusing to make an exhibition of itself, hanging charred and defiant from its pole, until a boy in beads and a headband pulled it to the ground and trampled it.

A Buddhist monk, the flames the same colour as his saffron robes. Then twisting and staggering as the fire took hold, blackened, horribly human still, falling, squirming . . .

They'd seen it all before.

'Well, blow this for a game of soldiers!' Hope flung down her duster. 'Look at us – like a bunch of old biddies at the WI.'

'It's *Till Death Us Do Part* next,' Nell reminded her.

'Big deal. I'm going to order a taxi. Who'll share it with me? We could go into Bagshot.'

'Bagshot? Wow!' laughed Juliet, tilting one perfectly curved black eyebrow. 'The centre of the universe. I can't wait!'

'If you can afford the fare to go further, that's fine by me. But I've got about 19/11½d to last until next payday.'

'It's ladies' night at the Pantiles and we can get in free.'

'Great – by my reckoning that'll leave us just about enough for one rum and Coke and five straws!'

'Is there anywhere else it's so easy to do something wrong?' Hope demanded. Careless of the double kick pleats in the back of her skirt (even at the end of a day spent sitting at a desk, someone would be sure to mention the creases), she spawled despairingly in an armchair, staring at an essay paper with more red scrawls on it than black ink. 'Doesn't matter what we do or how hard we try, it's always wrong. Whenever we think we've got it cracked, someone invents a new crime. There are more ways to be wrong here than I'd ever imagined. It's like a bad trip, all day and every day.'

Alison leaned over her shoulder and spoke quietly, but menacingly. 'No work in the anteroom, Hope. You know the rules. Just take those books out, would you?'

'Bloody rules. Bloody books.' Hope stood up and chucked the looseleaf binder in the general direction of the door. It split and spilled red-scrawled papers across the floor. 'Bloody petty.'

Alison's voice rose and cracked across the tantrum. '*Now*, Blakeney.'

'Just look at us. I mean, I can't believe it.'

Hope sat on the draining board, watching Nell placidly starching and ironing collars. The pile rose. They'd pooled ironing to save time and this was Nell's stint. Thirty collars, stiff as nuns' coifs, stiff enough to slice open the jugular if you gave too smart an eyes right, white as Reckitt's blue could make them, folded just so.

Juliet was loading the spin-drier with an armful of shirts. The load was off-centre when she put down the lid and the drier rocked and staggered around the floor, like a paralytic recruit on a Saturday night in Aldershot, until Juliet swore and snatched open the lid and adjusted the load.

'Just look at us,' Hope said again. 'We're out of this world. What're other people our age doing? Digging up the cobbles in Paris and chucking them at gendarmes, that's what. Lying in front of Russian tanks in Prague. Burning their draft cards. Sitting in. Dropping out. Storming the Pentagon . . .'

'And getting baton-charged for it,' Juliet finished for her, setting off the spin-drier again with a tooth-grinding clatter. 'I have no wish to get my skull fractured for a principle, thanks.'

'OK. Maybe. But what're *we* doing? Toeing the line. *Not* rocking the boat. Saying yes ma'am, no ma'am. Keeping our noses clean . . .'

'Oh, grow up, Hope,' snapped Juliet. 'I've got plans. I want to do things, go places, see the world – *not* with sandals and a sleeping bag and some hairy, unwashed man. I like clean clothes and clean beds and clean men. If the army pays me to travel, I'd be mad to turn it down.'

'God, listen to you, you could be forty, you sound just like my mother.'

'Stop whining. You get on my nerves, did you know that, with your everlasting complaints. If you don't like it here, do us all a favour and push off. Put up or shut up, why don't you?'

'Oh, fuck you,' Hope answered, but without any venom, as casually as shaking hands. 'I only meant we're not normal. We're aliens. Freaks. And what about you, busy little Nell? Don't you want something more meaningful out of life than ironing other people's collars?'

'I have to make a success of this,' Nell said, softly. She switched off the iron and squared up the pile of collars. They were perfect. Perfect. The sight of them gave her a strange pleasure. 'It's the one place I feel safe. I can't go back. And I might remind you that some of the collars are yours!'

After Hope had left, Juliet looked towards the door with a disapproving expression. 'The trouble with her,' she said, acidly, 'is that she isn't really one of us.'

Then she looked embarrassed at what she had

said and offered to put Nell's washing through the spinner.

It wasn't working. Ruth's plan of mutual support and care hadn't even got off the ground. But it could work, if they really tried. Isa thought she might go and have a chat with Ruth one evening about it all, but every evening she was just too tired.

All they had to do was try harder. Surely even Juliet was capable of that.

Hope had lain in her sleeping bag all night, on newspapers which covered the lino. Her bed was already made, its corners immaculately turned, its sheets pristine. The rug was vacuumed, rolled and standing upright in the corner. Hope groaned and rolled over inside the bag (polyester-filled – it wouldn't do to shed feathers). Her bones ached, particularly her hip bones. She'd spent half the night trying to find a position that eased them. Dimly, she was aware of the sound of a tolling bell, the chapel bell. Five minutes to eight.

Oh, Christ . . .

Hope sat up, unzipped the bag and ran into the corridor. Her hair was a wild, coppery fuzz – the Lady of Shalott on a bad trip. The long T-shirt she wore in bed had a blown-up front page of *Pravda* printed on it, with Brezhnev and his beetling brows in the centre.

'Fine friends you are,' she berated Ruth and Isa, who were on their way downstairs, already in berets and gloves. 'I'm duty cadet and I'm supposed to ring that bloody bell. Jesus Christ, I'll be bloody skinned . . .'

'Don't panic,' Ruth calmed her. 'Nell's doing it for you. Alison will never know.'

The bell's sound changed from a melancholy note to a frantic, one-minute-to-go clamour.

'Room all right?' asked Isa, sticking her head round the door. 'Great. Now, remember. Roll up and stash your sleeping bag first. No washing or dressing in here. Take everything down to the bathroom and do it there. You're not even to brush your hair in your room. When you're ready, walk backwards out of your room, picking up the newspapers as you go. And don't forget to put down your rug as well. Got that?'

Hope nodded.

'And if you don't have the best room in the place this morning, I'll stand you a drink tonight. The OC is going to be *dazzled*.'

'I don't know why I didn't just sleep in the bath last night.'

'You could have. Why didn't we think of that?'

Hope touched Isa's hand briefly. 'Thanks, Isa.'

'Go on . . .' Isa gave Hope a gentle shove, with a smile that eased the gesture. 'Get on with it. *Amaze us.*'

Of all jobs, Nell thought, she hated most locking up at night.

The kitchens were bad enough. She loathed the crumpled-paper rustle of cockroaches as she fumbled for the light switch. No matter how hard

102

the kitchen staff worked – and they worked extremely hard – the black brutes always found their way in somehow. And the kitchen always seemed to smell of gravy and custard and boiled dish towels. No matter what they'd eaten that night, the smell never changed.

Worse still was locking the hall and chapel. The long white building with its clocktower was all that was left of the Victorian orphanage on whose site the college stood. Her footsteps echoing hollowly, Nell would stride boldly through the dark under-croft, but her bravado melted once she was out of view.

Locking the first door behind her, she'd tiptoe upstairs and along the length of the hall, flashing her torch at each window to make sure it was closed, flashing the beam, too, at any shadow that seemed darker than it ought to be. The shadows seemed to fall into step behind her, but they weren't adult footsteps, they were light and soft and wary. Into the chapel for a quick breather, then down the stairs and out, faster than she'd gone in, locking the door on the sibilant silence.

Some people swore that they'd heard the orphans weeping and the bell tinkling when no-one was near. But that was just the wind. Wasn't it?

Worst of all, and for a very different reason, was checking the outside of Cadet Mess. If she was lucky, it would be a quiet night and there'd be no-one at the back. But Nell wasn't often a lucky person.

All too frequently, there would be a car parked

behind the building, sometimes more than one, the occupants using every last second until the magic hour of 2359. It was amazing what could be achieved in an MGB, with a little co-operation from both parties. Nell tried so hard to keep the torchlight away from the car windows. But it depended on how quickly she came round the corner and where the car might be parked.

Once – before she'd known any better – she'd swung the torch in a wide arc and the beam had shown her Jo Fiske, naked to the waist, her head thrown back. And a man's mouth, voracious at her nipple. Nell had run back into the building. The memory of the dark O of the mouth had come between her and the writing of her duty cadet's report.

Now she was more cautious. She would flick the light quickly round at tree height and hope that there was no irregularity she had missed, for it would be spotted, sure as sure, by the orderly officer on rounds later that night and Nell would be carpeted for lack of observation.

Now the weather was colder, any waiting car would have its windows steamed up. Nell wasn't certain if that was better or worse. Sometimes she knew that it was Juliet out there, with Simon if he'd been able to get any time off, or with that curly-headed subaltern from the RAOC Depot at Deepcut who was always ringing up. Or maybe Hope would be there and she'd come whisking in at the last moment, her hair rumpled and her cheeks roughened by late-night whiskers and her lips swollen and red.

So Nell would turn her eyes and her torch away from the steamed-up windows. She'd walk briskly back, her metal-tipped shoes crunching on the gravel, like a giant munching popcorn.

But Isa was never out there in the whispering darkness.

'Nell – telephone for you.'

Nell left her notes on pay and allowances open on her desk. A digestive biscuit marked the reference she'd just looked up in the textbook. She stuck her head out the door and yelled down the corridor.

'Who is it?'

'Didn't ask . . . a man . . .'

There was little privacy at the payphone tucked under the open-plan stairs. Nell picked up the dangling phone anxiously. A man? Suppose it were her father? Suppose she had to go home? Suppose her mother had gone off on one of her benders again and he was going to demand that Nell come home and sort it out?

'Hello . . .' she began, tentatively.

The reply was wiped out by the clatter of Hope's feet as she hurtled down the overhead stairs, late again, this time for a driving lesson. The outer door slammed and Nell could hear the engine gunned and the wheels skid on gravel.

'Hello . . .' she tried again.

'Nell? Oliver Hawtrey.'

The voice was confident, as though the name ought to mean something to her. She didn't have a clue.

'I'm sorry – who?'

'Oliver Hawtrey.' He was impatient. 'We met at a party at your mess. You were sent upstairs to take your trousers off – naughty girl!'

Heavens, Nell thought, *the blond Apollo. What on earth can he want . . . ?* 'Oh, yes, I remember.'

'Look – I was wondering if you'd care to have dinner.'

'Oh . . . I . . .'

'Don't sound *too* keen, will you. Awfully bad form.'

'No, sorry, I mean – yes. That would be . . . that would be very nice . . .'

'Next Saturday? Are you free? I'll pick you up at seven. Black tie. Oh, and get a late pass.'

'I'm not going.'

'What!'

'I don't know why I said yes. I wish I hadn't. All right?'

Nell stood at the door of her room and stripped off her filthy tracksuit and socks before going in. She padded barefoot across the newspaper on the floor and chucked the smelly bundle into the laundry bin. Barossa Common mud seemed to smell worse than any she'd smelt before – a mixture of peat, horse manure and a century of officer cadets' sweat. In their green Aertex and green knickers, the others crowded after her.

'Look at my shoes,' Nell moaned, holding up a scratched, mud-encrusted pair. Misreading the contours on her map, she'd slogged straight downhill into a bog and up the other side, instead of taking the longer, drier route around the top that everyone else seemed to have found. 'It's Remembrance Day parade tomorrow. How can I go out tonight?'

'You wore your best boots to go map reading?' Hope queried, with awe in her voice. 'Wow! You really *are* in the shit!'

'The other pair's being mended. I got a rocket from Sergeant Millett the other day for not having them heeled sooner. I know – I should have checked the timetable and seen we had map reading, but I didn't and that's that. I can't go. I'll be up all night polishing these.'

'I'd do them for you, but . . .' Hope offered hesitantly. She shrugged. 'But . . .'

'But they'd look like bacon rind, not leather, by the time you'd finished. I know. Thanks, anyway.'

'I'm going out with Simon,' Juliet said, but she had the grace to look shamefaced. 'Sorry. It's his first weekend off for two months, so . . .'

'Leave them with me,' offered Ruth. 'And I'll see what I can do with them. Call them a challenge, if you like, character building . . .'

'It's all right. Don't make a big thing about it. I'm not that keen on Oliver anyway.'

'No problem,' Isa announced. 'Wear a pair of mine. Plenty more where they came from. You can't be in the army as long as I have without picking up a few spares – extra collars here, shoes there – you know. Always worth having a good mate in the

QM's stores. They'll be too big, but you can stuff them up with paper. Who'll know, for an hour or two? I should think Oliver's worth a couple of blisters. So you shall go to the ball, Cinderella.'

Nell gave a soft sigh and tried to look suitably grateful. No way out, then. 'Thanks, Isa. You're a marvel.'

It was twenty-five past seven before Oliver appeared. Nell had been downstairs punctually, or rather, five minutes early, just as she ought. A good soldier is always five minutes early. If Nell ever chose a meditational mantra, it would be that.

'What do you think you're doing?' Juliet demanded. 'Get back upstairs.'

'But he said he'd be here at seven.'

'I don't care what time he appears, you don't come downstairs until five minutes after – or ten, even better. You don't want to look as though you care, do you? Well, then. Go on up. I'll call you. Hang on a mo. Take this with you.' And Juliet passed over a large G and T. 'Steady the nerves.'

'Oh, Juliet, that's really kind of you.'

'Isn't it!' She gave a gurgling laugh. 'It's on your bar chit, though!'

Back in her room, Nell was faced with both time to kill and the full-length mirror that she usually used only to check the straightness of her stocking seams and the back of her greatcoat for fluff. Its dark green melton cloth attracted stray threads like pins to a magnet.

Nell took a swig of gin. 'Oh, God,' she sighed,

staring in the mirror at a figure she scarcely recognized. 'I look like a Jersey cow.'

Juliet had taken her firmly in hand. She'd made Nell raid her Post Office book. 'But that's my savings,' Nell had protested. 'My rainy day money.'

'Funny, that rainy day is here,' she'd been told very firmly.

They'd skived off down to Camberley on a Wednesday afternoon when they should have been having a riding lesson from a cavalry corporal of horse in the Sandhurst *manège*.

In a dim boutique, set between a hairdresser and a motorcycle repair shop, an assistant who made Twiggy look positively robust was painting her nails maroon with glittery bits. She didn't look up as they came in. Probably she didn't hear them. The Bee Gees were at full volume, getting their message across. Disco lights wired to the sound flickered and strobed across the ceiling.

Juliet riffled through the rails of shoddily made dresses. She flipped expertly along, assessing their rainbow frailty.

'That's nice,' she said approvingly, hauling out a sliver of white plastic bordered in black, with a keyhole cutout round the belly button. 'Cute. I wouldn't mind that for myself. What d'you think?' She turned to a mirror, holding the dress against herself. 'Oh, no. Tarty.'

'You won't find anything in my size,' Nell moped. 'I never do.'

'Shut up, you. You're not a whale. You're just

normal. Anyone would think you don't want to go out with the best-looking man ever seen at Cadet Mess.'

'I don't. I don't know why he asked me. And I don't know why I said yes.'

'Thank goodness you've got *some* common sense. Here.'

She thrust half a dozen hangers into Nell's hand and pushed her into a cubicle that was screened only by a western saloon-style half-door. Nell's outraged face and jodhpur-clad legs could be seen above and below the door. The assistant had finished painting her nails and gazed with silent absorption at Nell's legs as she struggled out of the clinging nylon.

Nell could have wept. It was the sort of shop that she always avoided. Girls with hips and bosoms didn't bother with these racks of skinny dresses and supercilious assistants who laughed behind their hands as you sweated and strained. Why deliberately demoralize yourself?

'Buy yourself something worthwhile, something that will last,' her grandmother had said, pressing four £5 notes into Nell's hands when she'd left home. 'A nice outfit from Jaeger. That's always suitable. It would take you anywhere.'

So she'd spent it on a neat dress and jacket, heathery tweed, and a matching hat and it had taken her to every church parade that term, to drinks at the Commandant's flat and to lunch at Sandhurst's Old College – where a couple of hundred slavering young men had made eleven young women fear that

110

they might *be* the lunch. The outfit made Nell look not a day under thirty-five, but not even Juliet had told her that.

'Juliet,' she called over the half-door, feeling like Judy without Punch. 'I can't wear this. I can't even come out and show you.'

Juliet peeped over the top and sniggered. 'Whoops! I see what you mean. Two iced buns with cherries on top. I suppose you could always wear a body stocking under it. Well, perhaps not. Try that.' And she tossed something long and slippery over the door.

The assistant had said, when she'd seen Nell, 'Wow, like, really groovy!' But she'd been resticking her false lashes at the time, so perhaps that didn't count.

So, with Juliet twisting her arm, Nell left the boutique with a very flash plastic bag and a much depleted Post Office book.

'It'll probably fall apart after the first wearing,' Juliet had remarked cheerfully as they left. 'But who cares. Image is everything. No-one's going to examine the seams and you're not going to take it off. You're not, are you?' she queried, anxiously.

'For goodness sake, I'm not *that* sort of girl.'

So now she stood before the mirror, took another slug of her G and T, and appraised the new Nell.

Juliet had made her buy the subtly coloured panne velvet, full length, gently flared over the hips. It had a bloom on it like the finest hospital-patient black

111

grapes. The sleeves were long and tight. There was no superfluous ornamentation at all. Underneath she wore the threatened body stocking – it gave a lovely line, after all – with white lacy tights and chunky white slingbacks.

Her hair had been swept high and fell in spiralling ringlets of pale honey-brown – they won't last, she gloomed, waste of time. Should have just flattened the lot with the iron and brown paper.

Juliet had outlined Nell's wide grey eyes with a steady hand. Then she followed the curve of the eye socket with smudgy grey and filled in the space between with Nell's own sludgy grape shadow and pearly highlights. But Nell baulked at the false lashes.

'I won't be able to keep my eyes open. They make me look half asleep.'

'Rubbish. You've got marvellous eyes. Just like Jean Shrimpton. You look absolutely fab.'

Now Nell looked again at the result. Not even remotely like the fabulous Shrimp.

'Like a bloody great Jersey cow,' she repeated.

Oliver in dinner jacket and black tie was even more beautiful than Nell had remembered. The severity of the colouring pointed up his icy fairness. The way his silver-blond hair fell forward was too artless for words, Nell thought. Almost as though he'd planned it, as though he knew how devastating he looked when he flicked it back with a thin, long-fingered hand. But, watching him again, she was certain that his actions were completely natural.

There was nothing in the least effeminate about

the hard, bony profile or the frozen glitter of his pale eyes. A woman would have caked those light lashes in mascara or dyed them dark. In Oliver, the effect was like a wintry pool fringed thickly by frosted grass. Nell could almost hear the snap and crackle of the ice.

'You look nice,' he said, as she came downstairs.

Nice. What girl wants to look nice, for heaven's sake? Tell me I'm stunning. Tell me I sweep you off your feet.

'Pretty,' he amended, as she came closer. He lifted one or two of the ringlets with the tips of his fingers, stretching them and letting them spring back. And he helped her into the cuddly fun-fur coat that she'd borrowed from Juliet, then dropped a kiss onto her cheek that produced an effect that Nell remembered clearly from her childhood asthma attacks. Only nicer.

Nell hadn't done enough science at school (and much good Latin and Ancient Greek had done her since) to understand why, when they were travelling forwards, the draught came from behind and blew her painstaking ringlets all over her face. But there was something very exciting, primitively thrilling, in the surge of power that pinned her back into the dark blue leather bucket seat as Oliver slipped into first gear and stood so hard on the accelerator that the rev counter needle flipped right round the dial.

This is me, she thought, *this is Nell being whisked off in a fast car by a fantastic man to a black tie affair.*

'I should have warned you,' Nell shouted over the

113

growl of the engine, as the white E-type Jaguar hurtled down the drive (she'd be in trouble for that on Monday). 'We're not supposed to go to a pub or a restaurant or anything within a three-mile radius. So that we're not seen letting our hair and the side down, I suppose. Sorry.'

'Don't worry,' Oliver answered. 'We're going a lot further than three miles. Hey, don't look so anxious. I'm not selling you into white slavery. Couldn't be more respectable. We're going to see my mother.'

They hit a pothole at the same time, so Nell wasn't absolutely certain of the cause of the lurch in her stomach. His mother?

Worth it, she decided. Worth it to be wrapped in furs like Anna Karenina, hurtling through the winter night. Pinpoint stars and blurred lights and air too frosty to breathe and the sight of Oliver's hands, steady on the steering wheel, light and dark, light and dark. Worth it to feel cherished.

'So, you're in the army. Well – how interesting. Of course, during the war one was used to young women in uniform – I was a Wren myself, a better class of other rank, people always said – but nowadays, it's so . . . so unusual.'

Oliver's mother was a ghost of her son, a reflection in an ancient glass, with the gold turned to mottled silver and the sparkle faded.

Nell had survived the dinner better than she had feared, seated between Oliver and one of the Hawtreys' neighbours, a vet who point-to-pointed. The conversation had gone back and forth across her – who was trying to qualify their horses, Jack had broken his collarbone, silly sod, what were the odds on Cut A Dash for the Staff College Draghounds' event at Tweseldown. There seemed to be some running point-to-pointers' joke about Confined Maidens and Open Maidens that went right over Nell's head.

It had been all right, really. All she had to do was turn her head to the speaker, smile, nod and look animated. Easy. *At this rate*, Nell thought, *I shall get quite a reputation as a conversationalist.*

Across the table sat a gawky young man with an ugly nose who seemed, for some reason, to be familiar. And when he smiled, Nell remembered: *nice bristols, shame about the legs.* But tonight he was friendly, trying to draw Nell into the talk, asking questions about the college, but without the nosiness of other interrogations, smoothing over her stutters.

'Do they treat you like skivvies?' he'd asked. 'Everyone says you spend all your time cleaning bogs.'

'Not all the time,' Nell admitted. 'It just feels like it. I spent all one Saturday scrubbing out the loos at Crookham camp, while the seniors pretended to be officers. It wasn't that bad, though.'

'Pretty standard treatment. You can't answer back when you've got your head stuck down the pan. When I was at Sandhurst, I was put in charge of a row of urinals – best damn urinals in the place, though I say it myself. All the pipework polished. And I incised the trade name on each one with a razor blade – Shanks – stood out beautifully.'

'Harry, dear,' Mrs Hawtrey remonstrated with icy gentility. 'Is that *quite* the subject for the dinner table?'

Harry dropped his voice to a whisper that seemed to carry further than full throttle. 'Kept me out of mischief. That's about all I was fit for at Sandhurst. Cannon fodder.' He gave a hoot of laughter. 'Not like young Noll here. Sword of Honour for him. An up-and-coming young thruster, he was, even then.'

He was funny and jolly and uninhibited. Nell appreciated his kindness. She felt she might have misjudged him earlier.

Every time he leaned towards Nell, the girl on his right laid her hand on his sleeve. Oliver's sister, Nell knew, Fulvia or Flavia or Fabia or something similarly pretentious.

'Harry,' she'd begin in a thin, nasal whine that seemed to slice right through the conversation like a circular saw. 'Harry, be a darling and pass the redcurrant jelly . . . Harry, I hear you have a new posting, let me guess where . . . Harry, has Lavinia had her latest sprog yet . . . ?'

So Nell just ate stolidly through the inevitable kipper pâté, the pheasant that was high enough to have flown off the table (she managed to avoid the shot that crunched in her neighbour's teeth), the stringy braised celery, and the port jelly with flabby bits of banana imprisoned in it. And all the time she knew that the worst was still to come.

Mrs Hawtrey, with a compelling glance, gathered to her the attention of everyone at the table. With a murmured 'Well, shall we . . .' she rose and led the way upstairs.

Amazing how much noise so few women could make. They chattered contentedly as Oliver's mother led them along a threadbare corridor carpet. Nell trailed along behind. *Well, this is what you're supposed to do, isn't it?* she thought. *Ladies leave the gentlemen to their port and cigars. Like a Victorian novel. I expect even Anna Karenina had to do it. But this is 1968. Hope will never believe it. Juliet will, though. She'd be disappointed if we'd stayed downstairs.*

The bedroom was much like its mistress, Nell reflected. In Eng. Lit. at school, there'd been a term for that sort of coincidence, but she couldn't remember what it was. Her own mother's bedroom was warm, frilly and padded, peachy, softly lit and smelling always of Coty face powder, *Ma Griffe* and – beneath the perfumes – sourly of ancient whisky.

Oliver's mother's room was austere, somehow thin – it could only be a thin person's room – and very, very cold. Faded lilac wallpaper and a slippery eiderdown of lavender satin. A dressing table so polished that Nell couldn't imagine any feminine disorder of nail polish and spilled powder. One central light with a low-wattage bulb. The wind from the North Downs assaulted the long windows and whistled through ill-fitting sashes, billowing curtains of glassy lavender chintz.

Three women sat on the long dressing-table stool and repaired their makeup. The triple glass reflected them back like weird sisters. When one disappeared towards the lavatory, Nell could have slipped into her place, powdered her nose, joined in. But she didn't. Instead she hovered, alone on the outskirts of their feminine preoccupations. Ignored.

What could she know about that rather good hairdresser in Godalming or about propagating hellebores or making a cheat's crème brulée? She was a female soldier, an oddity, a man in a skirt. Or as good as.

When she got the chance, she locked herself in the bathroom. It was colder than the bedroom, white tiled, with arsenic green emulsion above the tiles, worn, green lino, and a tiny, frosted window eight feet above floor level. A matching green stain ran down the bath enamel below each tap.

Nell didn't dare look in the mirror. She could feel that the uncertain ringlets were slowly straightening out, but what she couldn't see, she couldn't be certain of, so it was better not to look and to keep her illusions intact – or at least, only slightly tattered.

So she pulled down the mahogany loo seat and sat there, leafing through ancient copies of *Punch* and *Horse and Hound*, until she heard the women go downstairs again.

'Those naughty men will have punished the port quite enough by now. High time we girls dragged them back to civilization.'

'Where's Oliver's little friend? Such a dull . . .'

'Oh, there you are. Goodness, I was beginning to think you'd got lost.'

118

Once Nell had settled in a chair that, somehow, seemed to be the furthest from a smoky fire in a vast grate, a smelly little Border terrier with death breath came over and dropped onto her feet.

'Oh, just give him a shove,' suggested Oliver's sister with the nasal voice, flopping into a wing chair that stood between Nell and even a sight of the fire. 'He's been stuffing himself with leftover pheasant, so he'll fart all night. Mummy spoils the foul little beast.'

'I don't mind,' Nell assured her and she didn't, because fondling its ears gave her something to do. She could look occupied rather than lost.

'Oliver tells me you're a soldier, too. How odd. Do you march up and down all day and wear enormous boots?'

'We do some drill,' Nell began, 'but . . .'

'Sounds awfully butch. You don't look it.'

'I'm not.'

'Then where's the fun?'

Flavia took a cigarette from a silver box on an exquisite little table by her chair, lit it and tossed the match into the fire.

'Oh, sorry . . .' She gestured towards the box. 'Do you? No?' She took a deep, satisfied drag. 'Actually, it's no secret if I tell you that Mummy rather sees you as the answer to a mother's prayer. Oliver's rather gone off the rails since Daddy died – you know, too much of everything. Lucky bugger. She's been leaning on him to find a nice, worthy girl. Someone biddable and not too bright, with good, child-bearing hips . . . only joking! . . . oh,

Harry . . .' As the men came in, flushed and noisy with port, she rose and crossed the room, fluttering in ice-blue chiffon. 'Harry, it's freezing in here. Put your arms around me, do.'

And now it was Nell's turn to occupy a car with steamed-up windows at the back of Cadet Mess.

'Thank you so much,' she began, politely, just restraining herself from the well-brought-up child's *thank you for having me*. She already had her hand on the car door handle. 'It's been a lovely evening . . .'

'Rubbish. I thought it was perfectly bloody and so did you – admit it. You were bored witless. Still, there are compensations. Come here . . .'

Oliver leaned over, skilfully avoiding the gear lever, and laid his lips on hers. Nudging and nibbling, he forced her lips apart. He tasted of port and Stilton and cigar smoke, but his skin smelt of the sea.

'I like you, little Nell,' he said, raising his head just a little. 'You're honest. You don't pretend to be anything you're not. I like that. But you really do need someone to teach you what's what . . .'

Nell found the feel . . . the *meatiness* of his tongue excitingly scary. Their exchange of saliva had an intimacy that she wasn't certain she was ready to offer.

But this is what you do, isn't it? This is the cost of the night out, she reminded herself. *There's always a bill to pay in the end*.

'Hey, little Nell,' he whispered hoarsely. 'Relax. It's like cuddling a poker.'

And a little later, his voice rougher still – 'God, what wonderful tits. I've been thinking about them all night.'

For a while, she lay awake in bed, in the dark, thinking, but with little coherence. Of the chill, high-ceilinged house and its wintry mistress. Of Flavia's grasping, greedy hands and Harry Dowland's ugly, charming smile. Of Oliver. Of the shivery excitement of his touch. She drew up her knees and curled, foetus-like, to still the unexpected ripple of memory.

He liked her. He had said so. Not exactly an earth-shattering statement, but it was a start.

A scattering of gravel across the window roused her from her drift into uneasy sleep. Then came a couple of hefty thuds and a grunt. Someone was trying to get into her window from the flat roof below it, the accepted entry for anyone who'd out-stayed her late pass.

Nell opened her window and Juliet tumbled through it and onto the bed.

'No, don't put on the light,' she commanded. 'I'm a bit dishevelled.'

'Juliet, you're mad. It must be after three.'

'Well past. So? How'd it go? Tell Juliet.'

'All right.'

'Only all right?' Juliet sounded as though the reply was a personal insult. 'After all my effort? Didn't he fall madly in love with you?'

'I don't think that was the original idea.'

'Did he kiss you?'

121

'Yes.'

'Did he do anything else? Stop wriggling and answer.'

'Well . . . yes . . .'

'All the way?'

'Certainly not! What do you think I am? Anyway, I shouldn't think it's possible in an E-type. Not that it's any of your business.'

Juliet gave a vast yawn. Her neat little teeth gleamed, disembodied in the darkness. 'God, I'm bushed. Not long till we get up again.'

'Then go to bed.'

'OK, grumpy. I'm going.' There was a pause. 'Nell . . .'

'Mmm . . .' Her voice was slurred with sleep.

'Simon asked me to marry him – again.'

'So what's new?'

'I said yes.'

Nell sat up with a squeak. 'You didn't! When?'

'Tonight, stupid.'

'No, I mean, *when*?'

'Oh, not for ages. It's going to be the all-time long engagement. There's no way I'm going to marry a doctor so junior he'd only be home once a fortnight and wouldn't even recognize me when he did get home. Might as well marry a sailor. I told him quite firmly. Not until you're a registrar, I said.'

'Poor Simon.'

'Poor Simon, nothing. He's lucky to get me. And anyway, I've got things to do first . . . plans . . . I'd love a posting to Cyprus, or Hong Kong, maybe.'

'Wouldn't we all. Bet you anything you like it'll be

Guildford for me. Or Mill Hill. Fate worse than death. Don't tell *them* about it, whatever you do. And don't get married too soon, Juliet. They'll make you pay your uniform allowance back. Juliet? Are you awake? Juliet . . . ?'

In the morning, Alison Barkwith stuck her head aggressively round the door.

'Still in bed? You ought to know by now that breakfast is a parade. It's Remembrance Sunday. You've got five minutes to get dressed and downstairs, ready for inspection. Oh . . . oh God, no . . .'

Juliet's head poked sleepily out from beneath Nell's eiderdown.

'Vernon – a little chat, if you please. In my office. Now.'

Obediently, Nell followed the Windsor company commander into her office. Captain Molly Greene straddled the corner of her desk, informally. Her heavy thighs strained against the straight lovat green skirt.

'Now, Vernon, a little bird has whispered to me that you were not alone in your room yesterday morning.'

Some little bird, thought Nell, remembering Alison's shocked face.

'Not only not alone in your room, but also not alone in your bed,' continued Captain Greene, with soft persistence. 'So – do you have anything to tell me?'

'I was alone *in* my bed, ma'am. Juliet – Officer Cadet Cleeve was *on* my bed.'

'I see. And why was she on your bed – or in it or around it or whatever?'

'We were talking late . . .' No need to shop Juliet by saying she'd climbed in the window '. . . and we were both very tired and we fell asleep. That's it.'

'Do your friends usually loll over your bed when you're in it? Vernon, you don't seem to realize the seriousness of this allegation. This could be big trouble for both of you. You and Cleeve were both found in the same bed in the morning and you expect me to believe . . .' Molly Greene leaned over and rummaged in her desk drawer. 'Here,' she said, offering a crumpled packet of Everton Mints. 'Have one. This is going to be a long session, as little chats go. Now, listen, Vernon. It's not the end of the world. You've just got to realize that what is required in the WRAC is public virginity. In other words, whatever you do, don't get caught. So if you and Cleeve have a . . . a bit of a thing going . . .'

The Everton Mint had as much flavour as a lump of coal in Nell's dry mouth. Wishing she'd had the sense to refuse it, she transferred it to her cheek, where it bulged like a hamster's leftovers. Nell looked down at her lap, at her hands twisted together, capable white hands with the tidemark of black shoe polish rimmed around two nails. And she looked up at Molly Greene, in time to catch an assessing gleam in moist black eyes and the flick of a pink tongue around red lips.

'. . . then be sensible,' she was advised, 'be discreet. A word to the wise. No-one cares what you do, as long as you don't frighten the horses! A public relationship will *not* be tolerated, but if you keep your heads down . . .'

'I'm sorry we were late for parade, ma'am, but we did both get extra orderly cadet duties in punishment.'

The older woman looked more carefully at Nell's face and suppressed a grin. 'Dear Lord – you haven't a clue what I've been talking about, have you? Vernon, I've just about persuaded the OC not to put you on warning.'

The sensation of nervous sickness that was never far from Nell these days welled up. A warning. Sent home as the next step. She couldn't bear it. She wouldn't bear it. Failure.

'Steady on,' the Company Commander urged. 'I don't think it'll happen, but you've been that—' and she held up a finger and thumb, barely apart '—far away from it.'

'Because of – what we've been talking about, ma'am?'

'No, not because of that. If Major Ottaway had the slightest suspicion, just the merest whisper that you and Cleeve were anything more than friends, you'd both be out of here so fast your heels would strike sparks. No, it's just that you seem to be lacking in every department, except the academic. You're a clever girl, Vernon, but you haven't got what it takes. No officer quality. At least, if you have, you've managed to disguise it pretty successfully so far. Well . . .' She paused to give Nell a chance to get a word in, but there was silence. 'It's all about the Corps motto. *Suaviter in modo, fortiter in re*. Gentle in manner, resolute in deed. Remember? I can see plenty of evidence of the *suaviter* bit in you, but not much of the *fortiter* so far. Grace under pressure, in other words.'

Nell looked again at the straining skirt. Plenty of pressure there, but not a lot of grace, as Hope had once pointed out. But this wasn't the moment to find herself grinning.

'Well?' her Company Commander pursued. 'Aren't you going to ask me anything?'

'I don't think I know what I've done wrong, ma'am.'

Molly Greene cast her eyes up in exasperation. 'That's the whole point, Vernon. You haven't done anything wrong. You're just a nice girl, but what you see is what you get. You haven't any spark at all. No initiative. No up and at 'em. No *joie de vivre*. No sense of humour – I bet you've never told a dirty joke in your life. You look scared to death half the time. If you were sent to a tough WRAC unit – the postal workers at Mill Hill, say, or the storewomen at Bicester – you'd be eaten alive before your first week was up. They'd have you on toast.'

'I'm sorry, ma'am,' Nell whispered.

'Dear God, what am I to do with you? You're teetering on the brink, girl. Get out and do something about it. Go on. Out.'

An elderly brigadier was supposed to be teaching military history. The lesson seemed to involve explaining the delights of dressing up in home-made uniforms and play-acting Civil War battles. He was passing around photos of re-enacted Edgehills and Marston Moors.

'Now, I want you all to think about joining the Sealed Knot Society. We could do with some more lively gels. Nurses and cooks and so forth. Camp followers. An army marches on its stomach, don't y'know.'

Typical, thought Hope. *The men do the fighting and have the fun. The women get the cooking and bandaging. All he's trying to do is enrol skivvies.*

Juliet shoved a note across the desks to Nell under cover of the pictures.

Did you get the third degree, too?

Not bad, Nell scribbled. *How about you?*

Effie McCall strung me up by the thumbs and lit a slow fire under my feet. Told them that if I fancied a woman, it wouldn't be you. That shut them up!

Nell had never realized that it's possible to be relieved and insulted at the same time.

And then it was end of term and, much to the surprise of them all, they'd survived intact. All for one and one for all, Ruth had urged, way back in the autumn, a time that now seemed hopelessly rosy, when they had been foolish and innocent and young and underworked. And now they were soldiers. Perhaps Ruth had done the trick. Something had kept them together.

There was all the flurry of the seniors' commissioning ball and their commissioning ceremony, preceded by endless rehearsals and complicated, in

127

this term, by a Christmas carol service the evening before.

'The RSM must be a masochist, that's all I can say,' remarked Hope, as they collected their books after the last lesson of term.

'It's a prerequisite,' said Isa. 'You can't be an RSM otherwise. It says so in the training manual.'

'I mean – all those chairs laid out one way for carols and then all to be moved before tomorrow. And the band first in one place and then another. The pioneer boys will be up all night shifting furniture.'

'That's the army for you.'

As they passed her office, the CSM popped out like the demon queen from a trapdoor. 'Just a moment, if you please, ladies. Miss Cleeve, Miss Blakeney – berets and gloves on. The OC would like a word with you.'

'Oh, Lord,' groaned Hope. 'It's the big heave-ho.'

'I kept back some tea for you,' said Ruth, when the two of them trailed back into Cadet Mess half an hour later. 'I thought you might need it.'

'Thanks, you're an angel,' said Hope, 'but I need a slug of something stronger than tea.'

'Well?' chorused three voices.

'I'm to be cadet corporal next term,' announced Juliet and they could all hear how hard she was trying to keep the jubilation out of her voice. All for one and one for all. 'And senior cadet.'

Into the silence came Isa's soft, Scottish voice. 'Well done. Congratulations. And Hope?'

'Back-squadded,' said Hope and burst into tears.

Isa sat in the congregation and listened to Hope's clear tones soaring into the hall rafters as she took a solo verse of 'In the Bleak Mid-winter.'

'*But only his mother . . .*' Hope sang, her voice sweet, soft and full, every word reaching right back to the duty stewardess, who was perched on a chair by the door, keeping an ear open for the hissing of the interval tea urn and wondering if last night's love bites showed above her collar. '. . . *in her maiden bliss Worshipped the Belovèd with a kiss.*'

Isa felt the tears she had suppressed so stoically for so long grow heavy under her lids. She looked up, blinking fiercely, daring them to fall. Not now. They could wait. They had to wait until she was on the train travelling north, the day after tomorrow.

Just below the bottom button of her jacket, she could feel a fragile fluttering, stirring, stretching, a little hiccuping jerk that anyone might easily have mistaken for the result of too many mince pies.

Isa knew better than that.

She had faced the reality, had met it head on. She had a choice, straightforward, it seemed in those first, bleak days of realization. She could abandon her hopes, her ambitions, the belief in herself that had carried her through the ranks so far. She could settle for what was left, making the best of it – as so many women do, trapped by their biological functions. As her own mother had done.

Or not.

She had confronted the future and found that it

129

was empty of love, whatever her choice. So she made the decision.

But it was a decision that became harder to justify as her body accustomed itself to new rhythms, new priorities, became slower, more defensive, inward looking.

And when the movement came again, harder and more insistent now – *I'm here, believe in me, feel me, acknowledge me* – she sat on her hands to stop herself placing them on her belly and stilling the foetal gymnastics. The last thing she wanted to do, dared to do, was to allow herself to think of the creature as alive.

She could feel it, sense its shape, knew its waking and sleeping. Random movement of the arms, experimental, like a swimmer testing the water, trying out new strokes. Legs that shot out spasmodically, searching for boundaries, sounding out the limits of their freedom.

I'm yours. Know me.

No. It was a cluster of cells. That was all.

On either side of her, she was conscious of Nell and Ruth and Juliet, of the stalwart warmth of their bodies, of the support they each owed the other. And she longed to confide, to say *Help me*, to test them and their friendship. But she knew she couldn't rely on them. Whatever they said, whatever they promised or believed, they would crumble beneath her weight. They barely had the strength to carry themselves through the next few months. The burden of Isa would break them, each one, separately. Even Hope.

As the congregation stood for the last verse of the carol, Isa could feel the weight of tears beading her lashes. Her vision blurred, broke up into a prism of light, a long vista of lovat green.

'*Yet what I can I give him,*' they all sang. '*Give my heart.*'

Isa folded her hands behind her back, away from temptation, in the At Ease position. She was over twenty-one, old enough to make her own decision and she had made it. She stood tall and slim and straight.

The perfect soldier.

1994

A time to lose . . .

'We really must do this again.'

'And not wait for the fiftieth anniversary!'

'Juliet, you've been marvellous. What organization.'

'Trust you to plan everything so efficiently, Juliet.'

'Whoops! Good thing I'm going home by train!'

'I'll call a taxi. We can share it to the station.'

'You're not driving, are you, Nell?'

'Well, yes, I am. P'r'aps I'd better stay on and have some more coffee.'

'Stay the night, more like. Look at the time.'

Oh, God . . .

'Well, I must get on. Alice will be gnashing her teeth and *starving*. Honestly, that girl couldn't shove a bit of bread in the toaster if her life depended on it!'

'Tell me about it. I can't think how Lucy even finds her bed at night, her room's in such a state. There are new fungal species waiting to be discovered in there – could be the cure for just about everything. Remember what our rooms looked like – like nuns' cells?'

'All except Hope's. That was a cross between a Mongolian yurt and a Hindu temple.'

And there were kisses all round and more promises of future meetings – at least once a year – and more kisses and goodbyes.

Then they were gone.

Look at the time. Oh, God . . .

Nell had been fine inside the hotel. Why did she feel so very woozy outside? It might be the drink. Anyone else would say it definitely was. But she knew better. She'd felt fine until she looked at her watch. The sensation of nausea didn't come on until then.

She extricated herself from the parking slot without too much difficulty, thinking it was just as well that wing mirrors are spring-loaded these days. There was a scrap of paper with a very ratty note from an under-chef stuck under a windscreen wiper – *you're in my parking space don't do it again YOU HAVE BEEN WARNED!!!*

Very slowly, she drove into Winchester's going-home rush. The early sunshine had deteriorated to a fine drizzle, too little to run the wipers at normal speed, too much to keep them intermittent. Just enough to make vision difficult. She drove very slowly, so as not to catch a policeman's eye. They're always there when you don't need them.

'I haven't drunk much,' she told herself. 'Compared to Juliet, I've been positively abstemious. Though, as Oliver reminded me this morning, it doesn't take much . . . But even if I were stone cold sober, I couldn't do more than grind my way around the one-way circuit. And Oliver has this absolute *thing* about drinking and driving, but I haven't been, not really . . .'

When she got into the wrong lane at a mini-roundabout, the pressure of traffic behind and the hooting as she tried to change lane forced her out along the motorway sliproad and she had to go as far as the next junction before she could find a roundabout to take her back again.

Round and round, like a hamster in a wheel.

You always were hopeless, Nell . . .

The silence closed around Isa as she shut the door behind her. Five storeys above the street, the traffic scarcely bothered her. She began to peel off her clothes as she padded through the flat.

Jacket.

Check the answerphone. No message from Mike. Working late, finishing off the last-minute ends before going on leave? Or already crawling around the M25 towards Dover, with poor Henrietta flipping madly through the map book, trying to find a shortcut for her impatient husband? *Rather her than me*, thought Isa and surprised herself by discovering that she meant it.

Earrings.

Flip through the rack and put Schubert's 'Quintet in C' on the CD player.

Shoes.

Turn on the kettle. Look at the clock. Switch off the kettle, open the fridge and pour a glass of Chardonnay.

Zip.

Put the plug in the bath and turn on the taps. Close the curtains.

Dress.

Back to the kitchen to top up the glass. Turn up the volume. The music was like driving through a dark wood and coming out suddenly into evening sunlight.

Wig.

Fluff up the golden sprouts underneath, sparse as seedlings in a hard spring.

Bra and pants.

Sprinkle into the bath a few drops of aromatherapy oil. Geranium for tranquillity. Rosemary for headaches. No looking at the scars, now. Not now. No averting horrified eyes. No anxious scanning, either. Just acceptance. You win some, you lose some. Time would tell which, in this case.

Isa balanced the glass on the edge of the bath, slid lower into the scented water and thought about the day.

A mistake.

Reunions were almost always a mistake, she had found. As the most senior woman officer, she was frequently asked to commemorative occasions: fifty years since the founding of the ATS; forty-five years since its disbanding; forty years since the founding of the WRAC; then its disbanding – a difficult one, that, to preside over. A wake. Too many tears at the passing of the girls in lovat green.

Not from Isa, though. To her, it was a natural progression. What other professional women sheltered behind a barrier of their own building, a self-imposed purdah? The exclusion that had been imposed on the Corps by the standards of the time – 1949 and let's get our girls back in the kitchen where they belong – had been embraced by them, welcomed, had been exalted into a means to an end. Ridiculous. Did women barristers only agree to represent female clients? Did women doctors limit themselves to female patients? Well, then.

She'd taken off her green one day and put on khaki the next, without emotion. She'd made a brief appearance on television that day – found herself popped in at the end of the ten o'clock news, in the 'and finally' slot. The woman who'll make men jump to it, they'd called her. There'd been pictures of her hanging up her dark green hat and trying on the more masculine one before a mirror. All rather trivial and she wished she'd never agreed to be filmed.

The following morning, the picture had been reproduced in the *Daily Mail*. Mike had seen it, looking over her shoulder as he went to refill the coffee pot. 'You can make me stand to attention any day,' he'd whispered, leaning over to nibble at the nape of her neck.

Now that she worked in the Ministry of Defence, as Director of Service Intelligence, she wore uniform only on specific occasions, out of London. It was a very civilian life – office hours, ordinary clothes (a bit of a bore deciding what to wear every day), a rented flat in Millbank, conveniently taken over from the last occupant of her job, a tiny weekend cottage in Wiltshire – amazingly unmilitary.

The point was – the point that the television people couldn't be expected to grasp – that she'd done what she'd said she was going to do.

She remembered that day at the WRAC College, the day when Major Ottaway had questioned them all about their ambitions. She remembered the hiss of indrawn breath, the gaze of absolute incomprehension. Isa had looked through the glass ceiling at a time when the phrase had not even been invented, and had seen what she wanted on the other side.

But it had cost.

That's the trouble with reunions. They start you thinking.

Some time during the lunch, someone – she wasn't sure who, but thought it was probably Juliet, it was her style – said, 'But did we all get what we wanted in the end? Here we all are, middle class, well off, successful husbands, still married to the same chaps after twenty-five years, which takes some doing these days, bit of a record—' she hadn't looked at Ruth or Isa as she'd said that '—all these silver weddings coming up one after another this year, one hell of a party. Sorry, Hope, I know you would still be married if . . . but the thing is—' She took a stiff swig from a glass that seemed to need topping up more often than most '—the thing is, it's not what we expected, is it? It's not what we set out to do. All those ambitions, all those dreams, all those images they'd peddled to us in the recruiting pamphlets – foreign postings, glamour, excitement, life like a great, big boiled egg just waiting for us to slice off the top and dig in. It wasn't like that.' She'd looked wistful, vaguely dissatisfied, the young Juliet again, with that touch of petulance that repelled or charmed equally. 'It wasn't like that at all . . .'

'Isa did what she said she was going to do,' Ruth reminded her.

'Oh, yes, Isa. But you were always different, weren't you, Isa? Tell us – have you really done everything you wanted?'

Isa had thought for a moment and then said slowly, her accent regaining for a moment that Scottish burr that she had drilled out of it, 'Yes, I did what I said I was going to do and I'm proud of it.'

Juliet could be very persistent when she felt like it. 'That's not what I asked.'

'No-one does *everything* they want, but – yes – most of it. Enough, anyway.'

'There's no-one following you, though, is there? There isn't another woman who'll take your place. It wasn't a breakthrough, after all.'

And Ruth, with her knack of soothing a situation, had said, 'Isa's a one-off, that's why.'

Isa closed her eyes and lay very still. The sound of the quintet's *Adagio* seeped into her. She'd said to Mike once that, if she were dying, she would like that to be the last earthly sound she'd hear. He'd looked at her in blank incomprehension.

'Bit morbid, old girl, eh?'

It was the silences Isa had noticed most. When the greetings were over, the exclamations at each other's appearance had died away, there had been a little silence. Perhaps Isa was the only one who'd noticed. And there were others later.

'Do you remember . . . ?'

And silence.

Ruth and Nell had both brought snapshots of their children and passed them round the table.

'Sorry. It's an awfully mumsie thing to do,' admitted Nell, 'but I can't help it.'

The responses were predictable. *Isn't he like you? Aren't they tall? Does she look like her father? What lovely children.* No-one mentioned Lucy's spots or Jessica's surly pout. And Jago was lovely, awkward and gentle with a smile that was his father's without the biting edge.

When the photos had reached Isa at the opposite end of the table, there had been another of those heartbeat-space silences. Or was she imagining it? Had she really seen Juliet lift that still perfectly groomed eyebrow and look across to Hope? Had Hope shrugged? Or was that just what she expected to see?

'They're lovely,' Isa had said quietly and had passed the pictures back.

People made choices every day, didn't they? Every day was a series of decisions, careful weighing of evidence or snap judgements. Little choices, like orange juice or apple juice for breakfast. Big choices, like am I going to leave my husband. Dammit, she was trained to make the biggest decision of them all

142

– will we go to war or not. Not that a woman would ever, *ever* be allowed to make that one. There were limits, after all, old boy!

You got used to making decisions and then you had to get used to living with them.

And in time you did, of course. Nothing lasts for ever. Not even guilt. Only . . .

Only sometimes the results of those choices come back when you least expect them.

Isa climbed out of the bath, wrapped herself in a huge, white bath sheet and turbaned her hair in another. Dark, damp footprints followed her across the ugly patterned carpet of the flat's living room. The music had finished. The only sound was the barely audible hum that came from the equipment. That, and the throaty rattle as the fridge's thermostat cut in.

Most nights were like that. After the easy camaraderie of work at the Ministry, the noisy debate of committee and sub-committee meetings, the intellectual clashes, the all-boys-together atmosphere, a cross between a St James's club dining room and a prep school – most nights were the same. She couldn't even fill in the dark hours with work, unless she stayed late at her desk. Nothing could be taken out in a briefcase. The security classification of her paperwork meant that it all had to be left in the Ministry.

If you get what you want, don't whine when the payment falls due.

She picked up the phone and dialled Mike's number. Then she put the phone down again before the first ring came back to her. Only neurotic women ring their lover's number when they know he's out, when they know that the phone won't be answered, but that just the sound of its ringing in his empty house is a perverse sort of comfort. If he'd had an answerphone, she could have listened to his voice.

How sad. She han't sunk that low yet. Deliberately, she turned away from the images of Mike and Henrietta wandering round the châteaux of the Loire with a green Michelin guide open. Instead, she forced herself to reproduce the memory of Mike's face that first time she'd felt brave enough to take her clothes off in front of him again.

He'd looked at the scars and then away. And in the microsecond before he'd got his face under control again, she'd seen it all. Horror. Shock. Pity – that was the worst.

And the end of their relationship. Its slow, terminal decline.

Serves you right, Isa.

Despising herself, laughing at herself, she padded through to the kitchen, scrubbed a potato, pricked it and popped it into the microwave. While she waited, she leafed through the notebook where she'd scribbled down addresses and phone numbers that afternoon. She sat cross-legged on the floor by the phone, with the glass and Chardonnay bottle handily sited in the crook of her legs, and dialled Hope's number.

*   *   *

Ruth and Juliet and Nell and Hope and Isa. There were too many things unsaid between them. They knew each other too well ever to be really comfortable together again.

'The General's hopping, ma'am.'

By the time Nell reached home, having taken it very steadily down the A303, she could have thrown up on the driveway. She had sneaked the car in the back gate to the garage and slipped in the staff-room door. Bombardier Kane's warning was meant to be jocular, but she knew it was the truth.

'Oh, dear, am I in disgrace?' she asked, with an attempt at bravado.

'No joke. If I were you, ma'am, I'd start today all over again.'

Nell could hear the sound of her assembled guests, the ones she'd neglected. They sounded happy enough. Her absence didn't seem to have clouded the atmosphere. After a few gins, no-one would notice that she wasn't there. Except Oliver.

Mrs Parr, neat in her best party black and white, elbowed her way backwards through the door with a tray of dirty glasses.

'You've made it, then, ma'am.'

'The traffic was awful, Mrs Parr.'

Damn it, why did Nell feel she had to apologize? Mrs Parr gave her a sour look, took a platter of shrimp vol-au-vents from the oven and went out again. In the doghouse all round, Nell.

'Should I go in now, do you think, Kane?'

'Not a good idea, ma'am. Why don't you just slip

up the back stairs, get changed as quick as you can – I'll bring you up a cup of tea as soon as I've got a breather – then down again and into the party and no-one'll know.'

'You're a wonder, Bombardier.'

'All the ladies say that, ma'am!'

Nell crept upstairs in her own house, aiming for the bedroom, but as she passed the door to their private upstairs sitting room Jessica bounced out. She was exactly the same shape as Nell had been at her age, so bounced was pretty accurate.

'Daddy's livid with you,' Jessica announced with relish. 'Where on earth have you been?'

'Out for lunch,' Nell replied, trying to muster some dignity.

'Lunch?' Jessica squeaked. 'It's half-past seven. Have you been drinking?'

'No. Not really.'

'You have. I can smell it. You're wrecked.'

'I am not. I only had . . . it's none of your business. I don't see why I should have to defend myself to my own daughter.' Attack is the best form of defence, they say. 'And you can start your time here by sorting out that disgusting pile of bin bags you call your luggage.'

Nell shut the bedroom door, but not quickly enough to avoid her daughter's reply. 'Daddy's really going to lose it when he sees you.'

No-one would have noticed. No-one but Nell, that is.

'Well done, darling. You made it,' he called across

146

the room as she sneaked in. 'Traffic awful? Never mind.'

His eyes were chips of obsidian, colourless and glittering, without light as they looked at her. His smile came nowhere near them. He crossed the room and took her by the elbow.

'Where the hell have you been?' he hissed as he touched his lips to Nell's cheek. 'You stupid bitch.' Then, aloud, 'Come and meet some people.'

Only Nell was aware that his grip paralysed her lower arm. He knew exactly where to press, where the vulnerable nerve endings were placed. He could kill with his hands. Quietly. Efficiently. No fuss. He'd told her so. He was trained to do it. But, for tonight, this was enough.

Nell kept smiling. Oliver took her over to a knot of people who stood by open French windows, admiring the garden. She smiled in welcome, in apology, a *yes, the sweet peas are coming on wonderfully, so early this year* sort of smile, a *so sorry, I got lost, I'm so stupid* smile. And when Oliver let go her arm, she looked down quickly to check – he'd left not so much as a red thumb mark. But her fingers were throbbing with pins and needles. A reminder.

She looked up and beyond the group and into the shocked brown eyes of Harry Dowland, now – and always, it seemed – Oliver's deputy. Dear faithful Harry, the perfect deputy, always helpful, always there, always behind, never quite catching up, never challenging, never going to make the top rung of the ladder and at last knowing it. Soft, dark eyes, like treacle – Oliver called them spaniel eyes – now darker still, black and bleak with anger. Harry was very still, very alert, his angular body caught in a freeze-frame of outrage. Nell realized he had seen everything, understood everything. The knowledge gave her an odd sort of comfort. And shame.

She turned away from his silent sympathy. She turned her back, missing the warmth that followed the anger. No-one must know. It was her business. No-one had a right to know. Not even Harry.

Most of the guests Nell knew already, of course, the small fry, the makers-up of numbers, who were there to boost the important people. These, she should have been at the door to greet. She was in the wrong; she couldn't wriggle out of it. She should have been ready to welcome their local MP – Macho Man, the tabloids called him – a man reputed to enjoy nothing more than donning camouflage kit and blasting off in a tank. He was reported to wear his camouflage kit at other, more intimate moments, too. With him was the woman who was now his third wife, but had been his parliamentary researcher. And then there was the GOC – General Officer Commanding – and his wife, a late bloomer, who was frantic about finding the right prep school for four-year-old Hamish, when the rest of her contemporaries were worrying about university interviews. The mayor was there, with the mayoress, and the chief executive of the district council and his wife. And there was the rural dean and *his* wife.

And Nell had been absent.

Harry was on his own, but no-one expected anything different from him. *Everyone* knew that Flavia didn't give a toss – about him or about the army – that she was far too taken up with running a busy maternity home for horses to make time to be nice to the right people, to give Harry's career a shove. Oliver's sister or not, Nell thought – and Oliver would be the first to agree. 'We're not having her round for Christmas, she's totally bonkers,' he'd say every year – Flavia was a cow and Harry deserved better.

The RC padre had been without a wife, of course. As had the host.

When they had gone, promptly at eight o'clock as all well-behaved drinks party guests should, Oliver shut himself in his study without a word. He didn't reappear until the staff had tidied up and gone home, leaving fifty-odd glasses washed up and gleaming, the carpet vacuumed, freshly washed tea towels drying and the table set for breakfast. Leaning over the banisters, Jessica saw him come out.

'Christ, I'm out of here,' she declared and slammed into her room. She turned the Chemical Brothers up to whining, sliding, pitch-bending full volume.

Nell heard him in the bathroom. She heard him in his dressing room. She waited for him to come to bed. Then she heard the click of the light switch next door and the slight squeak as he got into the spare bed.

She recognized the punishment. She was used to it.

It was the same sort of pressure that her mother used to apply to the teenage Nell. 'Lights out and no supper. And you can just stay up there, young lady, until you're ready to apologize.' And she always had apologized, brought to heel by darkness and hunger and the need – the *longing* – for forgiveness. Even if, half the time, she wasn't certain what she was apologizing for.

Nell lay in the dark and justified herself. *What am I supposed to have done, anyway? Had lunch with old friends. Had a giggle. Enjoyed myself. Got back a bit late. Bloody hell. Hardly the crime of the century.*

But she knew it was.

Selfish. Careless. Unthinking. Irresponsible. No consideration for others. Not playing the game. Thinking only of herself. Lack of loyalty. A loner. Lack of team spirit.

The words rattled accusingly around her head, like one of those terrible cadet lectures on leadership qualities. D minus for you, Nell.

She lay for half an hour or so, wondering whether she ought to leave well alone, then she got up.

'Oliver . . . '

He fumbled for the bedside light and switched it on. He blinked and focused on her, pushing back the heavy silver-gilt hair from his eyes. He'd been asleep. Damn him. Nell had been lying in the dark, alone and miserable, and he'd been asleep.

'Oliver . . .' She tried not to sound supplicating – and failed. 'Oliver, won't you talk to me? Please?' She came over and sat on the edge of the bed.

'That's enough, Nell.'

He tried to reach the light switch again, but she pulled the light across the table, out of his reach.

'Why are you doing this to me?'

'Go to bed, Nell. If I start now, I won't stop. So don't push your luck.'

'Look, I'm sorry. All right? I'm sorry. I didn't mean to be late.'

'Of course you didn't. That's the whole point. You just did what *you* wanted. Typical. I asked you to come home, sober and on time, and you didn't.'

'I'm sorry,' she said again, miserably.

'All you had to do was be here. Is that too much to ask? Just *be* here. With me. When I needed you. What do you do all day, for God's sake? What's the point of you? What are you for?'

'Don't . . .'

'You have staff to keep your house clean. You have a man to do the garden. You have people to cook, to serve the drinks, to do the washing up. The children are at school three-quarters of the year. You must spend your whole damned life flower arranging and drinking coffee. And all I ask is that you support me. That, now and again, you put in an appearance when I need you.'

His scorn was very bitter to her. Because she couldn't argue, couldn't stand up for herself. For, in so many ways, he was right. What use was she? Jessica didn't really need her any more. Oliver needed her to bolster his public image, but she didn't fool herself about how much she meant to him in private. Jago . . . oh, well . . . perhaps Jago still needed her. A bit. For a while.

'For once, just for once, I was with *my* friends. I forgot the time – OK? It's hardly a crime. I really meant to get back. But I never, ever see my friends. Only yours.'

'You don't care enough to make an effort.'

'Effort?' Bolder now, as though she fed on her own words and became stronger, Nell gave one of those short, sharp laughs that only women can make, mocking and crowing. A mistake. A laugh like that always is. It's trouble. 'I never stop making a bloody effort for you and your bloody career.'

'These were influential people, Nell. People who might be useful.'

'Ah, yes. I see what all this is about, now. Your knighthood. One day, very soon, you're going to be *Sir* Oliver. And nothing's going to get in your way. Not even me.'

'That's enough.'

Too far. She'd gone too far, this time. He stretched out his arm and Nell flinched away from it with a quick, involuntary muscular spasm, like a dog who can't help wagging its tail, even when there's nothing to wag about. But all he was reaching for was the light switch. The room was suddenly dark. A sliver of light from the landing sliced across the carpet. The bass from Jessica's CD player sounded very like Nell's own heartbeat.

'Go to bed, Nell. I don't suppose you'll find much to complain about when you're Lady Hawtrey.'

1969

A time to be born . . .

'You're the lowest of the low here and don't you forget it . . .'

Juliet spoke the words as though she'd never heard them before in her life. She spoke them with all the assurance of four months at the college behind her, with all the weight of her authority as Officer Cadet Corporal and senior cadet.

She'd come back from her Christmas leave driving a smart little Triumph Herald coupé, bright yellow, and had zipped up the drive past the station minibus, with a toot and a wave. Now she sat in the anteroom and surveyed the new entrants with an expression of absolute amazement.

Did this lot ever think they'd make officers? Some hope. Scruffy and cowed already. Still wet behind the ears. Pathetic.

I can't believe Juliet's saying that, Nell thought. *Can't she remember what it was like? They all look petrified. They look exactly as we must have done last September. And they're wriggling on the ghastly orange tweed G-plan and trying not to take sly peeps at each other and staring at us as though we've just*

155

descended from heaven complete with haloes and wings. She looked round at the rest of the seniors, trying to gauge their reactions to Juliet's speech.

When she saw Hope, she didn't look any further. Neither flesh nor fowl nor good red herring. Poor Hope.

Hope hadn't been able to work out where to sit. After her back-squadding, she wasn't a senior, so she could hardly sit on the side of the angels. But she was damned if she was going to sit with the rookies and endure Juliet's little pep talk. So she pulled a chair a little out of the circle and sat on her own, like a lioness cast out of the pride, neither one thing nor the other.

Lowest of the low! Bloody hell! Typical Juliet. That girl's got as much imagination as a haddock.

'For heaven's sake, don't pay any attention to all that twaddle,' Hope broke in, with a smile that was meant to defuse the situation, but only infuriated Juliet. 'She's only trying to put the wind up you. It's an old army custom.'

With the tension broken, Ruth felt she could join in.

'It's tough, all right, but we've been here four months and we're still in one piece. Just. So stick together. That's the best advice we can give you. Be a team. Help each other as much as you can.'

'And you can always come to us if you have any problems,' Nell added. 'We'll help you as much as we can. Particularly Isa. She knows everything. Isn't that right, Isa?'

'Mmm?'

156

Isa had been staring out of the floor-length windows, across the gravel paths, past the stark concrete façade of the Officers' Mess, over the tarmac drill square. Pin-hard sleet, like tiny beads of polystyrene, eddied and swirled across the slippery surface, before settling like litter along the bottom of the gymnasium wall. Beyond the fence, straggly pines stood black against the dying light.

'I said, we're all here to help, aren't we, Isa,' Nell repeated with some surprise.

'Oh. Oh, yes.'

'How dare you undermine my authority.' Juliet was so angry that her words tripped over themselves on their way past her lips.

'I didn't.'

'You did.'

'Look, grow up, why don't you. I'm not going to play *did–didn't* with you. I've got better things to do,' Hope declared. She opened her suitcase and began to unpack – books, underwear, records, a poster of Che Guevara, patchwork loon pants, a string of hanging chimes, a see-through cheese-cloth shirt, all in a mounting muddle. 'You were acting like a real little Hitler. Frightening those poor mites out of their skins. Can't you remember what it was like on our first day?'

'*We* had to put up with it. It was good for us.'

'No – don't say it – it's made men of us!'

'Very funny. It's good for them, too. Keeps them on their toes. Stops them thinking it's all going to be a walkover.'

'Bollocks. You know, Juliet, you're turning into a real military shit.'

'And you're still a junior, too,' Juliet hissed, 'and don't you forget it.'

'Just bugger off, why don't you. Go and polish something – how about the Commandant's backside!'

There was a sense, Nell thought, in which time stood still. She would watch the new girls scurrying around, absurd in stockings, PT skirts and plimsolls and half expected to see herself among them. She felt again that kick of tension in her guts. Their lost expressions and fearful anxiety were so familiar to her. Then Hope would come striding by, in uniform, but with her kick pleats crumpled and fluff on her beret, comfortable with neither the new nor the old. Nell and Ruth would join her, matching their strides with Hope's, trying to make her feel that being friends was nothing to do with which intake you were attached to or how long you'd been in the place.

'I don't think I'm going to make it, Nell,' Hope confided one day. 'The Corps and I just don't seem to have much in common.'

'I'd miss you,' Nell answered, but Hope noticed that she hadn't tried to argue.

'I'm hanging on by my fingernails, though. I think I might be quite good at this soldiering lark, if I could just get out of here into the real army. But it's going to be tough, seeing you all fly the coop ahead of me.'

'None of us has a cast-iron guarantee,' Nell said,

with a lightness she was far from feeling. 'They could chuck any one of us out between now and the beginning of May. I won't believe I've made it until I'm going out of those gates with a brand new pip on each shoulder.'

'You will.' Hope flung an arm around Nell's shoulder and gave her a squeeze. 'You will.'

But certain assumptions had to be made. The measuring of tailormade uniforms had to begin well in advance of the assumed commissioning date. The visit of representatives from Bernard Weatherill and Moss Bros was both exciting and demoralizing.

'Who are you going to choose?' Juliet asked.

'I don't suppose it makes much difference,' Ruth said, mildly. 'One uniform looks much like another in the long run.'

'Oh, no. That's where you're wrong. I'm definitely going for Weatherill's. They have so much more cachet. And while they're here, I think I'll have them measure me for a hunt coat. I certainly intend to hunt, wherever I'm posted.'

'How about Benbecula?' queried Ruth, barely concealing a snigger. 'Honestly, Juliet, you are the limit. You're not joining the Household Cavalry, you know.'

'I think I'll go for the one with the nicest tailor,' Nell decided. 'One of them looks like the ideal grandpa.'

The chosen tailors ran their tape measures impassively round the young female bodies, murmuring notes under their breath.

'Umm. Hollow back.'

Juliet was horrified.

'Dropped right shoulder.'

And Nell immediately tried to pull herself straighter.

'No, don't do that, please, madam. You've distorted the drop of that sleeve.'

Isa stood very still as the measurements of her bust, waist and hips were taken. 'A very nice figure for a jacket, if I may say so, madam.' Nell thought she looked thinner than before Christmas and there were hollows below her eyes where none had been before.

What sort of Christmas had Isa had? Nell wondered. At once she felt the familiar fluttering of her pulse and the tightening in her chest that always followed thoughts of home.

'Had a good Christmas?' the others had asked on that first night back.

'Oh, quiet, you know,' Nell had replied. 'Traditional.'

But a traditional Vernon Christmas was something else.

They'd had all the trimmings, an enormous tree, the turkey, the drink. They'd pulled crackers and put on the jolly paper crowns. Nell's mother had raised her glass in a toast to her husband across the table.

'Hail, king of the fools . . .'

Afterwards, Nell had quietly cleared away the remains of the smashed gravy boat and cleaned the grease off the carpet. Later she'd found her mother's wedding ring, where it had rolled under the sofa after it had been flung across the room. Later still, she'd tossed onto the fire the hunk of her father's hair that her mother had torn out and watched it sizzle and flare.

After that, coming back to the college had been like coming home. Nell had looked round the spartan room, empty of the family photos that the others displayed, and felt a deep sense of peace replace the grinding anxiety – like mental toothache – that had tormented her throughout her leave. They'd be split up in the spring, she knew that, but for now, Hope, Ruth, Juliet and Isa were all the family she wanted.

Right now, the only feeling she had was one of security. Dependence. Home. Safety. Friendship. Warm, rhubarb crumble and custard sort of words. It wouldn't last beyond tomorrow, she knew, but it was enough to feel it tonight.

A traditional Christmas? She wondered if Isa's had been any better. By the look of her, probably not.

It was exciting to have to choose between the merits of workaday white sateen or scarlet silk for jacket linings. The bottle green melton cloth for the great-coat was soft as sealskin. Everything fitted better, felt better, looked better than they were used to. Everything was of the best quality. The shirts had double cuffs and Juliet said that her father had promised her some solid gold cuff links, the size of gobstoppers, when he came back from Dubai.

'How vulgar,' Ruth murmured, most unexpectedly.

A fitter from Hillier's arrived to measure for their mess dresses, Norman Hartnell designed, those fantasy garments they would wear at formal dinners, when the men were decked out like peacocks in tight-fitting trousers and bum-freezer jackets, scarlet or blue or black or green.

Even the plainest man was transformed by the braid and the stripes, the tiny gold buttons and the miniature medals and the spurs. The good-looking ones were even more delicious than Terence Stamp playing Sergeant Troy in *Far from the Madding Crowd*. They'd all gone to watch the film one Saturday night just before Christmas and Juliet still hadn't recovered from the impact of Stamp's bright blue gaze.

'A walking bird trap,' was Hope's description of male mess kit. 'Sex on legs.'

The same couldn't be said of their female counterparts. The fitted white and gold brocade, embellished with a green, bullion-fringed sash sweeping from one shoulder, had been designed – they were told – to flatter all figures. Ruth, often so gawky, was turned by hers into a statuesque Juno. Nell felt lumpish and matronly.

On the days of the tailors' visits, the end seemed tantalizingly near.

Sometimes, it felt as though they were walled in behind the ladybird gates and would never get out.

*   *   *

Nell was allowed a weekend at home for her brother's confirmation. When she got back on Sunday night, Juliet popped her head round the bedroom door.

'The blond bombshell rang up for you last night,' she announced.

Nell's stomach gave a sickening, fairground swoop. 'Who?'

'You know perfectly well – don't be coy. It doesn't suit you. Only little women should be coy. When I told him you were away for the weekend, he asked if anyone else was free to go out for a drink. "Certainly not," I said, "what do you think this is? Rent-a-WRAC?" '

'Thanks a lot.'

'Do try to be a little bit grateful. I could have gone out with him myself – and then where would you be?'

Their drill sessions included officers' drill now. They learned how to take up their proper positions, at the command *March on, the Officers*. They learned how to behave, both when inspecting a parade and when being inspected. They learned how to take a platoon past a saluting base, giving the *Eyes Right* command as they passed the correct marker flag, how to march in a straight line while saluting and with the head turned smartly to the right (tricky that – Nell wavered like a drunk, even with Ruth behind her whispering left a bit, right a bit, steady on) and when to order *Eyes Front* again (what a relief!).

Sometimes, as she tottered along with her neck

twisted to the right, Nell would spot Hope hurrying off to another lesson, or see her through the classroom window, her attention wandering, her eyes avidly following the progress of the group she had once belonged to.

The sight made Nell feel guilty.

Nell had no idea what possible attraction she could hold for Oliver. Unless it was the one suggested by Flavia – that she was suitable mating material. And her pride wouldn't allow her to contemplate that idea (except when alone and in the dark and then it was obviously the only possible solution).

He phoned again a week later, suggesting that they should go to Larkhill for a point-to-point.

'Come and watch me break my neck, why don't you? Always good for a laugh.'

But it was Harry who turned up outside the door, in a half-timbered Morris Traveller with moss growing along the window ledges.

'Oliver's had to go on ahead, as he's riding. I say, you look jolly nice, but are you sure you're going to be warm enough? The wind fairly whistles across the course down there. Tell you what, you can borrow this. Get off, Madge, you silly bitch.'

Not on your life, thought Nell, as she watched him drag an aged brown Barbour from the back of the Traveller. It was splattered with mud, upholstered with spaniel hairs and smelt of ancient peat bogs.

She changed her mind once they reached Larkhill. A stiff northeasterly swept down off Salisbury Plain.

It whistled through the burnt-out tanks used for target practice by the gunners of the School of Artillery, then cut straight across the point-to-point course without pausing for breath.

Nell hauled the ancient Barbour over the snappy little trouser suit that WRAC regulations allowed her. She didn't look too out of place, she decided, warily assessing all the other women. Her only significant lack was a silk scarf knotted just above the point of her chin, like a guardsman's chinstrap. And everyone seemed to smell of either the accompanying labrador or springer spaniel, lolloping along on the end of a horse's lead rope, or of horse.

Only the horses were well turned out, sleekly groomed athletes, buzzing with health and energy, their skins bulging like balloons stuffed with muscle. The carpark was packed with muddy people letting down horsebox ramps and leading out clean horses or even muddier people loading sweating horses back in again. The air was pungent with sweat and whisky.

'Keep an eye on Madge, would you?' asked Harry, thrusting a rope at Nell. 'I must give Oliver a hand. Cut A Dash is playing up rather. Bloody nutter. See you at the paddock.'

'Silly bitch,' muttered Nell, as the spaniel tried to tug after Harry. Madge seemed to recognize the description and followed Nell happily after that. Nell slogged through the mud to the white-railed paddock.

Led by girl grooms who all seemed out of the same stable as Flavia, the horses walked round and round the paddock, while punters and connections assessed their virtues. They all looked beautiful to Nell, as they tiptoed with springy, elastic steps like dancers around the muddy circle, their ears pricked to the commentary, their nostrils redly flared to the wild winter smell blowing off the plain.

Hard-faced men in tweeds and ancient brown felt hats and women with cracked sheepskin coats and sharp, knowing eyes watched and made short, barking statements to each other.

'Brannigan Boy's never been a stayer . . .'

'The going's just right for Hulahoop . . .'

'Of course, Crispin's never been the same since he took that frightful purler at Maiden Bradley. Lost his bottle, silly bugger . . .'

Nell had the sense of being excluded from their world. Not, she told herself firmly, that she actually wanted to belong, but she would have liked someone – anyone – to talk to. All she had was Madge and *she* was making a dive for a pile of horse shit just within the paddock rails.

'Come back, you silly bitch,' Nell commanded, hauling on the muddy rope. 'D'you want to get trampled to death?'

And then there was Oliver, taking a leg up from Harry onto a leggy, bright bay who was trying to waltz backwards into his nearest rival. Oliver wore a knitted roll-neck jersey in his racing colours of black and purple and sat loosely in the saddle with cool assurance as he took the stirrup leathers up to jumping length, while Cut A Dash threatened to bite lumps out of an inoffensive grey in front.

'Nasty brute, that, pulls like a train,' Nell heard one of the knowing women remark. 'They'll either win or he'll go home on a stretcher.'

'Hey, little Nell,' Oliver called across the paddock. 'Come and give me a good luck kiss.'

Tugged by the ecstatic Madge who'd just spotted Harry, Nell made her way round the railings, know-ing – *knowing* – that there wasn't a girl around that circle who didn't envy her a kiss from Oliver Hawtrey. She ducked underneath and stood on tip-toe by the bad-tempered bay. Oliver leaned down from the saddle and put an arm round her neck. His lips were icy, firm and supple over Nell's trembling mouth. He tasted of toothpaste and whisky, such a heady mixture, and Nell caught the sharp, sexy tang of nervous tension as he leaned down. His kiss was long and exploratory, ended only when Cut A Dash aimed a cow kick at Nell.

'Very nice. You're getting better,' he said, with a tense, thin laugh. 'Have you been taking lessons?'

Like a knight, Nell thought in a romantic daze as the first riders cantered down to the start, and she wished she had something black or purple, some-thing in Oliver's colours to wear, to bring him luck.

'Is it dangerous?' she asked, ignorantly.

'No more than anything that's worth while. A few cracked skulls, maybe . . .' Cut A Dash pirouetted, taking away Oliver's concentration for a moment. 'But what's the point without the risk, eh? Anyway, you're my mascot today. Nothing'll go wrong.'

'What a responsibility. Good luck, then,' she called, as the remaining horses, by now almost all of them jitterbugging on the spot, plunged through the paddock gate towards the start. Nell and Madge slogged through the mud after Harry. He was making for the finish, with a pair of heavy, army issue binoculars in his hand.

'You can see most of the course from here,' he told her. 'And there they go.'

The riders hurtled past on the first circuit with a drumming of hooves and a blur of colour that woke a primitive thrill in Nell. The horses were bunched so closely that the fences didn't seem wide enough to take them all. One was squeezed out and forced round the fence wings, the rider yelling abuse at anyone who'd listen. The brushwood fences crackled under the attack. Clods of mud flew up and hit the ground with a soggy smack. And then they were through a narrow belt of trees and into the open at the far side of the course. Harry put up his binoculars.

'He's going well. Keeping out of trouble on the outside . . .'

'Let me see,' begged Nell.

'Took fence twelve well . . . ran on into thirteen a bit, bet that took the skin off his belly, OK though . . . steady up on the downhill bend . . . up and over . . .'

'Let me see. Let me see.'

Nell felt like a whining child. For heaven's sake, why did everyone treat her like a retarded seven-year-old?

'Coming to fifteen – oh God, he's down, up again, no . . . oh, bugger . . .'

And now Nell could see the runners as they came back round the curve towards the finish. Cut A Dash was up there at the front, broken reins trailing, empty stirrups thumping off his sides and driving him wild, mouth flecked with bloody foam. And the green military ambulance was bumping across the scarred turf and Harry was thrusting Madge's rope into Nell's frozen hand again and running towards the blowing horse.

Nell forced her way through the gaping crowds as the ambulance slowed over ruts gouged out of the chalky ground by tracked vehicles. She ran alongside it, ricking her ankles on the rough grass, panicky, thumping on the closed doors until they opened.

'What's all the fuss?' a medical orderly complained. 'He's not dying yet.'

Oliver lay on a stretcher with his legs immobilized by being strapped to each other and to the stretcher. Nell noticed that the beautiful, close-fitting leather boot had been cut away from his left leg and his breeches were slit beyond the knee. She didn't dare look too closely. Memories of a first aid demo at the medical depot in Mytchett, where Juliet had fainted at the sight of a mock-up compound fracture, were only too clear.

Oliver's skin had a chalky pallor and his lips were scarcely darker, blue-tinged. His eyes seemed to have sunk deeper into his head. There was a skim of sweat on his face. But he managed a smile at the sight of her.

'Dammit, my boots are ruined. Fine lucky mascot you turned out to be, little Nell.'

When the ambulance had gone, Harry found her again. She was clutching Oliver's crash hat, its black and purple hooped silk cover ragged, its left side cracked.

'Damn,' he said. 'And I had some decent money on him, too.'

'Harry . . .' Flavia was exquisite in chestnut-coloured suede hipsters, soft as velvet, worn with a green fun fur jacket – *ridiculous*, Nell thought, *she's dressed for the King's Road, not Salisbury Plain in March*. But Flavia wore the beautiful clothes with the total unconcern of those who never have to worry where the next outfit is coming from. Under the brim of a suede butcher's cap, her eyes were a swimming violet. She laid her grabbing little hand on Harry's sleeve. 'Aren't you going to help me get Cut A Dash home, Harry?'

'Why me? There's any number of chaps around who'd carry the brute home on their backs if you looked at them like that.'

'But I need you . . .'

'Do something yourself for once, can't you,' Harry snapped and Flavia looked as startled as though he'd stripped off all his clothes in public. 'Someone has to drive Nell home.'

'Oh, Nell . . . Oh, well, in *that* case . . .' Flavia's sarcasm was as subtle as a sledgehammer. 'Don't let little me stop you. I can manage that horrid beast all by myself, thank you.'

'Ghastly afternoon,' Harry said as they drove out of Larkhill. 'Disaster always makes me hungry. Let's go into Salisbury and have tea.'

*   *   *

He took her to the House of Steps, by the cathedral gate, dark and warm and resolutely cosy. Jammed against the wall, at a corner table, Nell found that she was able to sit quietly and let Harry's talk flow over her. He was a most undemanding companion. No sexual innuendo. No trying to belittle her because she was a woman in a man's world. No competition. No patronizing. He seemed to think he did his duty by stuffing Nell with tea and toasted teacakes. It was very restful.

So she could sit and worry about Oliver, and Harry would never notice that she wasn't sparkling and full of fun – like Flavia. Being vivacious had never been in Nell's line.

Supposing the break was a bad one? He'd looked so pale. He must have been in agony. Supposing he lost his leg? She saw herself bravely pushing a wheelchair (all the nasty business neatly covered with a blanket, of course), or steadying his faltering steps as he tried his new leg, saw his glance of gratitude, heard his words of love.

Without you, little Nell . . .

Poor Oliver . . .

Madge lay quietly under the table. Now and then, Harry would drop her a piece of teacake, murmuring, 'Who's a good girl, then?' The table would rock a little as she snapped it up then was still again.

Nell felt very sleepy. Worrying is awfully tiring, she decided, even worse than work. She'd been up until two that morning, anyway, roughing out her plan for the end of term history prize essay. 'Horrid swot,' Hope had called her when she found out. She leaned her head back against the wall, drowsing slightly, her eyes half closed.

Really, Harry was very ugly. If puppies are meant to grow into their feet, then boys are supposed to grow into their noses when they become men. Harry hadn't managed it yet. He was well over six feet, yet gave the impression that he was still trying to decide what size he ought to be. There were seams in his eyebrows that looked suspiciously like boxing scars. His mouth was wide and split into a ready grin at any excuse.

'You look just like a dormouse sitting there,' he said. 'Any minute now, I might stuff you into the teapot. Shall I order some more teacakes? Madge ate most of the last lot.'

But his eyes were beautiful, brown and soft and gentle, fringed with black lashes that Nell would have died for. He had a way of looking, sidelong, diffident, as though he didn't quite trust people to like him. A little like Madge. Yet Nell had the oddest feeling that he saw further with that tangential glance than Oliver ever did with his bold blue stare.

He's awfully nice, Nell thought. *What a pity he's so ordinary.*

And later, much later, she thought, *he's much too nice for Flavia.*

Sleep and work. There didn't seem to be much time for anything else. No-one crept through Nell's win-

172

dow in the middle of the night, now. The strain was showing. Ruth had a growling cough, rich with mucus, that kept her and her neighbours awake half the night. Juliet had cold sores and smelt of the surgical spirit she constantly dabbed on them. Nell had seconds of steamed pudding and custard every lunchtime and reduced the tailor to near tears as he had to adjust her uniform at every fitting. Hope upped her consumption of those nice herbal cigarettes. The whole corridor reeked of them, but she kept her smile. Isa turned inward. She didn't sit around and gossip at the end of the day. She didn't join in the shoe-polishing bees. She fixed a Do Not Disturb notice to her door. She was the only one Nell really worried about.

One more trial. Pass that and they'd made it. One weekend exercise away, at Browndown Camp, by Southampton Water, pretending to be the control team (God forbid!) limiting an oil pollution incident, and they'd cracked it.

Nearly there.

Hope was packing. Into an Afghan carpet bag and a couple of Tesco's carriers, she stuffed the few things she thought worth preserving. A sack of rubbish bulged at the door. Her uniform was scrappily folded on the bed. Already, the room was ominously bare.

Nell gaped. 'What're you doing?'

'What does it look as though I'm doing?'

'You can't.'

'Just watch me.'

Nell called on reinforcements and Ruth and Juliet crowded into the little room.

'C'mon, Hope, nothing's that bad.'

'It's not like you to give up on anything.'

'Where's your team spirit? We need you.'

'Look. I'm going. OK? It's *my* decision.' Hope turned her back abruptly to rummage in a cupboard, but Nell caught the glitter of tears on her cheek. Hope's voice came backwards and muffled. 'I'm not staying to be chucked out. I'm not going to give them the satisfaction.'

'But why now?'

Hope backed out of the cupboard carrying a pile of white shirts with their spare collars. She blew her nose heartily on a shirt tail, then threw them onto the pile of uniform and topped the lot with her forage cap.

'Green was never my colour, anyway! Because I don't fit in, that's why. I never did and never will. The OC made it perfectly clear today. "You're not one of us," she said. When I asked for a railway warrant home, I thought she was going to give three cheers.'

Not one of us, thought Nell. No – and she never had been. How did she ever imagine she could or would be? She was too vibrant, too alive, too . . . real. There was no way Hope could be squashed, like an ugly sister's toes, into a proper military shape.

But what will we do without her? Oh God, I'll miss her.

'Stupid cow.'

Nell broke in with such unexpected venom that Hope gave a delighted laugh, though the tears still showed as grubby tracks down her cheeks.

'Wow, Nell, you're growing up at last! But no, she's right. It's time for me to admit it. I'm never going to be a lady – a pretend one like Juliet . . .'

'Well, really.'

'. . . or a real one like Nell. I don't know, now, whatever made me think I could.'

A pile of military manuals teetered beside the rubbish. Scraps of paper jutted from them, scrawled with Hope's references. She pulled some folders from her desk and extracted the paper, tried to tear it across, gave up and tossed the lot into the bin bag. It rolled slowly over and spread its contents across the scuffed lino.

'There. That's that. All done. I feel better already.'

Ruth had disappeared as soon as she saw what Hope was doing. Now she came back in, carrying a bottle of whisky. 'I don't know if this is a wake or a celebration,' she said with a wry grin, 'but whatever – we deserve this.'

She'd brought glasses, too, stuffed into her pockets, and she poured a hefty slug into each.

'Hope,' she said, raising her glass. 'You're the best of a bad bunch. God bless.'

After that, it all got a bit vague. If they'd been sober, things might have been very different.

Hope's plans got wilder and wilder. Perhaps she'd be spotted on the news, demonstrating outside the chemical weapons establishment at Porton Down, or waving placards in Grosvenor Square. Perhaps she'd hitch to Samarkand, or find herself sitting at the feet of some wisdom-dispensing guru on the banks of the Ganges. Perhaps she'd hightail it to San Francisco and spend all day on the beach and all night singing. Anything seemed possible that night.

'Or perhaps you'll settle down,' Nell suggested.

'Blow that! But I suppose I'll have to earn some money somehow. What a bore. Still, other people manage. I could always sell my body, I suppose. Oh, Juliet, if only you could see your face! Your mouth looks like a dog's bottom!'

'I think that was crude and uncalled for and absolutely typical of you.'

'Right on all counts. Sorry, Juliet. Really. You know I always talk first and think afterwards.'

'Quite. Anyway, do try and plan something, for once in your life,' Juliet urged, barely forgiving. 'Never mind next month or next year. Where're you going *tomorrow*?'

'I suppose I'll turn up on Aunt Tabby's doorstep again – not for the first time. She runs a B&B in Salisbury. I'll hang around with her for a few days, wash up for my keep – just until I see what the scene is. You know.'

Hope sat on the floor with her back propped comfortably against the radiator. She opened an old Sharp's toffee tin and began to roll one of her skinny herbal cigarettes. The smoke rose in a thin, blue, barely seen spiral on the still, hot air. It was a satisfying smell, Nell thought as she sprawled across Hope's bed, like a summer hayfield or the barn which had stored the feed for her old pony. A comforting smell. Hope passed the cigarette up to her.

'Oh, I couldn't,' Nell objected. 'I don't smoke.'

'Silly. This isn't smoking. It's relaxing. Go on. Try it.'

Nell took a hesitant suck, holding the paper tube gingerly between thumb and first finger, ready to drop it. The smoke didn't seem to go down to her lungs. It seemed to find all the empty channels in her head. It drifted through her sinuses and eddied round her eustachian tubes. It swirled around the convolutions of her brain.

'It's not that bad,' she said and passed it over to Ruth, who was sitting in the sink, her long legs dangling almost to the floor. Ruth took a long, contemplative drag.

'That's good,' she agreed.

Then Juliet had a puff, but she tried to talk at the same time and coughed all the smoke back out again.

'That is *disgusting* – I'll stick to my Consulates, thanks.'

When it had burned away, shared around the three of them, Hope rolled another. They passed it peacefully around. Hope had turned out the main light and thrown a silk scarf over the white plastic table lampshade. Its colours split up, like shards of broken glass, like a cathedral window at noon, like the feathers of a pigeon's neck, like refractions around the moon on an icy night.

Nell had never before realized how beautiful her friends were. Hope always said her hair was like rusty barbed wire, but tonight it looked like spun sugar. It crackled with life. Nell could hear it. And Ruth was so graceful, so tranquil, Madonna-like in the way her head moved on a lily stem neck. Juliet was like a little black cat, furry and neat, with a pink tongue that flicked out between rose-red lips, as though she was tasting the air. But when she opened her mouth, you could see those sharp little white teeth.

The hard army mattress felt like marshmallow below her and the sound of their sleepy voices was sweeter than the music of the spheres.

I'll always remember Hope, Nell told herself. *And when I think of her, I'll think of tonight and her purple velvet waistcoat and the light winking off the tiny mirrors on it, like splinters off the stars, and her voice like the sound of bells . . .*

God, that sounds weird. Like, as if I was trying to write poetry. But poetry's not my thing – sensible Nell, thoroughly boring Nell . . .

Nell took another drag and knew that she loved them all, all . . .

And Isa. Where was Isa . . . ? Isa should be here, too.

Juliet went out to fetch her and when she came back she was very pale.

'I think you'd better all come,' she said.

You could rely on Isa. Isa was a sensible girl. Isa always kept her head in emergencies.

She'd stripped the bed and covered the mattress with a polythene sheet. She'd tossed around a lot since then and the sheeting had become wrinkled beneath her, but it was still doing its job.

She'd had a bath and put on her nightdress, her oldest one, of course, faded blue flower-sprigged Viyella. It was tangled now, rucked up, hauled up, further than was decent, almost to her waist. Nell didn't like to see her exposed like that. White and turgid. A mound crowned by a pale gold tuft. And between her legs, pulsing, almost winking at them, the top of a head.

'Oh, my God . . .' gasped Hope.

Juliet turned and hung over the sink, retching, but nothing came out except bile.

The air smelt of blood. It streaked Isa's inner thighs. Her bitten lips were spattered with it. It was a fat smell, thick enough to taste, to chew, flat and somehow metallic, a bland smell. The window was open, but it didn't go out. It hung around, mingling with Isa's sweat, with the fruity smell of whisky and the hay meadow smell of the reefers. It was the sort of smell that would creep around, out into the corridor, insidious, making people – making the juniors curious.

Ruth opened the window as wide as it would go. On a spring wind came the icy scent of daffodils and the sound of the record player from the room below, telling everyone that the age of Aquarius had dawned.

'It's too soon,' Isa whispered and her voice was engulfed by the music.

Her hair, fine as floss, its clover-honey colour darkened by sweat, clung to her head, revealing the

179

skull shape, narrow and vulnerable. Her eyes had receded into the bone, somewhere very far away, and the blueness had become black in the distance. At the centre, in the darkness, a tiny flame still burned, but only just.

'Too soon. I thought it wouldn't be until we got leave, until I was out of here.'

The mound of her belly – such a small mound, how could there possibly be room for a baby in there? – rippled and cross-rippled, as though stone after stone were being flung into a pool.

'I'll phone someone, fetch someone, the orderly officer . . .' Juliet turned to the door, but was halted by Isa, stronger now and urgent.

'No.'

'You need help.'

Isa struggled up and propped herself on her elbows. 'No. No-one.'

'But . . .'

'Do as . . .' She was silenced by another contraction. The head, blood-streaked, winked again, obscenely. 'Do as I say . . .'

Hope started to wash her hands, scrubbing vigorously at the nails. 'Nell,' she ordered, 'fetch some more pillows and some towels. Ruth, bring that whisky, what's left of it.'

'You've had enough.'

'I'm not going to drink it, idiot. I'm going to clean my hands with it. Come on, now, Isa. Let's make you more comfortable.'

'You can't do this,' Juliet insisted, once the other two had left the room.

'I can and I will.' Hope looked up quickly and the ferocity of her glare made Juliet step back a pace. 'If Isa kept quiet this long, she had a reason, and it's not for us to go running around like headless chickens, shouting for help. How long has she been lying here? No-one's seen her since five o'clock. Look at her lips – bitten to rags. Not a sound. Could you do that?'

Juliet shook her head. She was paler than Isa.

'Well, then. Shut up and don't get in the way.'

'But . . . but do you know what to do? Have you done it before?'

'No, but . . . well, people used to have babies in the fields. It can't be that difficult.'

Above the sound of the music, above the sound of their voices, came the quick puff-puff of Isa's breath. 'Ten green bottles hanging on a . . .'

'Suppose something goes wrong?'

'It won't. Ninety-five per cent of births are perfectly straightforward. I read that somewhere. I think.'

'There's a book,' said Isa and she pointed towards her desk.

Afterwards, Nell had only a jumbled memory, fragmented, a nightmare.

'Not long now,' Hope had said confidently, watching the head play hide-and-seek. 'I hope . . .'

It was like watching a silent movie.

Ruth sitting at the top of the bed with her arm around Isa's shoulders, encouraging, urging her on, but so quietly. How can anyone shout 'Come on, come on, nearly there, don't give up . . .' in a *whisper*?

Juliet in a corner, keeping out the way as she'd been ordered, her hands clasped to her mouth, the eyes above wide with horror. 'Never, never,' she muttered, over and over. 'I don't care what Simon says. He can have the babies. I'm *never* going to go through this . . .'

Hope kneeling at the business end, big, capable hands ready and waiting. Propped in Nell's hands, the book stood open at the relevant page. Hope tried to look as though she wasn't reading it, as though she'd done this a dozen times before, but she got Nell to keep turning the pages, all the same. No-one was fooled.

They'd taken the shades off the ceiling and table lamps and the light bounced back off the white-washed walls with surgical brilliance, making Hope's eyes ache. The print danced and blurred and as she wiped away the sweat that dripped into her eyes, her forehead was streaked with blood, like a child after the first hunt.

Supposing . . . she tried to ignore the insistent word . . . *supposing* . . .

And Isa . . . she was concentrating now, slipping far away from the bright white room, deep into herself where the others couldn't follow and the gasping breaths came quicker. 'And if one green bottle should accidentally fall . . .'

Weaker and weaker. Juliet could see that Isa was fading. *Dear God, suppose she dies, dear God, don't let her die . . . What would we do? What could we do?* In all the books that Juliet had read, a childbirth scene was accompanied by screams and hauling on towels knotted round the bedpost. But this was so much worse. The mess. The pain. The *silence*. She longed for someone to give a good, normal scream. If not Isa, then it would soon be herself. Juliet felt riven by every pang, stretched to bursting point by the tension. *How much longer? Oh, let it not be long . . .*

Isa gave a soft, sighing moan that seemed to come from somewhere far away.

'I couldn't do it,' she whispered.

'You can, you can,' urged Ruth.

'No, I mean . . .' She sighed again. 'I couldn't . . . I tried, over Christmas leave . . . but when I got to the place, I went out again. Terrible place. I couldn't do it . . .'

Outside the room, the evening went on as usual. Feet clumped up and down stairs. Doors banged. Showers gushed. Someone whined through the radio stations and fixed on Radio Luxembourg. No-one came near Isa's room. No junior ever challenged a Do Not Disturb sign on a senior's door.

Inside, the silence was uncanny. Someone must have turned down the volume knob. Nell thought she was lipreading. Hope's lips said, 'Now, Isa, now. I think . . .' But no words came out.

Isa's mouth opened in a great, soundless yell. And the mouth on the tiny, outraged face that appeared gave a matching yell. No wonder. Isa expelled the rest of the furious infant into Hope's waiting hands.

Greasy, vernix-smeared, blood-streaked, palpating

in Hope's grasp. No need for the traditional bottom-slapping. Greedy, rasping, sucking in of air. Jarring, crowing affirmation of life.

'Quick, turn the page, Nell,' Hope ordered. 'There's lots more to do.'

When it was over, Isa wept and smiled.

'Amazing,' said Juliet.

'Wonderful,' said Ruth.

'Fantastic,' said Hope.

'Beautiful,' said Nell.

And they were all crying.

And no-one outside heard a thing.

That's when the problems really began.

If they – they not we – if they hadn't all been stoned, Juliet often wondered, *what would they have done? Listened to me. I was the only sensible one of the lot. Done the right thing. Called for help. Recognized that things were getting out of control.*

I should have done it. I should have used my initiative.

But no-one listened to me.

She was such a healthy baby. She didn't understand the need for silence. Ruth turned on the transistor, as loudly as she dared. Juliet washed the baby in the basin, cleaning her of the birth blood and grease. She found the nappies and the few bits of clothing that Isa had smuggled in and hidden interleaved with her own clothing in a drawer, then she turned with the dressed baby in her arms and her face a ludicrous mask of fright.

'What're we going to do with her?' Juliet demanded, as the baby screamed again.

Isa held out her arms. 'Give her to me.'

The furious mouth was silenced at the touch of Isa's skin. With a life and purpose of its own, it rooted around, with a sound like miniature feet squelching through mud. When it found the nipple, it grabbed with a fierce intensity of purpose. Isa winced, then smiled, a silly, besotted smile.

Hope perched on the edge of the stained, rumpled bed. She laid her hand on Isa's arm. 'I'm not sure that's such a good idea, love,' she warned softly.

Isa didn't answer. With one finger, she stroked the damp, fair fluff that scarcely covered an angry red scalp and pulsing fontanelle. The baby's hair matched her own exactly.

'But Juliet's right,' Ruth said, watching the pair with troubled eyes. 'What *are* we going to do?'

'It's obvious, I'd have thought. Even to you lot.' Juliet scarcely bothered to disguise her impatience. 'Isa needs a doctor and the baby should be checked over.'

'It looks perfectly all right to me,' Nell remarked, looking towards the bed. 'Breathing. Eating. Two arms and two legs. Fingers and toes OK. I counted. What else do babies do but breathe and eat? I think we've done a jolly good job.'

'And Isa's OK, too. All in one piece. Nothing fell out. No stitching needed.' Ruth was quickly and efficiently tidying up. She already had Isa washed and decent and in a clean nightdress. The polythene sheeting was rolled up round the afterbirth – Nell

185

got a bit wobbly about that – and bagged. The bed was remade. But nothing Ruth had done had taken away the primitive smell of birth. 'You're right, Nell. We're pretty good at this. If they chuck us out of the army, we could get jobs as midwives!'

'You're mad!' Juliet accused. 'You're drunk or stoned or both. My God!'

'And you're not, I suppose.' Nell fighting back was as surprising as finding the mouse biting the cat. 'Fat lot of good you were, shivering in the corner. So shut up, unless you can say something useful.'

'But Isa might *die*. She might bleed to death in the night or something. We can't take the reponsibility.'

'Why don't we ask her what she wants,' Ruth suggested quietly.

Isa might as well have been in a different room, for all the attention she had paid. Ruth perched on the edge of the bed. She put out one tentative finger and touched the baby on the head, on the fingers, on the toes. Exhausted by the long passage into light, sated by the little that Isa's breasts had yet been able to produce, the baby slept, crumpled and red still, but with her newborn fury assuaged for a while. *Nell's right*, Ruth thought with an amazed rush of love and pride, *she's perfect, she's lovely. Aren't we clever?*

'Isa,' she began softly, unwilling to break into the mother's rapt silence. 'Do you want us to call a doctor? I think we should.'

Isa shook her head.

'Isa, what do you want us to do?'

Isa seemed to have lost weight during the hours of

186

labour. Her hair, though brushed now, still clung damply to her skull. There were bruises below her eyes and her skin seemed to be stretched very tightly across the bones of her face, as tightly, Nell thought, as the skin of a mummy she'd seen as a child, partly unwrapped in a museum, and had had night-mares about for weeks. Not that Isa . . . well, you wouldn't have nightmares, would you . . . she was still beautiful, of course, but there was some-thing . . . something ageless about that tight parch-ment skin.

The tears that hung on her lashes were not the easy tears of relief and joy. Her voice was muffled by a swollen, unruly tongue.

'Go and make her a cup of tea, Juliet – why don't you – with lots of sugar,' Ruth suggested. 'Her tongue's sticking to the roof of her mouth.'

'But . . .'

'Go on. Do something useful for once.'

'I like that! I'm the only one who's got any sense at all.'

When Juliet had gone, Isa let the tears spill over. They made stinging red tracks down her papery skin.

'Take her, Hope,' she whispered.

There was a shocked hiss of breath from Ruth and Nell. But it seemed as though Hope had been waiting for the request. She stood in the centre of the room, her arms hanging uselessly by her sides, her hands clean and scrubbed now, but still smelling of the whisky she had used as a disinfectant.

'Please, Hope.' Isa's voice was hoarse and

uncertain, as though the hours of silence had left her without a memory of sound, as though she knew she was reaching the outer limits of her control. 'My grandmother's name was Lydia. Please call her Lydia for me.'

And Hope nodded and held out her arms.

'Oh, no,' breathed Nell.

Ruth and Nell blurted out in shocked unison.

'We can't do this.'

'Hope, no . . .'

'Are you sure it's what you want?' asked Hope. She looked at Isa, and Nell had the impression that there was a silent dialogue going on, that she and Ruth were excluded from something – something past and secret. 'Think carefully.'

'Do I have a choice?' The baby stirred in her sleep, jerking suddenly with newborn lack of control. Her hands flew open, startled and wide, then folded again, with the thumbs tucked under the fingers. Her mouth suckled contentedly on nothing. Isa's expression, as she looked down, took root, deep in Nell's memory.

'There's always a choice,' Hope reminded her.

'Not for me. I don't have any home but the army. I was an army kid. My family followed the drum. I was born in Egypt, in the Canal Zone. I've lived in Germany, in Singapore, in Aden, in Hong Kong. I was seventeen before we came back to Scotland and then I joined up. I don't know how to live any other way.'

'But surely,' Nell began, 'your parents . . .'

Yet even as she said it, she tried to imagine her

188

own parents' reactions if she arrived home un-announced with a baby in her arms. And she shied away from the images . . .

'My father was so proud. His daughter – *his* daughter, Sergeant Cameron's daughter – going to be an officer. He'd kill me if I went home with a baby.'

'I can't believe . . .' But already Nell could believe.

'Nell, believe me. I know him. I've seen what he's done to my mother sometimes, for nothing, maybe for not having meat for his tea. She bumped into more doors . . . And I've nowhere else to go. Hope, please . . . tonight . . . before I start to love her.'

Hope bent over and lifted the baby out of her mother's arms. The munching mouth never stopped. 'I'll be good to her,' Hope whispered. 'I promise.'

Juliet came back with a tray and five mugs of tea slopping over onto it.

'I thought we'd all be better for a cuppa,' she said, briskly. 'Sober us up a bit and then we can decide sensibly what to do next.'

She walked into a shrieking silence. She looked at Isa, looked at Hope, put two and two together and came up with exactly the right answer.

'You've all gone mad,' she shouted and then, more quietly, conscious of listeners, 'you can't just walk off with a baby, just like that. It's illegal, must be. Kidnap, or something.'

'Shut up,' commanded Ruth. 'Can't you see you're upsetting Isa.'

'She should have thought of that before she . . .

before she . . .' Juliet looked at the three hostile faces and knew that, if she spoke the bitter words that were pushing their way out of her mouth, she would never be forgiven. 'Anyway, you can't possibly do it. You can't use a baby to play pass the parcel. I'm going to phone the orderly officer.'

For a big girl, Nell moved fast, faster than the PT instructors would ever have thought she could. She was at the door before Juliet and stood with her back against it.

'If you do, I'll tell them about your engagement to Simon,' she threatened. 'And then you won't be commissioned.'

'Don't be silly. I'll tell them I called it off.'

For a moment, Nell looked dashed, then – 'I'll tell them that we *were* in bed together that night.'

Juliet was about to shove Nell out of her way, but she stopped, her hand on Nell's shoulder, her face frozen in horror. 'You wouldn't dare . . .'

'Try me. Go on. I'm such a simpleton, they'll believe every word. I'll tell them how you seduced me, what we did . . .'

'You bitch . . .'

In the morning, Hope and Lydia were gone, driven by Juliet in her smart little yellow convertible to Farnborough, to catch the first train west on the main line.

She waited for the train with them. Hope's tatty baggage had been packed into one of Juliet's suit-cases to make it easier to handle. Lydia hung in an improvised sling around her neck. The crown of

190

Lydia's head, thin-skinned as a newly hatched squab, blue-veined and still pulsating, topped by a skim of fair fluff, poked from the smelly warmth of Hope's embroidered Afghan coat.

'I still think you're mad,' Juliet maintained. 'But I wish you all the luck in the world. And Lydia.' She gave Hope a hug that encompassed the baby. 'God bless.'

Juliet was back in time for parade. Isa was there, too, standing to attention, the perfect soldier.

'Good grief, Cameron,' said Molly Greene, as she ran her eye over the immaculate uniform. 'That must have been one hell of a party last night. You look like death warmed up.'

And then it was over.

They'd been able to tell for a week or two that they'd probably made it. The officers had suddenly begun calling them by their first names – no friendly shortenings, of course, so Nell became Eleanor and Isa was hardly recognizable as Isabel – as though they'd agreed a date for intimacy to be appropriate. *OK, if you're still around on 21 April, we'll call you Eleanor . . .*

Captain Hillcroft had shyly suggested that they could call her Jennifer, if they liked. Juliet did like. But to Nell, Ruth and Isa, it was like learning the true name of God. You might know it, but you wouldn't ever dare to pronounce it.

'It's like being the queen,' Juliet remarked, as she hauled her trunk along the corridor, bashing it off the whitewash as she rounded the turn in the stairs.

'This whole place is revolving around us – *us* – can't you feel it? We're the most important people in this entire unit. It only exists because we're here.'

The trunks, packed with new uniform like a dominatrix's trousseau, had to be addressed. And 'reporting for duty' letters had to be written. And so the final secrets had to be revealed.

All the old clichés about a breathless hush and pins dropping occurred to Nell as they waited for the Officer Commanding to unfold her papers. But it wasn't really like that at all. There was a motion – a commotion, silence made audible – in the air, made up from the hiss of pent-up breath, the tap-tap-tap of Juliet stubbing out her cigarette, the death watch beetle click of Ruth biting her nails, the rasp of nylon as legs were crossed and uncrossed, the surge of blood through congested circulation. It mattered so much . . .

'Officer Cadet Corporal Cleeve,' Major Ottaway announced, 'to the School of Signals, Blandford.'

Juliet grinned – Hope would have called it a smirk, but that would have been cruel. Accurate, though.

A plum posting. *Well, I've deserved it*, she thought. *I've worked hard and kept my nose clean. I've been the natural leader here and it's been noticed*. Only later did she think – *it's the other side of the country from Simon.*

'Officer Cadet Tedder to 3 Squadron, 10 Signal Regiment, Aldershot.'

Ruth couldn't have been more delighted. Aldershot might not be too exciting – it was so close that it scarcely seemed worth going to all the bother of packing a trunk – but it was the Home of the British Army, as the signboards declared, and it meant escaping from the dead hand of WRAC regimental duty.

'Officer Cadet Cameron to the Royal Engineers' Postal Depot, Mill Hill.'

Isa sat impassively, without a smile or a groan.

I worry about her, Major Ottaway thought, fleetingly. *She seems to have run out of steam recently. Too many late nights, maybe. I do hope we haven't made a mistake. You never can tell, with rankers. Could be brilliant or a disaster. Still, Mill Hill will iron out any problems. Kill or cure, there.*

'Officer Cadet Vernon to the WRAC Centre, Guildford.'

I can't, thought Nell, *I can't do it, I can't go there . . .* and she tried to look as pleased as Juliet or Ruth, but she knew that she'd failed. *I just can't . . .*

'We all feel, Eleanor,' Major Ottaway explained, 'that you need a posting where you'll be in touch with women and can really get down to some concentrated regimental work – no point in sending you off somewhere where you can simply be clever!' Her laugh invited Nell to join in, but there was no response. 'You need contact with servicewomen and you'll get plenty in Guildford. You'll learn a lot and leave all the better for it.'

It'll be like here, but worse. Two years of being watched by senior officers. Two years of being judged, being appraised, every action scrutinized. I can't . . . I won't . . .

But she knew that she would. She'd already learned that orders were orders. It would take a braver woman than Nell to question that.

'Mother's had a bit of a fall, I'm afraid.'

'Is she hurt? Is it bad?' Nell didn't have to ask how or why her mother had fallen.

'Not serious, but rather a mess. Leg cut about a bit. Can't walk, of course.' Nell's father was brisk, barely informative, as though he'd been given a dirty job to do and was determined to get it over with. 'Such a pity we shan't be able to be with you on your big day.'

'No-one? No-one at all? Daddy, can't you come? Please?'

'Don't be selfish, Nell. I couldn't possibly leave your mother. I'm surprised you asked.'

'But . . . but it's special. Everyone's families will be here. Everyone's. Could Alastair come?'

'Your brother wouldn't be comfortable amongst all those strangers.'

'*I'm* not a stranger.'

'Come on, Nell. You're a big girl now. A soldier. Where's that stiff upper lip, eh?'

The upper lip was anything but stiff. It's difficult to make yourself understood when your mouth wobbles into strange, unwanted shapes. Nell didn't trust herself to speak. She made a little, mewing sound that her father translated as acquiescence.

'That's my girl. What can't be cured must be endured, eh?' And then, with a twinge of conscience, 'I'm sorry, darling.'

When she'd replaced the receiver, Nell wanted to lash out at something, at someone. Anyone. She wanted to stamp, to shout, to kick like a spoiled toddler.

What about *me*, she wanted to cry. What about what *I* want? Don't *I* matter?

But, of course, she knew she didn't, really.

'Do they always travel in pairs?' Juliet asked, peering over the banisters as Oliver manoeuvred his way through the front door, shepherded by anxious, faithful Harry. 'Have they got a heavy thing going together?'

'Shut up. They'll hear. It's just that Oliver can't drive with that plaster.'

Nell ran down to greet her partner for the commissioning ball. In mess kit, Oliver was a Winterhalter portrait made flesh. In gloriously frogged short jacket and a scarlet waistcoat embellished with gold bullion, he might have charged the Russian guns in the valley of death or defended women and children with his dying breath at the gates of Lucknow. Replicas of his pale, stubborn beauty held off brutish native hordes on dining-room walls wherever the British army gathered to eat.

And if the left leg of his splendidly skin-tight trousers was slit along the broad scarlet stripe and held together by gold hunting stock pins, the result was not ridiculous. It turned him into a wounded hero.

'Hello, little Nell,' he said. 'Don't you look scrumptious. Just like a meringue. I can't kiss you and hold up these bloody crutches, so you'll have to come and kiss me instead.'

Even without using his arms, he seemed able to hold her. Mouth to mouth they stood, still and detached from the bustle of arrival. Nell could hear the lub-dub of her own heart. It seemed to have reversed its circulation, hammering in her ears and leaving her legs useless. The breath she shared with Oliver was the same breath, round and round, depleted of oxygen.

'I had a couple of fish just like you two. Sucker fish, they called them.' Nell opened her eyes to see Ruth hanging over the banisters, her mouth puckered in a fishy imitation. 'Don't you think you'd better split up before the Commandant throws a bucket of water over you?'

'Oh, God . . .'

Like a liner with attendant tugs, Colonel Marjorie Appleby, splendid in gold and white brocade, was escorted by her officers across the gravel towards Cadet Mess.

The tips of Oliver's crutches squeaked across the polished parquet, as he joined the other guests. Only then did Nell realize that Harry was wearing mess kit, too. The maroon and black of the Parachute Regiment was dreary beside the glories of infantry and cavalry kit, but the tiny gold parachuting wings were a distinguished glitter on Harry's right sleeve and, on his left breast, a sixpenny-sized medal told anyone who could read the green and purple scrap of ribbon and miniature campaign bar that he'd served in Radfan. The ribbon was embellished with a fairy-sized bronze oak leaf, a Mention in Despatches.

'Harry, what a surprise . . . I wasn't expecting . . . I mean, I don't want to be rude, but there's a guest list . . .'

'Harry's your dancing partner for tonight. Can't have you sitting out like a wallflower at your own commissioning ball and I'm not a bloody bit of good to you. Don't worry – you won't have to feed him.' Oliver laughed, carelessly casual, as though he'd brought a greedy Labrador to the ball. 'He's had some fish and chips. Haven't you, Harry?'

'Caused quite a stir in the chippie, dressed like this,' Harry replied, with that shy, self-mocking grin that Nell might have found so attractive, had she not been dazzled by Oliver's brilliance.

There was a heady sense of escape in the air. Tongues were looser, body language more relaxed. Silver, long burnished by stewardesses until any engraving was just a memory, glowed warmly. Candlelight softened Colonel Appleby's crêpey bosom, Molly Greene's moustache, the youngest cadet's acne. It glittered off earrings and medals, buttons and chains. It turned the decanters of port into carboys of ruby, like the ones that had glowed in the chemist's window when Nell was a child.

Everything was kinder, gentler, less threatening, more imposing.

Freedom. One more day . . .

God, he's *gorgeous*, thought Juliet as she looked

down the table towards Oliver. I can't think what he sees in that little mouse. If he looked at *me* like that . . . He wouldn't have to ask twice, that's for sure.

A little cough from Captain Hillcroft – Jennifer, now, Juliet reminded herself – recalled her to her duty, so she missed the flash of pain that passed across Simon's face, as he watched her watching . . .

Juliet, as President of the Mess Committee, handled the little gavel that called for silence with admirable femininity. She stood and caught the eye of Fiona, luckless, acned and only eighteen.

'Madam Vice – Her Majesty the Queen.'

Fiona's chair tipped backwards with a crash and a guffaw from the two Sandhurst cadets beside her. The little puddle of port by her glass followed the slope of the table towards its edge and trickled down her dress. She caught Captain Hillcroft's icy glare.

'Ladies and gentlemen,' she squeaked. 'The Queen.'

Dancing with Harry was like going on a long route march – backwards. Nell concentrated on the beat, trying to signal it silently to Harry, hoping that somehow he would absorb it by some mysterious process of rhythmic osmosis.

Where do you go to, my lovely? sang Peter Sarstedt and Harry joined in, off-key.

'You don't look very happy, little Nell.'

'Please don't call me that. I'm not your little Nell.'

Harry looked ludicrously chastened. 'Of course – sorry. But you don't look very happy whatever I call you. Is it my dancing? I know I'm not the greatest . . .'

'No, really.'

'And I know I'm no substitute for Oliver.'

'Don't be silly. You're very nice. You're just you . . . you're Harry . . .'

Suddenly Harry's worried face was blurring, shimmering, breaking up into a myriad rainbow-rimmed sparks. His eyes were brown no longer, but golden, like pale sherry. She tried to focus on them, but they wouldn't keep still, nothing would keep still, everything was wavering . . . like looking at the bottom of a deep pool . . .

'Hey, what's this?' Harry traced the tear down her cheek with one gentle, questing finger. 'This is supposed to be the best night of your life so far.'

'It is. Oh, yes, it is. Really. I'm having a wonderful time. It's just that . . . oh, damn. I wish I'd used waterproof mascara. Is everyone looking? I don't want anyone . . .'

Harry took her by the wrist and led her, half blinded, to the door. 'Come on. Let's go outside. And you can tell Harry all about it.'

They sat on the steps in the undercroft, below the orphanage building where Nell and her friends would be commissioned in the morning, in – she risked a glance at her watch – eleven hours. Harry opened his arms.

'Hey, come on . . . if I were a gentleman I'd

give you my jacket, but Paras aren't gentlemen by definition, so snuggle up – it's freezing out here.'

Nell cuddled against his shirt and Harry drew the edge of his jacket around her. He circled her with his arms. He made her feel quite small, quite fragile; not big, bouncing Nell, but someone completely different. Delicate. Female.

'Right, now – what's the problem?'

'Sorry. I was just being silly. I feel better already.'

'Good. But will you still feel better when you go back in there?'

Nell hovered between sensible lie and uncomfortable truth. 'No,' she admitted.

'So . . . ?'

'They're posting me to Guildford.'

'That's nice. You'll still be close.'

'It's not nice at all. It's awful. I can't survive a place like that. It'll be like here, but worse. I'll be watching the poor little recruits and passing judgement on them and all the time I'll know that I'm not fit to do it and all the time I'll know that other people are watching me and . . .'

'Hey, steady on. It won't be that bad.'

'It will. You don't know. In your army – the real army – the senior officers live out with their wives and come in to work every day. But in the WRAC, the senior officers are spinsters and they live in and watch you all the time and bitch about every little thing . . .'

His arm tightened around her. 'These old biddies

you talk about . . . they haven't – I mean, no-one's
tried anything – you know, *anything*?'

'What do you mean – anything?'

'Never mind. So what's the problem?'

'It's the watching. There's never any peace and
someone's always waiting for you to make the next
mistake, no matter how tiny . . .'

Harry heard the rising pitch of her voice, felt the
tremor that ran through her body into his. He held
her closer still, stroking her hair with broad, capable
hands, gentling her as he would a frightened animal,
as he'd stroked gun-shy Madge when he'd taken her
onto the rifle range.

'Sssh, sssh. It's all right. Look, I hated my first
posting, too. Everyone does. You're going to drop
all the clangers there are to drop. Everyone does. But
you learn. What's the good of getting older, if you
don't get any wiser? You've just got a bad case of
cold feet.'

But Nell knew it was more than that.

'Harry, I've made a terrible mistake. And there's
no way out. I shouldn't be in the army. There's no
place for someone like me. I've got no backbone. I'm
too stupid, too soppy.'

'I think you're lovely.'

Quietly, gently, he laid his lips on hers. Nell
stiffened, then, as she felt that he made no demands,
relaxed against his bony body. It was like leaning on
a toast rack. The bass rhythm from the disco beat
out of synch with Harry's heart. She was aware of a
warm glow, low in her belly, as comforting as
hugging a hot water bottle when you have tummy

cramps. She parted her lips just a little and waited for that dizzying, emptying swoop of desire, but it didn't happen.

Better than that, though. She felt safe.

'I shouldn't have done that.'

'Why?' she whispered. 'It was nice.'

'It just . . . makes things more complicated, that's all. You belong to Oliver and Oliver's my friend. You don't steal from friends.'

'But don't you like me?'

'That's the problem. I do like you . . . I like you very much.'

So he did it again.

And when they were both out of breath and Harry realized that more than enough time had passed, Nell asked, 'I don't suppose you have a cigarette, do you? Hope has these nice herbal ones that make you feel quite relaxed.'

Harry laughed loudly, an open, masculine sound, almost as rare in this enclosed place as in a nunnery – *oh, don't, supposing someone hears, supposing the RSM is prowling around making a last check on the seating* – and grabbed her and squeezed her more like a comrade than a lover – *well, of course, Nell you idiot, what else would you expect?*

Nell could feel every button on his clothes – tiny waistcoat ones, larger jacket ones, the embossed regimental crest imprinting itself over and over again on her breasts. Perhaps, when she undressed, she would find tiny parachute wings embellishing her flesh.

'Herbal? God, Nell, you're priceless! The best I

202

can offer you is a clean handkerchief to take off all that mascara.'

Obediently, Nell turned her face up to the light. Harry spat on his handkerchief and scrubbed none too gently at her cheeks.

'There. That's the best I can do. Let's go and face the music.'

On the edge of the swathe of light that cut across the darkened parade square, Harry caught Nell back.

'I just wanted you to know . . .' He tucked a straggle of hair that had unwound from her ringlets back behind her ear. Nell could feel that his hand wasn't quite steady. 'I just wanted you to know that if things don't quite – you know – if they don't work out the way you want them to, that I'll be around for you.'

She stretched up and kissed the corner of his jaw. 'I know you will.'

Oliver had settled himself in an armchair, close to the bar. His crutches leaned against the arm of the chair and the plastered leg stuck out in front of him, causing maximum interference to everyone who passed. They always apologized.

An impromptu conga was winding round the ballroom, through the dining room, in and out of the kitchen, watched indulgently by the senior staff – *you're only young once, it's just high spirits* – frowning as the chain headed for the stairs and the bedrooms. And as they danced, they sang, belting out more discordantly than the Animals . . .

We gotta get out of this place . . .

Oliver watched Nell and Harry come back in, assessed her rumpled hair and his crumpled shirt front, noted the swelling of her lips and the light abrasions on her skin. He couldn't quite place the emotion he felt. More than irritation. Nothing so mundane as jealousy. Whatever it was, it made his leg ache more.

Ridiculous. Nell and Harry. It wasn't right.

'I think I'll have to marry you, little Nell, before Harry beats me to it.'

'Oh, yes please,' she said.

It was an end and a beginning.

They were all crying. Out there, beyond the green and khaki ranks of official guests, Ruth's mother was turning her eyes up to the raftered ceiling and hoping that runproof meant waterproof. Juliet's mother stopped worrying about the angle of her hat and took out a lace-edged scrap of handkerchief. Sergeant Cameron, glittering from his cap badge to his toecaps, gave a sniff that he turned hastily into a cough. No-one was there for Nell.

And in a crowded kitchen not far from Salisbury's railway lines, Hope squinted at her watch before testing the temperature of the milk on the inside of her wrist. *Should be just about time*, she thought. *Yes. They've done it. They've done it. Good for you, girls. I knew you'd make it, all along.* And she popped the teat into Lydia's irate, gummy gape.

The WRAC staff band, red-cheeked and per-spiring in the elegant, dark green uniforms that had

204

just been abandoned by the rest of the Corps, had played stirring martial music throughout the ceremony. Now, they softened and the hardest hearts softened with them. To the sound of 'Auld Lang Syne', Ruth and Isa, Juliet and Nell slow-marched their way towards the door and the future.

1994

A time to refrain from embracing . . .

Hope was watering the garden when the phone rang. Only May and already the garden was turning into a dustbowl. The chalky soil held no moisture, despite the manure forked in liberally last autumn. She thought about '76 and the drudgery of lugging all the bathwater and using it to keep the water butt topped up. No chance of siphoning it off, when the ground-floor bathroom was lower than the garden.

Look on the bright side, she thought. *Global warming means not having to cut the grass all summer*.

She carried the washing-up bowl full of greasy, soapy water and tipped it from above, scrupulously fairly, right along the row of broad beans, drenching the tips of all the shoots.

'Bloody blackfly,' she muttered. 'This'll settle your hash.'

Talking to herself again. Lydia would have crept up behind her, teasing and saying that she was going batty. Was she really going to turn into a mad, lonely old woman who shouted in the street and pushed a pram full of mangy dogs around, like old Camberley Kate?

So what?

She didn't hurry back into the house when she heard the phone bell. Lydia was the only person she hurried for and it couldn't be Lydia, because she was bobbing up and down somewhere on the Solent. If anyone else wanted her, they had to want her badly enough to keep on ringing until she got there. If they rang off, she'd argue, it couldn't have been important enough in the first place.

Far too demanding, telephones. Loud, self-important, like disagreeable relatives, assuming that you'd drop whatever you were doing, because nothing – *nothing* – mattered more than their urgent summons. And who would it be? Double glazing. Life insurance. Just asking for a moment of your time . . . A sort of persecution, when you're up a ladder or in the bath. Bollocks to the lot of them.

Perhaps this time she wouldn't bother. Perhaps she'd just let it ring, until whoever was demanding her attention gave up. Bloody persistent, this one. She stooped through the low door and stood in the tiny lobby, listening to the phone, willing it to stop. She just didn't want to pick it up. The chill rose from the damp, red-brick floor, through the soles of her sandals and into her legs. She wrapped her arms around her body in an age-old defensive gesture and shivered.

Such a strange feeling. As though the phone itself had developed a malevolent streak. As though it wished her ill. As though, if she stretched out her hand to lift the receiver, she'd regret it. But the sound of the bell was tyrannical. She couldn't escape it. And it didn't stop.

She should have been surprised to find that Isa was on the other end of the line. She should have been, but somehow she wasn't.

'Hi, Isa,' Hope greeted her, pleasantly enough. She looked through the minute leaded window that allowed scarcely any light into the lobby. The sun was going off the garden. Long, smoky blue shadows were creeping across the grass, greedily reaching out, gobbling up the sunlit spaces. Past the fruit cage already. Only another few minutes – she was wasting precious daylight, damn . . . 'Didn't you have enough gossip this afternoon?'

'Hope, I have to see her.'

No preliminaries. Typical Isa. Straight for the jugular. And the voice was urgent. It demanded and begged at the same time. Supplicant and trespasser.

She'd guessed, of course. All the time the phone was ringing, all the time she'd stood and stared at it, she'd known. If not this phone call, then the next, or the one after that. Isa was back in her life.

'I don't think you should do that,' Hope answered, quietly, calmly, when all the time her instinct was to scream *No* and slam down the receiver.

'Please. I want to see her so much.'

'We agreed . . . you promised . . .'

'I know – but it was so long ago. Things change. She's not a child any longer.'

'What difference does that make? Look . . .' Hope

211

took a deep breath, caught hold of the spiralling panic. 'Look, we agreed that it was in Lydia's best interests for you to stay out of her life. That was twenty-five years ago. Now, this may sound hard, but I don't see that anything's changed.'

'Is she there? Just let me talk to her.'

'No, she's not. She's sailing, crewing for her boss and some of his business partners.'

'Really?'

'Really. Dammit, Isa, when have I ever lied to you?'

'Sorry, sorry, never. It's just that . . . But even if she were there, there's no way you'd let me talk to her. Right?'

'Right first time. It's not fair. To her or me. She doesn't need you in her life, meddling, complicating.'

'That's your point of view. But she's an adult now. She can make her own decisions. I don't need your permission to see her. I could find her any time I wanted.'

'That sounds like a threat.'

'It's not meant to. It's just the truth. She has a right . . .'

'She has rights. I have rights. The only one without rights is you. You gave them up. Remember?'

'Hope, I'm her mother.'

Jesus! That sweet, reasonable voice!

Fear drove Hope into a corner. She came out of it kicking and biting and gouging.

'Her mother? Where were you when the nappies needed changing, when she threw herself down on the shop floor because she wanted sweeties, when she puked all over the car? Where were you when she wet the bed, when she dreamed she was being chased by a million spiders, when the rabbit died? Where were you when she had her tonsils out, when she had her first period, when she fell in love with the wrong guy? Don't you dare call yourself her mother until you've been there and done that.'

There was a long, long silence on the other end of the line. Hope thought Isa had gone. She listened for the burr of a closed line, but it didn't come.

'Isa?'

'I'm here. I didn't want it to come to this.' She paused and Hope could hear a breathy thread of a sigh. It seemed to bind them together with a terrible strength, fragile and pitiless as a spider's spinning. 'Hope, I've got cancer.'

A strange thing, gravity. Hope felt as though it reached out and grabbed her. The lightheaded power of rage left her and she felt weighted to the ground, leaden, enmeshed.

'Funny, you looked well enough this afternoon.'

'I've got breast cancer.'

Trapped, then, no way out. And then awful remorse, because that wasn't the *proper* reaction. The instinctive one, yes, the gut reaction, but not the *right* one.

'God, Isa, that's awful. I'm so sorry. How are you . . . how, er . . . ?'

'How long? Go on. Ask it. Why not? It's what everyone wonders. Even me. After a radical mastectomy? That depends. They're throwing every chemical in the book – and some that aren't – at me and I'm doing well. They say.' Hope could almost hear Isa brace her shoulders and raise her chin, like she used to do on that long-ago drill square, as though some unseen sergeant had bawled *Squaaaad, squad 'shun*. 'You never know. I might get lucky. Or you might get lucky, Hope, and I might drop off my perch before . . .' She heard the gasp of horror from the other end of the line. 'I didn't mean that. I say things . . . I find I say things now that I don't really mean. Don't know why. Spite, I suppose. You looked so well today. I envied you – health *and* Lydia – envied you so much. But I didn't mean it. Pay no attention. Look, think about it, why don't you. You've got my number. Think about it and call me.'

When she had put down the phone, Hope balled her fist and thumped it against the wall. Flakes of unstable lime plaster floated to the ground.

Blackmail. That was the only word for it. Of the quiet kind. No threats. No extortion. But blackmail, all the same. *Let me see Lydia or . . .*

Or what?

Or you'll feel guilty for the rest of your life. Or you'll have turned your back on a friend when she needs you most. Or your daughter – our daughter – will never forgive you . . .

What sort of choice was that?

It hadn't been easy. But then, she'd never thought it would be. What no-one had warned her – what she'd completely underestimated – was just how difficult it could be to rear a child on her own. She'd been absurdly naive, culpably optimistic.

But she'd never – not even on the toughest days – regretted having Lydia for her daughter.

Hope had been meaning to tackle that patch of ground elder for ages and now seemed like a good time – better than most. Savagely, she rammed in the fork as far as its spikes would allow, bringing up the knots of roots and their fleshy white tendrils. Allow any to survive, even the tiniest fragment, and it would root again and again and spread and suffocate.

Now that the sun had gone, the midges were biting. They swarmed amongst the roots of her hair, minute black kamikaze, maddening and vicious. Hope swiped at them with her forearm and spread grime across her face. The sky was still bright, but beneath the low, thatched, cat-slide eaves it was almost dark. Hope still laboured, unable any longer to separate weed from flower, good from bad, but she didn't give up.

Aunt Tabby – more precisely, a great-aunt, Hope's grandmother's older sister – hadn't exactly been welcoming. That had never been her style.

She'd been scrubbing the scullery floor, a worn-out bath towel tied round her waist and an old sack for a knee pad, as Hope walked in. Tiny, tough, tenacious as an old badger and as whiskery, Tabitha Wilsher had scrubbed floors, her own and other people's, for well over seventy years and she couldn't be doing with all those packets and tubs with fancy smells and fancy ideas. 'They don't fool me. Paying a fortune for a smell. Just plain old washing soda by any other name,' she'd said and scrubbed on. She'd looked up at Hope and wrung out the floor-cloth with fingers reddened and cracked by years of soaking in scalding water and grunted a brief greeting. Kissing came hard to her.

'Chucked you out, then, did they? You don't want to fret about that, my maid. Didn't know a good thing when they saw it, they didn't.' Then she saw what Hope was carrying bundled against her chest. 'You never did. You stupid tomgudgeon. I thought all you girls was on that pill nowadays?'

And Hope set the first stitch in the tapestry of lies and deception that, a quarter of a century later, was still unfinished. It was surprisingly easy.

'The pill doesn't always work.'

That was the first lie, the easy one. Every one after that got tougher.

Hope dunked the tea bag in the mug, swilling it round. Disgusting. Waste of tea, too. You get into sloppy habits when you live on your own. Tasted good, though. Thick, sweet, strong. None of that virgin's pee that women were supposed to enjoy.

Polly looked up from her basket, her whiskery muzzle crinkled in surprise. She wasn't used to being woken up. She was the one who was supposed to get up first, to pad upstairs and lick Hope awake with a smelly, efficient tongue. She'd been caught unawares when Hope had riddled the dormant Rayburn into life, flung in some dusty coke and banged the kettle down on the hotplate.

Hope opened the back door – forgot to lock it again last night, but mad axemen were rare in Wiltshire – and stood on the step, leaning against the door frame, warming her hands on the hot mug, breathing in the rising steam.

It was true what they said – nothing ever looked so bad in the morning.

The sun was climbing just behind the slope of the Shellards' roof next door. The thatch was haloed. Every cell of the chicken wire that protected the roof from marauding birds was linked to the next by spiders' gossamer strands, beaded with dew, a honeycomb of diamonds.

A thread of smoke rose into the thin dawn air. Bill and Molly Shellard were up already, sorting the mail for delivery, writing names on newspapers, ready for young Craig Pocknell's paper round. Nice to know she wasn't the only person up. Trouble was, she hadn't been to bed.

There was no logic about the way she felt. There were no rules for this. For twenty-five years she had known that Lydia did not belong to her – known but not believed. She had known in the way that Christian fundamentalists know about evolution – because the facts are presented to them – but nothing will make them believe. Stubbornly, against all rationality, they cling to their faith.

And as the years passed, Hope had, very slowly, felt able to relax, to feel secure. Five of them had shared a secret, but not one had broken that implicit vow of silence. Not even Juliet. Perhaps they had forgotten. Perhaps it had been so unimportant that they had not even remembered that there was a secret to be kept.

But Hope remembered and she kept the knowledge in a private, unrecognized place, far from any temptation to share it. Even Chris had not known that the child he had raised with love and tenderness was no relation to his wife. He had accepted the baby she had brought into their marriage, never questioning, never grieving that Lydia was not followed by others, never loving her less. But never knowing.

A good man, Chris.

Hope shifted her position. The chill of the stone step had numbed her feet. A breeze that had risen with the dawn stirred her shrunken Viyella nightdress around her ankles. The tea in the mug had a milky skim over its cold surface.

Yes, a good man, Chris.

Neither Hope nor Lydia had taken up the offer of a trip to the Falklands when the war was over. They had not walked over the boggy, sheep-shorn, mine-spattered turf – Scotland with no-go areas – or stared across a grey sea from Mount Tumbledown. Hope had tried to explain, not knowing whether Lydia was old enough to understand financial pressures, that she couldn't afford to leave a burgeoning business to cross the world, even to say goodbye to Chris.

So they had watched on television as mothers, fathers, wives, children cast their flowers onto the

haunted water of Bluff Cove. The brilliant mass –
lilies, roses, chrysanthemums, some tossed free, some
still in their florists' cellophane cones, wreaths of
paper poppies – heaved on an oily, glassy swell,
splitting apart, then swirling together again and
soon, sodden, before the boat had reached the shore
again, sinking.

Hope sat before the screen, but her mind saw a
replay of those other pictures, images stamped as
brutally as a bootprint on flesh, so vividly that she
knew they would never fade. Her brain was damaged
for ever by knowledge she could never un-know.

Through an oily smog came the bobbing orange
life rafts with their blackened, suffering cargo.
Helicopters, lower than any pilot had dreamed he
might dare, used the wind of their rotors to shepherd
the rafts to shore. Carefully, nudging, butting, like a
cow with a backward calf, until the rubber rafts
grated safely on pebbles. But the clatter of the blades
could not drown out the moans of the wounded and
dying. Pitched below the hubbub and the shouting,
below the level of conscious hearing, was a long,
long drone of suffering.

The first all-televised, in-your-own-home-as-it-
happens war. Reporters as action men. Robert Fox
breathing heavily as he ran ashore with the Paras at
San Carlos Bay. Brian Hanrahan's catch-phrase – *I
counted them all out and I counted them all back*.
Ian MacDonald's curious monotone – *in the course
of its duties, within the total exclusion zone around
the Falkland Islands . . .*

Oh, this was life, all right. *Gotcha!* War subjected

to a nightly analysis. Performance evaluated as minutely as a football team's – *well, and how will our boys be feeling tonight, how do you rate their chances . . . ?* Death as entertainment for the armchair strategists. So real you could almost taste the burning oil catching in the back of your throat, smell the barbecued flesh.

Hope and Lydia had watched, aghast, too stricken for tears, as *Sir Galahad* burned and knew that Chris was burning in it.

Going back achieved nothing. Better not.

'It doesn't matter,' said Lydia. 'Going won't make us miss Daddy any less than we do. Leaving flowers won't make us feel any different.'

He had always been Daddy to Lydia and he always would be. But that night, Hope had heard Lydia crying and had not been strong enough to comfort her.

Underhanded? Making use of a good man? Making a fool of him? Hope didn't think so. She didn't see it that way. Chris and Lydia had given each other so much love, what did it matter who Lydia's birth parents were? Who cared? They'd been a family, a proper family. And that – Hope would often say to herself – simply proved that the end justified the means.

And if that was a cliché – well, so what? That was the way it had been. But what would that fiercely honest, uncompromising man have said now? How would he have advised her? Hope listened to the silence, straining to hear, desperate for comfort, but there was nothing.

Of course not. Life and death didn't work that way. Not here, anyway. This wasn't a scene from *Truly, Madly, Deeply*.

But then, what are friends for?

Hope mentally flipped through them, imagining their reactions, if she rang and asked for help.

Juliet? She'd be sound, sensible, full of good advice and oh-so-smug. If she didn't actually utter the words *I told you so* (and she probably would!) they'd hang in the air even after she'd gone, like the Cheshire cat's grin.

Nell? Sweet, sensitive, sympathetic. She'd say all the right things, make all the right gestures. And be as much real use as a chocolate teapot.

Ruth, then? Suddenly, Hope wanted to hear Ruth's slow, sensible voice, combining the gentleness of Nell with Juliet's common sense and adding her own, unmistakable, dry humour. Ruth always knew what to do and, if she didn't, she had the knack of making you think that you had known all along, anyway.

Hope squinted back through the door, trying to see the plastic pony clock with the wagging tail that Lydia had made so long ago. Still only 5.45. Really? Ruth wouldn't thank her for ringing so early. But they'd see each other at work. Hope would check the schedules and pop round to wherever Ruth was supervising that day. With a sense of relief, of a decision made, Hope turned to rummage in the under-sink cupboard for a tin of Chum.

*   *   *

But Ruth didn't come in to work that morning. She phoned to say that she couldn't make it.

'I'm sorry, Hope, I've let you down. And this really isn't a good time to talk. I've got to go.'

Engrossed in her own emotions, Hope didn't expect or want to hear the quaver of fear in Ruth's voice.

'Ruth, hang on. I won't take up much of your time, honest. I just want a quick chat. It's a bit important.'

'No, I can't manage . . . look, Hope, sorry, it's . . . oh, Hope, Tim was in an awful state when I got back last night . . .'

'What's wrong?' Hope could feel that cruel, little extra word *now* about to slip out of her mouth, but she swallowed it.

'He went to pick up Henry from school and – oh, it sounds so stupid, but it isn't, not to him – and he had a puncture on the way. And he couldn't fix it, couldn't even get the spare out of the boot, let alone loosen the wheel nuts. Can you imagine – a man like Tim, who used to be so fit – can you imagine what that did to him? We can't afford the AA, so he had to trudge three miles to the nearest garage for help. And when he finally got to school, Henry was still standing outside the gate, all alone and crying, and Tim started thinking about perverts and he just lost it and . . . oh, anyway, it was pretty awful.' Ruth's voice broke with the effort of remaining sensible, dependable Ruth. 'I feel so guilty that I wasn't there for him.'

'The one time in – how long? – that you'd been

out on your own. How often do you see your friends? He's got no right to make you feel guilty.'

'He doesn't. I can do that all on my own. And I'm so afraid he'll do something to himself, something stupid.'

'But why? I know he's not too well, but I've always seen you as the only really happy family I know.'

'He's so ill, sometimes in such pain. He despairs. He thinks he's let us all down. He thinks we'd be better off without him. He just doesn't believe . . .' There was a long and vulgar sniff. Hope could picture Ruth wiping her nose, picture her red and tear-stained face. 'He just doesn't believe that we love him, no matter what. Hang on a minute, Henry's just come in . . .' Now her voice brightened, taking on an upbeat tone that grated falsely down the line. 'No, it's not the doctor, love. Daddy's fine. No, of course not, I wouldn't hide anything from you. It's just Hope. Talk to her, if you don't believe me.'

'Hello,' Henry said, wary, suspicious, caught in the moment between a child's howls of fear and an adult's suppression of emotion.

'Hi, Henry, it's me – Hope.'

'Really?'

'Yes, really. How are you?'

'OK.'

'Look, why don't you come over and spend the day with me and Polly? Never mind about school. School's a bore. I need to tidy out the shed and I'm scared of spiders. I need a man to help me.'

223

'I don't want to.'

'Don't want to what? Tidy the shed or come and see me?'

'Come.'

'We'd have Chinese for supper.'

'I don't want to.'

'OK, whatever you say, Henry, love. Can I talk to Mummy now?' A pause, some mumbling, then Ruth was back. 'Ruth, what can I do? Shall I come over? Keep you company? Fetch and carry? Anything?'

'No, really, we're fine. I only rang to say I wouldn't be in to work for a day or two. Until Tim's on an even keel again.'

'No problem. Take as long as you need. Give Tim my love. And Ruth – call me any time, for anything.'

She wouldn't, though. She'd struggle on, saving Tim's pride, waiting for something to happen – a miracle cure, or, even greater miracle, government recognition that Tim had been damaged, was as much war-wounded as a man without legs.

If I was worth anything as a friend, Hope thought, *I'd be with her now, no matter what she said. I'd do her shopping, do the school run, anything, to let Ruth spend time with Tim. And nothing I could do would make it any better. It would be like sticking Elastoplast on a broken arm.*

But that's not a good reason for not trying.

'I'd love to see you for supper, Hope, darling, but Simon's got this ghastly dinner in Swindon of all places and I've got to be the dutiful little wife. Some drugs company promoting its latest wonder cure and hiring the Holiday Inn to impress us. As if . . . ! An awful bore and, frankly, I'd much rather have a night with toothache, but there you are. Some other time? We can have a good natter. Super . . .'

And honestly, it was rather a relief to Hope not to have to bare her soul to Juliet.

So that left Nell.

'Lovely. Come as early as you like. Oliver's visiting some exercise in Otterburn or Brecon or somewhere frightful. I'll give the staff a night off, so I can knock up some spag bog and we can be couch potatoes if we want.'

Nell led the way into the kitchen. Ferociously clean, spartan with shiny red lino and cream-painted cupboards and a view of an enclosed brick courtyard, it was an early Sixties modernization of the original Edwardian room. She began opening doors in a haphazard fashion.

'Pots. Where do you suppose she keeps the big pots? I know this sounds batty, but I never get into my own kitchen – not allowed! Mrs Parr was frightfully miffed when I said she could go off tonight. I think she thinks I can't cook – well, I can't really, only simple things.' Nell hauled out a heavy pot that had, Hope saw, a broad arrow – symbol of military property – stamped on its side. 'When we were first married, Oliver gave me a cook book called *One Hundred Ways to Cook Mince*. Trouble was – everyone else had a copy, too. Every supper party was some incarnation of mince. On a junior officer's pay – well, you remember what it was like – we never ever saw joined-up meat! We were lucky in a way. Oliver had his father's money, but he thought we ought to live like everyone else of his rank. So – mince all round. Sorry – I haven't even offered you a drink. Anything you like. We've always got oodles of duty-free. Corkscrew. Where's the corkscrew? Do you think we'll all go mad? I mean, all that mince. Do you think there'll be an outbreak of dementia amongst senior officers? All the generals and their wives suddenly going potty because they were paid so badly when they were younger they could only afford mince?' She paused, her hand in the drawer, rummaging for a tin opener, and Hope's laughter was silenced by the watery glitter in Nell's eyes. 'D'you suppose it's happened already? Could that be the spark that starts World War Three? BSE and the end of civilization as we know it? Heavens, I talk too much. Oliver always says I talk too much. Is that water boiling yet?'

Nell's stream of words wasn't silenced until she and Hope were curled up in armchairs with plates on their knees. By then, Nell had oversalted the bolognaise sauce and boiled the spaghetti well beyond *al dente*.

'God, I'm sorry, Hope. This is ghastly. I ought to have let Mrs Parr rustle up something for us. She'll only give me stick tomorrow for burning the pan, anyway. But it's so nice – I can't tell you – so nice to have you here and have the house to ourselves.'

'It's a lovely room.'

And, in its way, it was. In a floral, pastelly, curtains matching the covers, not a speck of dust sort of way. There were cream, almost-as-good-as-silk lampshades, nests of tables in undefined wood (so handy for all those visitors and their glasses), magnolia emulsion throughout, with a few good watercolours that barely broke the calm. Not for me, Hope acknowledged, but Nell in her pearl studs and velvet Alice band seemed to fit perfectly.

'Lovely. Isn't it. So refined, such good taste. But Hope – it's not *my* room. Not *my* house. Look . . .' Nell put her plate on the floor, slopping bolognaise onto the blue and cream speckled carpet, and wandered round the room, picking up and putting down. 'Not the carpets, not the curtains, not the chair covers, not the lamps, not even the plates we're eating off. I don't have a stake in anything here. It's just a tied cottage, like any farm worker's. One wrong move and we're out on our ears. Oh, but I did arrange the flowers. That's my contribution to our environment. Do you like them? Say you do . . .'

'Nell, sit down and eat your supper, for heaven's sake. OK, it's pretty disgusting, but think of all the starving millions and give thanks, as Sister Boniface used to say.'

'. . . I didn't grow them, of course. Harbridge grew them. And the photographs. Yes, of course, they belong to us. Our wedding – you remember that, don't you, such a perfect day – and here are Jago and Jessica at the cute stage and the me-and-my-bunny stage and the spotty, tramlines-top-and-bottom

227

stage, and now we've reached the I-shan't-need-you-much-longer stage.'

'Nell . . .'

But Nell prowled on, touching, patting. Her voice was very high, very controlled, with a musical note to it, like sheet ice that sings on a very cold night.

'Have you seen the stiffies on the chimneypiece?' She gestured in the direction of the crested, formal invitation cards. 'Requesting the pleasure of the company of Major-General and Mrs Oliver Hawtrey? They don't mean that, you know. Oliver is requested and I just tag along, too, because I'm joined to him, wife of – do you remember the abbreviation, w/o? – part of the package, like his medals and his shiny boots. It's a wonder he doesn't get Kane to give me a good spit-and-polishing each time we go out.'

Hope got up and put her arms around Nell's shoulders. They were very stiff, as though she'd forgotten to take out the coat hanger before she put on her jersey.

'Nell, come on, relax. You're a bit wound up tonight. Sit down, love. Talk about it.'

'Nothing wrong with me.'

'If you say so.'

All sorts of irritated platitudes sprang to Hope's lips – none the less true for being unkind – about how bloody lucky Nell was to have a husband and two healthy children and financial security and a warm, well-maintained roof over her head, no matter who actually owned the roof.

How bloody lucky to have all the things that Hope didn't have any longer.

But now didn't seem the right time to say it.

Instead she chucked out the congealing spaghetti – well wrapped up to avoid Mrs Parr's censure – and raided the duty-free.

'Vodka and tonic still your thing?' she called. 'Personally, after a meal like that, I need a stiff brandy to settle my stomach!'

When she came back, Nell was curled up in a chair, her legs drawn under her. She was hugging a cushion.

'Don't look so worried,' Nell said and her voice was her own again. 'I don't know what came over me. Yes, I do. Oliver and I had a bit of a spat last night and he went off this morning without saying goodbye to me.'

Hope flopped into her chair, adjusted the cushion behind her back, and took a slow, appreciative sip of her brandy before replying. 'That's all?'

'Of course,' Nell replied quickly. 'I was just over-reacting a bit. Sorry.'

'So you had a row? So what?'

'So we don't.' Nell raised fair, furry brows that were too light for her hair colour. They made her look perpetually surprised. Always had. Like Alice finding herself on the wrong side of the looking-glass.

'Come on, Nell.' Hope was scornful. '*Everyone* rows. When they have to. It's normal. Just because Chris is dead, I don't try to pretend he was a plaster saint. And *I'm* certainly not! So what was it this time – in-laws, children, money or sex? Bound to be one. Every row is a variation on a theme.'

'None of them. We don't row,' Nell insisted.

Hope looked across, taking in for the first time Nell's taut figure, the way she steadily kneaded the cushion that was still hugged to her chest. Looking closer, she saw that the nailbeds of the kneading fingers were ragged and raw. One was bleeding, leaving tiny red dots across the pale blue cushion.

'You mean it, don't you,' Hope said softly. 'Then I'm sorry for you.'

Nell followed the direction of Hope's eyes and flung the speckled cushion onto the floor with a little exclamation of disgust.

'You're making too much of a big thing about this,' she declared, with a lack of logic that left Hope without response. 'I promised Oliver I'd be back in time for a drinks thing last night and I wasn't and he was annoyed and I answered back. That's all. Much ado about nothing. Silly, wasn't it?' And she gave a little, helpless, deprecating laugh. 'It's just that . . . just that it's a bad time for me.'

'Never mind – we'll soon all be finished with that sort of thing. Have you thought of HRT?'

'I don't mean *that* sort of bad time. I can cope with that. I'm a big girl now! It's . . . Hope, I've never told anyone this before . . .'

Looking at Nell's face, at the almost fervent expression, Hope realized that there are secrets that should be shared and some that shouldn't. And suddenly she didn't want to have anything to do with this one. She'd had enough of secrets. She couldn't cope with another one. Nell looked too vulnerable, altogether too naked, too . . . too raw.

'Did you know . . . I'm not sure whether you – we all lost touch so quickly – did you know that Oliver and I started a family very quickly? Yes –' Nell gave a little shrug that exposed her as plainly as an X-ray '– the traditional honeymoon baby. Everyone was delighted. Oliver. His mother. And most of all me. I was so happy, so happy. You can't know . . .'

Oh, but I do know, Hope thought, with a surge of bitterness. *You can sit there and patronize me and suggest that I have never known what it is to love a child. But I know, Nell, I know . . .*

'. . . I nurtured that baby, didn't drink, didn't overtire myself, ate sensibly, never smoked anyway. It – he – was going to be the healthiest baby around. Then – it was early May, just about now, you see, that's why – we'd been to a regimental guest night, but Oliver wasn't drunk, he wouldn't do that to me, even the police said he wasn't drunk and they should know, only what other reason could there be? I mean, he was seeing things, for God's sake. I think I'd rather he was drunk than having hallucinations. I could understand drinking. Don't you agree? It wouldn't make it any more forgivable, but at least, you see, I could understand . . .'

'Nell, what?' Hope prompted gently.

'Oh, didn't you know? He crashed the car on the way home. It was the end of his lovely E-type. He said he'd seen someone, someone walking in the road, and had tried to avoid him. He was so certain. Oliver can be so *very* certain. Always. But, you know, Hope, there was no-one there, never had been. And the baby, our son, he was quite developed

231

enough – seven months, quite mature enough to have been born alive—' Nell's hand fluttered around her mouth, concealing the way it quivered and stretched out of shape, an ugly, tremulous square of grief. '—he was born dead the next day. Now, look, you mustn't be sorry for me. I've got two lovely children and they're my pride and joy – as people say. It's just that . . . just that round about now, I remember. I remember the perfection of him, Oliver in miniature, the blue veining of his eyelids, the transparency of the skin between his fingers – no fingernails, I remember he had no fingernails – the promise, the potential. They let me hold him for a little while. I remember wishing so badly that Oliver could have seen him, but Oliver had gone to Hereford that morning. It was the start of his SAS selection course – he would have stayed if he had known, I'm sure he would. But, of course, it was awfully important. To Oliver. Not everyone who wants to even gets on the selection course. And he wouldn't have another chance. The SAS *never* gives second chances. I knew that. So you see, he couldn't turn it down. He couldn't come home. I understood. I always understood. And then they took him away, my baby. I don't know where he went. There wasn't a funeral. He would have been called Henry. But now he's just called *he* . . .' Nell's voice tailed away. She picked abstractedly at the bloody hang-nail. Her eyes slid down and away, away from Hope's compassion. What use was compassion? 'So long ago. He would be twenty-three now, twenty-four in July. I often wonder about him. Not morbidly, you understand. I just wonder . . . Shall I make some coffee? Would you like some? I make quite passable coffee, even if my cooking isn't quite up to scratch.'

Hope realized that she would get no help from Nell. Remembering the past, remembering the bond that they had sworn would never be broken, she had turned for aid to her friends when the past had come back to wound her: to Ruth – who could not; to Juliet – who would not; to Nell – who never would be able.

She was on her own.

Sipping her brandy, watching the steam spiral above her coffee, listening to Nell talk about the thrift shop and the Federation of Army Wives and a life that was so far behind her now that it was almost incomprehensible, Hope had not heard the distinctive whine of a Land Rover's engine changing down, nor the crunch of gravel. But Nell had. Suddenly alert, like a faithful bitch that hears her master's whistle, she groped under the chair for her shoes.

'It's Oliver,' she said, unnecessarily. 'I didn't think he'd come back tonight. I didn't expect . . .'

And she whipped round the room, picking up glasses, straightening the crumpled loose covers, turning the bloodstained cushion to its clean side and managed to get out to the hall in time to greet him.

'Hope's here,' she said, following Oliver back into the drawing room. 'You remember Hope, don't you, darling?'

Oliver in his early twenties had been only the promise of the man he would become. Now to that icy beauty had been added maturity and physical strength and the calm certainty that power – almost absolute power – can give.

Even the clumsy camouflage kit, bulky in all the wrong places, could not hide the long, easy length of him. His hair, a few grey hairs blending into the silver-gilt brightness, had been ruffled when he'd taken off his beret and the leather band had left a dark pressure mark on his forehead. Below that, his face was leaner, sharper than Hope remembered, bold and imperious, unpredictable as a hand-tamed eagle.

Hope had lived without desire for so long, since Chris had died, for twelve years. But she recognized it. It hit her in the pit of her stomach like a well-placed boot. And she knew, quite suddenly, what was going to happen.

In a silence that crashed on her ears like waves, she saw that he was looking at her and the future bridged the gap between them. For a moment, she could see that he was startled, as though she had done something outrageous, had turned a cartwheel on the table or blasphemed in church or eaten her pudding with a soup spoon, something completely unforgivable. Then he smiled, recognized, acknowledged what was to come.

'Oh, yes,' said Oliver, softly. 'I remember Hope.'

1969

A time to keep silence . . .

The first lie was the easy one. After that it got harder.

Registering the baby wasn't too bad. Knowing there was a time limit and not knowing what it was, Hope took her next day to the Register Office in Bedwin Street and practised clumsy maternal dandlings on her knee while the registrar asked awkward questions. The baby was becoming familiar to Hope – her weight, the balance of it, the surprisingly strong wriggles, the spasmodic jerks of an immature nervous system, the sudden, scary lapses into sleep that was still enough to be death.

'Baby's name and date of birth?'

'Lydia. Lydia Tabitha,' Hope improvised. 'She was born on 14 April.'

'Mother's name and address?'

'That's me. Hope Blakeney. Meadow View, Mill Lane. For the time being.'

'Goodness. You are up and about quickly.'

'I am?' The first trap. Hope could sense it, but couldn't quite see where it lay.

'Only two days after the birth? When I had my

237

first, all mothers stayed in bed for ten days – two weeks, even. And *my* mother wasn't allowed to set foot on the ground for a month. I know that's not the modern way, my daughter was encouraged to potter around right from the start, but still – two days? It seems awfully soon to me.'

'I'm very fit.'

'You must be. And father's name?'

A little silence. The registrar sat with fingers poised over the typewriter keys. Then Hope brazened through. 'I don't know.'

'I'll have to write *Unknown*, then. Is that all right?' The registrar looked concerned. She was plump, motherly and – no doubt – the grandmother of half a dozen. None of *her* daughters, her look seemed to say, had presented her with a fatherless grandchild. Or else.

'If it's good enough for Lydia, it's good enough for me.'

'And place of birth?'

'I had her . . .' Hope could feel herself falling into the next bureaucratic trap. 'I had her at home.'

'Really. That's quite unusual these days for a first-time mother. She is your first, I imagine.'

'Yes. She was a bit early. A bit of a surprise, you could say. In more ways than one.'

Steady, Hope, don't get too chatty, too confident. You need to be faceless, characterless. The registrar must never be able to remember you, if . . . if what?

Nothing. Just if.

The registrar laughed. 'That's always the way of it with the first ones. Always early or late, they say.'

238

And then Hope was in the corridor, threading her way through a gathering wedding group, clinging to a precious piece of paper that told anyone who needed to know that she was the legally admitted mother of Lydia Tabitha Blakeney.

Still pretty easy. The lies were coming more naturally, now. You got good at them fairly quickly. Practice makes perfect. One just led to another. They skipped along in single file, at each other's heels, verbal follow-my-leader.

Hope felt an absurd rush of indignation. It wasn't right, was it, that you could register a baby as easily as that. Anyone could do it. Steal a baby from a pram. Smuggle it in a handbag, like a puppy avoiding quarantine.

Make a declaration and there you are. A mother – holy, haloed and selfless, sanctified by centuries of Christian art. Legal owner of a baby.

Adopting a child was more difficult, tangled about with legal niceties. For heaven's sake, buying a car was more difficult, or opening a bank account, or applying for a passport. Any of the mundane activities of life demanded more documentation. But get your hands on a baby and you could play living pass-the-parcel with her.

Not quite. Now the system had got her, nipping and worrying. Questions. Questions.

A district nurse turned up. Hope was upstairs, making beds. Lydia lay on her back on a pillow set on the floor in the bay window. She squirmed and kicked in the weak early sunshine, looking like a

frog turned upside down and pinned out on a slab
for dissection. Hope had given up biology at school
because she couldn't bear to mangle the helpless,
spreadeagled creatures. Lydia was making irritable
sounds that were growing louder. Hope stood very
still, listening to Aunt Tabby insist that she was
out, and hoping that Lydia wouldn't escalate her
demands.

'Busybodying around, sticking her neb into other
folks' business. I soon told her. Never could stand
that Pat Greaves, anyway. Her Uncle Arthur, him
that lost both his legs in Flanders – not in the
trenches, mind, he got run over by a rations wagon
when he was drunk – used to wait for me on the way
to school, round the corner where no-one could see
him, and try to pinch kisses off me.' Tabitha's
moustache seemed to bristle. She looked like a
spunky little terrier, too old for ratting, but with
blunted teeth still able to give a sharp nip. 'I soon let
him know where he got off, I can tell you. What's it
got to do with her, I'd like to know, whether or not
you've got a baby in the house?'

Hope just smiled and nodded and let her aunt
growl on, while she laid the tables for tomorrow's
breakfasts. The summer tourists were arriving,
regular as swallows, and the neat little house in Mill
Lane was full every night.

'All the same,' Aunt Tabby mused, 'that nurse did
say that you ought to register with a doctor here.
That baby needs to be looked at and you do, too, to
see if it's all going right and proper – down below,
you know.' And the old woman turned her creased,

240

virginal cheek away before Hope could see the blush. 'You ought to do that, maid. My cousin Edith died of childbed fever. One day she was right as rain, the next day her leg was all red and swelled up like a hot water bottle and the next –' she paused to emphasize the drama of the situation '– gone.'

'If I was going to get it, I'd be dead by now,' Hope retorted, not stopping to query the promptness of her own reply, half believing already the lie she was concocting. 'Anyway, that was a long time ago, before penicillin.'

'All the same,' Aunt Tabby concluded, darkly. She held a tumbler up to the light, breathed on it, then polished off the fingermarks with a corner of her apron. 'You get yourself round to that doctor.'

Suddenly, the simplest things became difficult. Pat Greaves didn't give up and on her third visit caught Hope unawares. The quick health check she gave Lydia was reassuring. It was a relief to know that she was a bonny – well, Hope knew that already – bouncing baby and that Hope was doing all the right things with the cord stump, which had dried up and looked as though it was about to drop off neatly.

'You want to put a half-crown over that,' Aunt Tabby had advised, peering mournfully over Hope's shoulder at the navel, 'and bandage it down tight. That's what my mother always used to do and it didn't do no harm. Mind you, it was a penny then. She didn't see a whole half-crown from one week's end to the next.'

'So much for Mr Wilson's pound in your pocket,'

said Hope, with a laugh, as she powdered Lydia's bottom. 'It takes half a crown nowadays to do the job of a penny!'

'But a half-crown would be better. Heavier. Stands to reason. Stop her belly popping out when she cries.'

'Looks all right to me,' Hope had answered, determined to do no such thing.

'Don't and that'll pop out like a rabbit out a hat. You just see if I'm not right.'

The nurse's probing questions about the labour and birth Hope was able to answer with convincing confidence, having been the person who delivered Lydia. She knew how long labour had lasted, she knew what condition Lydia had been in, whether she had been floppy or firm, blue or pink, breathing or not. She sounded, she thought, just as a mother should.

Then the questions became more immediate and personal – how did her breasts feel? Well, how should they feel? Hope used her imagination and was told very sharply that they'd feel better if she was feeding Lydia herself.

'Breast is best,' Hope was told, sententiously.

'But I was bottle-fed – I think – at least, Aunt Tabby tells me so. And it hasn't done me any harm. Just look what a big, bouncing girl I grew into!'

'I think you'll find that Miss Blakeney's opinions are several generations out of date,' the nurse replied, without a saving glimmer of a smile.

Then came a string of even more embarrassing questions and Hope improvised wildly about her

242

condition 'down there', as Aunt Tabby would have said.

With an exhortation to visit the mother and baby clinic at the Health Centre and not to wait too long before visiting the family planning clinic at the same place – we don't want another little accident, do we? for heaven's sake, get yourself seen to, love, the pill, they're good about handing that out these days, it's not just for married ladies now, or a nice little cap might suit if you prefer, you could be expecting again in weeks, especially if you're not feeding baby yourself, did you know that? you can't be too careful – Pat Greaves cycled off, her little round navy hat rammed firmly down and well skewered, the skirts of her navy mackintosh flapping and snapping in the stiff breeze that blew down the Avon and across the water meadows.

Hope bumped the door shut with her hip and held Lydia closely against her. *They* would take her away. As soon as a doctor got anywhere near Hope, as soon as she was examined 'down there' – and she had a wild vision of herself being spreadeagled on a doctor's couch and forcibly inspected – they'd know. And then the forces of right – and right was might and all right-thinking people, like Juliet, knew that it was wrong to walk off with a baby that wasn't your own, that she was no less guilty than if she had crept into a hospital and snatched one from a crib – would take her back and hand her over to . . . well, that was the problem, wasn't it?

Who wanted her? Without Hope, where would Lydia be? What would life hold for her? Taken into care? Fostered, if she was lucky? Tossed about from hand to hand, unwelcome as a grenade with the firing pin removed? Well, if she was going to be fostered, why not by Hope, who at least had the advantage of knowing her mother?

Hope propped Lydia against her shoulder and laid her cheek against the bony, bare, wobbling head. She smoothed the monkish tonsure of fair, feathery hair, so like Isa's. She fingered the folds of skin at the base of the baby's neck, loose as a dowager's, soft as crumpled petals. She breathed in the scent of Johnson's powder and dribble.

Lydia was a person.

Somehow, it was the last thing Hope had expected. Not yet, anyway. It was too soon. She hadn't taken Lydia because she cared for her, not even because she had felt sorry for her. It was Isa she'd pitied – Isa, who had been promised so much and was being offered so little, Isa, with the potential to be great and whose future held nothing but disgrace. A raw deal, Hope had thought, as Lydia was expelled, screaming and bloody, into her waiting hands.

So Hope, who was never going to be anybody, anyway, never going to amount to a hill of beans, had taken the burden upon herself. For Isa she had taken a baby, the baby, any baby. She hadn't realized – not then – that she was carrying away with her, in the sling under her afghan, a fully developed person.

'I don't know, Lydia. I don't know. Maybe I've done something terrible. It didn't seem so bad at the time, but now . . . maybe you'll hate me when you grow up. One day, poppet,' Hope promised the wriggling child, 'one day – but not until we're both ready – I'll tell you. No evasions. No lies. I won't pretend any longer than I have to. And in the meantime . . .'

In the meantime, she'd do her best and hope that it was good enough.

Hope kissed the top of Lydia's head, where the unformed bones left a soft, pulsing, vulnerable spot. The covering skin was almost translucent, fragile as tissue paper, beating to the rhythm of her heart.

If it wasn't for that, Hope thought, *I could see right into her brain.*

Sharp as a probe on a naked nerve, unexpected as winter lightning, pain and pleasure, joy and fear, the pang that sliced through Hope left her shaken and wondering.

She didn't recognize it – not then – as love.

And then there was money. When hadn't there been?

'Don't you bother about that, maid. Not yet awhiles. I make enough to buy a tin of Cow & Gate now and then.'

'It's more than that and you know it, Aunt Tabby. You feed me. You've given me a room that could be used by your B&B visitors.'

'And you work for it – you're a good little worker, I'll say that for you. The army's done that much for you. You know how to tackle a job, which is more than can be said for most of you young people these days. Soft you are, most of you. Different in my day. It was work or starve then, choose how. Anyway, I'm getting on, now.' She sounded surprised as she admitted it, as though the idea had only just occurred to her. 'I'd been thinking about getting in a girl for the bedmaking and laundry – that's heavy work at my age. And I'd have to pay her. Then you turns up. So we're square.'

'But if I found a job, I could pay you more.'

'And who'd look after this little mommet? Me, I suppose. And then I'd have to hire another girl to do the work I wouldn't have time to do no more. Oh yes, that makes right good sense . . .'

'I still think . . .'

'Not another word.' Aunt Tabby slammed cutlery into a drawer with a sound like a regiment of bayonets being fixed. 'You're making me mad and you wouldn't want me mad, would you?'

Hope shook her head and, laughing, gave a mock shudder.

'Well, then. Not another word . . .'

But the problem wouldn't go away.

'I say, don't I know you?'

Hope paused in her dance. From her position on the stage, she could see almost nothing of the crowd on the disco floor. The lights strobed across them – pop art shirts and straining flares, white plastic knee boots and chunky thighs – a psychedelic, epileptic tussle of fragmented body parts.

'I do know you,' the young man insisted. 'Hope? It is you?'

'Hang on,' Hope answered, 'can't talk now. I'm due a break in five minutes. See you then.'

She didn't expect to, of course. Being picked up was one of the occupational hazards of being a go-go dancer. Men thought you were available, just because your body was up there for inspection, for comment, for pleasure. They touched, some of them, sly, sweaty fingerings, strokings, pinchings. 'If you're not buying, don't handle the goods,' she'd snarl and aim a swift kick. And they almost always wanted to buy you a drink, claimed to know you, or know your sister, or tell you that – hey, did you know? – you looked just like Marianne Faithfull. Hope had developed a nice line in put-downs since she had started evening work at the Saddle Room.

She just danced. No extras.

Sometimes, it was quite easy. If the DJ was good and his music smooth, she could just drift along with the beat. Her body seemed to work independently, without command and control. She felt as though she were outside herself, watching another girl, a slightly familiar girl with a wild fuzz of coppery hair and firm, sweat-slicked skin, twisting and shimmering under a pulsing spotlight.

Sometimes – tonight – it was bloody hard work. She felt like a puppet with its strings tangled. Pull this one and the wrong bit moved. The DJ was stoned. He had a vacuous grin on his face and kept fluffing his changeovers. There was a raucous group near the stage that was already chucking cigarette packets and corks and looked as though it was about to start on bottles.

Well, it was money, wasn't it? Enough to give Aunt Tabby a bit of housekeeping and the leftovers bought Lydia a secondhand cot. Not before time. Aunt Tabby had been moaning for weeks about losing her big wicker laundry basket.

Clean money and cash, no questions.

But, oh God, she despised the stage gropers. This one was more than usually persistent. He was waiting at the side of the stage when she climbed down.

'I *have* seen you somewhere,' she acknowledged, taking in the gangling figure and the prominent nose. 'I thought it was just a come-on.'

'Harry. Harry Dowland. We met when you were at the WRAC College. I couldn't believe it was you.'

'Well, sometimes I can't believe it's me, either,' answered Hope, with a short, acid laugh. 'So we're quits.'

'Come and join our table. There's a crowd of us celebrating the last night of a staff promotion course, but it's more like a wake than a celebration. We've all failed.'

As Hope crossed the dance floor with Harry, the ultraviolet lights turned her tiny, white, fringed costume to flowing cobwebs, ethereal and ghostly. They darkened her limbs, making them somehow less rounded, less substantial, and hiding the sweat that slicked her skin like a channel swimmer's grease. But she could still feel the tickle of it between her shoulder blades and under her breasts.

Harry said something she couldn't hear, and the flash of ultraviolet teeth made him look like an amiable crocodile. Hope laughed and when he put his arm round her shoulders, she didn't mind.

He introduced her to the bottle-chucking group by the stage. Oliver, of course. Like David and Jonathan, she thought, or Laurel and Hardy, you never found Harry without Oliver, or vice versa. Mike – army rugby team and cauliflower ear. Toby – silk cravat and manners to match. Giles – dead drunk and asleep with his cheek in a pool of spilled wine. Chris – sitting in the shadow. She got a brief impression of bright, humorous eyes.

She could have been wrong about the names. Everyone was bawling over the sound of 'The Israelites'. Here the speakers were just a few feet from her chair. They didn't sound so loud on-stage. Her diaphragm thudded with the sound. The air vibrated. She nodded and smiled and tried to look intelligent.

The wine was terrible plonk. 'We're drowning our sorrows. First rung on the promotion ladder and we've all fallen off already. All fall down – load of bloody Humpty Dumpties!' Harry said, with a tipsy giggle, half in explanation, half in apology, 'Why waste good money, when the sole aim is to get drunk as quickly as possible?'

'Not so drunk that we can't pull a few birds first,' Mike corrected. 'Christ, look at that one. Her dress is see-through in this light. You can see her knickers shining through. Legs all the way up to her tits. Hang on, I must just . . .'

And he lurched across the dance floor towards an unsuspecting little blonde.

Oliver seemed to wake up then. He had been very far away, Hope thought. Somewhere deep and unreachable. His plastered leg stuck out sideways onto the tiny dance floor and he paid no attention when people stumbled over it. Their apologies were always embarrassed and profuse, but Oliver seemed neither to feel any pain nor to hear the regrets. He was looking, for the first time, from the far side of failure and he didn't like the view.

Ultraviolet light does strange things. It struck the dandruff on the shoulders of sleeping Giles, making it seem as though he lay, comatose, under a sprinkling of snow. It deepened the colour of the band of freckles across Toby's nose. He looked as though he was developing a severe case of acne. But then, reflected Hope, perhaps he was. Oliver's plaster had recently been replaced and was whiter than white. His toes looked so dark, protruding from the glowing cast, that they might have been gangrenous. Chris sat in the shadows still. Now and again, light caught his teeth as he smiled, but he didn't do that often. Mostly he sat and watched Hope. Hope knew he was watching, because the whites of his eyes were highlighted as he turned towards her. That was when he smiled. She made him smile.

'Jesus Christ, this is boring.' Oliver reached over and took both her hands in one of his. 'Don't you find lots of drunken men boring, Hope? 'Course you do. You're sober and so am I and all these others are boring drunks. I tell you what – why don't you take me away from here? That should be my line, shouldn't it? But with a leg like this I couldn't take you anywhere – except to paradise.' And he began to sing softly. '*If paradise is half as nice . . .*'

Hope tugged at her hands, but they were firmly held. 'My break is over. I have to get back to work.'

'Sod it,' Oliver spat out. 'Sod your stupid work. That's not work, that's flaunting yourself.'

'Oliver . . .' She wriggled, trying not to look as though she was struggling, trying not to make a scene. 'Let go. You're hurting me.'

'Am I?' He placed his face very close to hers, almost laid his cheek against Hope's, and whispered – yet she could hear him clearly above the pounding bass beat. 'Does that hurt, Hope? Oh, dear. Then you'd better come with me. Take me home, Hope. Take me to your home.'

'Don't be daft. I live with my great-aunt. I've got a baby at home.'

'A baby? A baby! Oh, Hope, have you been a naughty girl?'

Oliver took one hand off her wrists. He touched her lips, her chin, the point of her shoulder and then let one finger trail down the line of her breast. Under the glowing white nylon, her nipple peaked and he laughed and touched her again.

'Oliver, let go,' she pleaded.

'Come with me.'

'Leave the girl alone, Oliver.' Harry bent over the pair, his shadow falling between them and the dance floor. He tried to prise off Oliver's hand, finger by finger. 'Sorry, Hope, he doesn't mean it. We're all a bit OTT tonight. Come on, old chap, you're drunk. Let her go.'

'Oh, but you're wrong, Harry,' Oliver whispered, still with that eerie, carrying clarity. 'I do mean it.'

Oliver let go suddenly. Hope snatched her hands off the table and tried to massage back the circulation. Without turning his head, his body language giving nothing away, Oliver picked up a crutch that was propped against his chair and smashed Harry viciously across the shins.

'Bastard!' Hope shrieked.

Harry grunted and staggered, clutching his legs. He was saying over and over 'Bugger, bugger, bugger . . . I'm supposed to be at team training tomorrow . . . bugger . . .'

A dark, irregular circle was seeping over his right trouser leg and, as Hope watched, a smaller one appeared on the left leg. Giles woke up and puked over the table. Chris put his hand under Hope's elbow as she knelt by Harry and raised her to her feet.

'Come on. I'll take you home,' he said. 'No funny business. Promise.'

And when Hope looked at him, even in that distorting light, she saw enough to make her believe him.

'But I haven't finished my shift,' she protested, unconvincingly.

'I'll come back and make it right for you. Don't worry.'

*　　*　　*

Later, so late that it was almost time for Lydia to wake for her early feed, there were three things that Hope thought about as she lay awake waiting for that first muffled grizzle that grew and grew into furious demands.

The first was Chris's calm competence and good manners. He'd delivered her back to a grumpy Aunt Tabby, true to his promise of 'no funny business'. Yet he must have thought her easy pickings – a single girl with an admitted fatherless baby, making her living by gyrating half naked on a stage. He'd even asked if he could see her again, asked respect-fully, as though she were a decent girl. He was a decent man. There weren't enough of those around. But, for some reason, she'd said no.

The second was the lack of expression on Oliver's face as he had lashed out at Harry's legs. That frightened her. It wasn't normal. He had deliberately tried to inflict as much pain as he could, aiming with speed and accuracy at a vulnerable spot, yet his face had been impassive, almost iconic in its peaceful blankness.

And the third thing was the response that Oliver had awakened in her. Again and again, she experienced the touch of his finger as it trailed suggestively down her reluctant body. Like a trickle of water, like a feather, like a breath, like a red-hot wire. With a *frisson* of excitement and fear, she recalled the way he had seemed to sense exactly how she was feeling and enjoy the moment.

She drew her legs up to her chest and wrapped her arms around her knees. *Ignore it. It'll go away. He's going to marry Nell and that's that*. There was no way of rationalizing her feelings. She despised his behaviour. She hated him for what he had done to Harry, whose well-meaning intervention did not deserve such an attack. And she desired him. More than any man she had ever met.

She was still trying to make sense of it all as she stumbled downstairs, tousled and frowsty, to heat some milk for Lydia's bottle.

1994

A time to hate . . .

Nell was arranging sweet peas in vulgarly glorious multicoloured masses, cramming them into great silver trophy bowls. Arranging sounded a bit pretentious, she thought. You didn't do that with sweet peas. You just filled a container and they looked gorgeous – no problem.

The flowers throve on a nutritious diet of manure from the Saddle Club stables. She'd already donated an armful to decorate the Mess for that night's mess dinner, to be held on the eve of a parade to mark the presentation of new colours by the Queen to one of the garrison infantry regiments. She intended to stand one bowl in the hall, on the table where the visitors' book lay, one on the sideboard in the dining room and there were still enough left to fill a jug in the family sitting room.

Their scent was piercingly sweet. It masked the scullery smells of bleach and boot polish. She plunged her face into the moist bunches. The petals felt like babies' skin and smelt like all her good memories come at once. She breathed quietly and slowly and tried not to think about anything – not about Jago, or Oliver, or the Queen, not even about the pounds and pounds of overgrown beans the gardener had brought in with the sweet peas, all to be sliced and blanched and frozen. She was at peace.

Only one thing could make the moment better, and that was an end to the fighting between Jago and Oliver. Not that you could really term it *fighting*. No-one actually fought with Oliver, not if he or she had any sense, but from the early savage skirmishes, they had both settled into entrenched positions. Now Jago was stubbornly and fiercely holding his ground.

Their son had pitched up home around breakfast time two days earlier, bringing with him nothing at all. No luggage. No money. He'd walked most of the fifty miles home, as no-one seemed to trust a hitch-hiker as clean and wholesome as Jago – must be something wrong with him, must be a psycho in disguise. And when his mother had given up trying to force-feed him and persuade him into a hot bath and plaster his blisters, he'd made an announcement that had split the family apart.

'I've finished with Sandhurst.'

'Don't you mean,' Oliver had queried, looking up from the *Daily Telegraph* with dangerous calm, 'that Sandhurst has finished with you?'

'No. I've finished with it. I'm leaving. I want to go to agricultural college.'

'You want to be a shit shifter? You're mad.' There was the thud of the fridge door and Jessica wandered in from the kitchen, glugging from a carton of fruit juice. Cranberry juice left a rim of scarlet that made her look as though she'd had her lips collagen-enhanced. 'You've absolutely lost the plot,' she declared, rolling her eyes theatrically. 'Hawtreys don't *do* that sort of thing. So why didn't you just keep on walking – like off a cliff or something – and give us all some peace. Don't they shoot deserters, Daddy?'

And the battle of wills had gone on from there.

Jago was, in his own way, as bloody-minded as his father. He didn't rage and slam doors, the way teenagers are supposed to do. He'd grown out of that pretty quickly once he'd put on a uniform. He simply stated his case and wouldn't be budged. Oliver was the one left shouting the odds and he wasn't used to it.

Nell tried to mediate, but was left feeling like a net of hay between two horses, dragged backwards and forwards by every argument, each one biting lumps out of her.

'But you're so near the end of the course, darling, just another few months. Surely you can hang on a bit longer. You've worked so hard. Surely you don't want to throw it all away.'

'But he really isn't suited to it, Oliver. Surely you can see that. He's been miserable. You say yourself it's a life that requires dedication and he just hasn't got it. He's not . . . he's not a natural fighter. That's not a crime.'

'You really mustn't blame your father, Jago. He doesn't mean to be brutal. He loves you – yes, he does, don't you dare say that. It's been a bit of a

259

shock to him, that's all. He'll come round to the idea, in the end. Give him time.'

'It's all for the best, Oliver. Believe me. He's not . . . not the brightest of boys, you must admit. I really believe that if he wasn't your son, he'd have been asked to leave Sandhurst by now, anyway. No, it's not meant to be an insult to either of you. Just maybe they gave him more of a chance because of who he is, were more patient than . . . well, have it your own way.'

'Jago, you really must talk to your father. Now. You can't expect me to be piggy in the middle any longer. All I ask is that you sit down in a civilized fashion – no, I'm not joking and don't you dare laugh like that. I'm putting myself on the line here for you. Just talk. Try it. That's all I ask. He'll be reasonable. You'll see.'

'Oliver, this has got to stop. He may be only a boy to you, but to the rest of the world he's an adult. He's made his decision and I think it's a very sensible and brave and mature one. It took a lot of courage to come home and face the family – face you. Admit it. He's not another you. There's nothing you can do to make him a second Oliver.'

Dear God! The best thing she could do would be to shut them both away in the broom cupboard and keep them locked up until they could talk sense to each other.

And the Queen was coming tomorrow. So Oliver was more than usually tense, what with security men prowling the garrison and sealing up manhole covers along her route and the redecoration schedule of her personal lavatory, which was well overdue. Good timing, Jago!

It was the time of evening that Nell still liked best, when the port had been circulated and the loyal toasts drunk, when the mess staff had handed out cigars and liqueurs to those who still had any desires unfulfilled. Then she could lean back in her chair, comfortable in the knowledge that all had gone as it ought, as it always had done and always would.

In a moment, the speeches would begin. She didn't usually listen, not even when Oliver was speaking. The words didn't matter. They were always the same anyway, or as nearly the same as made no difference. Pride. Success. Tradition. Well done, chaps. The little in-joke that showed that the General was human and caused a ruffle of appreciative table rapping and a rattle of coffee spoons in saucers.

What mattered was the moment. Candlelight doubled and redoubled, pinpoint flames mirrored in polished mahogany. Red wood with a gleaming depth, unruffled as a fall of water, sliding down darker and darker, to the far corners of the room where sat the humblest subalterns. Familiar faces flattered, softened by the warm golden glow, reflected back from gleaming silver, distorted as a fairground image, relaxed, a little hot, perhaps, in the starched collar or the velvet dinner gown, a little red after five courses with wines, but dear all the same.

Friends. That was what the army was good at. That was what held it together. Respect and liking and trust and loyalty and faith and duty. Old-fashioned words. Untrendy. Certainly not latter-part-of-the-twentieth-century sentiments. Words that were illustrated by the vast oil paintings on the walls. Grisly, most of them, pictures of retreats or heroic last stands, enough to put anyone off a five-course dinner. Shoulder to shoulder, lads. Steady, that man. Back to back, now.

And that's how it is today, she thought. *Even now. There isn't a man in this room who wouldn't die for the man sitting next to him. And that's how it should be. That's the British Army. Gosh, I really am fuddled. It must have been the Cointreau. That's the most awful twaddle. True, though.*

She was conscious of the weight of tradition, not as a burden, but heavy and warm around her shoulders, like a father's arm. It comforted and cheered. It supported and encouraged.

There was Harry, pouring port for the woman on his right, attentively leaning over her cleavage – not Flavia, but no-one was surprised at that. There was the garrison doctor and the padre and the vet and the transport officer and the engineer and the quartermaster and the bomb disposer – no glamour, but hard grafters, all of them, who might never (in most cases, would certainly never) reach Oliver's exalted rank, yet who made the army tick. And there were their wives, miniature regimental brooches glittering, dressed up to the nines in their Sloaney, fashion-free way, with a sameness about them, a quality of reliability, steadiness that had served them well at Lucknow or Ladysmith or at the fall of Singapore and would do again, if necessary.

They could face enemy hordes or scrub out a kitchen with the same grace.

There they were, tomorrow's history. And, in that moment, Nell loved them all.

She watched Oliver speaking, not taking in his words, admiring the way he played the room. He should have been a politician, she thought. If he'd been standing on John Major's soapbox, he'd have had electors falling at his feet and begging to be trampled. Another, longer rumble of table rapping, distant thunder, and a few murmurs of appreciation. The candlelight erased the few signs of ageing in Oliver. His hair, so lightly frosted, was still thick and full of life. His body was honed by early morning runs and the need to pass his annual fitness inspection. He was perfect. The boy general. He could have asked his audience to roll over and have its collective tummy tickled and they would have done it, to a man, probably – and to a woman, certainly.

And tomorrow? Things would be better tomorrow. Surely. Oliver would have slept on his disappointment and must realize that Jago was right. The boy wasn't suited to a military career. Sandhurst was destroying him. He wasn't bright, wasn't thrusting, wasn't bursting to prove that he was as good a man as his father. He was just a lovely boy, with little or no ambition, who needed a quiet, steady life. Why couldn't his father understand?

Perhaps tomorrow they'd stop shouting and come to some arrangement. Oliver would act like a supportive father instead of a Victorian tyrant. He'd organize Jago's leaving Sandhurst and entry to

Cirencester Agricultural College. He'd pull strings, fix things. It could work. She was sure of it. And Jago would be happy. That's what it was all about, wasn't it? Happy families?

Nell's eye wandered round the room again. Oliver's brightness dazzled her. He burned with upright clarity, as a clear flame in a draught-free room. His rightness was wearying. His perfection wore her down.

Further down the room, at the lower end of the long table, in the outer darkness where the junior officers and their wives were seated, there was a flurry of movement. Heads were turned and turned away abruptly again, as though the watchers couldn't believe, or couldn't bear to contemplate what they had seen.

Nell sat forward in her seat, trying to work out what was happening. She saw . . . she saw a woman crawling, for God's sake . . . a pregnant woman, trying to attract as little attention as possible, crawling towards the door. She saw the other guests look at the woman with a ludicrous mixture of expressions – shock, horror, embarrassment, disbelief. The mess sergeant stood with his open box of cigars like a wooden Indian outside a tobacconist's, but his blink rate soared. It was absurd.

Oliver saw her, too. He paused in his speech, seemed for a moment to lose concentration, lose his place, then he picked up the thread again smoothly. With the merest hiatus, he carried on. But his eyes, Nell noticed, had frosted over. He had missed nothing. He would forgive nothing.

No-one – *no-one*, for whatever reason, heart attack excepted and perhaps not even that, ever left a dining room before general permission was given. Never had. Never would. It was a breach of self-discipline, showed lack of control. In the list of unforgivable solecisms, this one ranked high, somewhere up alongside adultery with a junior rank's wife and wearing your spurs upside down. The unfortunate woman's husband must have been suffering agonies.

Nell couldn't stand it. That poor, humiliated woman and her misguided attempt to get clear without being seen to break the rules filled Nell with rage and compassion. Dear God, she was pregnant, obviously so. She probably couldn't wait for Oliver's long-winded speech to finish to get to the loo. Why wasn't she allowed to stand up like a normal human being and just walk out the door? Because she was an army wife, that was why. w/o Captain Nobody. Not a real person at all.

Scarcely knowing she'd done it, Nell pushed back her chair and stood up. There was a wavering amongst the men, like a failed Mexican wave, as they half rose in acknowledgement of her move. Wives who had been expecting Nell, as senior wife, to give the signal for the ladies to retire, stood, gathered up handbags, wavered and then sat again as Oliver continued speaking. He didn't miss a beat.

Of course, she could have marched like a martyr to the lions, straight down the middle of the room, but, being Nell, she didn't. She squeezed apologetically around the edge, past all the chairs, until she reached the creeping woman. Everyone watched, but no-one looked. Nell bent and touched her on the elbow, recognizing her, as she did so, as Caroline something, the young wife of a junior staff officer. Gently, Nell raised her. Caroline was heavy and awkward, her pregnancy advanced.

'Gosh,' said Nell, lightly, but she could feel her own hand shaking as it lay on Caroline's arm. 'I'm absolutely dying to spend a penny. Aren't you? And those men do go on so. Let's leave them to it.'

In the lavatory that had been set aside for female guests by having the row of urinals draped in sheeting, Caroline began to cry.

'I'm awfully sorry – I couldn't help it – I waited and waited, but then I couldn't wait any longer. The baby's doing a tap dance on my bladder. I know it was awful of me. Roly was so cross . . .'

'Now, listen . . .' Nell sounded far more resolute than she felt. 'It's not a hanging offence, whatever your husband may have told you.'

'I was afraid.'

'Afraid your husband would lose his promotion because you needed to spend a penny? Hardly. Well, we're both in disgrace now, so we can hold hands in front of the firing squad.'

'But your husband was giving his speech and no-one ever, ever . . .'

'For goodness' sake—' Nell gave her a gentle shove in the direction of a cubicle. 'Go and do it before you burst. So what if we both find ourselves in the divorce court in the morning? At least we'll be comfortable right now.'

She kept up the fiction and went into the adjoining cubicle, waited a bit, pulled the handle and came out. Running cold water over her wrists, she squinted hopefully into a glaringly lit mirror. God – shiny and pink as a boiled shrimp. That poor woman – girl, really, she couldn't be much over twenty. She was absolutely terrified. As Nell would have been. As she was now, she admitted.

Slowly, slowly, as though a tiny spark was being fed and fanned and coaxed into flame, Nell felt the indignation that had first caught her by surprise kindle into rage. It fed on itself. Her hands were still shaking, but not now from fear.

They had watched her – poor, frightened Caroline in flower-sprigged Laura Ashley flopping over her swollen belly – gentlemen all, they had watched her crawl, and not one had remonstrated or dared to help her. They were as brainwashed as she – or she was as brainwashed as they – Nell's thinking was getting a bit too muddled to sort it out.

That was what tradition had done to them all. They would support each other to the death, but no-one was brave enough to be the one out of step, no-one wanted to be different. The thin red line had staggered, but had not broken.

Viciously, Nell dabbed at her shiny nose, but did more harm than good. She heard the lavatory flush and composed herself into a calming smile.

'Ready?' she asked. 'I think I hear everyone leaving the dining room, so it'll be pandemonium in here in a moment. Aren't we clever, we're ahead of the scrum!'

267

As she crossed the hall with Caroline, the mess sergeant appeared, with her coat held out in his hands, ready for Nell to pop her arms into the sleeves.

'General's compliments, ma'am,' he said, smoothly, 'and his car is at your disposal.'

'It is?' echoed Nell, stupidly.

'The GOC asked me to pass on to you that your presence won't be . . .' Poor man, he was trying so hard to be diplomatic and to upset neither the General nor his lady. Nell felt a very brief spasm of pity for him. '. . . won't be required for the rest of the evening.'

Dismissed. Nell plunged her hands into her coat pockets so that no-one could see how tightly they were clenched. Dismissed like a naughty parlour maid. Bloody hell.

Nell took off her makeup very carefully – well, to be honest, most of it had slid off during the course of the long dinner, but what was left she meticulously removed. She cleansed, toned and moisturised with more than her usual casual attention. Her dress she put by for the cleaners – there was a splash or two of red wine down the skirt.

And all the time, she thought.

She thought of Caroline something's crawl to freedom: she'd been as exposed as a lone wirecutter in no man's land when the Very lights go up – how scared must she have been to resort to such a desperate measure. And Nell faced up to the fact that she would herself have made that same, ignominious journey at Caroline's age, in Caroline's position.

She thought of the little eddy of movement, of the scandalized glances that had followed Caroline's progress. She thought of Oliver's penetrating stare, the way his hooded eyes had blinked slowly, the way the candle flames had left bright dots in the darkness where the pupils should have been. When she had stood up to cross the room, galvanized by shock into an action she would never have considered if she'd taken time to think, he had dared her, challenged her to move. And she had taken up that challenge.

She thought about Jago, trying and failing to emulate a man who had no match. She thought about the courage it must have taken for the boy to come home and admit he had failed. There are all sorts of courage and Jago's was a type that Oliver would never recognize.

She thought about all sorts of other things, too. And then she went downstairs.

The freezer needed defrosting, Nell noted with surprise. So there were some things that Mrs Parr neglected, after all. Once, the discovery of a flaw in the perfection might have given Nell a guilty spasm of pleasure. Now she just observed.

She carried the tub of ice cream upstairs and settled herself into bed, four pillows at her back and the duvet pulled up to her chin. Steadily, with no pleasure, she began to spoon the ice cream into her mouth.

Waitrose Stem Ginger. Her favourite. Ice cream always tastes better when allowed to thaw a little. But she didn't have time for that. This was freezer hard. It numbed her tongue and dulled her taste buds. The ginger had no kick to it. The little chocolatey bits were like pebbles. She hacked at the lump with her spoon. Fiercely. Intently. She didn't look up.

About half way through the 500-millilitre tub, Nell fought a surge of revulsion. This was disgusting. She was disgusting. But she didn't stop. She kept up her steady pace, because the quicker she ate, the quicker it would be over, but the sweetness gagged her, her throat tightened around the cloying, gelatinous texture.

Soon be finished, she told herself, *then I won't have to stuff in any more. Of course, I don't have to finish it. I mean, nothing's making me. I'm not a slave to ice cream. But what use is half a tub of ice cream to anyone? What's the point of putting it back in the freezer? Can't waste it. Only another few spoonfuls and then it'll be tidied up, out of the way. Nearly there.*

When she had finished, when she had scraped out every last lick, she lay, torpid and nauseous, clutching the soggy carton, irritated by its untidiness, by the condensation that had dripped onto the duvet, by her inability to clean the spoon to perfect brightness.

So she lay and thought some more. And, for once, her thoughts seemed to be getting somewhere. Usually, she was conscious of their lack of discipline.

They wandered about, picking up this, poking at that, like a toddler on a nature ramble – getting nowhere very slowly. Tonight – tonight, they did what they were told. She was in charge and the feeling was exhilarating.

But she could think more effectively, she was certain, if her surroundings were orderly. If there wasn't a splodge of melting ice cream on the pillow-case. So she cleaned out the empty tub with her finger, licking with the fierce intensity of an animal disinfecting a sore, until the inside was spotless.

When she could bear the reproach of her binge no longer, she went downstairs to dispose of the evidence.

The scullery was very dark, very quiet, after Kane had gone home. It smelt aggressively clean, of Ajax and Brillo, of Kiwi and Domestos, of the singed, satisfying, long-ago scent of generations of serge flattened under damp pressing cloths. There wasn't a trace of life in the smell, no body odours, nothing fleshly, only humanity ruthlessly repressed, all smells gone, all wrinkles smoothed, all dullness brightened.

Perfection.

Nell turned on the light and leaned against the door frame. Kane had left everything ready for the morning. Oliver's boots, rigid around their wooden trees, glittering spurs already fitted into the spur boxes in the heels, were on the draining board, with a clean duster laid over them in case a grain of dust should dim their black brilliance. Coiled beside them, under another duster, as polished and sleek as a healthy python, was Oliver's Sam Browne belt, which would support the sheathed sword that stood against the wall. Oliver's dress uniform, his blues, hung on the back of the door inside a plastic cover – hell to keep dust-free, blues, the slightest bit of fluff clung to them, making them the obvious military choice for a long day on Salisbury Plain, with armoured vehicles churning up plumes of white dust that drifted on a ceaseless wind. Still, it kept all the batmen of the British Army in employment and out of mischief: why choose an easy option when the difficult one was so much better for the character? And on the ironing board, inside their box, dark green stamped with gold letters – Spink & Son Ltd – gleamed Oliver's medals.

All ready for the early start. All ready for Kane to carry to the dressing room. While Oliver ate his one rasher and grilled tomato, upstairs Kane would box the trousers, known as overalls – how unglamorous – insert the Wellingtons into the legs, buckle the under-instep strap, button on the braces and roll the whole garment down to the ground, over the boots, ready for Oliver to step into and draw up. Absolutely nothing left to chance.

Nell thought of her own outfit: new, Alexon, from a Salisbury department store, to be outshone, in glamour, by Oliver. Perhaps the almond green had been a bit of a mistake, perhaps she should have gone for something a little – just a *little* – more dramatic. And the pleats – were they just a little bit *too* safe, too mumsie?

But she hadn't been invited to the parade in order to outshine the Queen. She was Oliver's consort, nothing more. If pleats were good enough for Her Majesty, they were good enough for Nell. I'll be neat, tidy and unremarkable, she thought, just what I ought to be. Let the men shine. It's their day, after all.

The hat was nice, though. She always looked good in hats. Some women did and some just didn't. Something to do with the angle.

She wandered into the scullery, letting her fingers drift across the green box, down the plastic cover, across the protective dusters. Clean ones, new ones, fluffy-chicken yellow, with no other purpose, never, ever sullied.

She lifted just a corner. Oliver's Wellingtons. Funny how boots and shoes always grew to look like their people. Rather like dogs – or was that the other way round? She couldn't remember and suddenly it seemed important. Dogs like people or people like dogs? And she was reminded of Alice tumbling down the rabbit hole, murmuring dreamily to herself as she fell, 'Do cats eat bats? Do cats eat bats? Do bats eat cats?'

Oliver's boots looked like Oliver and he was like his boots. Tall, straight, narrow, unbending, beautifully turned out. He had, as a hunting man might say, a beautiful leg for a boot. The slight curl across the toe reminded her of the way his nose wrinkled when she said something particularly stupid.

She picked up the right one to look at it more closely. A diamond glitter. Kane had outdone himself. Nothing too good for Her Majesty. 'I want to see my face in those when you've done,' Sergeant

273

Lofthouse had probably ordered Kane, the threat implicit, though unspoken – or else . . . She could see the reflection of the light bulb overhead, of herself, looking distorted – surely – surely she didn't usually have that faded smile?

She turned the boot round in her hands, but whichever way she looked at it, the same anxious face stared back at her. Nell?

As she turned the shining toecap this way and that, quietly intent, the boot slipped from her hand. Really. It just slipped. And she grabbed at it, terrified that it would hit the floor, scar that glittering perfection. Snatched at it, juggled for a moment, fumbled the catch. Hopeless Nell. Never could catch. Never picked for the rounders team. And her nails scored three deep, jagged lines across – no, *through* – the polish, right through to the leather.

Oh, God . . .

Nell stared at the damage, motionless as a rabbit in a cat's jaws. How to confess? How to explain? How to repair the damage before morning?

She breathed on the polish, trying to melt it, dabbed at it with the corner of the duster. But her old knack – like falling off a bike, she'd always thought, once you know how to bull up a pair of shoes, you never forget – had deserted her.

She stared, then slowly, carefully, with a feeling of absolute rightness, she scratched the other toecap to match.

And then she stared again.

Not good enough.

Nell looked round the room, opened the cupboards, searched the shelves. When she found a bottle of white spirit, she poured a measured amount over the remaining glossed leather. The polish dissolved, leaving a sticky, waxy smear. Then she did the same to the Sam Browne belt, dribbling the white spirit in patterns, loops and whorls and spirals, over the polish, watching it etch its way irreparably through the years of care and nurture.

Good.

Nell felt efficient, effective, useful. She was making a contribution to her own well-being. No spark, Molly Greene had once said – it seemed an awfully long time ago – no up and at 'em, no *joie de vivre*. And no initiative. But Nell rather thought that she was showing quite a bit of initiative now.

She walked briskly upstairs to their sitting room and rummaged in her work basket for the large scissors. No point in trying little ones. Things had to be done properly.

She drew up the covering plastic bag from Oliver's uniform and cut the crotch out of the trousers. It was quite difficult. The cloth was good quality, a very firm weave. And while she was at it, she thought she'd better make a decent job, no half measures. So she cut out the SAS wings from the right sleeve. Not cut off – cut out. Oliver despised half measures.

Her thumb was a bit sore by the time she'd finished. The loop of the scissors had left red marks on the skin. She stood and assessed her work, head on one side, appraising.

Better.

She looked around the room, her eyes flicking from boots to belt, from belt to clothes. It all looked a bit untidy and she didn't want Kane getting into trouble in the morning. He'd left everything just so. A very particular man, was Kane. So she replaced the protective dusters and put away the white spirit, carefully mopping up the spills with kitchen paper. Then she threw away the ragged circle of blue serge, embellished with fly buttons, threw away the flaunting gold wings and used the dustpan and brush to tidy the fragments of blue thread that lay on the red tiled floor. She pulled down the plastic bag over Oliver's blues. All tidy again.

Just as she was about to leave the scullery, Nell spotted the green medal box on the ironing board.

Good, better, best. Never let it rest, till the good is better and the better best.

So she snipped each glittering embossed metal trophy from its supporting scrap of ribbon, making certain that the ribbon was sufficiently mutilated to prevent emergency repair. That's not being vicious, she thought, just sensible, taking precautions.

Separated, the ribbons and medals were disarmed, unmanned, the conflicts they represented long over, long forgotten by a civilian population unused, thank God, to war.

Who Dares Wins and no-one could say that Oliver had not dared.

Dull red ribbon, with narrow blue edgings, the Distinguished Service Order, won for – Nell didn't know for what, the SAS was far too secretive, but she knew he'd been in the Falklands at the time –

and now it was separated from its white-enamelled cross. That was when Jago was sent away to board at a seaside prep school and Nell had cried for a week, until the second-in-command's wife had told her to 'Buck up, old thing. We all go through it, you know.'

Two broad white stripes flanking a purple one of the same width and the silver Military Cross lying forlorn on the cotton wool that lined the box. That was Northern Ireland, she remembered, border operations and we all knew what that meant, but no-one said a word. That was when Jessica was born, the year that Oliver had been around only long enough to impregnate his wife. But that was duty.

Salmon pink, edged silver, rather gaudy. A gold cross, this, decorated with the miniature profile of George V. An Officer of the Order of the British Empire. For being an all-round good egg. And for the successful relief of the Iranian Embassy siege. And for having a wife who could run a thriving Wives' Club and keep the girls on the straight and narrow when their men were away.

Purple and green, dull-looking, but hard won, she knew, the General Service Medal, a great disc of silver, heavy, impressive, like an old half-crown. The ribbon carried a silver clasp that bore the words, very tiny to fit into the space, South Arabia. That was when Nell was still at school.

She arranged each medal carefully under its corresponding slashed ribbon and closed the box lid.

Best.

When she was putting away the scissors, she

realized that she hadn't completed her task. That was careless. If a job's worth doing, it's worth doing well. Procrastination is the thief of time. Never put off till tomorrow what you can do today.

So she went into Oliver's dressing room, opened the cupboard door and gave all his uniforms the same treatment. There wasn't another six-foot-four major-general with size 12 feet for – Nell tried to calculate the number of miles, mentally going through her address book and discarding entry after entry – all too short or too fat or too far away – then recognized that she was wasting time. There would be nothing he could borrow. He would have nothing to wear to meet the Queen in the morning.

'Finished,' Nell said softly and meant it.

She sat on the bed and did a bit more thinking. Her thoughts were very clear, pin-bright, but wobbly, rather difficult to catch hold of. It was like looking, she imagined, through a very old window, through rippled, bottom-of-the-sea-green glass. You could see everything so plainly, but nothing stood still. The flaws in the glass altered your view. Move your head and there was an entirely unexpected angle. The perspectives were all wrong.

Her breathing was quite shallow. There didn't seem to be enough oxygen making its way to her lungs. And she knew that you needed oxygen to think. So she started taking bigger breaths, huge breaths, great gulps, dragging in air to power her brain until her chest muscles hurt. And she thought.

After a while, she went through to Jessica's room, knocking punctiliously, taking the answering growl as permission to enter. Jessica sat sideways at a table. A table lamp turned her hair into a silver halo, spun around the profile of an angel painted by one of the more saccharine Renaissance painters – a Filippino Lippi perhaps, all sugar and no spice. Her head was tucked onto her left arm and an exercise book lay diagonally on the table. She was filling the page with a spider chart. Its convolutions reached right to the edge of the page on one side, but the top left corner had only one wavering thread leading to it. Something wrong there. Henry VII sat in the centre.

'I don't know how you can write like that, darling,' Nell said quietly, scarcely daring to break into Jessica's unusual concentration. 'Twisted round so far. You'll hurt your back.'

''Course I won't. You always say that.'

Nell laid her hand on Jessica's hair, feeling the spring of it from a crooked centre parting under her hand, loving the slippery, shiny, washed-every-day health of it.

Jessica shrugged her off, tossing her head so that her face was hidden by a bright veil.

'Don't. I just washed it. What *is* it with you? You nag me to study and when I do, you wander around disturbing me. It's so spooky. Who said you could come in, anyway?'

Jago was stretched flat on his bed, earphones in his ears, with closed eyes and a beatific smile on his face. A tiny, tinny leak escaped from the headset, audible phantoms, as though private angel voices whispered promises in his ears only. There was a packet of Coco Pops on the floor, alongside a bowl with the dregs of chocolatey milk and three Penguin wrappers.

He hasn't looked as peaceful as that since he came home, Nell thought. It would be cruel to disturb him.

She began to pull the door closed, but Jago must have caught the wind of movement, because he raised his head and pulled back one earphone and gave the smile that was so like Oliver's – so like Oliver's that Nell felt the stroking finger, no more than a touch on the back of her neck, of fear.

'You're back early. Everything all right, Mum?' he queried.

Nell was tempted to answer that everything was far from all right, but she didn't have the heart to burden him or the courage to begin a major discussion. So she nodded and smiled, hoping that he'd be able to hear her, or at least lip-read.

'Fine, fine. Good night, love.'

And she closed the door and leaned against it and thought that, maybe, hearts really do break.

Harry had two or three attempts at getting the key in the lock. Not that he was drunk – far from it – not in his terms, anyway, although a traffic policeman would have had a different view. Luckily, they didn't prowl the roads of the garrison much. They left dealing with army personnel to the military police, who weren't likely to sneak around the Officers' Mess after a guest night.

He had the door open and was reaching for the

light switch, when he thought he heard a small, breathy sound in the darkness behind him, just a parting of the air, a sigh. He didn't turn round. He pulled the key slickly out of the lock – far more quickly than he'd put it in – darted in and slammed the door.

That's what conditioning does for you, he thought sheepishly, as he leaned against a side wall, well clear of any possible blast. Action or reaction or over-reaction? You don't wait to find out. You don't wait to ask who's out there in the darkness. You get the hell out of his reach.

Then you feel stupid. This wasn't Aden. This wasn't Belfast.

All the same, he didn't open the door again. He slid along the wall and flicked the light switch. He felt more comfortable in the darkness. Then he listened.

'Harry.' The knock was timid and the voice uncertain, wobbling nervously. 'Oh Harry, let me in. Please.'

'Sorry for the unfriendly welcome.'

'That's all right. It's a funny time for social calls.'

Harry looked comfortable in his own kitchen, Nell thought, in a way she never did these days. He banged around like an enthusiastic spaniel, retrieving little trophies for her – a mug, a milk jug, a plate of chocolate digestives – and placing them on the table, giving the impression that he'd rather lay them at her feet. But at least he knew where everything was. At least he . . . She spooned a generous

281

amount of sugar into her tea. Yuk, she hadn't taken sugar for ten years, at least.

It was very peaceful in the kitchen: the only sounds were small, unobtrusive ones – short whimpers from the dreaming spaniel, one of the long line of Madge's successors (and all called Madge – so much simpler), the kettle lid rattling, the tuned metallic chink of teaspoons and of Harry's miniature medals as he moved. Safe sounds.

He pulled out a chair opposite Nell and spooned a matching amount of sugar into his own tea. He'd untied his bow tie and opened the stiff, winged collar. The gold stud had left a tiny bruised circle on his throat. Nell wanted suddenly to touch it, to lay one questing finger on that place, to feel the pulse beneath it. Her hand began to move forward, but she diverted it and took a biscuit.

'Sorry. Didn't mean to slam the door in your face. I thought you were the IRA,' he said with a rueful smile. 'I know it's unlikely – I mean, what could they want with me – but it's happened: look at that poor bugger in Germany. That's how you stay alive, anticipating the unlikely.'

'I thought you were quite restrained, in the circumstances. Oliver would've throttled me first and asked questions later,' said Nell, taking a bite out of her second biscuit.

'You sobered me up pretty damn quick, anyway. Is everything all right . . . I mean, say it's none of my business if you like, but . . .'

'But what the hell am I doing here in the middle of the night?' Nell completed for him.

'More or less.'

Nell looked across at the face of the man she'd known as long as she'd known her husband. The years had not been as kind to him as they had to Oliver. Oman had left his skin leathery, with a tan that never seemed to fade. A rugby injury had meant the end of his active parachuting days and left him with an awkward right knee. He used to joke that a tour at the Parachute Training Depot in Aldershot was responsible for the grey hairs. Not too many, just enough to balance the fan of lines at the corner of each eye. The eyes were the same, though, warm brown, like treacle toffee, and painfully honest.

A friend. That was all and, just now, that was everything.

He looked at her for a long time. 'Forget it. You don't have to tell me anything,' Harry said softly.

But if Harry was home – the thought came to her like a vicious kick on the ankle – if Harry was home, then Oliver would be too. They would have left the mess together. Oliver would be searching . . . would be raging . . .

'Don't worry,' Harry reassured her, as though he had looked past her eyes and seen the panic, a gathering cloud, purple-edged, moving fast, obliterating reason. 'This is the last place he'll look for you.'

'Harry, I think . . . oh God, I think I'm going to be sick . . .'

Nell shoved back her chair and headed for the cloakroom, with her hand held hard against her mouth, but she didn't make it.

There wasn't a hint that a woman had ever entered this room – this house – before. Early light, pale and colourless, struggled through blue unlined curtains. When she was small, Nell had used to hold her nose and sit at the bottom of the swimming pool. For a while – quite a long time, because she practised a lot – all she could see was her own limbs, distorted, wavering and whitely blue, all she could hear was the bubbling of her own breath. *I am here*, she would think, *I am breathing and no-one knows*. It was a strangely comforting idea, safe. Bubbles like silver frogspawn rose from her lips and dispersed before they reached the surface.

Secure in the flickering blue light, Nell lay in the army-issue bed and looked at the army-issue furniture. She looked at the bare, highly polished surfaces, at the walls without a picture and the chairs without a cushion and wondered when Flavia had last lived with her husband.

Then she wondered how she'd got into this bed. And when she remembered, she shrank with shame.

Harry had carried her upstairs. He had wiped her face as tenderly as ever she had wiped Jago's or Jessica's. 'Sorry, sorry . . .' she had muttered, over and over.

'No need. Soldiers do worse after a night out.'

'But I haven't *had* a night out,' she'd wailed.

She'd heard, coming from downstairs, the running water, the rattle of a bucket handle and the sound of scrubbing. She had curled up on the bed, turned her face to the wall and closed her eyes.

Oliver was right. She was a disaster.

'All right?' Harry had stuck his head round the door ten minutes later and, even in her misery, Nell had wanted to laugh. He'd looked as though he was afraid that she might be trying to cut her wrists with a pair of nail scissors. 'I brought you these.' He held out a toothbrush and toothpaste and a long Omani jellaba, white and fiercely starched, to wear. 'Feeling better?'

Nell sat up and smiled, a warm, deprecating little smile, unaware that it stripped away the last of her onion-layered protective barriers. 'Mmm. Better and ashamed.'

'Doesn't matter. You ought to rest.'

He'd kissed her briefly on the cheek. Nell had turned her head away, afraid that he might be disgusted by her breath, afraid that he was just displaying a martyr's kindness. But when he'd kissed her, he'd done it again, slowly and reflectively. He held her by both shoulders and looked carefully at her face, seeing more there than she realized, more than she had ever meant to show. 'No. Not a good idea. Good night, little Nell. Sleep well.'

Contrary to her own expectations, she had slept, soundly and dreamlessly. Her last thought had been that she was bound to have a dreadful night, it would serve her right . . . and then it was daylight.

The spartan room had held her attention. She lay very still, as still as once she sat at the bottom of the

285

pool, assessing the charmlessness of Harry's home. Flavia visited for the social functions, for the Christmas and summer balls, for the beatings of retreat, for the parades (but only if they were to be held before a royal personage – God, she would be arriving today), the band concerts and massive cocktail parties, but had she, Nell wondered, even spent one night in the house that was let to Harry as a married quarter?

There were so many rumours. Garrisons were all the same – little, inbred, introspective worlds of gossip. Once Nell had overheard speculation, cautiously expressed but damning, that Harry must be a closet homosexual whose marriage was a blind, to protect him from being chucked out of the army. But no-one – well, perhaps only Oliver – knew the truth about Harry's marriage. *What a very private man*, she thought.

'I've brought you some tea.' Harry opened the door and gave a rattling tap at the same time. He wore his dressing gown, firmly tied, and his hair was slicked back and wet from his shower. 'Early start, I'm afraid. Parades are always like that. Feeling better?'

'Better than I've any right to. No, don't go.'

She held out her arm, expecting him to put the mug into her hand, but her hand was hidden beneath the too-long sleeve of the jellaba. She flipped the cuff back and Harry took the suddenly exposed fingers within his own. His touch was cool and his skin smelt freshly of soap. A mistake, of course. A misunderstanding. He hadn't meant to touch her. It was the way her hand had suddenly shot out from the starched white folds. It had surprised him.

She let her fingers lie in his for a moment. To withdraw them too quickly would be prudish. Harry was a friend. Just for a moment, then. She was in control. She could decide when to draw back. His touch felt . . . comforting. No more.

His fingers were long and very bony, not like Oliver's at all, yet, somehow, familiar, steadying. Their warmth entered hers, seeping through the skin, then branching, flowing through each tiny capillary, a sort of osmosis.

She gripped his fingers tighter, with an urgency that caught him unawares. She watched his eyes darken as the pupils widened. She sucked in his warmth. She was greedy for it. It burned, now, threading like lava through ashes, bright and dangerous.

It was like coming up for air. She felt as though she had been under the water, not seen, not heard, not noticed, for so long that she'd almost forgotten what it was like to breathe. She had sat crosslegged on the cement at the bottom of the pool until the little stream of bubbles that issued from her lips was nearly exhausted. Now she was surfacing, rising, coming up to the light, to where the air was sweet and pure. She would take great gulps of it. She would taste the freshness of it, the newness. And though the suddenness of her surfacing might kill her, she didn't care.

When he slipped beneath the covers beside her, she wasn't even surprised. She slid to one side, to make room for him in the narrow, hard bed. They lay very still, side by side and silent, still as a marble couple on a monument. Harry looked at her and Nell looked back at him, gravely, calmly, giving and accepting consent.

With just the tips of his fingers he touched her, as though they were learning her, as though every pad had a separate memory and the whole of her was being committed to each. The line of her neck. The angle of her shoulders. The way the fullness of her breasts tapered away under her arms. The little bump of each individual rib. The swoop inwards to her waist and flare of the hips. He felt the graininess of the skin of her belly, stretched by three pregnancies. He felt the dimpled inner flesh of her thighs. And she was not ashamed.

Nell waited, patiently, content for him to know her.

The phone was ringing. It rang for a very long time before the caller gave up.

She responded, touched him, delighted in the power she had to give him pleasure. It was like exploring a country she knew well from guidebooks. The length of him, the boniness, the toastrack ribs, all was familiar, but nothing was quite as she had expected. Like rounding a well-known corner and finding that everything has been altered. Such surprises. His tenderness. His solemn curiosity as he discovered her hidden places. Her own awed wonder. The shared laughter. She had never laughed before.

She was still smiling when he entered her. She felt

herself melt around him, dissolve until she was nothing but pure sensation. No speech. No hearing. No sight. Just a dual pulse that seemed to spread, ripple after ripple, like grasping fingers, throughout her whole body.

They were both very still for a long time. His heart hammered against her ribs. Their breathing steadied, slowing to a shared pattern. Then with a small, sucking sound, like a distant kiss, Harry slithered out of her. He smiled, his comfortable, ugly face soft with memory, and pushed the damp hair back from her forehead.

'Whatever happens next,' he said, softly, 'don't regret that. Or if you do, don't tell me.'

Nell curled into the crook of his arm. Perfectly happy. How few moments can really be described that way. Perfectly – nothing to mar the moment, no echo to the ticking of the clock, no looking over the shoulder, no dustcloud on the horizon that grows as it swirls towards you – happy. No past. No future. Just now. And the heat of Harry's skin under her own and the rise and fall of his chest with every breath. Some things are so simple that they can't be anything but right.

She must have dozed – they both must have – so the fierce ringing of the doorbell took some time to reach her.

She knew. No-one else would ring at this time, in that imperious way.

She closed her eyes and dived back down to the bottom of the blue pool. Safer there. The sound of Harry's feet on the stairs was muffled by the whistle of her own escaping breath. The two voices – one raised, thick-tongued with rage, one quiet, contained – barely reached her in her asylum. She lay quite still, breathing very slowly.

Flavia's husband. Oliver's sister's husband. Nell's brother-in-law. This could be sin. She wondered whether the relationship was banned in the Table of Kindred in the back of the Prayer Book. It had had a gruesome fascination at school. She remembered girls poring over it between lessons, appearing holy but looking for smut. 'Yeech! Fancy wanting to do it with Uncle Reg – can you imagine the teeth in the glass! Or Grandpa – you'd need to be dead from the neck down to do it with Grandpa.' So that was one sin that had seemed unlikely. But what about this? She resolved to check as soon as she could lay hands on a Prayer Book. In fact, why not now? Harry must have one. She decided she'd better get up and have a look.

Then Harry came back. He pulled back the bed-clothes very gently and looked at her with a new admiration.

'My God, you knew how to kick him where it hurt! He's raging. He's taking the garrison apart, looking for you. Not exactly discreet. And Kane's been sacked. He's talking about sending the poor bugger to Bosnia.'

'Oh, no.' Nell sat up, clutching the sheet modestly across her breasts, as though the man beside her hadn't recently caressed every square millimetre of her skin. 'He mustn't do that. It's not Kane's fault. He wasn't even in the house when I . . . when I . . .'

'When you made it impossible for Oliver to meet the Queen in two hours' time.' Harry began to laugh. He sat on the edge of the bed and wrapped his wiry arms, whipcord strong, around Nell, drawing her close against him. She could feel the vibrations of his laughter run through her like the warnings of a long-anticipated earthquake. 'God, you're wonderful. There's more to you than anyone guesses.' He tightened the arm around her shoulder and glanced quickly across her at his watch. 'Christ – Her Majesty will be halfway down the M3 . . .'

He rolled off the bed and ran through to his dressing room. Nell followed, trailing the wrapping sheet after her. She watched him shave, watched the tiny, brisk, intimate movements of blade across skin, the certainty of his hand.

I have committed adultery with this man, she thought, with a calm that she was able to regard with detached surprise. *For the first time in my life, I have known a man who is not Oliver*. She waited for the hot flush of guilt, but it didn't come. The fact that it didn't gave her something else to think about, apart from Harry's long, lean back and the stretched profile of his throat, as he scraped upwards towards his chin.

And when he looked into the mirror, she saw his eyes narrow in amused recognition of her gaze.

'Bugger,' he swore and dabbed at the blood that oozed from the nick in his neck, just where the high collar of his tunic would sit. 'D'you think the Queen will mind a bit of loo paper?'

291

Nell sat on the floor, her back propped comfortably against the wall. They were easy together, almost too relaxed for a man and a woman who had just seen each other naked for the first time. She anticipated just how he would twist his neck as he fastened the upright starched collar with its studs. She understood that the only way to get the narrow blue trousers on was to insert the boots into the legs first and then step into trousers and boots at the same time. She knew that he would take two or three attempts to pin the medal row precisely straight.

Everything had an awful familiarity. It was like watching Oliver.

When he was ready, he turned to her and smiled – and that gentle, awkward smile had a quality of innocence, strangely at odds with the greying hair and weathered skin, that wasn't a bit like Oliver's. He held out a hand and raised her from the floor, trailing the protective sheet, holding her nakedness tightly against the speckless dark blue of his uniform. The tiny, embossed parachute wing buttons reproduced themselves again and again on her flesh. There was a moment when she thought . . . when she seemed to remember a time . . . no, it was gone, it was nothing . . .

Yet that phantom memory left behind it an unexpected warmth, a feeling of safety, of security. It was like a hand reaching out to her across a gulf. *Take it. Hold it. I won't let you fall. Hold tight.*

'I don't want to leave you, but . . .'

'But you can't keep Her Majesty waiting,' she finished for him.

'As deputy, I have to be her escort now that . . .' He laughed delightedly, with a boyish sense of mischief. 'Now that Oliver can't be there!'

'It's all right. I've followed the drum long enough to understand that. Go on. It'll be a splendid parade.'

'You will still be here when I get back?'

'I don't know . . . I haven't thought . . . I haven't done any thinking at all since I walked out of Kabul House.'

'Stay here,' he urged. 'It's the only place that's safe. It's the one place he won't think of looking for you. You've got your reasons – I don't need to know them – but Oliver is going to take this county apart. You need to be absolutely certain what you're going to do next before you leave here. Besides . . . besides, I don't want you to go. We'll think of something, little Nell. When I come back. We'll sort it out.'

'But not now. I know. Go and do your duty. Go on – off you go.'

She kissed him lightly, not whining, not clinging. She was calm, sensible Nell again. She smiled as he clattered downstairs, sword rattling.

He stopped at the foot of the stairs and looked back up at her, still tousled, still naked. Her plump limbs were still rosy from the pressures of his own body. Her trusting smile was too heavy for him. He felt the weight of her reliance as much as he felt the physical weight of the metal and gold braid that adorned him. Responsibility? What else had he been

293

trained to handle all his adult life? But this time it was different. This time, responsibility and guilt were the matching burdens that Nell had brought with her, as though she had carried them in suitcases and dropped them at his feet.

'Be here,' he said.

She had gone long before he returned.

Hope had had a filthy day. She'd had to shuffle work rosters because chickenpox was scything through the local primary school and her workers were mothers first and cleaners second. Two of the vans had been in for service, so, of course, another broke down, leaving Hope to run a mad shuttle service all round the county. She'd picked up a useful little group of jobs, because a gunner regiment was moving to Germany, but she didn't have the transport to get her cleaners to Bulford on the most popular day. Ruth was still away from work – presumably Tim was still in bed with his face turned to the wall . . . God, no, that was bitchy, she didn't mean it, it wasn't his fault, he really felt ill, even if he wasn't – and the VAT inspectors suddenly decided they'd like to have a look at her accounts.

On days like this, Hope wondered why she hadn't just settled for a quiet, steady job when Chris had died. An income was what she had needed, not a challenge. A library would be nice, she thought. Or a nunnery. Better still, a mortuary. Somewhere hushed and peaceful. Somewhere she wouldn't be tormented by a mobile phone. Somewhere that the letters VAT simply meant a large barrel.

It was nearly nine o'clock that evening before she got home. By then, Nell had been sitting in her garden for a very long time.

'Christ! You gave me a scare. What're you sitting in the dark for?' Hope turned on the kitchen light, snapping the switch to show her irritation. Light sliced across the garden, as though a knife had cut a wedge out of the sky to let in the day. It reached Nell's feet as she sat on the bench, but left her body in comforting darkness. 'Nell? That is you, isn't it? Are you all right? What's wrong?'

Nell rose stiffly. Her arms and legs moved jerkily, as though she had been tied to the bench. 'Fine. Sorry. I didn't mean to scare you.'

Hope looked sharply at her as she came into range of the light beam. 'Doesn't matter. Come on in. Had any supper? I can rustle up an omelette or something.' From the fridge she brought two-thirds of a bottle of wine and divided the contents between two tumblers, pouring the major portion into Nell's.

Nell took the glass and clutched it as though it was holding her up.

'So?' Hope demanded, taking a slug from her own glass. It had been a hell of a day.

'I've committed adultery.'

'Is that all?' Hope gave a quick, sharp laugh. 'God, sorry. I mean, so it's not the end of the world . . . not murder.' Nell shook her head with a tremulous smile. The colour was coming back to her face. 'Not rape or pillage?' Hope continued. 'Not grand larceny?'

'Not that either.'

'Oh, well. There's hope for you yet. C'mon, sit down and tell me all about it. Sure you don't want anything to eat?'

Nell shook her head. 'I rather overdid it yesterday.'

'Mind if I do? After a day like today, what I really need is a big plate of stodge. Shepherd's pie would be lovely, but I suppose a lettuce leaf will do just as well.'

She scarcely had to move around the tiny kitchen to reach everything she wanted. Her busyness was comforting, somehow normal. She laid a place for herself at the kitchen table, opposite Nell. From the cupboard under the sink she produced another bottle and rummaged for the corkscrew.

'Might as well carry on as we've begun, I suppose. Hold out your glass. Right, I'll eat. You talk.'

Nell gave a soft, deprecating laugh. 'I got my priorities wrong. I should have said the most important thing first. I've left Oliver.'

That did give Hope a jolt. 'No! I always thought – well, you always looked like the perfect couple. Practically childhood sweethearts – the next best thing, anyway.'

'Twenty-five years. It's been a long time.' Nell mentally reviewed those years, but they all blurred together. One long sameness. Or was that the wine on an empty stomach?

'But what happened?'

'Nothing *happened*. That's the whole point. I'd had enough,' Nell said simply, then corrected herself. 'I've had enough.'

Hope recognized the sound of truth when she heard it. *She must have flipped. Women like Nell don't just walk out of their own lives. They never simply get bored, or tired, or want to be unmarried. They dig in their sharp little British bulldog teeth and hang on, for better or for worse and even worse. Unless something . . .*

Unless she knows. She must. But then why would she come here? Why isn't she scratching out my eyes? I would be. Dear God, don't let her have found out. I don't deserve that You should even be listening, but this isn't the time for selective deafness. Oliver is – is what I needed, for now, but not for ever. He's funny, sexy, gorgeous by any woman's standards. He makes me feel good. He makes me feel young again, wanted. And I think I do the same thing for him. We're suited in a way that's purely for now. Even tomorrow might be too long. It's different. Separate from ordinary living. A fantasy. How many years since the sound of the telephone bell could make me run to pick up the receiver? It's living. But not at the expense of hurting Nell.

That's what they all say, isn't it? The mistresses. The stealers of other women's husbands. *I didn't mean to hurt her.* So you carry around another woman's baggage, another woman's sensitivities. She is your burden. At times you feel her, as though she and not her husband owned the body weighting you down on your mattress.

And at some point you have to decide whether the pleasure is worth the accompanying backpack of guilt. You might just feel like dropping the lot and getting on with your own life again.

'. . . maybe something like this, not very big,' Nell was saying, 'somewhere I can just get on with my own life again. Hope, are you listening?'

'Sure. What else could I possibly be doing, when you're only three feet away?'

Nell looked around the kitchen at the junkshop cupboards painted by Chris long ago, yellow and blue and purple and green, gypsy caravan colours though chipped along each edge now. She saw the seed trays balanced on the windowsill, the black Rayburn with its soothing hiss. The little room was bright with assorted patterns – china and curtains and cushions in an old basket chair clashed and jostled for attention. Beyond the open window, honeysuckle ramped up an unpruned apple tree. Its perfume, stronger than the smell of Hope's omelette, was heartbreakingly sweet, heavy with memory.

'It's lovely. And it's yours, you see. I've never known what that's like. Everything in a married quarter had to be perfect and if something wasn't, I'd whip it into the Exchange Stores and swap it.'

'Some people do that with husbands!'

'If only . . . No really – I want to be able to drink out of chipped mugs because I like their pattern.' She laughed, a more natural sound than Hope had heard since she'd arrived. She sounded hopeful, eager, younger. 'Not exactly a world-shaking ambition! Still, it's a start.'

Hopelessly romantic. Poor, silly Nell. She had no idea. Life was tough on your own. It wasn't all thatched roofs and honeysuckle and quaint little kitchens. Like a Monopoly player, you dip into the Community Chest and pull out roof repairs or income tax payments or council tax assessments. Still, she'd find that out for herself soon enough.

'What else?' Hope encouraged.

'A spare bedroom, just a small one. I don't fool myself that Jessica and Jago will want to come and live with me – why should they? I won't have much to offer – but they might decide to visit me now and again. I hope.'

'And?' Hope prompted. She had to know.

'Oh, and a job, of course. There must be something I can do. Type? Scrub floors? I don't suppose you . . . ? No, of course not. Well, something, anyway. I have all sorts of skills.' Nell laughed shyly. Her skin was very flushed, a hectic red, appealing in a young girl, most unattractive in a middle-aged woman. But her spirit was strengthening all the time. She was beginning to believe in herself. 'You know what they are – you've been on the same treadmill. I can whip up a supper for forty people out of a tin of tuna and some condensed soup. I can spot a packet of OMO detergent – On My Own – in an other rank's kitchen window at a hundred paces and rush in and save a wife from sin. I can sort thrift shop offerings at a glance into pricey, worth a bob or two, and filthy rags. I can clean someone else's grotty oven while singing all the verses of the National Anthem. There must be a market for skills like that. D'you know – I haven't earned a penny since 1969. Do you suppose that's a record?'

'I didn't mean that. I meant – what about him?'

'Who?'

'*Him*, you goose. The man. Whoever . . . '

'Oh, I don't suppose I'll be seeing him again.'

Oh, God. More responsibilities. Had she driven Nell into the bed of a complete stranger, or some slimy married toe-rag?

'There are times . . .' Hope slammed both her hands palm down on the table. 'There are times when I could shake you till your teeth rattle!'

'What have I said?'

'Oh, come on! You met this man and hopped into bed with him and that's that. D'you expect me to believe that? It's just not you. We're supposed to be friends. You might trust me with the truth.'

'But I didn't say that. He's not just any man. What do you take me for? I'm not a whore. He's someone I've known for a long time and liked and . . .'

'And lusted after?'

'No. No. I don't think – I don't remember ever lusting after anyone, not even Oliver. I'm not like you, Hope. Sex doesn't come easily to me.'

'Well, thanks for making me feel like a slut.'

Nell leaned forward and took both Hope's hands in her own. Their grasp was firm and steady. She felt, Hope thought, stronger and stronger as they talked. She began to wonder who was comforting who, on this strange night when both women were pretending to be open, but each was keeping her own secret.

As the air chilled, the scent of the honeysuckle

became steely, a clean, pure smell that had lost the softness of early evening. A distant tawny owl shrieked and the answer came from so close by that both women jumped.

'Listen, Hope. You're strong and brave and determined. You know what you want and how to get it. You're not afraid of anyone. I'm a wimp. I'm not like you. But this time, I can be. I went to bed – once – with someone I like very much. And that's that. I shouldn't have done it. My only excuse is that I was feeling . . . alone.' She looked down and away, but not soon enough. Hope could see that she was fighting the tears. 'Tit for tat, you could say. Oliver's got someone. He's been pretty good at covering his tracks, but I know . . .'

Here it comes, thought Hope: *everything I deserve*. She braced herself. But she was wrong, this time, at least.

'But for me, it wasn't like that,' Nell continued. 'Not revenge. Not lust, either. Something better. Something special. Amazing.' She smiled, a sweet, remembering smile, and Hope had a glimpse of the depth of feeling that Nell seemed to have for the unnamed man. 'But wrong, all the same. I don't have to make things worse by doing it again.'

'And how does he feel?'

Nell looked as though she had just been asked the most unexpected question, as though the idea that the man had any feelings – had, indeed, any right to any feelings – had only just occurred to her. 'I don't know.'

'Does he care about you?'

'I don't know. But, Hope – oh dear, Hope – I'm scared that he might love me.'

Sometimes you drift apart; sometimes you argue; sometimes the breaking of a friendship is a kind of seismic rift from which you never really recover, however much you think you may have healed. When trust is broken, nothing is ever the same.

They sat in the kitchen most of the night. Every so often, Nell would say, 'I'm being so selfish. You've got to get up for work in the morning. Just tell me to shut up and go to bed.'

Yet she wouldn't move and Hope would say, 'Good idea. Come on. I'll show you your room. It's Lydia's, when she's at home, but she won't mind if you don't.'

But she wouldn't move either, except when the glasses needed refilling.

And Nell took her marriage apart and laid it out for inspection and Hope kept silent.

The gulf between them was as impassable as the shark-infested coconut matting in the gym at the officer selection board in Westbury. They'd had to pass over it, then, or fail. So they'd invented ingenious methods of crossing, involving ropes and oil drums and too-short planks and pulleys. Triumphantly, they'd reached the other side, carrying the mock casualty. But that had been long ago, when they were young.

Silence was more dangerous than sharks.

*   *   *

It might have been the wine. It might have been relief. Or reaction. Nell began to giggle.

'The perfect wife, military style. In approved wifely uniform, day and night. My God – I even wore a velvet Alice band for that man! Can you believe that? I can't believe myself sometimes.'

Hope lay very still and watched the square of her uncurtained bedroom window lighten to grey, then silver, then blue. The bars of lead around each pane divided the shape precisely, ruling neat lines between the bands of colour.

She heard the waking rustle of the doves perched on the windowsill. The feathers didn't sound soft. They snapped and rasped, like a pack of cards being shuffled.

She thought about the tough day she'd just had and about the one to come. She thought about her untrustworthy alarm clock, which would fail to alert her after she'd fallen asleep – as she would – half an hour before she ought to be rising.

She tried not to think about Oliver.

A dangerous man.

Hope tried to visualize his reaction when he found that Nell had gone. She shivered as she imagined that quiet savagery, that determination, that will to succeed all turned on Nell. The qualities that had taken him to the top so quickly were not qualities that would make a harmonious private life. But it had been seen as such. The image had been important to him. Generals had to be happily married. That was a prerequisite of the rank, the price of privilege. Conformity was part of the package.

Yet he must have loved Nell once. He had, she was certain. He must have wanted her, or why the phone calls, the visits, the outings, the pursuits of their cadet days? She remembered Oliver's intensity, Nell's shy smile when she saw him enter a room. And maybe, maybe – here Hope sat up and pummelled her pillow into reluctant submission – he loved Nell still in an absent-minded fashion. Losing her would be like losing a front tooth, losing a shadow, losing a mate, losing the soft side, the human side of his complex nature. Now that Nell had splintered his image of the conventional family, his fury would be terrible.

She shouldn't have done it, Hope thought, and, in that muddled, between sleeping and waking confusion, she wasn't quite certain whether she was thinking about Nell or about herself.

Hope shivered. And acknowledged with disgust and delight the dark, secret, innermost stirrings of desire. No point in pretending that the sex hadn't been good – as good as it gets, she admitted. But that was the by-product, for Hope, at least, if not for Oliver. The value, the point of it all had been – not to have a point at all.

She had waited, patiently, certain that he would come. It was like floating, like lying on a red rubber Lilo, bobbing along on the top of the waves, going where she was driven and, all the time, knowing that the next wave, or the one after that, or the one after that, would engulf her, knowing, too, that if she struggled, she would drown.

Of course he came. She never doubted that he would.

It was an end of summer thing. She was quite prepared to admit to that. Her personal summer had reached late August, maybe even early September. She felt like a dahlia, or a chrysanthemum, like the sort of flower she hated to see in her own garden, blowsy and floppy, perfumeless, prone to earwigs and liable to be blown over in a gale. Her days were growing short – she hadn't even noticed their passing until they had gone – and the long, long night was ahead.

Not very original, she thought. *It happens.* Supposing every woman did something about it when she realized that the swallows were gathering on the telephone lines. What a shuffling of partners there would be. Every suburban street would be a middle-aged sexual eightsome reel. Perhaps we all feel the ache, the sense of loss at the passing of youth, at the shortening of the days – only most of us don't do anything about it.

Not as far as she knew, anyway. But then there was Nell and her inexplicable admission of adultery. Had Nell, that most unlikely of adulteresses, had Nell, too, heard the twittering of the swallows?

If not Oliver, then someone. He had just been there, at the right moment, when Hope needed him. But she wished he had been almost anyone else. Only the truly heartless takes away a friend's tomorrows to lengthen her own today.

It wouldn't hurt her. I won't hurt her. We've been so careful, so discreet. Laughably so. She can't

305

*know. And if she does . . . if she does, well, Nell is
one of us now. No longer pure. No longer waiting
and watching. She has joined in the dance and must
change partners as often as the music changes. She
doesn't know, yet, that the dance goes on until her
shoes drop apart.*

But I won't hurt her if I can help it.

When she rose, late and puffy-eyed and stuffy-
headed, Nell was still sleeping. Hope looked in with
a cup of tea, but didn't have the heart to wake her,
so left the mug on the bedside table. It was there,
white-skimmed and unappetizing, when Nell opened
her eyes.

Nell would have woken earlier if she had known
that she wouldn't see Hope alive again.

Instead, she read the note that Hope had tucked
under the mug. *No need to go. Stay a bit and find
your feet. Lydia will be back tomorrow, but she can
doss down in a sleeping bag. Take Polly for a walk,
if you've got a moment.*

She found a scrappy heel of a loaf in the bread bin,
a couple of tea bags and some UHT milk at the
bottom of a carton. Hope obviously didn't believe in
the benefits of a nourishing breakfast. But there were
pots and pots of home-made marmalade glistening
along a pantry shelf. One of them was open. It had a
knife stuck messily into the rich amber jelly. Nell
acknowledged the brief image of Oliver at his neatly
set breakfast table, with the marmalade in a little
crystal dish and the folded *Daily Telegraph* flanking

306

his plate. She wondered how he would have coped if he'd married a woman like Hope. Absolute chaos. Everything he hated.

Then she wondered – but wouldn't allow herself to enlarge on the thought – whether breakfast would have been quite so important to him if he'd married a woman with a bit more zing in bed.

Had there really been a time when she'd flung an arm across Oliver's naked body, holding him back as he'd tried to rise? Had he ever turned the alarm clock face down as it rang, muffling its summons with a pillow? She noted automatically that Hope's fridge badly needed defrosting. Ice was pushing out the freezer compartment door. A four-pack of yoghurt bulged, seeping its fermenting contents.

Breakfast or exciting sex. They seemed to be mutually exclusive.

So she settled for a mug of tea, dunking the tea bag, dropping it into an overcrowded bin.

Hope might make a living cleaning other people's houses, she mused, but old habits die hard. The cottage reminded Nell of the next-door room that Hope had struggled to maintain to the orderly officer's satisfaction.

Good, though, the tea. Sitting under the apple tree made it taste a lot better. Nell clasped the mug in both hands, enjoying the ripples of the thrown pottery under her fingers, exploring the waviness of the rim with her tongue.

Good.

She stretched out her bare legs to catch the sun. Polly snuffled round her ankles, tickling with stiff, military-style whiskers. Nell scratched the little terrier behind the ears and was rewarded when Polly circled three times and flopped beside Nell on the grass.

She felt curiously empty. She had woken in the morning, blinking in muzzy confusion at the unfamiliar curtains and unrecognized pictures on the wall, and thought *Now I must be afraid, now I really have something to worry about*. And she had waited, expectantly. But the feeling had refused to appear.

Absence of emotion was alarming in itself, she found. As though something important was missing, something she was certain would be vital, if only she could remember what it was. She felt she ought to rush around and look for it, like searching for Jago's rugby boots on the first morning of term. He probably wouldn't have a games lesson for two or three days, but he *had* to have the boots. Now.

After a while, however, she grew used to the untenanted spaces within herself. Smooth and glacial they stretched, untouched, unmarred, with no clutter in the corners. Her mind bore no footprints. She felt it grow spartan and strong.

No-one is going to make any demands on me today, she thought, in some wonder; *no-one is going to want anything from me. Ever again*. And if the words wandered rather forlornly around the space, Nell ignored their echo.

The first thing I'll do is get my hair cut. No more bloody Alice bands. And the second thing I'll do is . . . well, I'll make a list, of course. I'll just have some more tea and start a list while the kettle's boiling.

And that's how Isa found her, with the back door wide open and probing beams of sunlight examining the neglected corners of Hope's rainbow-bright kitchen. Nell hunched over the kitchen table, staring at a piece of paper headed THINGS TO DO, while the dry kettle popped and banged on the Rayburn hotplate.

Isa leaned over Nell's shoulder. '*Item number one,*' she suggested, '*Stop kettle melting.*'

'Oh, my God . . .' Nell lost her pencil and grabbed at the kettle. 'Oh, my God . . .' she said again, louder, when she'd dropped the crackling kettle into the sink and run cold water onto it. A volcano of steam erupted, engulfing her face and hands in scalding clouds.

'You're not safe to be left on your own, Nell,' Isa remarked, when she'd checked Nell's hands for burns – only superficial – and put her back in a chair in the garden. 'I'm surprised Oliver doesn't lock you away and only let you out with a bodyguard.'

'Why not a ball and chain?' Nell suggested, stiffly. 'Since everyone knows that I'm such a pathetic creature I can't even be trusted to boil a kettle.' She blew on her fingers and shook them in the air. 'In fact, I wouldn't be surprised if he had turned out the guard to ransack Salisbury Plain for me.'

'Hey – Nell, dear – it was only a joke.'

'Then – *frankly*, Isa dear – your sense of humour stinks. Anyway, I wasn't joking. I've left Oliver.'

'What?'

'I've left Oliver,' Nell repeated, stubborn and defensive.

'At last . . . No, don't look so surprised. I'm not – surprised, that is. Well, only that you didn't do it years ago.'

'What are you talking about?'

'Well, I mean, after all . . . I'm sorry, Nell, but after all Oliver is a bit of a bastard.'

'I've been married to that bastard, as you call him, for twenty-five years and had two . . . three . . . two children with him.'

Nell sucked her fingers and hated Isa for that casual dismissal.

'Sure, sorry. None of my business. No, I mean it. Sorry. Anyway, I came to see Hope.'

'She's out, of course, working. You won't find her at this time of day. She has a living to earn. The real world isn't like the army, you know. You can't just skive off work to go to the bank or pop round to see a friend on the off-chance.'

'OK, OK. I just wondered. I don't suppose Lydia's in, is she? By any chance?'

Cool Isa. So casual, so right for any occasion. The perfect touch. Nell looked at the well-pressed black jeans, the perfect white shirt, the well-cut ash blond hair, gossamer silky – if there was any grey, she couldn't see it – and wasn't fooled by Isa's relaxed air.

'Lydia isn't here,' she said, warily. 'You know what the young are like these days. Always busy. Never have time to clock in at home. I don't suppose Hope sees her all that often now.'

'No. Of course not. I don't suppose she does. I just wondered. You know. She might have been . . .'

'I know exactly what you wondered, Isa.' The natural softness of Nell's voice maddened her. She could never sound angry enough, never sound as fierce as she felt. But, oh God, she meant every word. 'Leave her alone. Leave them both alone. They don't need you. What's past is past.'

'I know that,' Isa replied, calmly enough, but Nell noticed that her eyes were ranging the bedroom windows, wondering, checking. Just in case.

'What's the good? What's the point? After all these years? Think of the distress you'll cause.'

'I don't know why you're getting yourself all steamed up like that, Nell.' Isa soothed her as though she was a not very bright child. 'I've no intention of causing a scene. I simply want to pop in and say hello in a civilized fashion. Where's the harm in that?'

'Isa, you promised.'

Isa looked at her then, pale eyes frosted and snapping, eerily like Oliver's. Nell shivered.

'I promised nothing,' Isa whispered.

Director of Service Intelligence. It sounds very hush-hush, Isa mused, as though I might be a spymaster, someone from the pages of John le Carré or Ian Fleming. Nothing so glamorous.

She wound down the car window an inch or so to clear the glass. Drizzle drifted through the opening, beading her lashes, turning her hair into a gilded spider's web.

Dull mostly. Routine paperwork, too much of it. Decisions to be made, but none of them world-shaking. Responsibility without power. Priorities to be assigned. Meetings to be attended. Budgets to be planned and agreed. No Cold War to keep us all on our toes.

Hardly Mata Hari stuff.

None of it had prepared her for sitting in a car on a misty evening, covertly watching a house. A friend's house. And there was no-one at home.

Briefly, she acknowledged a sense of shame, but it was no more lasting than the stabbing charge that attacks sensitive teeth in contact with ice cream. The ice cream is worth the shock. Outlast that momentary discomfort and you receive your reward. Isa's guilt was as instant and as easily overcome.

It must be pretty easy to keep an eye on someone in a city. How simple to be an anonymous watcher in a swirling mass of people. All those doorways to skulk in and windows to gaze at. The excitement of reflections in the glass. Here, in a village, she felt both conspicuous and vulnerable. Her car was pulled into a convenient layby opposite and a few houses further north than Hope's cottage. The sporty little 4x4 looked too clean for the country lane, as exotic, amongst the mud-splattered Land Rovers, as an albino in a flock of crows. But if she moved the car and walked back on foot, perhaps to sit on the bench encircling a horse chestnut that stood in the centre of a little triangle of rough grass, she would be as good as naked.

She had wondered whether it might have been

safer to set up a covert watch from the abandoned railway line, used now as a cycle track, that ran along the back of Hope's garden. She would have been unseen, might have set up a camouflaged hide amongst the elder bushes that bordered the track. With dark clothing and some good field glasses . . . After all, what had been the point of all those uncomfortable training exercises when she was younger, if she never got the chance to put theory into practice?

She'd given the idea serious consideration before rejecting it. It was too military, too laughable, too . . . too safe.

She looked at the clock on the car dashboard. How long would it be before a zealous Neighbourhood Watch member called the police?

She hadn't thought it through, she acknowledged. She hadn't thought at all, actually. She had simply acted. That impulsiveness was entirely foreign to her. It made her nervous. She recognized the emergence of an emotion that had been absent for as long as she could remember. All her life – almost – she had had a reason for doing something. If she had deviated from her own strictly organized lifestyle at any time, she had regretted it sooner or later.

Control, control. That was the answer. Keep your tabs on every detail. Facts at your fingertips. Don't let things slip. Be certain. Be in command. Or else. Or else what?

Mike, the one fling, the one womanly indulgence in a career in which she had had to out-man the men, to be, if not stronger, then quicker, sharper, cleverer, more ruthless . . . Mike had made her feel like a woman and a desirable one, too, beneath the collar and tie. Without thinking, without planning, she had fallen in love with Mike, not because he was good looking, not even because he was particularly kind – he had been, still was, she could admit to herself now, a bit of a shit – but because he made her feel whole.

Then, when she was at her most vulnerable, he had recoiled from her mutilated self and gone back to Henrietta. A lesson learned, she told herself, a valuable lesson: planning and purpose are vital; emotion is messy and not to be trusted.

So here she was, sitting in the dusk in a car in a layby, all messed up with inconvenient emotions and not feeling at all tough. She hadn't thought things through again and the feeling made her nervous, as though the ground was sliding away from her feet.

She tried to look as though she might be consulting a map. Then she put away the map book and leaned back against the headrest, the weary motorist snatching a quick snooze before setting off up the A338, northwards. But she was watching the rearview mirror and Hope's cottage. And waiting.

So when Lydia came . . . *Oh, God, it's her, what do I do, what shall I say? Damn, damn, damn, she's not alone.*

Isa thumped the rim of the steering wheel with clenched fists.

She watched Lydia get out of the passenger door

314

of a black Golf. No mistaking her. The blond crop
was spiky, clipped savagely around an elegant skull.
Black Lycra clung to a body that was still angular,
with much of the heart-wrenching supple awkward-
ness of youth. From the confines of the little car, she
unfolded knees and elbows with all the grace of an
unfolding origami sculpture. The young woman's
heritage shrieked out to Isa. How *could* this girl
imagine that she was Hope's daughter?

Isa's eyesight seemed to have been unnaturally
sharpened, as though she circled, a waiting bird of
prey, high above the cottage, alert for every betray-
ing movement. She saw that Lydia dangled frail
silver spiders' webs from her ears and that she
wore a silver nose stud. Isa frowned. Tacky. Hope's
influence, of course. She'd always had exhibitionist
tendencies. Even in uniform, she'd managed to look
like a gypsy. Didn't this girl know that she was too
beautiful to hang these tawdry decorations about
herself?

Her daughter. Not Hope's. And Hope was trying
to keep them apart.

Lydia banged into the house and came out a few
minutes later, carrying a bulging backpack. The
young man got out from the driver's seat to throw
the backpack into the rear. Isa barely registered
him. She saw only that he was young and slight and
dark. She saw his hand run familiarly down the long
curve of Lydia's back. She saw Lydia cup his face in
one hand, sensed the rasp of dark stubble on her
own fingertips, imagined the firmness of the lips that
Lydia brushed briefly.

315

And then they were gone, heading north, without a glance in the direction of Isa's waiting car. The house was empty again.

Normal. Living a life without her. Not needing her. Not knowing or caring.

Twenty-five years.

Isa hungered. The impact of the feeling left her weak. *Not thinking again*, she told herself. *You've gone blind into this and look what's happened*. When once – last week, last month, last year – she had wanted to see, just to see Lydia to satisfy a vague, irrational craving, now that she had seen her . . . oh, now she needed to know her. Now she needed to talk, to touch, to hear, to smell.

To embrace? Too early for that. Too overbearing. Too paperback romance. But, yes. One day soon. Before it was too late. You can't just barge up to a grown woman and say *OK, forget everything you've ever believed, I'm your mother, so love me*. These things take time. But Isa didn't have time.

Isa had a pain. But it wasn't the usual sort, the sort that could be – barely – kept under control (for how much longer? she wondered). This was different. This was a dull, insistent ache, located, unaccountably, in her guts. It had arrived in tow with a fluttering panic, the kind you get after four or five mugs of strong black coffee, the panic that hangs around and fills you with foreboding on even the brightest day.

Isa was losing control and she hated it.

'My daughter,' she said, experimentally, trying

the words for fit. They sounded good. They fitted comfortably around her teeth and tongue. 'My daughter, Lydia.'

She could introduce her like that, quietly, without obvious pride, but everyone who knew her would sense the underlying emotion.

Jesus Christ, Hope, I gave you everything. Can't you give me just a little in return?

Oh God, it hurt. It hurt so much.

Dusk fell too soon on this late summer evening darkened by low cloud and drizzle. Lights flicked on in a few of the cottages, but Hope's was dark. Time to move. On a sunny evening, she would have been more conspicuous to people at work in their gardens, but even in this miserable weather, she must have been noticed. The most exhausted traveller must have finished snoozing by now. Isa was cramped and stiff. She switched on the ignition, but delayed a moment before turning the engine, taking a last look in her rearview mirror.

Hope's little red van turned into the gateway. Isa watched Hope lock the van, open her kitchen door. She watched the light flick on in the kitchen. And still she didn't fire her engine. She saw Hope come out again almost immediately with a dog lead in her hand and Polly pattering along beside her, sharp black claws clicking on the pavement. They passed right by her without looking into the car.

Hope never looked, never sensed the gaze that followed her, never felt the emotion that had built up like an aura around the vehicle. Isa went to roll down the window, but she stopped with her hand on the button.

She watched Hope and Polly turn right onto the footpath that led to the canal. Then, locking the car carefully, she followed at a discreet distance.

1994–5

A time to die . . .

Lydia wasn't certain when the sound of the telephone bell changed into the sound of the doorbell.

'Mum's left her key again,' she said to herself and called, 'It's open.'

Then came the misery of remembrance.

It was often like that. You'd think it wasn't possible to forget, that there never would be a moment again when she could think about her mother in the present tense. But she did and when the real present, the present without her, intruded, the loss became fresh and new and unbearable all over again.

'It's normal, love,' Daniel would say, stroking the spikes of her hair that lay down flat these days, too miserable to be aggressive. 'Everyone feels like that. It takes time.'

'How long?'

'I don't know,' he admitted. 'But it has to get better.'

'How do you know?' she'd demand, sitting up and pushing away his comforting arms. 'Maybe I don't have enough time left.' She was a curled, miserable hedgehog of a girl, her head on her bent knees, her arms wrapped defensively around the back of her neck and he couldn't reach her.

So after a while he stopped offering rejected words of comfort and, a while after that, he stopped offering physical comfort, too.

She'd let him read the letters, piles of them, too many to answer.

'All these people,' she'd said. 'They thought they knew my mother. But no-one did. Not even me. Me least of all.'

Daniel sifted helplessly through the sheets of paper. The sight depressed him. The words of comfort left him with a bloated, overindulged feeling.

'It's as though, as though . . .' Lydia swept the letters into a box, mixing up page numbers – a sheet from someone who had known her parents in Germany in the Seventies, a sheet from someone who had worked for Hope when Lydia was a baby, a sheet from an ex-soldier who remembered her father (father?) from a long-ago posting – hopelessly muddling Daniel's attempt to fold them neatly and insert each back into its appropriate envelope. '. . . give me those . . .' She snatched back the last few pages, leaving a corner of blue Basildon Bond still between Daniel's finger and thumb. '. . . as though they've tried to pin her down with words, turn her into a verbal icon, give her all these attributes she never really had. She was human. Sometimes she'd be a real shit, especially – you know – in the morning. Just like me. And sometimes she'd fall asleep in the kitchen, because she'd worked all day and half the night. And then she'd say *What's the point of waking me up to tell me to go to sleep?* Then she'd chase me upstairs. And sometimes we'd both laugh about the silliest things. And she'd never let anyone – not a teacher or anyone – come down heavy on me if she didn't think I deserved it. And I could tell her anything and know she wouldn't be shocked. And now I've got no-one.'

You've got me, Daniel wanted to say, but the sentiment was so trite and the unstrung floppiness of her body so alarming that he didn't dare utter the words.

After a while, he didn't look for chances to say them.

Now she doesn't belong to me any more, Lydia thought. *There was before, when I had a mother, even though she was dead. I was an orphan, a grown-up orphan, and people understand what that means. Those letters were sent to that person, Hope's daughter. But Hope's daughter doesn't exist. And then there was after, when she'd been taken away from me. When she turned into Hope Strickland, television big name, public property, victim. She never had me and I never had her. Not really.*

All those long-ago jovial comments made sense at last. Visitors would look at Hope's tangled rusty frizz and then at Chris's thinning brown strands and they'd maybe raise one of Lydia's thick silver-gilt plaits and say, with a heavyweight twinkle, 'And whose little girl are you? The milkman's?'

'Oh, no,' Lydia would say seriously. 'I'm only my mummy and daddy's little girl.'

And she'd join in the laughter that didn't really seem very funny.

Because it was true. She didn't belong to anyone.

By the time she realized that the sound of the phone bell had been replaced by the sound of the doorbell, the caller had given up ringing and was thumping on the door.

'Lydia? Open up. It's me.'

'Daniel?'

'Who else? For Christ's sake, let me in.'

'It's not locked.'

'Are you mad?' Daniel banged the door behind him harder than he needed to and made a point of turning the key in the lock. 'You're sitting here alone in the dark and the door's not locked?'

'Why should it be? My mother never locked the door.'

'Yes, and look what . . .'

And he ground down into silence. They both knew what he had nearly said. The unspoken words shocked Daniel almost as much as the sight of Lydia sitting on the floor, surrounded by the stirred-up contents of a cardboard box. Polly lay on a pile of photos, with her pink-freckled tummy turned towards a feeble fire. The cut ends of the logs were fizzing damply with a sound like frying sausages. No warmth reached the far side of the rug where Lydia crouched. She'd pulled a table lamp onto the floor as close as its lead would allow and removed the shade to light her rooting.

'You weren't going to come,' she stated, as a fact not a question.

'You banned me from the funeral,' Daniel answered softly, 'not from the rest of your life.' He looked pointedly at the bottle of vodka that stood, open, on the tiled floor beside Lydia. The level hadn't dropped too far yet, he noted with some relief. 'Look at you. When did you last eat?'

'Oh, you know – ham sandwiches and sherry in the village hall. The girls at Houseproud Cavalry insisted, said it would be disrespectful to my mother's memory not to and I couldn't let them down. Why? Are you hungry? There might be some tins in the kitchen. Soup or tuna or something.'

'I'm all right. You're not.'

Daniel squatted on the rug beside Lydia. He took her chin gently in one hand and turned her face towards the harsh light. The bare bulb threw strong shadows along one side of her nose. Her fair brows and lashes merged into the skin colour. Underlit, her face was all bare planes and hollows, like one of the scary faces children love to make with a torch under the chin.

'When are you coming home?' Daniel asked.

'I am home.'

Daniel sighed, trying to be patient, trying to be understanding, trying to be all the things he wasn't naturally intended to be.

'You know what I mean. I miss you.'

'I miss you,' she responded automatically. It was

one of the things you said. Just good manners. *Always be polite*, Hope used to say. *It costs you nothing.* Not true, of course. Sometimes it cost you your integrity. Like now. Daniel was calmed by her answer, so it had been the right thing to say – right for him and wrong for her.

'Then why not come back with me tonight? Put all that stuff in the box and take it with you. You can sort it out later.'

'There's Polly. She can't live in a flat.'

'Then – oh, I don't know – find a kennels or something. A friendly neighbour. Isn't everyone in the country supposed to be supportive and caring? I'll stay tonight and help you look for somewhere in the morning. We can be back in London by the middle of the day.'

Lydia shuffled backwards on her bottom across the rug, away from Daniel and towards Polly. Her face was beyond the range of the light. Now the beam was concentrated on her hands. They lay very still in her cross-legged lap, fingers interlaced, knuckles white.

'I'm not going back yet.'

'Oh, Christ, you can be stubborn when you want to.' Daniel poured a shot of vodka into the dumpy tumbler Lydia had been using. It went down like water. 'OK, OK, I'm sorry. I know it's been dreadful for you . . .'

'You don't know,' she said, softly and firmly. 'You have no idea.'

'. . . but a funeral is – is a sort of tidying up, don't you see. Last page of the book. Tying off the threads. And all that sort of symbolic crap. It's over. Now it's time to start again.'

'But that's what I'm doing. You want me to go back to what I was before. And I can't. I want to go forwards, not backwards.'

Daniel sighed again. He balanced the glass on the sloping floor, tried to come closer, tried to put a sympathetic arm around Lydia's narrow shoulders. She repelled him. There was a sort of force field around her. She was untouchable, straight-backed and formidable. He got nowhere near her.

'Look, everyone at work knows you've had a rough time. They're all sorry you've lost your mother, really sorry. But you've got a job to go back to, you know, and they won't keep it for ever. Human Resources rings the flat every evening to check. Like, the queue outside the door for vacancies gets longer every day. So if you're not back sitting in your chair soon, you might find someone else in it when you do decide to reappear.'

'I know.'

'And you don't care?'

'I care about something else more. Maybe . . .' And she genuinely believed that she hadn't thought this thought before, that it had, just now, arrived in her brain without preparation. 'Maybe I don't want to go back. Maybe I'll just stay here.'

She leaned over and pushed Polly gently, rolling the terrier off the pile of photos. Polly grunted and snapped with unconvincing ferocity. Lydia rummaged for a moment, then held out one of the pictures to Daniel.

327

He saw five women – girls, younger than Lydia now – in a dated, stuffy uniform, three seated, two standing behind. The poignancy of their soft youthfulness inside the hard shells reached out from the half-tones of the print across a quarter of a century, even to Daniel. They all looked at the camera with wary expressions, as though they expected the firing squad to come marching round the corner. Their shoes were immense, Minnie Mouse like. Their names were neatly typed on slips of paper stapled to the bottom of the print: Vernon; Blakeney; Cleeve; Tedder; Cameron.

'I wanted to show you this. One of them might be my mother.'

'I know that. There in the back row. The one with hair like a haystack. She didn't change much, did she?'

'But I don't mean Hope . . .'

Murder victim Hope Strickland, battered to death while walking her dog, was today buried at her home village church. Six weeks after her death, police admit that there has been little progress in the case. In an effort to jog the memories of possible witnesses, police today re-released a taped reconstruction of Hope's last walk, with her Border terrier Polly, from her thatched home towards the canal towpath where her body was found. One villager reported a white car which he said had been parked for some hours in a layby near the cottage, but is unable to remember the model or to give a description of any person in it. Police urge the driver of this

328

car to come forward so that he or she may be eliminated from their inquiries.

There followed a telephone number on a blue background of mingled shadowy figures, telephones and flashing lights. Daniel had watched the local news report, transfixed by the grieving face of Lydia, as she had followed the coffin through the lych gate of St Andrew's. She had seemed stunned, vacant, shrink-wrapped, a husk of the vibrant girl she ought to have been.

'I should have been there. I should have been with her. Why wouldn't she let me come?' he questioned.

Then he had watched further, appalled now, as a woman who looked nothing like Hope had walked, trailing a reluctant Polly, along a muddy track towards the towpath. Polly seemed to know where she was going. She dug her little paws into the mud as the woman tried to imitate Hope's usual jaunty stride.

It was a travesty. Who could possibly connect this laboured scene with Hope's last evening stroll? Daniel wanted to shout at the screen, 'Don't be ridiculous. She was nothing like that. You're just wasting time . . .' He thought wildly about phoning the television company to complain. 'You're hurting her,' he would say. 'Let her forget.' Then he heard Lydia's footsteps on the stairs and quickly switched off the television. But he still looked oddly, illogically guilty when she reappeared.

They came one by one, each bearing gifts in kind, like pilgrims bearing votive offerings to a shrine.

*　　*　　*

'Hi, I'm Ruth. I used to work for your mother.'

The woman was tall and gaunt. She stooped below the low door that Lydia held reluctantly open and entered the kitchen. She looked as though she'd come straight from work. There was a sort of I-last-brushed-my-hair-eleven-hours-ago look about her that Lydia found endearing. She hadn't tried to make an impression. She'd just come to do what she thought was right. The problem was that Lydia didn't want to become anyone's charitable intent.

'I came to see if you were all right.'

'I'm all right,' Lydia replied abruptly.

And all the time she was watching and assessing. *Is it this one?* She watched the movement of the head, its balance, the angle of the neck, the way Ruth's elegant, work-worn hands were used naturally to emphasize her comments. She saw the quirk of her lips, the way Ruth folded them in a positive way when she had finished a statement.

Do I do that?

Is there anything of me there? Is there a clue, a suggestion of a shared gene pool?

She listened critically to the way Ruth said the word *mother*. She didn't really listen to what Ruth was saying.

'I should have come much earlier. I don't like to think of you being on your own, with memories – sorry – well, it must seem lonely.'

'We're fine. Polly and me. We're fine.'

330

'I would have come . . .' Ruth was too tall for the kitchen. Her head hung below the beams in a way that made her seem unnecessarily apologetic '. . . but my husband hasn't been too well. He's – to be frank, he's impossible – I don't know how we . . . but it's not his fault. He's disabled and he finds it hard to accept. He used to be so fit, you see, a skier and a climber, so . . . and now, I find I hardly dare leave the house without worrying whether he'll do something . . . final. But I'm not making excuses. I ought to have come sooner.'

Lydia made up her mind and stopped staring. 'Would you like some coffee? I expect I could . . . somewhere . . . there must be . . .'

She stared helplessly in the direction of the cupboards, as though she knew perfectly well that they were nearly empty. Ruth looked carefully at Lydia. 'Yes. That would be nice. There are things we need to talk about.'

Ruth watched Lydia rinse out a couple of mugs from the dirty pile in the sink. There was a scraping of coffee in the bottom of a jar. They shared a teaspoon between them.

'Milk's off, I'm afraid,' Lydia announced, sniffing at the top of a jug, then pouring the contents into Polly's bowl. 'She won't mind, though.'

'I like it black,' said Ruth. 'You're . . . you're quite different from my imagination, Lydia. Sharper, somehow. Brittle. And thin. Not that it's my business. But are you eating?'

'Oh, yes. Like a pig. Spider-legs, Daniel calls me. He's my partner.'

'And is he staying with you?' Ruth's enquiries were too mild to be considered intrusive, but sufficiently determined to ferret out the answers she wanted.

'No, we have a flat in Battersea. He couldn't stay away from his job for too long.' Lydia stirred and stirred her coffee, but Ruth hadn't noticed that she'd put any sugar into the mug. 'He's in hospital administration.'

'That's . . . er, interesting,' Ruth answered brightly. 'Lydia, we need to talk about something rather important.'

Useful, Lydia might have answered at another time, *when you want to get hold of a forensic report.* But she didn't say it. She was too busy wondering about what Ruth was going to say next.

Is this it? Is this the moment?

'It's about the Houseproud Cavalry . . .'

'I see.'

'Things haven't been going too well since Hope – since we lost Hope. The bank has been paying minimum wages, of course, and we've been ticking over, but that's all. Almost zero cash flow now. There's no-one taking decisions. There's no-one going out and getting new business. And, frankly, it's not looking good.' She paused, obviously waiting for some sort of response from Lydia. When the wait grew embarrassingly long, she continued. 'It's all yours now and, of course, you must do as you wish, but I wonder . . . would you let me take on some sort of managerial role? I wouldn't make any big decisions without you, no changes, but it's day-today managing that's needed. I could make it work again.'

Her voice trailed away on an upward, optimistic beat. The longing in it was unbearable. Lydia looked down at her grubby coffee mug.

'I was thinking of selling.'

'Selling! Yes, I see. Of course you are. I should have realized . . . I wasn't going to ask for any more money, you know. I'd do it for the same.'

'I mean, it's no use to me.'

'No, of course. But Lydia, have you thought how many people used to depend on Hope. And now they depend on you. They *need* you.' She looked at Lydia, reaching across the table, trying so hard to convey the message that her words were failing to do. 'We're all hard-working people. We wouldn't be any trouble to you – really.'

'That's not a responsibility I'd enjoy.'

'*I* need you, Lydia. I'm forty-four years old, I've got three children still at school, a husband who spends his waking hours looking forward to the next dose of painkiller and I need a job. Is that plain enough? I'm begging. OK?'

Lydia drew an idle pattern in spilled coffee – a meandering maze, but once she had drawn it she saw that she had given it no exit at all. And all the time, she thought she could hear the frightened, erratic beat of Ruth's heart.

She was being cornered, forced into a role that didn't suit her, and all because of the frayed web of connections that strung Hope and Ruth and Nell and Isa and Juliet together. And now Lydia. What had they to do with Lydia? They were ancient history. The line had been severed, but still she was expected to carry Hope's burden because it was there, because she was there, because . . .

Is it you? Are you the one?

Hope wouldn't have let Ruth down.

'I really do have to sell, but, I suppose, until then . . . you could, you know, keep things going, keep it hot.'

She tried to disguise the resentment in her voice, but Ruth was sensitive to it.

'Oh, yes. Yes, I could. I could make it work for you.'

'And a going concern sells much better than a dying one.'

'Exactly. It's best for you, as well as everyone else.' Like a flower battered by autumn gales, Ruth leaned to kiss Lydia's cheek. 'It's the right decision.'

As she rose, Ruth's eye was caught by a photograph pinned to a cork board on the back of a cupboard. She put on little half-moon glasses and bent again to look at it.

'How extraordinary,' she said quietly. 'I used to think that none of us had changed a bit, but now I see that we've changed almost beyond recognition.' She straightened, still keeping her head bent in the gap between the ceiling beams. 'I'm not certain if they were happy times, but they were certainly interesting.'

What must it be like to be so desperate, Lydia wondered when Ruth had gone. How must it feel to beg someone twenty years younger than you for a job that you've been doing perfectly well for years anyway?

What was she getting involved in? It had never been part of her life plan to own a domestic cleaning company. The idea was absurd. Daniel would think she had really lost the plot. For heaven's sake, she was young, she had a good job (still had one, she hoped), she had a flat with a joint mortgage, commitments. She had it all worked out. So how did she find herself saddled with the welfare of a gaggle of middle-aged people she didn't even know?

Juliet came to the front door. It seemed more appropriate, somehow, for a visit of condolence. She'd decided not to look too formal – it might be intimidating for the poor child. So she just smartened up the trousers and shirt she was wearing with a Daks jacket, some big gold earrings and a dash of makeup. About right, she thought, the proper touch. Casual and smart. She had, after all, a position to keep up.

She was shocked when she saw Lydia, though. The door opened stiffly, as though it hadn't been used for some time. Weddings and funerals, Juliet thought irreverently, typical working class. She was assailed by the image of Hope's coffin passing through the door and was still shuddering when Lydia managed to scrape the door back on a dragging hinge.

'My dear,' began Juliet impulsively.

Then she stopped. Good lord, the child looked

positively anaemic. Probably the result of all that black. All the young wear black these days, of course, but there's black and then there's *black*. And that fearful hair. The spikes were growing out and the result was much like a road casualty animal. And the colour – it couldn't be natural. She remembered Isa's ash blond, but Lydia's must have been chemically aided to reach that ice-touched gold.

She tried again. 'My dear child, I'm so sorry. Of course, I wrote . . .'

'Did you?' Lydia answered vaguely. 'So many people did.'

'Oh, yes. I did. At once. I'm Juliet Cottrill. You'll remember me, I imagine. I was a great friend of your mother and I remember *you* when you were . . . well, terribly tiny.'

Is this the one?

Such a neat little cat person, a little black cat with a little pink mouth and such sharp white teeth. Nothing there that spoke to Lydia at all. But how would she know?

Juliet aimed herself through the door before Lydia had a chance to invite her in. The room was very dark – spooky, Juliet thought – with tiny leaded windows and grim ceiling beams that very probably hid a monstrous regiment of spiders. And just look at that dust billowing around in the sunbeams. It only took a flash of sun to show up your housekeeping. *Not* the sort of place to encourage recovery from an unhappy event. Juliet made up her mind on the spot.

'I've come to invite you to stay with us,' she said.

'Now don't even *dream* of refusing. It's absolutely no trouble and the least I can do.'

'Why?'

'Why?'

'When people say *It's the least I can do*, they're usually trying to make up for something they've done wrong.'

Juliet was momentarily thrown by Lydia's level stare. It was as though – as though she was trying to look beyond the now, as though she was trying to catch a glimpse of something just beyond the range of her vision. It was unnerving.

'Well, I don't really think that I have any need to put the past behind me. *My* conscience is clear,' she said firmly. 'So you can get rid of that idea right now. The offer's there. Take it or leave it. But if I were in your shoes, I'd welcome a little normal family life. I can guarantee that you won't be badgered by that ghastly daughter of mine. Oh, I don't mean it, of course. She's really quite a sweetie, in her own way, but she'd die if she thought I said so. Now, tell me . . .' She sidestepped Lydia and went on into the kitchen, stopping to stare incredulously at the dirty dishes and the open empty tin of Chappie. 'Who's looking after you?'

'I don't need looking after. I'm not a child.'

'Oh, my dear, I remember exactly how old you are. All I mean is that when you've – lost a loved one . . .' She made it sound as inconvenient as losing a glove. '. . . you need a little pampering. I prescribe light nourishing meals, fresh air and plenty of sleep. And I'm a doctor's daughter and a doctor's wife, so

I ought to know what I'm talking about.' She held out both hands, appealing, irresistible. How could Lydia say no? 'Now *do* say you'll come. Hope would have wanted it. Come for your mother's sake.'

Lydia opened her mouth to shout *She wasn't my mother!* Instead, she said, 'Thank you. I'll remember that. At the moment I'm quite comfortable.'

Although the words were mild, they were spoken with a firmness that convinced even Juliet that she hadn't made her point. Juliet turned, defeated, and her eye caught the photo pinned to the cork board.

'Oh, look!' she squealed, as though she had made the discovery and Lydia had no idea it was there. 'It's us. Oh, aren't we young. Just babies. I think that was taken on our first day in uniform. It was a Saturday morning and I know I was dying to pop into Camberley in the afternoon and spend my princely wages, but the photographer took absolutely ages. Who would have guessed that little more than a year later we'd all be married. Except Isa, of course. Mad. Oh, well. Happy days. I think!'

Was that the one?

God, I hope not.

Nell came carrying her guilt.

She timed her arrival for the Sunday that Daniel came down. He'd brought with him a bag full of goodies from Harvey Nichol's fifth floor, little tempting things that even the most queasy stomach might be persuaded to eat: stuffed vine leaves, rolled no larger than Lydia's little finger; yoghurt completely unlike anything that came from a plastic

338

tub, delicately coloured green by chopped mint leaves; tiny flaky pastry rounds stuffed with minced chicken; marble-sized meat balls; fragrant tabouleh; alpine strawberries that must have cost each as much as whole punnets of wishy-washy Spanish ones. And he brought champagne and managed to persuade Lydia to sit in the garden with a glass, while he arranged a table for two under the apple tree.

He achieved what he set out to achieve. Lydia smiled and ate and was as nearly normal as she had been for a long time.

I'm winning, he thought. *She's coming out of it. I knew she would get better once the funeral was over. It's been hanging over her head for far too long. Now we can go forward.*

Afterwards she took his hand as he led her, as thoughtfully as he might lead a virgin bride, upstairs.

Then Nell arrived. Daniel heard her calling, an uncertain voice from the kitchen.

'Christ, do you never lock your door?' he asked, irritably.

Lydia swung her legs out and sat on the edge of the bed. Daniel saw with shock the ridges of her spine, like grooves on a washboard. Her shoulder blades were like budding wings and the tops of her arms scarcely thicker than below her elbow.

With just the tip of a finger, he touched her backbone. Her skin was cold.

'Hey,' he said, 'stay there, keep warm. I'll go down and scare her off. Shall I go down like this? She'd run a mile!'

He stood naked in the centre of the room, barefooted on bare boards, caught in a sunbeam, with his arms outspread and his legs apart. Each of the black hairs on his body seemed to have a life of its own, springing and curling and holding the light. His erection had not been tamed by the interruption. Rather, he seemed even more exuberant.

Lydia stared. Unexpectedly, she felt a bubble of happiness rising, breaking into a giggle and then bursting before it had time to become a full-blown laugh. He was vibrant and beautiful and, at this time and in this place, altogether wrong.

'I'll go,' she said, pulling on a T-shirt and trackie bums.

'Don't be long or I really will come and get you.' Daniel caught her by the wrist as she passed him. 'It's not a crime to laugh, you know.'

'I've called at a bad time,' Nell stated. She had heard the noises from upstairs, but hadn't worked out how to extricate herself – write a quick note and run? – without making it obvious that she *had* heard before Lydia came down.

Lydia had the diamond-bright look of a woman who is about to be loved very thoroughly. Her cheeks were rosy from the rasping of Daniel's afternoon beard, her lips were puffy and looked almost painful. They moved stiffly. Nell was certain that there would be tiny nicks on the soft inner surfaces.

Goodness, how crass can I be? Nell thought. *I never checked, never phoned – just barged in and expected to be welcomed. She has a life of her own. Somehow, I never thought about that. Stupid.*

Lydia stared back levelly, meeting Nell's flustered gaze and mumbled apologies, assessing the woman.

Is this the one?

So conventional. So ordinary. Everything about her was average. Average height. Average weight. Bland colouring. Should Lydia ever be asked to describe Nell, she would have to say *I can't*.

Soft, Lydia thought. *She wouldn't have the guts to say no. Not to a man. Not to the pressures of a different society from this one. She wouldn't have the nerve to face up to having an illegitimate child. It might be . . .*

She waited for the spasm that she was sure would accompany recognition, some spark, some call. She didn't realize that what she was waiting for was a revelation. But there was none.

'I should have rung,' Nell said apologetically. 'But I was afraid that would give you a chance to tell me not to come. You see, it was all my fault.'

Somehow Lydia found herself forgetting her promise to Daniel that she would get rid of her visitor. They sat in the chairs that Daniel had placed under the apple tree in heatless, heartless autumn sunshine. Lydia was suddenly cold. The warmth of Daniel's skin against hers had faded and a thin mist was beginning to move across the sky. She was leaden with anticipation, heavy with the fear of what she was about to find out.

'It was my fault because, you see, I was supposed to be with her. I was supposed to be staying here and

341

if I had, we would have gone for that walk together and then it wouldn't have happened. Would it?' Nell's tone craved confirmation. It was as though she longed to be blamed. 'I mean, no-one attacks two women at once. So Hope would have been safe. So it's my fault that she died.'

'Is that it?'

'Isn't that enough? I was with . . . with a man. I'd left my husband, you see. Oh, it's a long story, none of it very nice, and no-one comes out well. Especially not me. A bad case of calf love, never outgrown . . .' There was a wistfulness in Nell's expression that might have torn some sympathy from Lydia on another day. 'I've gone back to him now. My husband, that is. Well, it was for the best. The children, you know. Anyway, then . . . your mother had invited me to stay on until I'd sorted out what I wanted to do. But instead I spent that night with a man and she died. Are the two facts connected? Am I being punished through her? That seems very cruel. Or would it have happened anyway? If not then, another time. The police say that some unbelievable percentage of murders are committed by someone the victim knew, so maybe Hope . . . but I can't help feeling . . . it was all my fault.'

Lydia fixed her with an unblinking stare. She looked right past the frantic hands, the submissive body language. She felt let down, unassuaged, hungry still.

'Is that all?'

'Yes. What else?'

'I thought you were going to tell me . . .'

And the shock on Nell's face mirrored the loss on Lydia's.

'Oh, my dear. Oh, no. I have no idea who . . . I couldn't possibly . . . I told the police everything I know. I didn't hide anything.'

So Lydia let her go on thinking that was what she'd expected to hear. Stupid woman. Stupid, soft, *hopeless* woman.

Before Nell left, she asked permission to look for a photograph that she had left behind during her brief attempt at freedom.

'Jago and Jessica at Legoland – it's in a little leather folding frame – we went there when Oliver was posted to northern Germany. Jago was seven and Jessica was three. Such a happy day. I meant to come back here the next day, but then *it* happened, so of course . . . but I don't want to lose it.'

'I think I've seen it,' Lydia volunteered. 'I'll fetch it for you.'

She wasn't certain what Daniel might do if Nell went upstairs – leap out from behind a curtain, naked and growling, perhaps. Or swear and throw his shoes at her because his enthusiasm had died away during the time he had been waiting.

When she returned, Nell was looking at the photo pinned to the cork board.

'Hope kept it,' she said, with wonder. 'I would never have thought it. She was so unhappy there, so misplaced. And I missed her so much once she'd gone. All the colour seemed to go out of the place with her. But then there was you. You were the best thing that ever happened to her.'

And if Lydia hadn't known better, if the evidence of the post-mortem hadn't been so conclusive, that remark might have made her happy.

'Look, why don't we go away,' Daniel suggested. 'It would do us both good. Especially you.'

'Aren't you the one continually telling me I have to get back to work and that I'll be lucky still to have some work to go to when I do?'

'I know, I know – but let's wring the compassionate angle a bit harder. Tell them you need more time. God knows it's not a lie. You look like death.'

'Thanks. You really know how to make a girl feel good.'

Daniel ignored her. 'We could go to . . . to Venice, or somewhere quieter, if you prefer, maybe to Gubbio, or Spoleto. You can look at all the frescos you want and I *promise* not to moan about all those bloody churches.'

'You're trying too hard, Daniel.'

'Maybe you need some sun to perk you up. How about Penang? Or Bali, maybe? Australia? Lydia – darling – say something.'

'I'm quite happy here. It's home.'

'But it's not *my* home, is it? Jesus Christ, Lydia, you're driving me round the bend. I'll be as mad as you are soon.' Lydia flicked a warning look, a dangerous look, but he didn't recognize the moment to stop. 'What makes you think one of these women is your mother? And why the hell does it matter, anyway? Maybe you are adopted. You could be anybody's, any by-blow off the streets, but it doesn't *matter*. Hope was your real mother.'

She turned away then, with a cool, dismissive shrug. 'I need to know.'

'You're obsessed. I love you – but I don't understand you.' Daniel took her by the shoulders and turned her to face him. Unresponding, she allowed him to hold her, to straighten her tangled hair, to kiss her closed lids, her damp cheeks, her compressed lips. 'Lydia, Lydia, you're driving me away.'

Lydia was expecting Isa. After all, the others had come, hadn't they? Why should the last one be different?

She was, of course. Firstly, because she telephoned in advance. She didn't just turn up and expect Lydia to be at home, grieving or making cakes for the WI. Secondly, because she invited Lydia to lunch at a decent restaurant in Salisbury.

'Neutral ground,' she explained over the phone. 'We can both say what we feel without territorial protocol getting in the way.'

Impressions were important to her, Lydia could tell by the tone of her voice, by the precision with which Isa organized date, time, place – no time wasted, nothing left to chance. Instinctively, Lydia felt that this was a woman who wouldn't appreciate sloppiness, who wouldn't make excuses for lack of preparation and who certainly wouldn't consider that mourning was a sufficient reason for not washing up.

So Lydia made an appointment earlier that

morning to have her hair cut. And when it was finished, she looked in the mirror and saw how much she had changed. The lengthening hair had disguised the alteration. Now it was back to the old, in-your-face length and she saw that it topped a woman she scarcely knew.

There was an expression behind her eyes she knew would be indelible. All the features she remembered were still there, but subtly remixed. It was as though Death had held out his hand for her. He was far away still, in no hurry to claim her, but she knew, now, that she belonged to him. He had touched those she loved. Both Chris and Hope had died violent, painful deaths, and the knowledge had altered her for ever.

It was the unkind light, surely – shouldn't a hairdresser light his clients in a more flattering way? – that threw shadows where none should be, that made her look so haunted. Lydia looked again and a healthy, strong young woman looked back, but the strangely colourless eyes were hooded and withdrawn.

Isa was already waiting. *Of course, she would be*, Lydia thought, feeling uncomfortably late, resentful, although she was in good time.

'Lydia,' Isa said, standing and holding out a hand: not the emotional two-handed salute of Juliet, not the pleading hands of Ruth or Nell's guilty wringing, but an open greeting, almost manly in its simplicity. Lydia liked her better after that.

The feeling increased as they ordered lunch. Isa was decisive and straightforward. She deferred to her guest, but was prepared to make decisions. She didn't rush to offer condolences or utter mawkish sentiments and have to stop, flustered, when a waiter arrived. She got on with the business in hand.

Not until the ordering was over, after the wine had been tasted and poured, in the gap before their food appeared, did Isa make any reference to Hope.

'Look,' she said, turning a pale-eyed gaze on Lydia, 'I'm not ignoring all the terrible things that have happened. Hope was a friend, perhaps the best friend I've ever had.' A little silence, a twitch of that stubborn chin. *God, she's going to cry*, Lydia thought. Then – 'We had our differences. There were things we didn't agree about. Of course. But that didn't change us. She was a marvellous woman. Now, that's all I'm going to say, or we'll both end up crying and making exhibitions of ourselves. You loved her and I loved her and we don't have to prove it to each other by seeing who can wallow the most.'

Lydia nodded, unable to find words to match Isa's straightforwardness. Her throat seemed to have clamped up, leaving her scarcely able to swallow.

'So let's not be afraid to mention her,' Isa continued. 'She was the best person I knew.'

Some time during the meal Lydia realized that she had not once – not once – felt that niggling ache, that intrusive, questioning voice.

Is she the one?

The thought had not occurred to her. And when it did, deliberately brought to the forefront of her mind, she dismissed it without further consideration.

347

There was nothing, nothing at all, that seemed to link her to Isa Cameron. Was Isa her mother? Impossible. The woman was too open, too pragmatic to be able to hide a secret of such significance, too confident to care what other people thought.

Raising a glass to her lips, she looked across the table at Isa. The colouring was there, certainly. They shared the same blond hair, although in very different tones, and they both had fair, fragile skin, that in Isa was already showing the collapse of youthful firmness. Lydia knew that her own would look the same in twenty-five years' time. Both, she acknowledged, were painfully thin: Lydia because, during the weeks when nothing seemed to make sense, she had neglected herself; Isa because . . . because, Lydia thought, that's the way she was. Her face was all hollows and planes, almost yellow, as though a heavy suntan had faded imperfectly, with bluish thumbprints beneath each eye. Her lipstick was a courageous gash. The sleeves of her fluid grey jersey dress were long and the neckline high, but Lydia had the impression of a body consumed, of flesh burned away, leaving the perfect outline of a human being.

And nothing else. There was no link. There was no feeling between them.

Lydia had the oddest idea that she might be some sort of hybrid, a composite, that in some inexplicable way, each of five women had given her something of herself. She was a freak.

From Isa she had inherited her colouring. From Juliet her irritability; she was quick to anger and quick to criticize. Ruth had given her stamina and an ability to last, to see problems through. From Nell she had inherited the soft core that no-one, not even Daniel, was allowed to suspect. And Hope – Hope had given her life, if not literally, then in every other way that mattered. She had nourished, nurtured, guarded and loved until she was no longer able to do it.

Lydia's throat closed again. She couldn't swallow the mouthful of wine. It swilled around her tongue and palate, bitter with remembrance and loss. She felt her eyes fill with tears. The plates, the cutlery, the flowers in the dumpy glass vase sparkled in an unbelievable way. Winking rainbow prisms of light blurred all the crisp outlines.

She looked across the table at Isa's unknown yet familiar face. Her sight cleared. She swallowed the wine.

'Good girl,' Isa said, softly.

'I like her best,' Lydia said to Daniel. She cradled the telephone awkwardly between chin and ear while she danced a twist of paper on a long string in front of Polly. Polly sniffed and scorned it. 'She's sensible and intelligent – which is more than can be said for any of the others. She didn't make me feel like a little girl in need of mothering.'

'And is she the one?' he asked.

'Of course not.'

Hats, hats. Today Nell hated hats.

'Why do you always need a new hat?' Oliver used

349

to grumble, when they were poor and living on mince.

'Because we go to so many hatty occasions,' she'd reply. 'Because every one I buy is always a last-minute mistake, so I can't wear it again, so I need a new one. Only this time, I'll be more careful.'

'You always say that.'

Oliver hadn't grumbled about this hat, Nell realized as she fixed it at the proper angle – not tilted, not clinging to the back of her head like a stray pancake. Perhaps he didn't complain because we aren't poor any more (not by any means), perhaps because he doesn't notice any more – I could be wearing his beret for all the impression I make. Or perhaps he believes that any expense is justified for Buckingham Palace.

Kane, reprieved from his hasty sacking, was downstairs with the staff car already. She could hear Oliver's greeting and the driver's cheerful reply. Fearful of being late, Nell went down and allowed Kane to see her into the car for the tedious journey to London.

Sir Oliver and Lady Hawtrey, she thought. Oliver finally got what he wanted. Promotion, the knighthood that went with it, like milk and cornflakes, and a posting to SHAPE – Supreme Headquarters Allied Powers Europe – in Belgium. It was all going to plan.

And a wife to go with the job, a hostess for visiting politicians and diplomats, to keep his social diary and grace his table with wit and charm. What more could a man want?

Lady Hawtrey. She doesn't sound at all like me. She's another woman.

Nell stared out of the left-hand passenger window at the vanishing M3. Oliver had opened his briefcase and was working on papers, reading with a frown, signing with a flourish or writing pungent comments in the margin. Once he grunted and scored a long red line right across a page. Kane was singing, soundlessly, but Nell could see the rhythmic tap-tap of his fingers on the steering wheel.

It would have been so nice if Jago and Jessica had come, too. Palace rules allowed one child and special dispensation could be granted for a second. But, after a tense Christmas, Jago was still keeping out of Oliver's way and Jessica had frankly stated that she'd rather have toothache than spend all day in a hat. All the same . . . Nell sighed and shifted in her seat, trying not to crease her skirt. She wished they had come. They ought to have come.

There was silence in the Rover even when they had joined the queue of cars grinding up the Mall towards the palace – private cars directed towards parking in the park, official cars dropping off passengers under the palace portico. Nell tried not to be awed – she had been here before, when Oliver had been awarded his OBE, and yet . . . and yet this was the home of the Queen who had described Nell herself, in the words of her commission, as *Trusty and Well-beloved*. That sort of wording tends to stick around and surface at unexpected moments. She tried to act as though she were surrounded by gold leaf and red carpets every day, but it was difficult not to gape, as Oliver was led off for instruction and she was directed towards the ball-room and a spindly gilt chair.

I must remember all this, she thought, *to tell Jago and Jessica. She'll shrug and tell me it's all so naff, but she'll be furious if I don't recall every detail – just so that she can sneer. And I must remember for me, too. It's my day, as well as his. I worked bloody hard to get Oliver here. He might not think so, but it's true. The army's had its pound of flesh from me, all right.*

A Guards string orchestra was playing hits from Lloyd Webber musicals. Contentedly, Nell rubber-necked, confident that everyone else was doing the same. Her eyes ached from the dazzle of white and gold. Her bottom ached from the rim of the tiny chair. She was enjoying every moment.

The atmosphere changed to solemn anticipation as the orchestra played the National Anthem and the guests rose to greet the Queen. Nell had seen her several times in the past, but she guessed what many of the other guests were saying. Her neighbour, a councillor, Nell had learned, from Sunderland, nudged her and whispered, 'Isn't she tiny? And you'd think she'd have bothered to dress up a bit more.'

Later, the same woman muttered, 'That queue's longer than the gate at Roker Park on a Saturday afternoon.'

One by one, divided into groups by the honours hierarchy, the great, the good and the worthy shuffled towards their sovereign. A quick nod of the head or a dip scarcely worthy of the word curtsy, a few words from the Queen, a glint of metal, bright blue eyes, a smile, a handshake. Memories are made of this.

Nell began by giving every recipient her full attention – John Major's school crossing ladies and bus drivers, good, hard-working people – but the effort and the numbers were too great. They merged into a blur of lounge suits and floral two-pieces (very appropriate – just like Her Majesty), broken now and then by uniforms and a great deal of stamping. The Queen was still smiling, as though each nervous person were the first of the day.

The recipients for each honour were becoming fewer as the grades became higher. It was worth paying more attention now, as there might well be someone she knew, or had known in the past. That was always interesting, to discover what had become of old acquaintances – who had prospered and been promoted, who had failed and taken redundancy. There was a short string of older men for the CBE – Commander of the Order of the British Empire – a grateful nation's last gift to colonels about to go into distinguished retirement.

And, amongst them, Harry. Unmistakably Harry. Nell knew of his award, as she, in common with most military wives, read the Honours Lists as avidly as the Hatches, Matches and Dispatches. But one never knew to which investiture anyone might be invited.

Harry. His countryman's all-year-round tan. His

slight limp, noticeable only when he was tired. His hair, brutally cut for the occasion, more grizzled than she remembered. Nell found that she had risen slightly from her seat, poised, as though he only had to call and she would go to him.

'All right, dear?' the Sunderland councillor queried penetratingly. 'Not long now. I'm dying to spend a penny myself.'

The last time she had seen Harry . . .

'Be here,' he had said and she had obeyed. She had never meant to, never intended to detach herself from one man, only to hook herself to another, like a troublesome burr. This was the chance to go where she wanted to go, for God's sake, be who she wanted to be. It was freedom.

She thought of his smile, as he had looked back from the bottom of the stairs, she thought of the shared memories, the might-have-been. And she chose Harry. She had spent one night with Hope, but the following night she returned to Harry's desolate married quarter.

One night more. That was all. One night to feel that someone cared for her. Was it so much to ask? Too much.

Harry had made her feel valued. He had made her feel young again. No, not again, she never had been young. Harry made her feel young at last.

She remembered his tenderness, his inquisitiveness. She remembered his silence as he learned the ways of her body. He concentrated. He made sure

354

that their pleasure was a shared one. Most of all she remembered the shared laughter.

She had spent one more night with Harry.

In the morning, they had sat in bed together, drinking coffee and making plans.

'Why don't I feel guilty?' Nell had asked, watching the way the sunlight lanced off the dimpled, black surface of the drink. The liquid trembled with the motion of Harry's breathing and the light broke up into bright splinters. Nell lay quietly in the sheltering curve of his left arm. She was content to wait for his answer.

'Because this is right for us,' Harry had replied, in his straightforward way.

So Hope had died.

And Harry had been given a sudden and unexpected posting to York. It might have been the Falklands, or Otterburn, or Benbecula, or the outermost circle of the Inferno. Nothing was too bad for those who committed the ultimate military sin of adultery within the ranks.

Be sure your sins will find you out, Nell's grandmother had always warned her. And they had. Oh, they had.

Waiting for Oliver. Waiting for the summit of his ambition. Or was it? There were still false peaks to climb. And he would. He had the talent and the ruthlessness, both requisites of success. But he already knew that he wouldn't make Chief of the Defence Staff and the knowledge was bitter. He'd worked out that, by the time he was ready for the post, the notorious 'buggin's turn' system, by which a sailor, a soldier and an airman were selected for the post successively, would be working against him. Unless, of course, the prospective incumbent should blot his copybook. It had happened. *The Air Marshal and the Call Girl* had made good tabloid headlines before now. So there was always hope.

With a start, Nell recognized Isa standing before the Queen. Isa – a dame. Nell could have laughed out loud. The official payoff. Poor Isa. Her retirement hadn't been announced, but it was a certainty after the award. Given her ambition, it was surprising she was retiring at such a relatively early age, but perhaps, Nell reflected, even Isa had her limits. The old boys' network had won and there never would be a woman in the highest echelons.

She looked impressive, Nell mused. A good advertisement for women in uniform, neither butch nor twee. But Nell knew – they all knew, Hope and Ruth and Juliet and Nell – what it had cost her to be allowed to play with the big boys. Only Isa knew whether it was worth the sacrifice and she wasn't about to tell.

Oliver at last. Definitely – Nell tried to tell herself that her opinion was purely objective – the most distinguished man of the day.

She stirred in her seat, craning for a better view. It was all over so quickly. Oliver knelt with eye-catching grace on a low stool, there was a brief flash of the sword handed to the Queen by a courtier and it was all over. Sir Oliver and Lady Hawtrey.

In the throng afterwards, Oliver found her. He had Harry at one side and Flavia at the other.

'Amazing, isn't it, darling,' said Oliver with a wide, ingenuous smile. 'Two old reprobates honoured on the same day.'

Flavia and Nell kissed, hat brims clashing awkwardly.

'Congratulations, Harry,' Nell murmured awkwardly.

'Oh, it's the end of the line, of course,' put in Flavia, with a bright little laugh. 'We all know that. Next stop the dole queue. Harry's never going to make the top, is he, Oliver?'

'Oh, I wouldn't say . . .' Even Oliver looked embarrassed.

'Well, I would. I should have been clever and married someone like you, shouldn't I?'

'If you *had* been clever, Flavia dear, you'd have been a good wife, done all the right things, cultivated all the right people. A man needs a good woman to steady the ladder while he climbs it – like little Nell here. When she thinks I've gone off net, she has a most ingenious method of bringing me to heel. Hasn't she, Harry?' Oliver laughed loudly, turning heads around their group, and, putting his arm around Nell, he gave her a boisterous squeeze. 'Where would I be without you? Mmm?'

'Isa was there. Did you see her? You remember Isa, don't you?' Nell said, not answering Oliver's question. 'I don't suppose you can see her, can you, Harry? You're so much taller than me. Oh, Isa. How amazing to meet you here. Congratulations. I can't

357

remember whether it's proper to kiss you in uniform or not. Remind me. Oh, to hell with it, this isn't just any day.'

'Oh, look, photographers,' exclaimed Flavia. 'Do let's have a picture, shall we? All of us together?'

Oliver in the centre, with Nell and Flavia, one on each arm. Isa behind, tall enough to be seen over Nell's head, very straight and distinguished, every inch a new Dame of the British Empire. Harry hovering and somehow out of it, not even looking in the same direction. Linked arms and proud smiles. The palace portico as a backdrop. One for the album. A day to remember.

'Lunch. We must all have lunch together,' Oliver announced. 'Isa, you must join us, too. I have a table booked at the In and Out. There'll be no problem about extra bodies.'

Oh, no. Oliver, no, Nell pleaded silently. *How can you do this? How can you make me sit with him, look at him, be with him? Sheathe your claws, this once. Make me suffer tomorrow, if you must, but, just for today, leave us alone.*

Flavia twitched at Nell's sleeve. 'Now you must forgive me – I just have to ask – you're not just a tiny bit tiddly, are you?'

'Oh, of course, Flavia, dear. I was tippling out of a hip flask all the way through the ceremony. Didn't you notice? In fact, I was passing it up and down the row. Oh, don't be so ridiculous.'

'There's no need to take that attitude – I just thought – well, you do seem just a little bit OTT. Not at all your usual self.'

'How would you know what my usual self is? We've scarcely seen each other for twenty-five years. Oliver's always done his best to avoid you and now I can see why.'

'Oh.' Flavia blinked and looked well-bred and offended, like an elderly brood mare bitten unexpectedly by a particularly common little pony.

This is a nightmare, Nell thought. *Something that Oliver has devised for his own amusement. He is such a good host. He knows how to get the best out of his guests.*

'A decent champagne, don't you think? Now, Nell, don't look so disapproving, darling. It's an occasion. There won't be another day like this again.' He raised his glass in the Scottish toast, but he spared them the cod Scottish accent. 'Here's to us, who's like us? Damn few, and they're all dead!'

He sits at the top of the table, laughing, tweaking the sensitive spots and watching us all twitch. What does he get out of this, apart from the pleasure of tormenting me?

Harry was behaving with a calm dignity, carrying on a conversation with Isa, so that she should not feel excluded from a family party. They had covered all the safe topics, catching up with the years – people they knew, where they had been posted, future plans for the early retirements or redundancies they both knew were inevitable.

But sometimes Harry looked across the table. It was there, the pain, in the twist of his lips, in the shadows behind the soft brown eyes – the spaniel eyes that Oliver mocked. Too late. They had left it

all too late and now there was no way out. Nell
couldn't believe that the others couldn't see, couldn't
understand, couldn't hear the silent conversation
that crossed the silver candlesticks and the scarlet
carnation centrepiece.

Why did you go back to him?

As restitution. Because Hope died.

Was he good to you?

*In his way. He took my chin between his finger
and thumb and turned my face up to his and said,
'This is not something we need to speak about
again.' And I covered the bruises with extra foun-
dation – they weren't big ones, you know, just
enough, one each side of my jaw. And that night,
he . . .*

Tell Harry that? Oh, no.

No need to tell him of that night, when Oliver
reversed the meaning of the word love-making. It
was about power. It was about victory. It was about
possession. No need to tell Harry of her shame that
her body had so quickly fallen into the familiar
rhythms of twenty-five years' intimacy.

Spare Harry that.

It wasn't meant to be like this.

*We both made mistakes when we were young. We
had a chance to begin again.*

Too late.

Flavia didn't seem to notice, but when had she
ever noticed anything about Harry? She noticed
her dogs more often. A quarter of a century had
not been as kind to her as it had to her brother,
Nell noted with some satisfaction. She looked

360

increasingly like her mother (be sure to look at the mother before you marry the daughter), long-nosed and with a long upper lip that made her resemble the horses that she bred (didn't all foreign men think that Englishwomen looked like horses?). Her skin, fine and fair in youth, had crumbled into a subway system of lines. *An elderly thoroughbred,* Nell thought, *a bit long in the tooth, though with breeding in every line of her, in the long, slender hands, heavy with her mother's good rings, in the long legs and the trim ankles. It might have worked. Harry could have been happy with her, if she had loved him even a tiny bit,* Nell thought sentimentally, *if she hadn't grabbed at him as a substitute for the glamorous brother she couldn't have.*

And Isa. Nell hadn't really looked at her until now. She hadn't seen her since the day of Hope's funeral. Now she saw that Isa was dying.

Somehow, the truth wasn't a shock, but a confirmation. It was as though she had absorbed the clues during the months since that carefree reunion last summer, as though her subconscious had taken note of the changes in Isa at each meeting since then and now presented her with the evidence. That hair, perfectly cut and dressed. She never had a hair out of place. It wasn't her hair. Of course. Isa moved as though her very bones hurt, as though the marrow within them lacerated her internally. She still smiled, even at Harry's jokes, but seemed now to have too many teeth for the rest of her face.

She was discussing her retirement plans with Harry.

361

'Oh, I'm not really a country person,' she was saying. 'I'm not going to wallow in organic vegetables and good works. I think I'll trade up my cottage for a flat in town, go to all the concerts I want, see all the plays, you know, spoil myself . . .'

She looked across at Nell, caught her staring and gave a little shake of the head, imperceptible to the others, but her message was plain. This was the woman who had borne a child in grim silence and now she was facing the future with the same courage.

Nell had a dream.

She dreamed that Hope was alive. She saw Hope standing in her garden, with a trowel in one hand and a basket of beans in the other. Not a ghost. Alive. Nell knew that because Hope's hands were ingrained with soil and she was sweating. Ghosts don't sweat.

'Of course,' Hope said. 'It was all a silly mistake. You got the wrong end of the stick, as usual, you goose.'

Oh, the relief. All a mistake. Of course. Nell could feel the tension drop from her, like Christian's bundle. Her dream self laughed and hugged Hope.

'Typical of me,' Nell said.

'Never mind. We all make mistakes,' said Hope, putting an arm around Nell's shoulders. 'Let's go in and tell Lydia. She must have been so worried.'

By the time they reached the kitchen door, Hope's face had, terrifyingly, metamorphosed. The skin had stretched over her bones like tanned hide. Her hair fell in tufts. She had too many teeth for her face. In her dream, Nell screamed as Hope's dead face turned into Harry's.

And when a sweating Nell woke up, she knew what she had to do.

THE GENERAL AND THE GO-GO GIRL
MURDER VICTIM WAS HIS MISTRESS
TOP NATO OFFICER IN SECRET LOVE
NEST SCANDAL

Sources today revealed that the British general newly appointed to a top NATO post had been having a long-standing affair with a murdered one-time go-go dancer. Lieutenant-General Sir Oliver Hawtrey (48), knighted by the Queen only four days ago, has served in the Falklands conflict, the Gulf War and in Bosnia and is one of Britain's most decorated soldiers. He is tipped for a top Ministry of Defence post in the future.

But the sexy soldier has been on manoeuvres of a different kind. He was caught visiting a secret love nest in a Wiltshire village not far from the official married quarters that he shares with his wife and two teenage children.

The General, SAS-trained and an 'above average' marksman, set his sights on buxom former go-go dancer, Hope Strickland (45). But their camouflage was faulty and they were spotted on several occasions on night exercises at a local country house hotel.

Mrs Strickland's battered body was found on a canal towpath in May last year.

At her Tidworth home yesterday, Lady Hawtrey said 'No comment'.

Juliet spotted the headline when she went to her village shop to complain about their delivery of the *Guardian* instead of the *Independent*. She was standing by the newspaper rack, waiting while child benefit was paid from the post office window to a string of young mothers. *And not one of them wearing a wedding ring*, Juliet thought, turning away. She never would have admitted that she was actively reading the headlines in the *Sun*. 'Just gazing in that direction,' she might have said, 'and my attention was caught by the picture, of course . . .'

What she actually said was, 'Oh, my God . . .' And then, 'Poor Nell.'

She thought about buying the paper, but, just then, her turn came up in the queue and she didn't have the nerve to buy such a sensationalist rag (as Simon would have called it) from a shop where she was known. So, later that morning, she drove into Romsey and bought the *Sun* from a newsagent who didn't know her. The journey used over twenty miles' worth of petrol, but this was an emergency.

'Oh, my God,' she said again, when she had the paper spread out on the kitchen table, along with a cup of coffee. 'Poor Nell.'

Then she tilted her chair and picked the cordless phone off its rest.

'You poor dear,' she said to Nell, as soon as her

364

call was answered. 'What a brute. And as for her . . . well, shooting's too good for her. Or it would be if . . . oh, God, what a mess. Nell? Are you there?'

'I'm here.'

'You sound absolutely drained – and no wonder. You're very quiet. Are you alone?'

'I'm never alone. Not a chance.' Nell gave a little laugh that Juliet thought was quite out of place in the circumstances. 'Bombardier Kane is polishing the silver. Mrs Parr is cleaning windows and is just outside my door, probably tying herself in knots to hear what you and I are talking about. Sergeant Lofthouse is trying to get five newspaper reporters off the doorstep before Oliver comes home for lunch.'

'Oh, my dear. Look, why don't you just slip out the back door and come here for the rest of the day – or a day or two—' Juliet added, in a flush of generosity. '—just until things blow over.'

'Because there are another two reporters at the back door. I can't face them.'

'Ghastly. Look, you haven't said anything to them, have you?'

'Of course not. Oliver would kill me if I talked to them.'

'Because you mustn't. Dignity is all you have left, now. Absolutely the last thing you must do is say that you're going to stand by him and allow one of those put-up happy family photos – like what's-his-name, you know, that MP. Fatal. Makes you look such a gullible fool when you do finally leave him.'

'But I'm not going to . . .'

'Oh, yes, you are. Wives always do, in the end. But who would have thought it? I mean, Hope, of all people.'

'I know . . .'

Nell's voice was so feeble that Juliet could barely hear her. *Absolutely shattered*, she thought, *and no wonder*. Mind you, Oliver was always too good-looking for his own good – or her own good, rather. That sort of man can never be faithful. She would be very surprised if this was his first liaison. Made you grateful that you were married to a dull man – worthy, of course, but dull, all the same.

'I wonder,' she said, slowly, probing . . . 'I wonder how the papers got hold of the story. Just bad luck for Oliver, I suppose.'

'I told them. I've known for ages he had someone else.'

'What?'

'I told them. Of course. But – oh, Juliet – I swear that I never knew the woman was Hope . . .'

Ruth was visiting her (or Lydia's, she had to keep reminding herself) work teams. She made a point of visiting each one at least once a week, to keep an eye on standards and to allow the workers to air worries before they became grievances. She arrived in the middle of a coffee break. The *Sun* was being passed round.

'He's just broken Number One of the Queen's Regulations – it doesn't matter what you do as long as you don't get caught.'

'I wonder if they pay for these stories – I wonder what they'd pay me if I told them my Kieran is knocking off the girl at the farm shop.'

'Never. That barrel of lard? Is he? But your Kieran wouldn't look as good as this in a photo, would he. I wouldn't mind a spot of target practice with *him*.'

'Here, Ruth – don't you still get chucked out the army for having it away? Conduct unbecoming or something?'

'I don't know. They can be pretty tough on adultery. And I think it's even more unpopular if it involves someone else in the services – you know – it's a rank thing, subordinates' wives and all that, maybe someone you write a confidential report on.'

'It all comes down to rank in the end. Doesn't it always?'

Ruth craned forward to see the article.

'So who's been a naughty boy now, then? Oh, my God,' she said. 'Poor Lydia.' And then, almost as an afterthought, 'Poor Nell.'

Lydia began to reassemble the torn pieces. She pulled them out of the wastepaper basket and tried to turn them back into a page of the *Sun*. *That's mad*, she thought, *it doesn't work*. They should fit, but they don't. Can't ever have. They just don't seem to make the right shape. The whole thing's too large.

For a while, the remaking was enough. It stopped her from thinking, like a jigsaw of ponies had diverted her from scratching when she had chicken-pox and was nearly better and grumpy. It was enough, for the moment, to marry up the right heads

367

and bodies, the proper legs into a pair, the correct hands on the ends of arms.

And when she had put them in order, she looked at the picture for a long time. It had been taken quite recently, under the portico of Buckingham Palace. Isa and Nell she recognized. The caption told her that the others were *family friends* – Harry Dowland and his wife, Flavia, and *love rat and security risk* – Oliver Hawtrey.

This man knows more secrets than most people have hot dinners. The nation trusts him, but his wife can't.

It still didn't look right. Lydia began swapping heads and bodies; the result was funny enough to make her laugh – as funny as Mr Potato Head – if she'd felt like laughing: Nell's face on Harry's body; Flavia's body under Harry's head; Oliver's face on Isa's body. Mix and match. Pick 'n' mix.

Then she stood up and looked in the mirror.

Oliver's face on Isa's body.

Now it was beginning to make sense.

WHO MURDERED HOPE?
IS THIS WHY SHE DIED?

Police sources refused to confirm or deny that murder victim Hope Strickland, revealed yesterday in a **Sun** exclusive as the long-time mistress of British top brass Sir Oliver Hawtrey, may have died because she knew too much.

Hope, a one-time army officer trainee during

the Swinging Sixties, was forced to leave the army when she became pregnant with her only child. Friends speak of her and the young Oliver Hawtrey as 'inseparable, definitely an item' in those days.

'Who said that? Who have they been talking to? Oh, my God, can't they get anything right?'

Nell pushed the newspaper across the table and leaned her head on the wood. She could feel the edge biting into her skin. The feeling was a good one, uncomplicated, perfectly straightforward. Simpler than people. Simple enough for Nell to understand.

Around her, the sounds of morning carried on without interruption. The vacuum cleaner was droning somewhere. The gardener was hoeing below the dining-room window, preparing the earth for the summer bedding plants that Nell would choose in a few weeks, and the rhythmic scrape-clink of the hoe through stones was steadyingly normal. She could even identify, through the dining-room hatch, if she sat very still and didn't breathe too loudly, the gentle swish-swish of boot brushes, as Kane buffed up Oliver's boots.

And, at the centre of all this activity, was turmoil. Nell could imagine, in every other senior officer's house, in every other garrison, a steadfast, calm, unflappable woman going about her morning duties – answering invitations, holding coffee mornings, frightening the younger women into becoming acceptable replicas of herself. But in Oliver's house his wife was chasing reporters off her doorstep.

Everything was going too fast, as though she had accidentally knocked out the bath plug with her toe. She could fumble about under water, think she had stanched the flow, but still it escaped. Too fast. Too fast. It was out of her control.

'I wish, I wish . . .' Nell balled her fists and thumped the table. The china leapt off the surface and landed again with a confused rattle.

At the unexpected sound, Mrs Parr stuck her head around the dining-room door. Nell saw her look at the paper, then at the disturbed table setting, and draw her own conclusions.

'No, thank you, Mrs Parr, there's nothing I need at the moment.'

She hated being out of control. She couldn't bear the way events had slid away out of her grasp, slippery and determined and deceptive. Despairing – or, as Hope might have said, completely off her rocker – she had struck out at Oliver in the only way she knew that would really hurt him. Threaten his career and you really put the man under pressure.

But she ought to have known better. Those whom God hath joined together, let no man put asunder; they two shall be one flesh. And in lashing out at Oliver, she had done greater harm to herself.

She had started this, but she wasn't at all certain that she could finish.

General Hawtrey, who joined the SAS in 1970, is described by colleagues as a hard man with a soft centre and an eye for the ladies.

An MoD spokesman said yesterday that no

breaches of security had come to light and that no action was currently being considered.

Isa lay curled up on the edge of her mattress. She was sick, so sick . . . *sick unto death* . . . the words floated in and out of her recollection.

It will pass, she told herself, it always passes.

She stretched out her arms and looked at them steadily, at veins so collapsed it was difficult now to find anywhere to put a needle. She looked at the medley of colours in the spontaneous bruising, turning her wrists this way and that. Nothing particularly to worry about (as though everybody looked as if they'd been trampled by a horse). Quite normal, she'd been told, in cases where platelets were being destroyed and clotting was being impaired. So the splendid new blood they'd given her was going the way of the old. No progress. And there were the pills, and the pills to counteract the side effects of the pills.

It had seemed quite straightforward, at first. The tests, the tension, the waiting and then the news, the surgeon's encouraging expression . . . *right*, she'd thought, breathing slowly and thoughtfully, as if absorbing the news, spreading it with the oxygen throughout her body, *so I've got it, so I'll get better, you never hear about the people who get better. It's early days, caught in time . . . maybe they'll be able to cut it clean away, maybe I'll have to lose a breast, but we can beat this . . . no reason why not, if caught in time, lots of people live, why not me, what're the odds . . . ?*

A year ago, two years, three – she couldn't remember.

So sick now, so sick . . .

But I am going to win, she told herself. *I'm going to beat this bloody thing. Lydia needs me even more now.*

But what if I can't . . . ?

She let the newspaper slip off the edge of the bed, without the energy or desire to catch it as it fell.

Ruth would have gone to see Lydia. She really meant to go. But what with one thing and another . . . you know how it is.

Henry had mumps. Just as well to get it over with at seven, of course, Tim said. But all the same, his timing was scarcely helpful. He was off school and fractious and Tim was no help at all.

Not that she held it against Tim. How could she? He had more than enough to put up with. Lydia had offered – shyly, as though she didn't have the right to make the suggestion – Ruth extra money for the increased responsibility she had taken on since Hope's death. Not that it wasn't welcome. But Tim regarded it almost as an insult. He couldn't bear Ruth being the breadwinner and he could bear even less her being a successful one.

'What does that girl know about running a business? Barely out of school. Handing money around as though it grew on trees.'

'You don't want it, I suppose? And Lucy expects to go on a geography field trip to Normandy next month.'

'What's wrong with British rocks, I'd like to know? Can't she study them? We don't need charity.'

'I work bloody hard for that money.'

And she'd begun peeling potatoes with a fierce concentration, wielding the scraper in a manner that made Tim creep out into the garden to see if the lawn mower needed doing up before the grass started growing again.

'You want to get out of that,' he said, just after Henry's mumps had been confirmed.

'And do what exactly?' she queried. Snappy and exhausted after Henry had grizzled half the night, she sounded sharper, perhaps, than she realized.

'Henry needs you. Children need their mothers when they're sick.'

'He's got you, hasn't he? Won't you do? How many parents does he need to fetch him Ribena and pick up his comics?'

'I don't have time to hang around. I'm looking for work.'

'And I'm *doing* it. Tim – oh, Tim – I'm sorry. I didn't mean it like that.'

'You meant it how it sounded. Christ, you know how to make a man feel useless.'

So Ruth stayed at home and concocted sloppy meals that Henry wouldn't eat and picked Jasmine's second litter of kittens out of the boy's bed every five minutes. Tim's skin condition erupted again and she knew he blamed her – stress always brought out the rash. And his joints never stopped hurting in damp weather.

But she really had meant to see Lydia.

373

*   *   *

Juliet privately thought that Nell was as dangerous as a loose cannon. So she rang up Ruth to say so.

'We all ought to get together and do something about her. She's going to hell in a handcart. We owe it to her to stop her.'

'Do you know, Juliet,' said Ruth with a weariness that struck Juliet as new and worrying – when had Ruth ever been too tired to muck in and help? – 'I really don't think there's anything we can do. If Nell is determined to bring Oliver down, then we have to let her.'

'I never thought – never – that you'd be the first of us to say that. What happened to all that old musketeer spirit? What about standing up and being counted, never letting each other down and all that?'

'That was then. And this is now. We've all changed.'

'And Lydia?'

'She's a grown woman. She'll get over it.'

Oliver didn't read the *Sun*: he couldn't be counted a *Sun* reader, that is. Wouldn't buy it. He saw it, of course. He always 'just had a quick look', as he would put it, at Kane's copy on the short journey between house and office.

'Don't know why you waste your money on this trash, Kane,' he'd say without fail. 'Read a decent paper, why don't you?'

But Kane knew which side of his bread was buttered. On this particular morning he told the General that he'd taken his advice and given up the *Sun*. Oliver didn't believe him, but he appreciated the man's thoughtfulness.

'Too late, Kane,' he said. 'I've already seen it.'

Kane wondered whether he ought to express sympathy, but decided that would be a distinctly dicey move. There are limits to chumminess, after all, beyond which no sensible bombardier would trespass and he had no wish to goad his boss into fixing a retaliatory posting back to regimental duty – Shoeburyness, say, or Manorbier, or any other far-flung firing range.

It was the wife he felt sorry for, mind. Married to him, for starters. But maybe she'd got used to that by now. All the same, it was fucking awful to see her, holed up in that miserable house, with no-one to talk to but miseryguts Parr and Sergeant Lofthouse, who made Oddjob look like good company.

And did all her friends come round to see her? Did they hell. You'd think she had something catching. Where were all those stuck-up buggers who'd sat around eating their food and drinking their drink? Nowhere, that's where. Typical.

He wondered if he'd ever get used to calling her Lady Hawtrey. And then he thought that maybe he wouldn't have to. The way things were going, the boss would be packed off, sharpish, somewhere he couldn't make any more trouble. Bosnia might be a good one.

So Kane stepped on the accelerator, fixed his eyes on the road and tapped his fingers on the steering wheel to a silent rendering of one of the James Bond themes. A man can dream.

Oliver wondered briefly if he might have indigestion. Never having had it before, he wasn't certain if he'd recognize it. No, it was more than that – a black, black churning of his guts, a vile brew that he longed to spew out. All the venom, all the bile, all the cant and hypocrisy that had been hurled in his direction in the past few days had lodged in a unreachable place where it seethed around and got between Oliver and his sleep.

The tabloids he could take – just. Who paid any attention, anyway? Only people like Kane. Only people who didn't matter. He could wait – until the next celebrity footballer went on a drunken spree or yesterday's pop idol molested a child. If there was one lesson he'd learned in the SAS, it was the value of patience. Never show your hand too soon. Never blow your cover. Keep down, keep quiet, stay alive.

But this morning he had read *The Times*.

Questions were yesterday asked in the House regarding allegations that a British general with a possible senior position within NATO had a sexual relationship with a murdered woman. Shadow Defence Secretary, David Clark, at Question Time, asked the Prime Minister whether he could confirm reports that a major breach of security had taken place, one that, if proven, ought to result in wide-scale resignations, not least of the Secretary of State himself.

Mr Major replied that none of the allegations

had been proven, but that, of course, he always bore in mind that the security of the realm was of paramount importance to Her Majesty's government.

Little people. Little people with little, piffling, dirty minds.

Oliver sat in the rear seat of the Rover with a view of the back of Kane's shaven neck. The bonnet pennant that designated Oliver's rank jerked stiffly in the wake of their progress. He acknowledged the salutes – automatically noticed even when he was thinking about something else – that were snapped in his direction by officers and soldiers going to work and alerted by the flag and the red bumper plates with three gold stars.

Did they really think that he was going to jeopardize everything he'd been aiming for since he'd won the Sword of Honour at Sandhurst? Just for a woman? Did they really think that he and Hope had talked military secrets when they'd been face to face on a pillow? Jesus Christ.

A *possible* senior position in NATO. Only last week it had been as good as his. Nell could have taken a trip out to see what needed doing in the residence, organize a kitchen update, choose colour schemes or whatever women thought was important.

And after Mons, almost certainly a position on the Army Board and the Defence Council. Everything slotting into place. Just as he had always believed it would. Neat. Inevitable. And now . . .

Jesus Christ – a man couldn't trust anyone these days. Not Nell. Not even – and this hurt even more than his wife's betrayal – not even Harry.

Always the same picture. Someone must have syndicated it. Always the wrong one. Who would know her?

Everywhere seemed to sell newspapers these days: village shops, garages, supermarkets. Lydia tried to avoid them, but she had to live. Polly needed her tins of Chappie. Even buying a pint of milk was an expedition loaded with meaning. Headlines, vulgar or restrained, leapt out at her. The Shellards did their best and moved the paper rack away from the till, so that Lydia could wait her turn without her mother's face staring back at her, but there were other places she could not avoid.

Always the wrong picture.

Lydia remembered her mother as often laughing, occasionally ferocious, always loving. Sometimes all three at once. She remembered her foxy hair, grey-sprinkled, like a tough old vixen's. She remembered the collection of inappropriate chandelier earrings that had mesmerized her as a child, the raggle-taggle-gypsy-oh clothes – velvet and silk and home-spun wool – the texture as she buried her face in her mother's lap, the comfort, the security, the fierce protectiveness. She remembered herself, at eight or nine or ten years old, sitting by the fire, clutching a mug of hot chocolate, while her mother read *Jane Eyre* and *Vanity Fair* aloud, never skimping a word, never making patronizing allowances for Lydia's age. Most of all, she remembered the laughter.

What has this to do with the go-go dancer in the skimpy, fringed costume who looks back from the pages of the newspapers? She is caught in a long-ago camera flash, startled, red-eyed, trapped in a movement that looks self-consciously seductive. Where is the connection between this girl and Chris Strickland's widow and Lydia's mother?

THE WOMAN WHO KNEW TOO MUCH

Suggestions were raised yesterday that Hope Strickland, battered mistress of one of Britain's top brass, may have been murdered by British intelligence agents. In a leaked memo to this paper, suggestions were made that pillow talk between Hope and Lieutenant-General Sir Oliver Hawtrey may have compromised British military secrets. Trained-to-kill Sir Oliver is a member of the elite SAS and due to take up a senior NATO appointment shortly. Police investigating Mrs Strickland's death are working on a theory that she may have been killed because she knew too much.

A Ministry of Defence spokesman said last night that 'The British don't work like that', but other sources admitted that Sir Oliver would have access to information of an extremely sensitive nature.

There was no question mark in the headline, but Lydia recognized the implicit one. No-one really *knew* anything. But the supposition was delicious, was gripping tabloid headlines day after day. It had everything – sex, uniforms, a closed society, codes of honour, rituals as arcane as the Free-masons', secrets, scandal, another chance for the Opposition to chant 'Sleaze' across the divides of the House of Commons. Oh, they could keep worry-ing at this one for weeks. There'd been nothing like it since Profumo.

No-one had cared until Hope's relationship with Oliver Hawtrey had been made public. She had been brutally murdered, had been battered until her comfortable, laughing face was unrecognizable and no-one had given a toss, not really. Breakfast shudders. 'Oh, dear, isn't that awful? Walking the dog. Makes you think, doesn't it. Is there any more marmalade?'

Now . . . now suddenly, she was a martyr.

'Come on, Ruth. You must remember some-thing.'

'No, really, I . . .'

Lydia saw the closed expression, the eyes that slid away, defensive, shuttered. Not for the first time, she had the sense of being on the outside looking in, of being an alien trying to break into a society she didn't understand.

'You're holding out on me. Don't you under-stand? This isn't some stupid barrackroom honour thing, like not turning in your mates when they've missed their guard duty. This is important . . . Ruth, you *owe* me.'

A mistake. Lydia sensed that at once. Unforgivably clumsy. She had gone too far, had presumed an allegiance that Ruth didn't share. Ruth's loyalty was to Hope, not to Hope's daughter.

'If that's the way you feel . . .' Ruth stood up with a quiet dignity. 'I thought I was working for you because I did a good job, not because you wanted something in return. Well, I can't give it to you, Lydia. I don't know anything. But if I did . . . Do you want it in writing or will you accept this as a verbal resignation?'

Old loyalties die hard, Juliet thought. She had urged Hope to tell the truth, had, indeed, believed that it was owed to Lydia. But to say it herself? That was different, somehow. She wasn't involved. It wasn't her problem. It had been Hope's. It was Isa's. Now, it appeared, it was Nell's. But not Juliet's.

They were bound by ties as invisible as a spider's web and as enduring. Tightly wrapped, they had not struggled or complained. All except Juliet. She had stood outside the pack, always looking in, always censorious, always critical of the closeness. Incestuous, it sometimes seemed. Friends were friends, for heaven's sake, but not one of them had the right to demand perfect love, perfect silence from another. It wasn't normal.

And now death was loosening the bonds and the pain from the returning circulation was felt by them all. Even Juliet.

Nell. Isa. Hope. Ruth. Juliet. What did they have in common? Suddenly the answer was blindingly

381

obvious. So obvious that Juliet gave a sudden, delighted laugh.

'Oh, my God,' she gasped. 'Of course.'

Simon looked up from the crossword with an irritated expression.

'If you're going to imitate a hyena,' he suggested, but mildly – Juliet's response could be sharper than he could put up with, first thing in the morning, 'perhaps you might do it in the garden.'

'If you would get yourself off to work, I could get on with clearing the table. I have a sunbed session booked this morning, followed by lunch with Ruth in Salisbury, and a host of things to do before I go out.'

Juliet felt very hot. She knew she was unbecomingly red. Was this what the Americans called a *power surge*, she wondered? If so, it was very unpleasant. That made sense, of course, because when had an American ever called a spade a spade?

Or was she simply excited?

What was the link between them all? Why, Oliver, of course. Oliver had married Nell. He had been Hope's lover. He had – here she became quite a bit redder and began to clear up noisily around unsuspecting Simon, dropping a spoon and clashing plates together, chipping one – well, it had been a long time ago, before she was married (although engaged, she had to admit), and only the once, of course, scarcely sinful, but still . . .

If three, why not four? Or five? Had Oliver had all of them? Ruth? Unlikely – rather like rogering the Statue of Liberty, she imagined – but not impossible.

382

Isa? Ah, Isa . . . who always gave the impression of untouchable virginity, but we all knew better, didn't we? Dame Isabel was no better than she ought to be.

'Alice?' Juliet stood at the foot of the stairs and called up. If the little baggage wasn't awake yet, it was time she was. 'Alice, what was the name of that goddess, you know, the virgin goddess, the one who wore armour and sprang out of her father's head, or something?'

There was a lot of thumping and quite a bit of grunting.

'Alice?'

'For Christ's sake, Mum, what . . . ?'

'You heard. No point in pretending you didn't. What was her name? The goddess?'

'Athene. Don't you know *anything*?'

'I was a linguist at school, you might remember. And what were *your* French and German grades?'

Athene. Yes. The soldier goddess. A virgin, fully armed. Untouchable. But someone had touched her. Lydia was the evidence of that. Oliver?

She thought of Oliver like a leggy, black spider sitting in the middle of a web, winding in five little flies on his sticky, shining, irresistible threads.

The implications made Juliet shiver beneath her lavender cashmere rollneck.

She had to get Ruth rather drunk before she could ask her. And that was quite difficult. Ruth was in a stubborn mood. She clung to her wine and mineral water spritzer for an irritatingly long time.

'Oh, come on. You're not even driving. So no

excuses. A girl's lunch out isn't the same without getting a little tipsy. That mineral water must be absolutely flat by now. Horrid.'

She pushed the half-filled glass to the far side of the table and filled Ruth's empty wine glass to the brim.

'Well, just the one. It's rather good, isn't it?'

'Delicious,' Juliet agreed. 'Can't you just see that lazy, romantic Loire? Those wide, sandy banks and the vines above, grapes ripening, smoke and honey and flint. All the bus passengers will be green with envy when you go home smelling of that.'

'They'll just think I'm a boozy old bag lady!'

Ruth laughed and sipped and Juliet kept her glass just topped up, subtly, so that Ruth had no idea how much she'd actually drunk.

It was Juliet's treat, to cheer Ruth up after she'd lost her job. Not that *lost* was a completely accurate description. She hadn't been told everything, but Juliet was of the opinion that Ruth had probably been very silly. So out of character. Not that she was going to say so, of course. What sort of a way would that be to cheer up a friend?

'What you need is comfort food,' she urged. 'None of that nibbling a radiccio leaf. Nursery food is the only cure for disappointment. Or so Simon tells me. I wouldn't know.'

Not *too* much to eat, of course. That would only mop up the alcohol. The idea was to relax Ruth, to make her responsive to an outrageous question. When the moment was ripe. *Before* she was sobered by coffee. Juliet thought the opportunity would

384

never come and, when it did, the result was satisfyingly instant.

'Did Oliver ever make love to you?'

'Good God.' Wine slopped over the rim of Ruth's glass and left a trail of spots down her shirt, like a spill of broken beads. 'What a question.'

But Juliet was quick to spot the two hectic circles on her cheeks. Did Ruth, too, suffer from power surges?

'Not so strange. Think about it.' And she leaned forward to replace the wine that Ruth had spilled. 'An attractive young man – no, let's be honest, a *gorgeous* young man – with open entry to as many girls as he wanted. Predatory. But aren't they all at that age? Wouldn't it be strange if he . . . ? No, wouldn't it be strange if he didn't . . . ?'

'Do you mean . . . ?'

'All of us? Mmm. That's exactly what I mean.' She leaned forward again, conspiratorial, coaxing, her lips only inches away from Ruth's own. 'A secret? But it was such a long time ago. Secrets don't count when they're very old. Nell. Hope. Me. Yes, I admit it.' Juliet gave a little, reminiscent giggle that ended in a sigh. 'As I said, it was a long time ago. What about you? Go on. Fair's fair. Tell.'

'Well . . .' Ruth turned her face away, but not before Juliet spotted the curve of her lips. Memory was sweet and her smile reflected it. Juliet remembered the young Ruth, her slow movements, uncertain, like a statue coming to surprised life, but never clumsy. She remembered the lily stalk neck and the large, competent hands, the air of repose that seemed to surround her when everyone else was rushing around in a panic. And look at her now . . . Tragic, really.

'I was duty cadet one night. You were all out at some party somewhere – you remember what it was like.'

Juliet nodded, controlling her excitement. 'Oh, yes. I remember.'

'And Oliver came round and his leg hurt and I felt sorry for him and opened some wine and we were all alone and – well, you know. We shouldn't have. But I don't regret it.'

'Of course you don't. Don't be daft. No-one regrets an *experience*!'

'Mmm.' Ruth laughed. 'It was that all right! His plaster was like a battering ram!'

'I knew it.' Triumph. A theory proved. Or almost. 'All of us?'

'*All* of us.'

'Isa?'

'Of course Isa. Isa, above all. Isa first, foremost and without a doubt. All we have to do is get her to admit it.'

WOULD YOU TRUST THIS MAN
WITH A SECRET?
CALL FOR LOVE-CHEAT TO RESIGN

Harry closed the paper with a sound that was very close to a groan.

Oliver was finished. There was no way out of this mess.

Alone among the services, the army still clung to its ancient attitude towards adultery. In the RAF, as far as Harry could gather, everyone was doing it to everyone else. In the navy, he was pretty certain they would, if only they were in one place long enough to make a conquest. But in the army's scale of wrong-doing, adultery still rated somewhere above the sin against the Holy Ghost. It was an attack on the sacred principle of the regimental family, an under-mining of the trust that must exist, high and low, if that principle is to survive. A man has to be able to go to war, secure in the knowledge that his wife isn't being rogered by her next-door neigh-bour (or vice versa). Adultery was a flouting of revered tradition, nearly as bad as trampling on the regimental colours. Adultery was still, in extreme (or extremely unlucky) cases, a court-martial offence.

In other words – do it if you must, but don't get caught.

Oliver had broken both rules. Oliver was finished.

Harry pushed aside his bacon and egg. The split yolk had already congealed into a sticky puddle spotted, like a plague victim, with Worcestershire sauce. The knife slid off the plate and bounced off his trousers on its way to the carpet. Harry dabbed at the stain, but he wasn't really concentrating.

'You're just making that worse,' Flavia snapped. 'Can't you get anything right?'

'If I want to spread butter and marmalade on my trousers and eat them,' Harry retorted, 'I'll do it.'

It was the nearest to temper that Flavia had ever experienced from her mild-mannered husband. The expression on Flavia's face was gratifying, but he felt deeply ashamed to admit the pleasure it gave him.

Christ, Oliver must be at rock bottom. He would be as ostracized as a leper. Failure is a disease. Publicity is the finger of death. No-one would go near him for fear of contagion. All those up-and-coming young thrusters who'd emulated Oliver's cut-throat ways would be wishing they'd modelled themselves on a duller, safer *beau idéal*. The retired, yet still influential men who had been his patrons, who'd sought out the best jobs for him, who'd recommended him for this and that – they'd drop him like a rotten egg. Bastards.

Oliver would be fighting mad and dangerous.

There was only one place to be, Harry decided, and that was with him. That's what friends were for. Back to back in a broken square, fending off the fuzzy-wuzzies together. Oliver might not want him, but he was going to get him, anyway.

'Mum, is something wrong?'

Jessica gave a snort of disgust. 'God, you can be *really* thick.'

'Shut up, Jess. We don't need you trying to be clever. I meant, is anything *more* wrong?'

'What could be wronger than having your father accused of being a love rat, a spy and probably a homicidal maniac, all at the same time?'

Jessica slammed out of the room, leaving half a mug of hot Ribena and a mangled slab of chocolate brownie, still in its foil tray. The table was sticky with chocolate crumbs. Comfort food, Nell thought sadly, beginning automatically to clear the mess. Once Jessica could rely on Oliver and me and now even chocolate fails her.

Spread on the table was a newspaper, open at a cartoon. There was a uniformed, miniature Oliver, begging bowl in hand, before a writhing, anonymous go-go girl. *Please, ma'am*, read the caption, *I want some more*. Poor Jessica. No wonder she had shrieked at her brother. Nell closed the paper and pushed it to one side.

'Mum? Well, is there?'

Cautiously, Nell dabbed at the crumbs with a damp fingertip and licked them away. They were nauseatingly sweet – she needed to tidy them quickly away. She looked at her son, noting his wariness, the delicacy with which he was trying to approach a problem that was so far beyond his comprehension. She saw, too, the heart-stopping resemblance to Oliver, which seemed to increase as Jago grew wider and taller. Sandhurst had begun the physical change from boy to man and now constant outdoor work was completing it. But his face was still that of a troubled boy who felt the world of childhood shifting beneath his feet.

'Should there be?' she asked, carefully.

'It's just that Dad's been in his study for hours. I heard him go in and I'm certain he hasn't been out since. I just wondered if – you know – if things had got worse.'

'Don't worry, love,' Nell reassured him. 'Things have already got just as bad as they could possibly

389

be.' And she gave a little laugh that was designed to prove to Jago that she was only joking.

'You don't suppose he would . . . you know . . . *do* something?'

'Of course not. Don't be silly. Your father's a fighter.'

All the same . . .

Nell stood for a long time outside the door. She knew he was in there. Not a sound penetrated the stout Edwardian timber, but she knew.

She nibbled her fingernails for a while and listened more carefully. Then she raised her fist and let it lie on the door, ready to knock, but unwilling. Oliver was not a man to disturb if he didn't want it. She dreaded the rough dismissal, or, worse, the casual, uninterested one. But he had been so quiet for so long.

She could sense him. On the far side of the door she could feel Oliver's presence, as surely as though he had stretched out a hand and touched her. The tension, the ferocity. Unmistakable. So he was still alive, she was certain of that. Jago's worst fear, his unacknowledged fear, could be dismissed.

'Oliver?' She tapped lightly, then went in, without waiting to be sent away. 'Oliver?'

He sat in one of the worn but highly polished leather armchairs. At his elbow, on a low table, was a decanter of whisky, with a telephone beside it. The room was unlit, but a reflection from the pale spring sky was caught up and cast back, tranquil, clear as water. The level of the spirits, Nell noted, was ominously low.

'Shut the door,' he said and the expected tone of command was still there, but oddly muted.

Nell closed the door and leaned against it, uncertain of her welcome, uncertain of her purpose.

'I'm finished, little Nell.'

He raised his head and gave her a fleeting smile, so un-Oliver, so rueful, so defeated, that it brought her to her knees at his feet.

'Surely not,' she reassured him, not believing her own words.

'The Adjutant-General rang this afternoon. On behalf of the Army Board. Very subtle. He's not actually going to leave me in a room with a loaded revolver, but . . .' He laughed at his bad joke. '. . . as good as. He's waiting for my resignation now.'

'Oh, Oliver . . .'

The chair seemed too large for him. He was shrunken, diminished, all authority excised like a dangerous tumour.

'I've lived for the army since I left school. Thirty years and I'm as expendable as a pair of worn-out boots.'

Pity. Remorse. Regret. All of those she felt. And guilt. Most of all, guilt.

She had destroyed something that was, in its own way, as nearly perfect as it could be. His way was not her way, yet it had worked. One morning, like wantonly pulling the wings from a butterfly, she had picked up the phone and smashed him. What use is a butterfly? What use is a soldier? But isn't it enough that something is perfect? Shouldn't it be allowed to exist for the simple reason of being itself, because there isn't another like it? Does everything have to have a purpose? Oliver had been the example, the ideal of his kind, the very perfect knight. Not now.

From far away, farther away than seemed possible, Nell could hear Jessica screech.

'You! Yes, *you*! Who do you think I'm talking to? Get off the fucking doorstep!'

There was the sound of a slamming door. *I ought to go*, Nell thought, *I ought to see what has happened now*. But she didn't have the will to move.

'Satisfied? Is this what you wanted, then?' he said. Nell shook her head, then laid it on his knee. Gently, he smoothed her hair, stroking it with quiet, regular movements. 'You must have hated me so much to do this.'

'I didn't, don't . . . this wasn't supposed to happen.'

His fingers were soft, strong, absent-minded, as though he fondled a favourite dog's ears.

'I didn't think it had been that bad – our marriage. I thought you had everything you wanted. Has it been? Bad, I mean?'

So difficult to answer truthfully. Good years and bad years muddled around in Nell's head, bumping into each other, treading on each other's toes in an effort to be noticed – *me, me, remember me, remember the time when . . . remember when you . . . when he . . . ?*

She had loved him once, she remembered that. No – adored, worshipped him. She had laid herself at his feet, a willing sacrifice, to raise or to trample as he chose. And since she had given him the choice, how could she blame him for the way he had followed? Was it all her fault then? If she had loved him as a woman loves a man, rather than as a bride of Christ loves her Master, would it all have been different? Would Oliver not have been sitting in a fast-darkening room contemplating the ruin of his career?

Was she, after all, to blame?

It hadn't always been that way, she was certain. So, logically, it must all be her fault – all, all of it, the muddle, the mess, the fading of love. She had failed to be what he wanted her to be. She had failed to be the life's helpmeet he had needed. As the years passed, she had become less and less able to meet his requirements.

'I expect,' she answered slowly, trying to be truthful, to be fair, 'that we've had the good and the bad.'

'Don't most people?'

'I suppose so.'

'Then why? Why now?'

'Because . . .'

She couldn't say it, not to his face . . . because you humiliated me once too often, because you took me for granted, because you thought I'd always be there . . . petty reasons, petty woman to destroy a man for this . . .

The truth was all of these and more, too complicated, too painful to face. How many times can a man expect his wife to turn the other cheek?

She felt the misery seep from his fingertips through her scalp, stealing its way into her brain, numbing and depressing.

'What're you going to do?' she whispered.

'Resign, of course. What else is there to do? I'm too tired to struggle any longer. Will that get the hacks off my back, do you think? Will they turn on the next victim then?'

'I don't know.'

'And what then? What about us?'

'I don't know,' she answered again, as close to the truth as she dared to come. 'Maybe we've . . . perhaps we've come to the end of the road.'

But he had stopped listening. His misery was a private place. Nell sat for a few moments longer, unable to give or receive comfort. Then she rose, awkwardly, her legs already numb with pins and needles. She didn't think he noticed her going. At the door, she turned to look at Oliver again. The energy, the spark, the brightness were dimmed. She remembered Madge, Harry's Madge, first of the long line of that name. Madge had looked like that at the end. She'd given up living, climbed into her basket and died.

And with the memory of Harry came the remembrance, sweet and bitter and probing, of all she had given up.

As she turned the door handle, Oliver looked up briefly.

'The police want to interview me. They want me to make a formal statement.'

'I was afraid they might.'

'I didn't kill her, you know.'

'I never thought you did,' Nell replied and closed the door on him.

*　　*　　*

Lydia didn't throw away the scraps of newspaper jigsaw that she had created. She straightened out their crumples and tucked them away, safely, in the drawer of the table that stood by her bed. No-one would find them there. Not even Daniel. And Daniel never came now. There were a hundred, a thousand reasons that Lydia could find to stop him. A man can only take so much rejection.

Oliver's face on Isa's body.

Simple. It made so much sense that Lydia couldn't bear to be wrong.

Sometimes, at night, when she had stared at the cracks in the ceiling for long enough, when the creaks and strains of the old building settling down had kept her awake unbearably long, Lydia would go downstairs and rummage in the fridge for the supper she had forgotten to eat before she went to bed. She would toss sleepy Polly a few Bonios, then stare at the open fridge door, as though she wondered who had left it like that. So she'd slap the kettle onto the Rayburn hotplate and make some more tea, sit hugging the mug in blue-tipped fingers, feeling the chill of bare tiles seep up through her uncovered feet and into her legs. Then she'd search out the random pieces of the photo and rearrange them, trying to persuade herself that there was another combination, another answer that made sense.

But she always came up with the same solution. Simple.

Her father had killed her adopted mother. Anyone could see that.

Perhaps she had threatened to expose him. (But why, after all these years?) Perhaps he had feared that Lydia would come looking for him, now that she was an adult. (As if she would, as if she had not been perfectly happy with the parents that had been chosen for her. Who needed natural parents, after all, especially ones that turned out to be like hers?)

It didn't all make sense. Sometimes, in her better moments, she'd admit that it didn't make sense at all, but then lots of things didn't. That didn't make them any less true.

And anyway, she told herself, lying again in the dark, listening to the cottage breathe and settle, listening to the scurry of mice across her ceiling that was their floor, the reason wasn't that important. It was the fact that mattered. That – and what she was going to do about it.

Juliet was flattered. Lydia could have chosen Nell or Ruth.

But who would choose Nell, of course, especially now. 'A broken reed,' she'd said to Simon, only the other day, nodding to emphasize her point, to demonstrate her sympathy. 'Poor Nell.' Simon had nodded, too, and wondered whether that chap really was going to sue for malpractice. Bluffing, probably.

And Ruth and Lydia had fallen out, Juliet had heard. Not surprisingly. Ruth could be amazingly stiff-necked when she'd set her mind on something. And stubborn. Lydia probably felt that she'd been railroaded into handing over more responsibility in the Houseproud Cavalry than she'd intended to.

So that left Juliet. But Juliet was absolutely convinced that Lydia would have chosen her, in any case. If she wanted sound, sane, unbiased advice, she'd come to the right place.

She couldn't help feeling, though, that Lydia was just a little overwrought. More than a little. Simon would have said – doctors can be surprisingly crude – definitely a basket case. Lydia refused a sherry, refused a little something stronger, although it wouldn't have been out of place, in the circumstances.

'I want you to tell me,' she said, outright, no beating about the bush. 'I want you to tell me if Isabel Cameron is my mother.'

Well . . .

'Why do you think I know?' Juliet questioned, stalling.

Lydia was pacing up and down the room, crossing and re-crossing Juliet's Kazakh rug, ruffling the fringes, catching her toe on the worn patch that Juliet had intended to have repaired for ages.

'If you must stalk around like that, would you please choose another part of the room. You're damaging that rug.'

Juliet felt better, more in control. Nothing like having a quick snap at someone – about anything, it doesn't matter what, it's the quick surge of power that's important – to make you feel in charge.

Lydia stopped, stood quiet and still.

Dangerous, Juliet thought, *this girl could be dangerous.*

'Well?'

Time to make a decision. At last. Time to set things right. Time to get it all sorted out once and for all. If the others didn't have the guts to face the truth, Juliet certainly did.

'Of course she is.'

'Are you certain?'

'Certain?' Juliet gave a quick, brittle laugh that managed to be both patronizing and defensive at the same time. 'Of course I'm certain. I saw you appear, so to speak. No denying where you came from. We were all there.'

'All?'

'Me, Ruth, Nell. And Hope, of course. We saw you born – and a perfectly ghastly evening that was, too. Hope should have told you long ago. I told her to. It wasn't fair to you or to any of us. I warned her what would happen if she didn't. Secrets are dangerous, I said.'

Funny, that was the second time in as many minutes that word had popped into her mind.

'And my father? Is that your secret, too? What else did you all bury between you?'

'Well, really, that's scarcely necessary – are you sure you wouldn't like something to drink? You look as though you need it. No? Lydia, I can assure you that I don't know who your father is. None of us does. Not even Hope knew that. At least, I don't think so. Isa, of course – I hope she does, at any rate. No, she wasn't that sort of girl. Isa knows – but no-one else.'

'And I know.'

Lydia stood very still, at last. *Thank goodness*,

Juliet thought. *If she hadn't stopped pacing I'd have screamed.* The young woman stood in a shaft of watery spring sunshine, sunlight with a greenish pallor that warmed nothing, heartless, revealing all that the winter gloom had kept decently hidden.

'And I know who killed Hope, too.'

Juliet was taken unawares by a feeling she had rarely, if ever, encountered. She was afraid that she might have done the wrong thing.

'You had a visitor while you were asleep,' the nurse said when she came to change the drip in Isa's arm.

Isa didn't turn her head towards the speaker. She didn't use sentences any more, when one word took so much less effort. Everything she did and thought and said was pared down to its essence. Perfect, in its way, she sometimes thought. Perhaps we ought all to communicate with fewer words.

'Who?'

'She wouldn't say. Said you would realize who she was. Tall girl, fair – a bit . . . a bit scary, to be honest. Does that sound familiar?'

'Yes.'

'We said she could stay until you woke, but she only stayed five minutes or so. She said she'd come back.'

'Then she will.'

When she was alone again, Isa closed her eyes. It wasn't dark in there, of course, behind her lids. The sunlight was filtered twice, once through inadequate blinds and once through her lids, but, like tissue paper, they allowed the light to reach her brain. She could see, randomly imprinted on her inner eye, the shape of the window, the position of the door, the bunch of red carnations and the huge, colourful card (from the clerks and typists who worked for her at MoD), the pot of scented jonquils with a discreet card signed in loopy feminine handwriting *Best wishes from Mike and Henrietta* (a conscience-appeaser from Mike?), the panic button, the trolley carrying the equipment that would stop her from dying if she decided to do it. And she could see Lydia – not as she had last seen her, but as she had become. Lydia, scared and scary, blighted by the truth.

Juliet's panicky phone call had preceded Lydia by two hours, about as long as it would take Lydia to get to London immediately after leaving Juliet.

'I really thought it was for the best,' Juliet defended herself. 'I mean – what good would any more lies do? She's old enough to handle the truth.'

Isa nodded, forgetting Juliet couldn't see her. Then she managed 'Yes', but her tongue was sticking to the roof of her mouth, so the word came out strangely muffled. But Juliet had seemed to understand.

'It's all your fault, anyway, yours and Hope's. That ridiculous bargain. Quite unacceptable. I said at the time that no good would come of it. And now, look. Hope's dead. Lydia's snapping on your heels. And she seems to have got some mad idea . . . She has a right to be told who her father is, you know. Isa? Isa – are you still there? I said . . .'

'I heard.'

'You can't keep it from her.'

Isa reached over to the side table and moistened her lips with water. Some dribbled down her chin and wet the front of her gown, but it felt good, all the same. She made an effort. Juliet seemed to demand that much.

'If you're angling to get me to tell you who he is, Juliet, you're wasting your time.'

'I wouldn't dream of it.' Juliet sounded comically indignant. 'It's none of my business. I've guessed, anyway. I'm not stupid. But I warn you – you and Hope started something that Lydia is going to finish.'

So Isa knew what Lydia had come to say, knew what she wanted.

I ought to have woken but I wasn't strong enough, she thought. *I should have realized that she was there.*

Lydia had sat beside the bed and looked at the sleeping figure. What had she thought? What had she felt? She had seen a sleeping woman, bloated, now, with drugs. A stranger, unconscious, breathing lightly, almost not breathing at all. She had seen tubes and needles and all the impersonal paraphernalia that was devoted to sustaining one life. But what had she felt? And what had she thought?

Isa closed her eyes again, fighting the overwhelming sense of nausea, fighting the weakness and deadly lethargy, and thought about Lydia. She thought about all the events that had occurred since she had rung Hope and told her, insisted, that she wanted to be back in Lydia's life. She thought about Juliet's emotional assessment of Lydia's character. She worked her way through the facts as Lydia saw them to come to the same conclusion that Lydia had reached.

Then she knew that she had to make one more, perhaps a final, effort. She leaned over and picked up the phone again.

Harry had read the notices tacked to the peeling cream emulsion so often that he almost knew them by heart.

DRINK KILLS

COLORADO BEETLE IS A NOTIFIABLE PEST

KEEP RABIES OUT

HAVE YOU SEEN THIS WOMAN?

He had stopped pacing around the perimeter. The steel toe and heel tips of his shoes sounded too melancholy, too lonely, altogether too dispiriting.

Oliver had been gone a long time. How long did it take to make a formal statement and how formal was formal, anyway?

Harry tried to make himself comfortable on a tubular steel-framed chair, but the back was too low and the seat too shallow. His legs stretched uncomfortably far across the stained carpet tiles. A Formica-topped table held a selection of leaflets on spotting the symptoms of drug abuse in children, a polystyrene cup half full of tepid instant coffee and an overflowing ashtray. The air was still and dead, almost weighty on his head and shoulders, and bitter with the flavour of long-cold tobacco.

A cigarette might be nice, he thought. He hadn't had one for twenty-three years, but the concept seemed suddenly appealing. Something to do. More interesting than police station coffee, anyway, and probably better for him.

Oliver had been astonished to see him. Gratifying, really. He never imagined that there would be anything he could do that would surprise Oliver. Harry had just strolled in through the unlocked back door of Kabul House. He could hear the sound of vacuuming, somewhere. Downstairs, there was almost complete silence.

Security's slipping, Oliver, he thought. *I shouldn't be able to do this. Looks as though the rats have already abandoned ship.*

Madge's claws click-clacked along the polished floors as Harry opened door after door, looking for Oliver. He found him in the study.

'Just thought you might need someone to mind your back, Noll,' he said, giving an awkward, forgive-me grin.

'Harry . . .'

Harry was shocked by the shrunkenness of him. Dear God, this was worse than he'd imagined. Oliver was sitting in a room made gloomy by drawn curtains – it reminded Harry of the room his grandmother had lived in for the last ten years of her life, mourning, keeping at bay sunlight and warm breezes and the smell of grass and anything that made her

403

think that life was worth living. The only smell around Oliver was whisky.

The table was littered with photographs and letters and old diaries. *Going through his memoirs, bad sign*, Harry thought. He pulled back the curtains violently and shoved up the sash window as far as it would go. The cold scent of freshly turned earth met the stink of whisky and pushed it back.

'Harry . . .' Oliver said again. He sounded bewildered. 'What're you doing here?'

Pity sliced through Harry with a thin, wicked blade, but he knew Oliver too well to give his feelings voice.

'Civvie life doesn't suit me. No-one wants to give me a job – too stupid, I suppose – it's all very dull. So I thought it would be more fun to see what you're up to. Coffee? Yes. Don't argue.'

Leaving all the kitchen cupboard doors ajar, Harry scrabbled around until he found some decent coffee. He made a potful – very black, very strong, no milk and lots of sugar – and set a tray with a couple of mugs and some custard creams.

'Here you are, old girl,' he said, tossing a couple to Madge. 'Make those the last today. You're getting fat.'

And that was how Nell found him – leaning casually against a worktop, one hand held high, with Madge at his feet, quivering, ready to jump, her floppy ears tense with desire.

Nell stood in the kitchen doorway, perfectly still, watching Harry. The sight of him kicked the breath out of her. A jumble of emotions fought for her attention, all clamouring, with the urgency of Madge, to be the one to catch her eye, the one to be tossed the biscuit.

He was so relaxed, so unaware of her gaze, so naturally happy in the unguarded moment. Nell realized that she hadn't seen anyone who looked happy for a long time. Everyone in Kabul House was tense and strained, unable to talk freely without giving away too much, unable simply to put out a hand to someone else and say *I need you*.

Oliver and Nell, Jago and Jessica were caught up in a framework of good manners. Be polite. Keep yourself to yourself. Don't shout. Don't cry. Don't give way. Don't give anything away.

For a little while, it seemed as though Jessica might challenge the rules, but even she had retreated into silent endurance. She had refused to go back to school after spring half-term – Nell didn't have the heart to force her and Oliver didn't notice; now she practically lived in her bedroom, coming out only to pick around morosely in the fridge. The music that blasted along the corridors and down the stairs was like a scream of protest.

And into all this came Harry – uncomplicated, decent – and happy. He had the capacity – rare indeed – to enjoy the moment. What had gone before might be tragedy, there might be disaster to come, but Harry stood in a shaft of sunlight and fed custard creams to Madge and that fraction of time was perfect.

Then he looked up and Nell saw how wrong she was.

Their shared past had marked Harry as deeply as it had everyone. He had not forgotten, he had not forgiven, but he understood. Oliver held them both captive. As long as he had need of Harry or of Nell, they would give themselves and he would use them. For each other, they could allow only what Oliver spared.

The knowledge kept them both silent. Nothing that was important could be spoken.

Then Harry said, 'Thought he looked as though he could use some coffee. How long has this been going on?'

'I . . . I'm not certain. Days just seem to run into each other recently.'

Harry grunted. 'Well, that's over now.' As he passed her, tray in hand, he continued with unshakeable certainty, but gently. 'It'll be all right, little Nell. You'll see.'

When he returned to the study, Oliver was sweeping into files the mess of papers that littered the desk. He had looked up with a new air of confidence and grinned.

'You're right. It's time to get a grip of things again. Regroup and advance,' he'd said. 'Welcome back, Harry.'

Oliver looked relaxed when he left the police station. His heels clicked along the shabbily tiled corridor, an echo of class and power and confidence, with Harry's in long-striding counterpoint, making the softly soled policemen seem to shuffle by contrast.

Once in his car, the illusion collapsed. Oliver

clasped the steering wheel with both hands and laid his head upon them.

'I'm to make myself – in their words – available for further questioning. Not to leave the country. Not to be out of contact. Not to disappear, in other words. Damn nearly asked me to surrender my passport. Where the hell did they think I'd go?'

'Could be worse,' Harry comforted. 'They could have taken . . . Oliver, just start up and drive, will you. There's a chap coming over, looks like a reporter.'

Oliver gunned the engine and drove out of the carpark, narrowly missing the approaching man.

'I don't think that's any way to get the press on your side,' remarked Harry, looking back through the nearside wing mirror.

Oliver drove with single-minded speed. He cut across the top of the downs behind Collingbourne Ducis, along the straight, fast, unclassified road that chopped miles off the A road and picked up the Hungerford route near the Wilton windmill.

'A mystery tour?' Harry queried. 'Where're we going?'

'London,' Oliver replied, briefly.

We should go and see Isa, Ruth thought as she sat late, balancing books that stubbornly refused to be balanced, stabbing at a calculator that offered her a different answer each time. The house was still and quiet, Tim asleep at last, but groaning in his sleep and twitching, as though he lay on a bed of nails. The eczema patches in the folds of his elbows, knees and groin were red and weeping. Ruth sighed, rubbed her eyes and adjusted her new, ready-made reading spectacles. The end of the tax year was coming up and the company accountant was asking for all sorts of things that Ruth didn't know where to find. *All the same*, she thought, *we must find time to see Isa. Together. I'll give Nell and Juliet a ring, soon, when I've got a spare moment.*

We should go and see Isa, Nell thought. *If she doesn't have us, she doesn't have anyone.* Perhaps when things had settled down a bit, when she could open the door without finding tabloid hacks camping on the doorstep. It must end soon. Now that Oliver was to resign, the family must be left alone. What more could they want? There must be other victims out there to throw to the lions, someone else to tear apart. Surely? This couldn't go on. *All the same*, she thought, *we must find time to see Isa. Together. I'll give Ruth and Juliet a ring, soon, when things quieten down a bit.*

We should go and see Isa, Juliet thought. *Lydia makes me nervous.* Not that Juliet held herself in any way to blame. Why should she? If anything, the blame was Isa's. After all, if she hadn't – you know – and if Hope hadn't . . . well, things would be a lot smoother all round. She wouldn't go as far as to say that Isa's illness was a judgement on her. That would be the sort of reaction one might expect from one's grandmother. All the same. It made you think. Now Isa needed all the protection she could get – and from her own daughter, too. It could be an appalling shock to a fragile system to find that prickly stranger at her bedside, demanding, accusing. None of my business, you might say. *All the same*, she thought, *we must find time to see Isa. Together. I'll give Ruth and Nell a ring tomorrow. Oh, no, not tomorrow – it's Alice's parents/teachers meeting – oh, God . . . the next day, then.*

When Isa woke again, Lydia was there.

Lydia watched the tissue-paper lids, veined like a baby's, flicker once, twice and open. Lydia could feel the discomfort of the tubular-framed seat, bonier than her own hips, beneath her, smell the aseptic hospital smell, decay and corruption kept fiercely in check by Dettol, yet she wasn't entirely certain that she was actually there. Part of her seemed to be suspended, watching a young woman, in a chair, who was watching another woman go through the ritual of wakening.

What links us? she wondered. *I feel nothing more than the abstract pity one feels for the dying. There is absolutely nothing that we share except genes. And those are not enough.*

'I've been waiting for you,' Isa said. Her voice was brittle as the last leaf tapping against a frozen twig. 'I didn't think you would take so long.'

'Did I need to hurry?' Lydia asked, moved by pity, moved by courage, but not – yet – by love.

'It would have been a pity if you'd waited too long.'

What do you say, Lydia thought, *in circumstances*

like these? What are you supposed to say to your mother, a new mother whom you have only just discovered? And when she is dying, should the words be different? Am I supposed to be less bitter, less aggrieved because she is weak and I am strong?

'How are you feeling?' Lydia asked. Wasn't that the sort of banality you addressed to a sick stranger? Where were the rules for a confrontation of this sort? Who had decided what could and could not be said?

'Better today. Stronger.'

And Lydia could sense the brave lie. She could see that Isa's body had begun to die, was already far advanced in its own shut-down procedure. As though her cells could sense that their dissolution was near, her system was closing off. But that stubborn will was the last to let go. The will that had allowed Isa to bear Lydia in secret and without a murmur still kept its grip.

The brightness of Isa's blue eyes, once steely, had faded, but their glance was still as keen. She looked at Lydia hungrily, as though trying to make up for all the years of absence, as though sucking in her strength and independence. They had met before, but then their relationship had been unacknowledged. Now, she could take in, without fear of disclosure, the hidden places of her daughter.

Lydia focused on those eyes, trying to shut her mind to the trailing tubes and wires, to the body that was dissolving before her. Isa's inspection unnerved her.

'Well?' she demanded with defensive aggression. 'Am I what you expected?'

'Exactly.'

'Am I like you or am I like my father?'

Lydia thought Isa had fallen asleep. Veined, crumpled tissue-paper lids slipped over the blue gaze, masking Isa's emotion. The silence was profound. The ceaseless hospital noises seemed external to it. Trolleys clanked. Bells rang. Feet squished along polished floors. None of this intruded. The two women were isolated in a sound vacuum.

Oh, God, Lydia thought, *is she . . . ?*

But Isa was looking a long, long way back – beyond the spiky adult Lydia in that bone-pinching chair, beyond the greedily suckling infant whose perfect pink fingers, each one very slightly blue-tipped, had paddled furiously, if for such a short time, at Isa's reluctant breast.

There wasn't much to do here, apart from thinking. She had done a lot of that, waiting for Lydia to come. She knew what the questions would be, anticipated them and tried out different options, permutating questions and answers in a tangle of right and wrong. All of them were painful. All of them involved hurting someone. It was a matter of supplying the answer that caused least damage.

'I don't know who your father was.'

Would that hurt Lydia more than the truth?

It was Isa's last, her only gift to Oliver.

Disbelieving and angry, wanting to hurt as she had been hurt, Lydia blurted out, 'I didn't think you were a whore. She said you weren't that sort of girl.'

Isa coughed, a soft, mucousy cough that robbed her of breath for a moment or two. 'Too much lying on my back,' she explained and coughed again. The cough gave her valuable time to gather up her own hurt and anger and stow it out of sight. There hadn't been any need for that accusation. Lydia had wanted to wound and had succeeded. But Isa would rather cough than betray her hurt.

'She? Who? Juliet? Of course, Juliet. What does she know?'

'She said you would tell me.'

And the voice was almost a wail, a child crying in the dark – *I want, I need, come to me, make me better.*

'I can't tell you what I don't know.'

Isa seemed to be gaining strength. When Lydia arrived, she'd looked as though any effort was beyond her, as though she was letting life slip through her grasp. Now she placed hands no more powerful than a loosely bound bunch of twigs against the mattress and heaved herself into a more upright position. Lydia half stood, hovered, feeling she ought to offer assistance, but uncertain whether it was needed or wanted.

'It's better this way, Lydia. Believe me.'

Her acknowledgement of her own lie was implicit, her determination to hold to it invincible. Hurt and angry and rejected. That must be how Lydia felt, Isa believed. Robbed of the parents she had thought were hers, she had been deprived at the same time of all the stability that her childhood had given her. No wonder she was rocking. All Hope's nurturing, her

412

care and love had been tossed away. Adrift, Lydia was snatching at anything that floated by and trying to use it as ballast to pin down a past out of control.

Isa felt the blame, as weighty, as final as a coffin lid. She wouldn't have blamed Lydia if she had walked out then, rejecting the relationship, clinging to a past that had been, though false, at least happy and secure and unchanging.

Twice – only twice – is that too often? she thought, *I've allowed emotion to overrule common sense. I'm not like other women, I haven't stumbled from one emotional highlight to the next. Yet I have left chaos behind me. I'm not good at passion. Obviously. I have started something that I can't finish.*

'But I know,' Lydia argued. She leaned forward, laying her hands, clenched into fists, on the bed, long-fingered, fine hands, copies of Oliver's and now rigid with barely suppressed fury. 'I know who he is. You're trying to shield him, put me off . . . whatever . . . there's something . . . you're not telling . . . But you can't fool me. My father is Oliver Hawtrey. Well,' she shouted into the shrieking silence that followed. 'Isn't he? And he killed Hope. He killed my mother.'

'No.' Isa's voice was astonishingly strong, the parade square voice, the voice of command. 'I don't know why you believe that, but you're wrong – on both counts.'

'He is. He did it. I know.'

'I swear.' Exhausted, Isa laid her head back against the pile of pillows. 'I swear to you, Lydia, that I don't know who your father is. And Oliver had not the least reason to kill Hope.'

'But if I don't believe that,' Lydia said, so softly that Isa had to strain to hear her, 'then there's nothing left for me to believe.'

'Believe that Hope loved you – and Chris, too. Believe that I would have loved you if I had known you. Isn't that enough?'

Lydia thought about this for a while, considering the possibilities. 'It doesn't seem to be,' she acknowledged, but more calmly. 'Not at the moment. Some day, maybe, but not now.'

Isa leaned over and pushed a button on the other side of the bed. 'Sorry,' she said and her voice was juddery with pain. 'I need . . . they're so good here, make sure we don't suffer too much, give us all the pain relief we need – and then some more, if we . . . really . . . need it.'

'I've tired you. I'm sorry. I shouldn't have come.'

'Things need to be said. Don't go yet,' she added, as a nurse carrying a small metal dish entered the room, 'unless you have to.'

Lydia walked over to the window, averting her eyes as the nurse gave Isa her pain relief. The mechanics of illness scared her. Isa was never meant to be helpless, never meant to be dependent. Lydia looked down, across a little patio below with a miniature fountain and benches for visitors, and over into the carpark. It was full. And each car represented a family coming to terms with death and loss. A woman came through swing doors and onto the patio. Grey-haired, ordinary, foreshortened by

414

height, she looked around to check that she was alone, but she didn't look upwards. She sat on the nearest bench and laid her forehead on the back rest, in an attitude of absolute despair. Lydia watched, curious, layers of loneliness cocooning her from the touch of humanity, isolated by glass and by her own peculiar circumstances. One day she might weep for Isa, too, but not yet. She was still grieving for Hope.

She listened to the rattle of metal on metal, to Isa's sigh, to the squish-squish of the nurse's departing shoes. Only then did she turn. She saw that Isa's skin was a dingy yellow as though sunlit, yet the sunlight did not fall on her, that her arms were a mass of bruises, that her oddly flat, mutilated chest barely rose with every inhalation. She wondered if the drug had knocked her out. But Isa was still alert, though her speech was less clear.

'Sorry. Thought I could last a bit longer.'

'I'm sorry, too. I didn't mean to drag all my hang-ups into view.'

'Things needed saying.'

'Later. No hurry. We'll always have later. Isn't there anything – I mean, I read about people having different drugs, amazing new ones, or laser treatment or alternative therapies . . .'

'No more clutching at straws. Not now.'

'But you could have . . . what about a bone marrow transplant . . . a donor?'

Isa made a soft sound that Lydia thought might have been a sigh or might have been a laugh. 'Not now,' Isa repeated. 'There was a possibility once –

maybe it wouldn't have helped, anyway, who knows – but that was when I still thought that I could beat this thing – a sort of arrogance, I suppose. I had done everything else I wanted to do. Then why not this last conquest? And then, was I going to get in touch with you and say *Hey, I'm your mother and, by the way, could I borrow some bone marrow from you?*' This time the sound was quite definitely a laugh and it moved Lydia more than tears could ever have done. 'I've always been too arrogant for my own good.'

'Well, that's definitely something you've passed on,' Lydia admitted and her laugh joined her mother's.

Isa lay still for a while after that. Lydia sat by the bed, close, watching, but not feeling justified in holding the withered hand that lay on crumpled sheets. *That would be hypocrisy*, she thought; *we've a long way to go before we're ready for that. Too much has happened and too little has been explained.*

She remembered the liking she'd first felt for Isa, when they'd met shortly after Hope's death. This was someone, she'd thought then, that she could deal with, this was someone with her own sense of balance, not fluffy or wishy-washy or bitchy.

So much had happened since that meeting. Lydia had had too much to absorb in too short a time. One day, perhaps, that liking she'd felt would be translated into respect. Who knows – perhaps – into something more. They had a basis to work on. Not yet. One day. In time. If there was time.

'Perhaps you'd better go now,' Isa said and her voice was barely audible.

'Shall I come again?'

Almost reluctantly, urged by an emotion that she didn't understand and couldn't stand up against, Lydia took Isa's hand, feeling the papery skin, withered beneath her own smoothness, fearing that it might tear beneath her grasp, sensing the twig-like bones within. She was startled by the strength of the responding grip, by its almost aggressive masculinity. Isa hadn't quite given up.

'Could you make it soon?'

'Soon,' Lydia promised.

When she was alone, Isa, drifting between morphine-induced insensibility and the terrifying, wakeful torpor that made her nights unbearable, wondered how she could have made things different. At what point had she gone wrong?

When she had allowed Oliver to make love to her? Nowadays, she thought with some amusement, she could have blamed her loveless childhood. No-one has to shoulder responsibility any more, she reflected, no-one is guilty. That's awfully convenient.

But the truth had been simpler than that. She had been curious and Oliver had obliged, disposing of her virginity skilfully and satisfyingly. Scarcely a sin, in that era of newly free love. Their enjoyment had been mutual and no-one had been hurt – or so it seemed.

Yet it had been more than that. At some deeper

level, Oliver and Isa had recognized each other as kindred spirits. She represented his feminine angle, he her masculine side. They matched. Theseus and Hippolyta. Together, they could have scaled unnamed heights. Or they would have torn each other apart in the race to reach the top first.

Or had she gone wrong when she had given Lydia away? Unmarried mothers simply *didn't* keep their babies in the Sixties. And she had done her best for Lydia. She hadn't given birth and forgotten. Would it have been better for Lydia to have been born in some morally pure unmarried mothers' home? Would deprivation have made her birth more socially acceptable? Does the mother have to suffer to cleanse the child? Isa hadn't handed her over to some disapproving local authority representative to be homed who knew where. She had behaved – as she saw it – responsibly. She had made certain that Lydia was going to a good woman to be cherished and nurtured and raised as she deserved to be.

Perhaps . . . had it been when she had failed to keep her promise to Hope, when she had tried to force her way back into Lydia's life? Harder to vindicate, that.

Hope had seen that action, with some justification, as an act of emotional vandalism, breaking up something that had worked for a quarter of a century, destruction for selfish ends. Isa could plead that she was frightened by her illness, that she wasn't completely responsible for such an irrational action. But that would be less than the truth. She had been scared by passing time – yes – panicked into

418

acknowledgement of how little was left. But she had been totally in control at every moment.

And when she had followed Hope along the towpath that last evening? Isa twisted in her bed, crumpling the sheets into ridges that dug into her fleshless body, less irritating than toast crumbs to a healthy person in bed, unbelievably painful to Isa and her stripped bones.

And that is guilt, she thought. *Guilt is a punishment worse than the death penalty: guilt is eternal.*

The fact that she had not meant to kill Hope made her response – almost – more damning.

If I could do something like that without trying, what could I do if I really meant to cause harm?

Seared on the back of her eyelids, sharper and clearer and less muddled than the actual event had been, she saw again the chain of circumstances that had led to Hope's death.

She saw herself leave her car, carefully locking the door, orderly, in control, certain that no-one would notice her, leaving nothing to chance. She could feel the grating slide of chalk, the many-sided sharpness of flints beneath her feet as she left the road and started on the track that led downhill to the canal. She had blundered against a stand of nettles and their sting was welcome, a deserved scourge. Ahead of her was Hope's unaware figure, striding easily along, saying a few words to Polly, tossing a stick, bracing and jolly. Isa had kept Hope in view, but far enough ahead to prevent her from hearing her follower. Even Polly was too interested in rabbits and coots to realize that they were not alone on the long, straight, lonely towpath.

But with what purpose had she followed? There must have been a reason; Isa never did anything without clearcut analysis and decision. She was trained for that. She didn't just muddle along in a helpless, hopeless, female way. Why had she left the car, why followed Hope those critical yards behind?

An ordinary woman would have thought twice about walking alone in such a place, at such a time, when the light was balanced between day and night, when the birds were roosting in the spindle and elder bushes and bats flittered low across the glassy surface of the canal. But Hope was not an ordinary woman. She lived by her own rules.

The air was heavy with the pungent scent, like sweetened cats' pee, of elder. The blossoms hung, heavy white umbels, luminous in the half-light, across the path and the women brushed against them as they passed, picking up dew and pollen particles on their left sleeves. Isa had walked faster, but Hope was turning for home before they met. Isa was aware of momentary alarm in Hope, who expected to be alone and who had not immediately recognized the pursuing figure, then the quick surge of relief as she knew the friendly face.

Isa twisted her head, trying to escape from the memory. Her pillows felt as though they had been stuffed with rubble. This time, the morphine had not offered oblivion, but left her with a dulled body and a sharpened mind, a mind that was out of her control. A sort of justice, she acknowledged. Hope did not deserve to be abandoned in her grave.

She saw Hope's alarm give way to a welcoming smile that faded as Isa pressed her again to allow access to Lydia.

'I don't need to ask you,' she had insisted. 'It's only a courtesy between us. If I want to speak to Lydia, I will.'

'It's always been what you want, hasn't it, Isa? You want and you get. No matter who gets in the way.'

'I don't understand you, Hope, I really don't. How can you be so selfish? What harm can a meeting do? You're acting as though I'm going to seduce Lydia.'

'Well, aren't you? In your own way? Leave us alone. We don't need you.'

Stubborn women both, each convinced of her right to another's body and mind and love. Neither would give way, neither would compromise. You said this. But *you* agreed that. You promised this. But *you* promised that. And in the end . . .

'Over my dead body,' Hope had declared.

And so it had been.

That was the end of the argument for Hope, her final word. Exasperated. Hemmed in by Isa's demands and physically by her tall, strong body blocking the path. She pushed against Isa, to move her out of the way, not hard, not violent, but positive, her hands against Isa's chest, sensing through her palms the flatness, the absent breast.

And Isa, off balance, felt threatened. Chalk is very

slippery and the canal bank was wet, slick with flattened weeds and white, sludgy mud. Isa thought she was slipping in. She could feel her right foot losing purchase on the mud, sliding, sliding. Hope was pushing her in. She knew it. Hope was going to kill her.

'For Christ's sake, Hope, what're you doing?'

She remembered saying that. It was important to remember those words, those exact words.

'I said *For Christ's sake, Hope, what're you doing?*' she would tell herself, over and over again, rehearsing the exact tone, the precise meaning.

It hadn't been murder. How could it be? They were friends. They had shared so much, dared so much. They loved each other, in their way.

Isa remembered her own cry of fear, remembered the way it had been caught up in the tunnel of trees that overhung the water and extinguished.

Taller, stronger, fitter and angrier, she had picked up a many-angled flint, deadly as a medieval mace, and with telling aim, swung it against Hope's temple.

Dead people fall in such a positive way, as though they really mean it. They don't gently sink, like in the movies, or fall forward neatly. They simply drop, crumple, as though someone has just cut the string that ran through the tops of their heads to an unseen hook in the sky. Flop. Just like that.

Isa could see that Hope was dead, just by the way she fell. She was there. And then she wasn't. There wasn't any Hope left in the body, not any more. A shard of bone had been driven into her brain and she just died.

Isa didn't mean that to happen. Did she?

Angry. Angry. Angry with Hope for dying. Breathless and weeping and angry. Your fault, your fault. Why did you push me? Angry with Hope for making it happen.

Angry enough to destroy her. There was nothing of Hope's face to recognize when Isa ran back along the path, shielded by darkness.

Your fault, Hope, your fault. You shouldn't have touched me. All I wanted was my daughter. All you had to do was say yes. You should never have touched me.

Not a feminine way to kill. Women poison, gas, knife, suffocate, shoot sometimes – even, desperate, run over a victim. They don't strangle, or batter an upright, conscious person. The police never looked for a woman.

But neither was ambition a feminine trait. Isa had seen what she wanted and had gone out to get it, taking on the men at their own game. Why not? Who decreed there had to be men's roles and women's roles? Ambition had led her to a position to which no other woman had ever aspired. It had caused her to give up her baby. She could have been married, several times over and to decent men, all of them, but had chosen to remain single. Even if Mike (so unlikely, but still, imagine . . .) had freed himself of Henrietta and asked Isa to marry him, she'd have smiled a clever smile and said, 'A little late in life, don't you think . . .' And then, just when she had everything she had always wanted, she discovered that her life was to be taken away from her. In return, she decided that there was one more thing, just one, that she wanted.

Having it all. They said the Nineties woman could have it all. Career and marriage and children. Well, she'd left it too late for the marriage thing, but surely – surely it was not too late to regain her child.

Isa and Oliver. The child of their union must surely be so special, so different. Such bright darkness. As though stars had collided. Yet Lydia had turned into an ordinary, if perfectly nice, young woman, banal as her adoptive mother. How unexpected, but for the best, perhaps.

Only . . . sometimes, in the blackest part of the night, when she couldn't breathe lying down or when the latest cocktail of drugs caused even more severe nausea, Isa feared that she had supped with the devil and that her spoon had not been anything like long enough.

Oh, yes, she and Oliver were two of a kind. They deserved each other.

But now Oliver was suffering.

He must have done plenty of things that other men would have been ashamed of on his swift climb to the top. How many fingers had he stamped on, when he felt them on the ladder rungs beneath his boots? How many rugs had he pulled out beneath how many feet? But those faults were trivial, technicalities, just things that happened when you were on your way up. There were winners and losers. Everyone knew that. And Oliver was always going to be a winner. That's what power does to

424

you. There's always something else, something more, something better.

Until now, he had deserved all he got. Isa, puritanical Scots Isa, had been shocked to her Nonconformist depths by the revelation of Oliver's affair with Hope. That was a whole batch of the seven deadly sins piled into one. An affair? It happened. An affair with your wife's best friend? Or an affair with your best friend's husband, depending on your viewpoint? That was unforgivable. An affair with the woman who had raised your love child for twenty-five years . . . OK, OK, so he didn't know that – and neither, fortunately, did the tabloids or he would have been pegged out naked on an ant heap – still, Oliver was a shit. But Isa had always known that and hadn't held it against him. She was one herself.

Now, it was different. Some people might have found it satisfying to think that Oliver was to be destroyed by something he hadn't done. Now, with an accusation of murder being added to every other crime in the book, he was going to go down, all the way, and there might be a sort of rough justice in that. But Isa could stop it. If she wanted to.

So Isa lay back against her mounded pillows and waited for Oliver to answer her call.

Lydia felt the coffee cup cool beneath her fingers. She had twirled it, stirred the contents, made messy concentric rings of dark liquid on the surface of the table, done everything but drink.

And think. She wasn't thinking at all. She was

aware of the opening and closing door of the let's-all-pretend-we're-French café, of the gushing rush of the coffee machine, the smells of coffee and all-day croissants. She could sense the basketweave chair threading its patterns across the backs of her thighs. She watched, through steamy windows, cars jostle for precious parking spots on dotted yellow lines. But she didn't think.

She felt, though. She felt the gnawing need to say the things that had been left unsaid, the urgency of unfinished business. She felt a conflicting longing, equally urgent, to let things rest, to have an end to it all, to be at peace at last. That was the direction in which Hope would have encouraged her, she knew. Sensible, forgiving Hope.

Let it be, she would have said. *No good will come of tearing your heart out.* Lydia could hear her, or she would be able to if that bloody coffee machine would just stop spluttering. *You've got a life to live and it's the only one you've got. Don't let the past sour it.*

But . . .

Isa might well have been telling the truth when she said she didn't know who had fathered Lydia, but the one statement didn't lead to the next. Just because she wasn't certain that Oliver was her father, it didn't follow that he wasn't. And it certainly didn't make it impossible for him to kill Hope. Isa believed him innocent, but that didn't make it true. Necessarily. You just had to think things through, logically. All Lydia's reasoning was still valid.

Their business was still unfinished.

Choose, Lydia, a voice seemed to say; *choose now, stay or go. Sit here and drink the bloody coffee. Then turn right outside the door and walk down to the station – and home and Daniel – and don't look back. Or turn left and go back to that shaded room, to the slow rasping of breath, to the terrifying power of that woman – and finish it.*

Oliver had paid no attention to Harry's assurances that no-one was following and no-one cared a toss where they were going.

'And I don't think being had for speeding on the M4 is going to increase your chances of anonymity.'

'Long word, Harry, are you sure you know what it means?' Oliver answered, with a grin that worried Harry more than the speed.

'I wish you'd brought Kane with you. At least I could be certain of getting wherever we're going in one piece.'

'Too noticeable. I don't want to be spotted.'

'There's a fault in your reasoning there, some-where!'

They had snaked their way through outer London back streets, slaloming around parked cars, shooting red lights, holding pelican crossings to ransom. They took out a couple of wing mirrors on the way. Harry couldn't believe they were getting away with it.

'Bloody hell, Noll. If I so much as tripped over the speed limit, I'd get collared.'

'I've had too much bad luck for too long. It's about time it changed.'

When they drove into a carpark, discreetly signed as belonging to St Barbara's Hospice, Harry wondered how that could possibly be true.

'Want me to come with you?' he asked, not knowing where, but half opening the car door in preparation.

'Not this time. Sorry. No reflection on you. But this is something I have to do on my own.'

And Oliver left Harry in the car, waiting and wondering, sweating slightly beneath his tweeds after the pace of the journey.

Oliver was himself again. And Harry wasn't at all certain of what he thought about the alteration. Oliver's near-surrender had shocked him. It had been like watching a glacier melt, watching great slabs of protective ice slip and slide into a boiling sea, leaving a diminished remnant. How could he have allowed that to continue? How could he not shore up the wreck?

Yet all the same . . . the image of Nell slid shyly into his mind. Nell asleep, her lips just parted, childlike, honey-brown hair feathering across flushed cheeks. Nell in her kitchen, watching him with silent, desperate courage as he organized coffee to sober up her husband. Nell, managing to hold onto a very public smile, nursing bruises on her arms.

Whichever he chose, he would betray the other.

Oliver suspected that they had been trying to keep him out, but when he stood in the door of the room, he saw that he had not been told lies.

428

The stillness was frightful. Not a breath stirred. Isa seemed to be sustained by something other than oxygen. Willpower, he wondered; bloody-mindedness? Oliver could see no evidence that she was breathing at all. Yet she must be. He knew that if she stopped, all the wired-up monitors would screech in alarm, bringing staff running. Or would they? Had the decision already been made to let Isa slide away when her time came? If so, who had made it? Isa, herself, he was certain. No-one had ever been able to make decisions in her name.

He stood, neither in nor out of the room, a hand on each jamb, too big for the room, too healthy for the atmosphere of degeneration. Death wasn't new to him. It never is, to a soldier. It's always waiting – on the streets of Belfast or the mountains of Bosnia, in sand or snow or mud, or, carelessly and cruelly, by accident in training. But the deaths that he had seen had been sudden and bloody, struggled against. Lives had been fought for and given up only when every option had been tried. He was aware that there were no rules for this meeting, no certainties this time.

'Oliver?'

'I'm here.' He stepped in, closer to the bed, but not yet close enough, not yet committed.

'Recognized your walk.'

And she laughed. He was sure of that. It was no more than a puff of breath, but there was humour in the sound.

He hovered. It was still possible to run, still possible to dish out a few comforting platitudes and take the easy way out. Then he made up his mind and pulled up a chair, close enough to allow Isa to say whatever she had in mind with as little distress as possible.

Her chest was heaving. So much effort for so little gain. The air barely stirred around her nostrils, but her chest muscles laboured. No ventilator. She'd made her decision, then. Oliver admired her for it.

Oliver watched her struggle, his own chest aching in sympathy, feeling as though it had been shrink-wrapped. He had no idea why Isa had called so urgently, but he was pretty certain that he would be the last visitor she would ever have.

Something – there must be something she needed, something she wanted, but he couldn't think what it could be.

She didn't say anything else. Oliver sat for a long time, not too quietly, in case she thought he'd gone. He rustled a bit, let her know that he was listening, let her know that she wasn't alone. But Isa was facing up to her final struggle and words were beyond her. A soft, bubbly plop-plop came from her lungs, like the sound of rice that has been left too long to boil and has turned the water thick and starchy.

He left when pins and needles had deadened his legs, bending his long, lean body over the high bed to leave a kiss on a forehead that seemed already cooler than it ought to be. But she was still there, her essence was there, somehow. An awkward kiss, from a man who hadn't made up his mind what he was trying to say with it. A complicated gesture, that combined what-might-have-been with what-had-been, that tried to give her courage and then backed off, confusing pity and grief, afraid of the commitment, afraid of what might be read into it.

Then he clicked out over the lino as quietly as he could, leaving the flat, sheet-covered body and the frightening sound of the bubbling lungs.

Harry was dozing, his head awkwardly balanced against the window, his neck ridiculously twisted, when Oliver reached the car again. He sat up, blinking childishly, confused. Oliver slid into the driving seat beside him. Harry simply looked his query and Oliver nodded.

'I think so. I think it was nearly over when I left.' He laid his head on the steering wheel. His knuckles were clenched and white. When he sat up again, there were tears in his eyes, two or three heavy, painful, male ones that plopped off his chin and left spreading dark splashes on his shirt.

'Oh, God, that's a bloody way to die.'

So much of their shared past seemed to be dissolving, Harry thought, as though everything was being wrapped up and finished off. Was that what it felt like to get old? Hope gone. Isa gone. Himself and Flavia fighting like two ferrets in a bag. Oliver and Nell keeping up appearances and not very successfully, at that. Everything changing. Everything uncertain. Nothing remaining the way he wanted it to be.

Oliver was too proud to apologize for the tears. Without embarrassment, he wiped his face, loosened

431

his tie, unbuttoned his collar and started the engine.

'Bloody shame,' he said, sniffing, as he slipped the car into gear.

'You could stay. Don't mind me. I'll go up with you, if you like. She shouldn't be alone – not now.'

'No point. I don't think she realized I was there, not after the first few moments.'

'But what did Isa want?' Harry asked.

'That's it. I don't know.'

'It must have been pretty important to make you fly across the country like that.'

'She said on the phone it was something about Hope, something I had to know. I'll never know now. Perhaps – I don't know – perhaps she was confused. All those drugs. I'll never know.'

As they threaded their way out of the carpark, Harry looked back at the hospice building. It seemed to him gaunt, functional, despite attempts to make it appear more welcoming with bright paint and flower tubs. He thought about Isa, alone. He thought about her single-mindedness, about the way she pursued what she wanted. He had admired her formidable intelligence and been awed by the way it was combined with such elegance of body.

And, at the end, she was alone. Oliver, the last person from her old life to see her, had walked out because she was taking too long to die.

But I wouldn't have left her, he thought, *I would have stayed until the end – no matter when.*

And then he thought, *But I didn't – did I?*

*   *   *

432

Lydia left the café without having made up her mind. When she was a child, it would have been so easy to make the decision. *If the first dog that comes along is a spotty one, I go to the pictures with Gemma. If there's a pink pair of stilettos in that shop window, I'll finish my geography prep first.* Simple. The more outrageous you made the *if* principle, the more likely you were to get what you really wanted in the first place.

But now she was hardly likely to say *If that cat on the wall miaows three times, I'll go home.* Grown-ups don't make their decisions that way. How much better for all if they did.

Right or left? Home or hospice?

In the end, it was a simple thing that made up her mind for her. A road drill started up to her right, smashing through paving stones with earsplitting determination. The operator, his ears undefended against the noise, vibrations juddering up and down his body, almost rode the machine like a particularly macho motorcycle. Smoke and powdered stone rose in a choking cloud. Most of the pavement was blocked off by red-and-white-striped barriers, forcing pedestrians into single file past the worker. Lydia felt the sound slice into her, cutting the last threads that linked her to reality. She turned left.

Urgency pushed her into a run. Isa did know. She knew all along. Isa would tell her. But Isa was dying. She was dying alone. There was no-one – no-one – who cared enough to be with her in her last moments. Hope had been alone. Lydia had left her, had gone away with Daniel, been happy, laughed and loved all night and let Hope die. She wasn't going to abandon Isa in the same way.

Panting slightly now, tapping along in unsuitable shoes, bouncing off an old woman with a tartan shopping trolley, tripping over an uneven flagstone – about time they were replaced – she rounded the corner before the hospice gates.

And he was there. Oliver Hawtrey. Driving out of the gate, coming out fast and accelerating away. Lydia knew him at once, even though low sunlight was slicing across the windscreen. It lit his face, caught the ruffled silver gilt hair that was, she could see now, exactly like her own, throwing an un-earthly halo around an imperious profile.

Isa knew. Isa had always known. What else did she know? What else had she concealed?

Lydia stepped off the kerb, from behind a waste collection truck, and flung an arm up into the air in an arresting gesture. She saw Oliver's face turn to her. His expression was frozen into a snarl of disbelief. The confidence, the authority ebbed. He was only a man, after all. He was so close that she could see his dilated pupils, could almost smell his fear. She sensed that she was what he feared. The realization was a rush of pure power that seemed to burst out through the top of her head. So much power that she felt as though her very hair was sparking. She sizzled with energy.

He had killed Hope and he was afraid of her knowledge.

Then everything seemed to happen with the measured pace of certainty. It had to be.

He turned the steering wheel frantically. His mouth was open. She could hear his cry. She felt it lance through her brain at the instant the car wing caught her and tossed her into the air and back onto the pavement. The car kept turning, in an arc that became slower and wider, with a terrible inevitability, as she watched. When it hit the yellow waste lorry, it was concertinaed into half its length by the impact.

EPILOGUE

A time to heal . . .

They had given him a military funeral. Forgiven, it seemed to say, received back into the fold. One of us again. After all, it was pointed out, nothing had actually been proved. No admissions. No last-minute guilt. He hadn't actually resigned. Not quite.

Nell stood in the Military Cemetery in Tidworth and looked along the neat files of identical headstones. The wind that whined off the plain carried on it the distant growling of tank engines and bore away the sound of bugles to be heard along the lines of red-brick barracks and jerry-built married quarters. The shorn grass, like a recruit's haircut, around the graves barely stirred under the attack of the wind.

Jessica was sobbing and leaning on her mother's shoulder, a dead weight, all arrogance dissolved. Jago was on her right, being the man, but Nell could feel the tremor that ran through him as though it travelled along the ground and into her own body.

The need to be strong for her children kept her in check. That – and the formality – saved her. The

Garrison Church of St Michael and All Angels had been stiff with dignitaries. The men who had pegged Oliver out to dry had come to add their condolences to the hundreds of letters she had, somehow, to answer. The road outside had been crammed with black military cars. The aisles had echoed to the chink of medals and the bullion rustle of aiguillettes. Good rousing hymns, chosen by the padre because Nell couldn't make up her mind. A brisk, down-to-earth eulogy that made much of Oliver's early life and mentioned nothing about those last days – those *difficult* days as some less than tactful correspondent had called them.

Everything done properly. Everything as it should be. The ranks had closed around Oliver again and repelled outsiders.

Worth dying for that, he might have said.

Strangers, most of them. Nell had looked around and wondered who they all were. Strangers. Khaki clones. Flavia was there, of course. She was his sister, why shouldn't she be? But she had looked at Nell with ill-disguised disgust, as though she held her to blame for everything those difficult days had brought.

And Harry. But separately from Flavia. They had arrived fifteen minutes apart and sat in different corners of the church, as though they were strangers. Harry had propelled his own wheelchair up the central nave and positioned it close, but not too close, to Nell. She heard the squeak of its brake three or four rows behind her. Drugged up to the eyeballs, but determined to come. Harry with his shattered,

440

pinned legs and homely face scarred by its contact with the dashboard of Oliver's car.

But he looked worse than his injuries would warrant. He looked as though he had left his heart in Oliver's coffin.

She hadn't understood.

'It shouldn't have happened, Harry,' she'd said when she visited him in hospital and the bleakness in her voice sliced through the muzzy veil of pain-killers. 'Why did it happen?'

Her hands were helpless, fluttering things that he would have taken and stilled and comforted with his own if he could have moved without crying out.

'It was almost as if he knew, as if he'd been waiting all his life for her to step out. Expecting her. Rehearsing. I don't understand.'

But Harry did.

He could have told her about the pre-dawn drive back from Hamburg, about the packed-in rowdy subalterns who'd fallen asleep one by one and been dropped off by Oliver at their various messes, with barely time to get showered and changed and on parade. About Oliver looking at his watch and saying, 'Christ, we've got to step on it now.'

He could have told her about the early morning shift worker who'd stepped sleepily into the road. About the panic and the blood and then the silence. And the conspiracy of silence that followed.

And Oliver, never drinking and driving again, haunted by phantoms in overalls stepping out from roadsides. But Lydia had been no phantom.

He'd known that would be no help to Nell now. So he'd said nothing.

They hadn't all risked the wind. Most had left after the church service. *Well, it's a long way back*, they'd say, *heavy traffic and we've done our duty. Best thing in the end, you know. Could have got very nasty indeed, if it had been allowed to drag on. As it is . . . best thing, really.*

Nell's veil snapped around her face, lifting and lowering in the gusts, revealing her frozen expression to Harry's gaze and then concealing it again, as though she were ashamed to be seen.

Somehow, the sedatives she had been given sharpened her vision. She hadn't expected that. She had hoped to get through the day in a merciful blur. But everything stood sharply defined under a wind-washed sky, as though cut out and stuck on a field of smooth green felt.

There was the tall white cross at the top of the slope, the same Cross of Sacrifice that stood in every war cemetery. The Union Flag that draped the gun carriage whereon Oliver lay was a bright thing, gaudily striped, jolly in a bleak white light that was the same colour as the heaped chalk around the open grave. His buff SAS beret, not his dress hat, lay on the flag along with medals that Kane had polished brighter than they had ever been. Their many-coloured ribbons clashed with the red, white and blue of the flag.

Too cold to snow, Nell thought; *typical Salisbury Plain spring*. Sharp pinpricks of sleet eddied in the wind like polystyrene beads. They drifted into ever-changing patterns, like a pure white kaleidoscope, but never settled anywhere for more than a second. They made the padre's surplice look greyed.

And the faces. Nipped and blanched. Set against the chill, turning shoulders against the blast. Flavia, her nose red-tipped with tears and cold, her face pinched with grief and anger. Behind the ring of khaki, Nell could see Ruth and Juliet. *Why, Juliet is growing old*, she thought, with some surprise. *Oliver's death has added years to her.* Ruth had her arm around Juliet's shoulders, as though she was protecting her from something. *From guilt*, Nell concluded. *We are all guilty. We have all colluded and the result is here.*

Beyond Ruth and Juliet, standing apart, almost in a different plane, as though she inhabited a different sphere . . . Isa. *Oh, my God . . .*

And then Nell looked again and recognized Lydia. Lydia in stark black as though she had been bereaved.

Nell's immediate reaction, that snap, in-the-gut spasm that no-one can ever quite avoid – *how dare she?* – lasted no longer than the time the words took to flash through her consciousness. It was replaced by *how can she dare? Where has she found the courage?* Without Lydia's presence at Oliver's funeral, there would have been a void that Nell would have sensed without ever being aware of the reason. Things would have been left unsaid, unfinished, with raw, unravelling edges. But how had she dared?

443

Nell recognized a spirit that was sterner and stronger and freer than her own could ever be, a spirit that combined Isa's bottomless physical control with Oliver's unique blend of daring and risk-taking. And suddenly it all became clear . . .

Lydia stood awkwardly, as though parts of her still hurt and she wasn't certain from where the pain would stab next. Her hair was caught by the wind and ruffled into boyish, platinum spikes. Her face, still bruised down one side, was pinched by cold and pain and grief into hawkish, unfeminine angles. Nell could see how she would be in twenty years' time.

So obvious. Everything just slotted into place with a comfortable click, telling her that – this time – she was facing the truth. She had been so stupid, so deliberately obtuse. Why hadn't she realized? Strangely, the revelation didn't hurt. Nell waited for some warning jab, but nothing happened. It was almost a relief. As though everything that had seemed random and hopeless had just been given a shape. She didn't have to like the pattern that suddenly presented itself, but the fact that it was there at all was oddly comforting.

Everything fitted. There could be no other way. That didn't make it better, or easier to bear, or more just or equable. Simply clearer. And as the pieces snapped together, Nell glimpsed a time – distant yet – when she would be able to think again, when she would be able to give her children the support they deserved, when the sharp edges would be blunted.

Not yet, but some day.

Jessica and Jago stiffened around her before she

heard the warning click of the rifle bolts. The sound of the repeated volleys crashed against the chalk mounds of Sidbury Hill and Windmill Hill, reverberated and was absorbed. And afterwards the silence was so final.

As though they were being thrown out by God calling time, the last mourners hurried to shake Nell's hand, some to kiss her, tangling with her veil, most muttering unheard sympathies. Always behind her, and never too close, sat Harry. But whether he was watching for Nell or taking up his allotted place as guardian of his friend's grave, no-one would have known.

Nell waited and watched. Juliet had wept and kissed her. Ruth managed to hug her and Juliet at the same time. Only three, now. They clung together, shipwrecked remnants. And, at last, trying to slip past in the confusion, came Lydia.

Gently, Nell put aside Juliet and her sniffles and tears. She held out her hands.

'Lydia . . .' she began and then ran out of words, because she had never intended this moment to arrive so soon.

Too soon. Too soon. Lydia shied like a nervous horse. The expression that flashed across her strangely pale eyes was so like Oliver's that Nell flinched from her, then immediately regretted the motion. It had been insensitive, as good as telling Lydia that she was an outsider, that she would never belong, never be one of them.

No wonder she hurt. What had they all done to her? Isa and Ruth, Nell and Juliet, yes – and Hope, too, in her way. They had pursued their own secret aims within the protecting walls of their comradeship. And all had suffered, but none like Lydia. How she must hate them all.

She remembered Juliet's once cruelly casual remark about Hope. *Of course, she was never really one of us.*

Here was Isa's daughter, Oliver's daughter, only very slightly older than Nell's own first-born would have been. Her first son. *He would have been called Henry*, she remembered herself telling Hope that night last year when everything had begun to spin out of control. *But now he's just called he . . .*

Nell hurt. Of course she hurt. But she mustn't imagine that her pain was unique. Lydia had been treated – by everyone who ought to have cared, who ought to have known better – as though she had no feelings at all. And the result would punish them all for years to come.

You have to leave in the end, leave the fresh mound and the wreaths, leave your years of youth and love and laughter and disillusionment and grief.

Jago and Jessica first, clinging together for a while, thrown together by sorrow for a few days longer.

Nell and Ruth and Juliet. Not many of them left now. But still side by side. The strait-jacket of twenty-five years is a hard one to throw off.

Harry, behind, pushing his chair more slowly now, in pain, leaving the days of his youth, along with Nell's, in Oliver's grave.

446

Further back still, Lydia, proud and alone, even though Daniel hovered beside her, trying to comfort her, but aware of the limits she imposed, of how far he could go. Patient Daniel, waiting for the Lydia he remembered to come back to him. One day, he told himself, and he had to believe it because without that there wasn't much left. One day.

Then the sound of running feet. Lydia took the handles of Harry's chair, briskly and without pity, giving them a little, admonitory shake.

'Come on, you'll never get anywhere at that rate,' she said, still angry, still abrasive, daring them to reject her. Harry heard the tone and understood the craving that lay beneath. And for Harry, too, the truth became suddenly clear and didn't surprise him. The gesture, the voice, reminded him so much of Oliver. He could follow every convolution of her thought, just as once he had been able to do with her father. 'I can do this better than you.'

And she pushed Harry alongside Nell and walked with them together down the long tarmac path. Nell stretched out her hand and laid it softly on Harry's shoulder. Harry raised one of his now-free hands and put it on top of hers.

THE END

A SELECTED LIST OF FINE NOVELS
AVAILABLE FROM CORGI BOOKS

14060	0	MERSEY BLUES	*Lyn Andrews*	£5.99
14570	X	FORGED METAL	*Lesley Campbell*	£5.99
14447	9	FIREBIRD	*Iris Gower*	£5.99
14448	7	DREAM CATCHER	*Iris Gower*	£5.99
14537	8	APPLE BLOSSOM TIME	*Kathryn Haig*	£5.99
14567	X	THE CORNER HOUSE	*Ruth Hamilton*	£5.99
14410	X	MISS HONORIA WEST	*Ruth Hamilton*	£5.99
13872	X	LEGACY OF LOVE	*Caroline Harvey*	£5.99
14686	2	CITY OF GEMS	*Caroline Harvey*	£5.99
14535	1	THE HELMINGHAM ROSE	*Joan Hessayon*	£5.99
14692	7	THE PARADISE GARDEN	*Joan Hessayon*	£5.99
14543	2	THE COLOUR OF SIN	*Janet Inglis*	£5.99
14332	4	THE WINTER HOUSE	*Judith Lennox*	£5.99
14603	X	THE SHADOW CHILD	*Judith Lennox*	£5.99
13910	6	BLUEBIRDS	*Margaret Mayhew*	£5.99
14693	5	THE LITTLE SHIP	*Margaret Mayhew*	£5.99
14499	1	THESE FOOLISH THINGS	*Imogen Parker*	£5.99
14658	7	THE MEN IN HER LIFE	*Imogen Parker*	£5.99
14752	4	WITHOUT CHARITY	*Michelle Paver*	£5.99
10375	6	CSARDAS	*Diane Pearson*	£5.99
14577	7	PORTRAIT OF CHLOE	*Elvi Rhodes*	£5.99
14655	2	SPRING MUSIC	*Elvi Rhodes*	£5.99
14636	6	COME RAIN OR SHINE	*Susan Sallis*	£5.99
14671	4	THE KEYS TO THE GARDEN	*Susan Sallis*	£5.99
14657	9	CHURCHILL'S PEOPLE	*Mary Jane Staples*	£5.99
14708	7	BRIGHT DAY, DARK NIGHT	*Mary Jane Staples*	£5.99
14502	5	THE LONG ROAD HOME	*Danielle Steel*	£5.99
14637	4	THE KLONE AND I	*Danielle Steel*	£5.99
14640	4	THE ROMANY GIRL	*Valerie Wood*	£5.99
14740	0	EMILY	*Valerie Wood*	£5.99